THE
SILENT
GIRL

BOOKS BY KELLY HEARD

Before You Go
The Girl I Thought I Knew

THE SILENT GIRL

KELLY HEARD

bookouture

Published by Bookouture in 2021

An imprint of Storyfire Ltd.
Carmelite House
50 Victoria Embankment
London EC4Y 0DZ

www.bookouture.com

ISBN: 978-1-80019-436-6
eBook ISBN: 978-1-80019-435-9

For Isla Jane: I adore your imagination, your willfulness, your incandescence. The world needs your fire—don't let anyone tame it.

CHAPTER ONE

A man's voice speaks into a transceiver. "Female. Thirty, maybe. Send an ambulance. And check for missing persons, anything on the news. Strawberry blonde, blue dress. There's—flowers in her hair." With a whispered curse, he turns away. "Hang on a minute," he says.

I hear a different voice telling me that help is coming. That I need to hold on a little longer. But I'm not ready to leave the flowers yet. The blossoms surrounded me, a thousand red moons bobbing on delicate stems. I'm pushing back consciousness, trying not to wake up. Whatever I did wrong, whatever landed me here, I know the flowers would forgive me, and I wish that I could stay.

There is a sickening pain in my head. Blood has dried on my face, my eyelashes are sticking together, and I wonder, distantly, about time, about the pale light and the distant bird calls. I can feel scratches along my shoulder and down my right arm that scream every time I breathe. Fear, like a wild horse, runs through my veins. All of this I know, not as facts are known, but in my body, the way a fledgling bird must know which way to fly when the nights get cold. What I don't know is where I went wrong. The red of those flowers has erased whatever came before. I stare up at glossy green leaves and, without needing to close my eyes, slip gratefully away into a field of numbing red.

"Can you tell me your name? Where are you from?"

"Head injury, see? She might not even be able to hear you."

But they're wrong. I didn't answer because I don't know.

All I know is that I don't want to go back. That wherever I came from there was nothing waiting for me but my own end, and some worse pain than dragging myself through the woods half-dead. That, I know, is something beyond what I can imagine, even now.

CHAPTER TWO

I open my eyes to bright fluorescent lights that send a shock to my pupils. Squeezing my eyes shut, I turn my head and tug at my arms. I feel resistance and throw all my weight against my elbows and try to sit up. This was a mistake. Suddenly, everything hurts. A pulse of pain in my head, constellations of pain lighting up my limbs, even down to my fingertips.

I can't move.

They've found me.

At my side, a mechanical tone sounds at an increasing pace. Something slithers at my side, between my arm and my ribs.

If there's no sin in your heart, the rattlers won't bite you.

I didn't do anything wrong, I plead. *I'd never betray you.*

Then prove it.

The echo leaves me with a shiver. I stare down at the writhing, gray forms, too afraid to move.

When a nurse walks in, it takes me several seconds to realize that I'm in a hospital, with IV lines that trail from both my arms. She speaks into a phone clipped to her collar: "Room sixteen's awake." Then, she seems to be everywhere at once. She adjusts the IV, checks the straps that hold my limbs to the bed, all the while looking into my eyes.

"You're safe." She checks an IV bag. "Sorry for the restraints. Didn't want you to fall out of the bed." Again, I try to sit up, my head jerking side to side. I rock my knees back and forth, trying to free them from whatever holds them in place. With a tearing sound, a tie loosens and they are free. I swing my feet down and find the floor, cold tile under my feet.

"Some help?" The nurse's voice rises and an attendant rushes in. But I don't make it far; she catches me before I hit the floor altogether. I'm still thrashing, trying to escape, as they lift me up. "She's short," the nurse explains. "Got out of the restraints."

"Please," I say, gritting my teeth. "Let me go."

"I can get you something to help you calm down, miss." They ease me back onto the bed. The nurse rests a hand on my shoulder. "Do you know where you are? You're in the hospital."

"I know," I gasp, wheeze another breath. "I have to get out of here."

"To where?" Now she's listening, as if I might know something she doesn't. "Where do you need to go?"

"Away," I answer.

"From what?"

I think my heart stops for a moment, and in that moment I settle into her gaze. Her eyes are golden brown, dark hair, kind but serious mouth. I don't have an answer.

"It's alright," she repeats. "You're safe. Promise." She glances to the doorway. "See? They put security outside your door."

"Why?" I ask. This, apparently, is the first question of mine the nurse wasn't prepared for.

"Well—since…" She busies herself with the IV, disconnecting the bag, putting on a new one, checking the port in my arm. I realize I can't feel much. "How much do you remember?" I blink, purse my lips, feel a splash of pain.

"Tell me," I plead.

"Don't worry about that right now," she says. "We're going to try to help you get some more rest, okay?"

She turns her attention to small tasks, straightening things around the room, adjusting the blankets over my legs, updating a chart on a dry-erase board that hangs by the door. I begin to feel light, as if I'm floating away. What a relief it is, to feel less, and then a little bit less than that. Though I watch her write, the letters swim and fade before my eyes. All I can make out is the line at the top. It reads 'Jane Doe.'

CHAPTER THREE

The next time I wake, it seems to be morning. With a remote calm, I see that my palms are wrapped in gauze, that both arms are either stitched or bandaged. Beneath the hospital gown, there's a row of stitches down my chest, the dark thread like ants crawling over a red welt.

I sense the absence of pain, and realize there's either some medicine at work here, or I've already died. What a cruel trick, if the afterlife looked like the inside of a hospital room.

Beyond the foot of the bed, a window offers a view of blue-edged mountains that rise above the sleepy town below. I watch the stoplights changing, which they do slowly, as if there's no reason to hurry. As if from far away, muffled through water, I hear the door open. Then, a woman in blue scrubs is opening a dressing on my arm, cleaning the skin beneath.

I watch the nurse working, feeling my dry lips crack as I smile. "Thank you."

Startled, she almost drops the gauze. "You're awake!" She seals the bandage with a light touch. "I'm going to get the attending."

I try to nod my head, but my neck is stiff. Instead, I return to the window. Beyond a row of trees, there's a pond, and from here it looks as shallow and reflective as a hand mirror.

A white-coated woman with graying brown hair enters the room, followed by a younger man I take for a student of some sort. The attending pulls up a chair and sits at my bedside.

"Good morning. How are you feeling?" she asks me.

"Hard to say." I begin to study my body: the bandages that cover one arm, the cuts and scratches that line the other. There's a jagged wound on my chest, neatly held closed with tiny stitches. When I lift a hand, I can feel half-healed marks on my face, too.

When the forest cooled at night, the dew settled on the leaves. Like a chill mist, a realization settles over me. I don't know where I am. My shoulders tense and pain reverberates up my neck. I reach up to touch my head and feel a bandage at my temple. The doctor gently pulls my hand away. "We'll get to that. What's important is that you're safe now." I pull back, rest my hand on my knee.

"First, maybe you'd like to introduce yourself?"

Why are they asking me this? The whiteboard still reads 'Jane Doe', and I wonder if they really don't know, or if this is some sort of test.

"Or maybe you can tell us what year it is?"

"Two thousand and ten."

"That's good," she answers. "June 3, 2010. You've been unconscious for three days."

The doctor nods to the student standing behind her, and he takes a step forward. He's holding a clipboard and wearing an ID tag that reads 'Resident.' "We'd like to find your family. Maybe you can try to tell us about where you're from. What do you remember?"

"My brother." My mouth forms the words as if from muscle memory. When I say them, I'm suddenly aware of a charge in the air, almost as if I expect speaking so to conjure something. I wait for the words to call up an image, a voice. But there's nothing.

"So—you have a brother." The resident nods and makes a note. "What's his name? Do you know where he lives?"

"Miles," I breathe, realizing with some despair that I don't. My chest feels heavy and weightless both at once, and I say it again. "My brother. I have to find him."

"Yes, but any specifics that come to mind?"

I raise both hands to my temples, as if I can squeeze the thoughts loose, and feel a sharp jolt of pain. The doctor gestures at one of my bedside monitors with her pen. "You see, this is a stress response. Heart rate up, BP up, but her pulse ox is steady. Miss?"

It's something less than comforting to hear them discuss me while I'm sitting right here. At least the resident makes eye contact with me.

"You're about thirty years old. You don't have any tattoos or identifying scars. The police returned something of yours. We—"

"Police?" I interrupt. "Why?"

They exchange a glance, and the attending answers. "It's standard procedure. Would you like to see?"

"Standard procedure for what?" I ask. The resident opens a plastic bag and takes out something silver, which he offers to me. I wrap my hand around it, a tarnished metal charm on a length of twine. It looks like a symbol, a semicircle topped with two crisscrossed lines, one bold dash underneath. Though it's fascinating, smooth and cool to the touch, it calls up no thoughts in my mind, no memory.

"I can't remember anything," I stammer, turning it over in my palm. "This was mine?"

"You were wearing it when you were found." The resident answers me without looking up from his clipboard.

"Found?" I demand, holding back stronger language. "Is anybody going to tell me what happened?"

"You see," the attending says, barely raising her eyes to mine. "We were hoping you might be able to tell us." She nods to the younger doctor, who reads from his clipboard.

"Unnamed patient, discovered roadside by a motorist, who then called emergency response." His pen runs down a list of text, and I see that he's skimming. "Negative for sexual assault. Negative for drugs and alcohol—although, some drugs are in the system only for a few days, so that might not give us the full picture." I move to cover my face with my hands and see red seeping through the gauze on my palms. I can't help but feel there must have been a mistake. That these hands can't belong to me.

The attending clicks her tongue and indicates the monitors again. "See, you need to keep an eye on these. BP's still up. We'll let the nurse know about that when we're done here. What notes do you have?"

"Head injury," the resident answers. "Considering all of the circumstances, I'd say—amnesia, likely related to brain injury."

The doctor shakes her head. "Incorrect. You've seen the MRI. The concussion was determined to be mild." They speak as if I can't understand them. "The scan did not return brain injury that would be consistent with memory loss."

"But—"

"Dissociative amnesia, most likely," the attending says. "Repressed memories, essentially. You'll see this in instances of trauma or intense stress. But," she adds, "the good news is that it's virtually always temporary." She turns a neat, professional smile my way. "We'll send the nurse back in. Get some rest."

"No snakebites?" I ask. The doctor turns to me with a quizzical, annoyed glance.

"No," she answers. "No snakebites." The doctor tilts her head. "Why?"

"A—a dream, maybe." The doctor leaves the door open when she walks away.

The nurse must have been waiting just outside the door, because she returns immediately.

"Sorry," she says, leaning close and moving the collar of my gown to look at the stitches there. "Just checking on this." She's in constant motion, returning the chair to its place, checking the monitors, adjusting the blanket over my legs. Though I realize she's doing a job, that doesn't make me appreciate it any less. "It's a teaching hospital," she says. "They forget patients are people, sometimes."

"You heard all of that?" I grimace with embarrassment.

She purses her mouth and checks my blood pressure again.

"What happened?" I ask her, holding the necklace. "Why did the police have this?"

"Your injuries don't look accidental." She pauses, holding her hand out. I put my hand in hers, and she turns it over, indicating scratches around my wrist, a couple of broken nails, the cuts that reach up my arm. "These are defensive wounds. Put all of that together, it's safe to assume you're a victim of a crime."

"But what happened?"

For the first time, the nurse sits still, turning her warm brown eyes my way.

"We don't know. But you put up a fight. You don't get cuts like that unless you gave someone hell. And you heal fast," she says.

"Thanks—I guess." I'm not sure that it was a compliment, but it's something concrete. With a surplus of nervous energy, I notice that the doctor left her pen at the bedside tray. I pick it up, twirl it in my hand.

"You'll be feeling better before you know it," she assures me. "My name's Anjali."

"Nice to meet you."

"You too. Can I get you anything?"

"Do you have anything I could write or draw on?"

"Let me see what I can find," she says, walking out of the door.

Anjali returns with a lined notepad and a packet of colored pencils. "I borrowed these from the pediatrics unit," she says. "But you can keep them. They have plenty."

I thank her, and she leaves me to my thoughts.

The pencils seem to jump into my hand, to move with their own instinct when I hold them to the paper. I can't grip the pencils the way I want to, the cut in my hand threatening to open when my palm bends, so I sketch loosely, and the motion of doing so is enough to bring some comfort. I draw shadows and lines, which soon take form, beginning to draw out the images in my mind. I fill a page, then flip to the next. Looking down at the pencils in my hands, I feel a warmth, nearly a presence. I blink, and a recollection comes to the surface of my mind: a hand around mine, a piece of construction paper on a tabletop, a figure with soft hair. Just as quickly, the sensation flees. I don't know how, but I'm certain that I have a mother, that she taught me how to draw.

With the paper beneath my hands, the cuts that line my wrists and hands seem fainter, less demanding of my focus. When the day shift ends, Anjali comes back to tell me goodnight. When she sees my work, her face softens into a smile.

"See? You haven't forgotten everything." She admires the notepad. "You're an artist."

I wish Anjali a good evening when she leaves, then sit the pencils down, take a moment to study what I've drawn.

A woman reclines in a bed of flowers. She's in shadow, but I know her dress is blue. Above and around her, red flowers blossom, like great, shimmering fish. And then, uninvited, the thought springs into my mind: I'd like to be there now. Back there in a meadow of flowers so red, they could make the blood in your veins seem less than real.

Through the glazed window, I can make out faint shapes in the hallway. I hear footsteps, then see a silhouette. Male, light hair, with sturdy, square shoulders. Before I know what's happening, I can feel my heartbeat in the back of my throat, and I'm stumbling to my feet. Colored pencils scatter across the floor, and I slip on one as I crawl for anywhere to hide, finding only the dusty space between the bathroom door and the wall. I see a man's face, hard eyes, a line of a scar through one eyebrow. Behind the door, I crane my neck to look at the window again. From this angle, I can't see anything. When half an hour has passed, I slowly creep out, collect my pencils and paper, and sit holding them against my chest, watching the door. When the morning nurse comes in to check on me, I've fallen asleep huddled over my knees. I don't know why or how, but I know I'm not safe here.

CHAPTER FOUR

Days pass, but my memory does not return. Instead, I have to build things from scratch, and I collect facts with determination. I know that my body is strong. That I heal quickly. Within days, I'm walking on my own, and not long after that, a nurse removes the stitches from my temple.

I learn that I'm in Hazel Bluff, South Carolina. That it's a kind of joy to watch the sunlight changing on the little town beneath my window, the shifting shades of green on the mountains rising toward the west. The nurses offer to let me walk outside, but I pace the halls instead. I don't like the idea of being alone.

But I'm still working on mirrors. It takes a physical effort not to flinch when I see myself, even now the swelling has improved. Ginger-blonde hair, which is the exact color of dust when it needs a wash, but has a warm spark to it when it's clean. Eyes blue, or almost blue, though it seems to depend on the light. And I have a cut lip, and a rainbow of bruises around my cheekbones and eyes. I comb my hair twice a day in the bathroom, trying not to look in the mirror. I part it on the side to cover the line where my stitches came out. The truth is, there are marks all over my body, although I try just to focus on the fact that they're healing. That's the only reason I look at them, keeping a daily catalogue, a roll call. When it gets to be too much to know, I color in the blank pages of the book.

On the first morning of the second week, tired of sitting in bed, I bring my colored pencils and notepad to the upholstered chair in the corner. Hearing a knock at the door, I put down my pencil.

"Good morning." A woman stands in the doorway, tall and slim, with an upright posture and a measured tone that lets me know she's either law enforcement or military.

"Hi." I'm not sure I like the idea of any kind of unexpected visitor.

"I'm Selena Radford. Police detective." Without asking if she can come in, Detective Radford crosses through the doorway and sits in the chair nearest to mine. I'm correcting my own posture, straightening my hair, something about the precision of her appearance making me self-conscious. Her dark hair is in a low, tight braid, and she wears a blazer over a crisp dress, and I see the flash of a badge on her collar. "I'd like to talk about what brought you here. I understand another officer came by several days ago, but you were still unconscious."

"Nice to meet you, Detective."

"You too, ah—" She glances up at the dry-erase board, then turns back to me. "You're probably tired of Jane Doe, aren't you?"

"I should be used to it by now," I answer. Her manner isn't very friendly, but there's something I can appreciate about someone who isn't trying to win me over, so I put my notepad down to show her I'm listening. "I don't know how much help I'll be. I still don't remember anything. Nothing useful, at least." Her smile is measured and professional, but I notice the curve of her cheek, the striking line of her brow.

"You'd be surprised what might be useful," she answers. As commanding as she is, I almost didn't notice that she's also terribly pretty.

"I remember family, a little bit," I tell her. "My mom. And my brother—Miles."

"Anything else?"

I shake my head. With nervous hands, I pick up my notepad again and open my unfinished picture, begin to draw. "It's calming," I explain. The detective glances at the picture, then back to me.

"Sophia, right?"

"No—no." For some reason, my voice jolts out before I realize I'm answering. "I meant to say, I don't know. Why?"

"Not you," she says. "You were found wearing a necklace, with a distinctive charm. This is that symbol, isn't it?"

"Yes," I answer. I cross the room and take the necklace from the bedside tray, then show it to her from where I stand.

"Do you know anything about it?"

"Astrology," she sighs, shaking her head as if she's embarrassed to admit she knows it. "That's the astrological glyph for an asteroid, a faraway one. But the name of the asteroid is Sophia. Which, in turn, is involved with ideas like knowledge. The feminine aspect of the divine. It's nonsense. I just happened to recognize it because my grandmother thinks she's some kind of mystic." She taps her fingers against her knee.

"Sophia," I repeat. I like something about this name, about its soft consonants. To hear Detective Radford say a name, for a moment, almost made me feel as if I had my own.

"It means something to you, then," she says, picking up her pen and making a mark in her notebook.

"Maybe it did once." It's clear enough she doesn't entirely trust me.

"This isn't an interrogation," she says, as if she's reminding herself as well as me. "The circumstances being what they are, it's important we consider every possibility."

"Nobody's told me what the circumstances are. I see that you know more than I do."

I hold my chin up and turn my face to the window. I haven't shed a tear since I woke up here, and today is not going to be the day I do.

"I see," she answers. "Apologies. I'll go over the report with you. Is that alright?"

"I'd appreciate it," I answer. Detective Radford begins to read from her clipboard, using the same measured, practiced tone. Several times she starts a sentence, then cuts off, seems to skip down a few lines. I watch her with eyebrows raised.

"You were found in the mountains a couple of hours from here," she says. "Near the side of the road. If only we could know—do you live nearby? Or did you get here from somewhere else? Whatever happened, you did not sustain your injuries there at the roadside, so we know that something happened."

"How do you know?"

"Well, one, there are abrasions general on your right side." She gestures with the tip of her pen. "Your shoulder, your arm. It suggests that you fell from a vehicle." She pauses, seems to check my response. "More accurately, that you were dragged from a vehicle and then fell. The debris didn't match the gravel on the road where they found you." I listen to her without wincing. She's honest, something I am far more grateful for than an attempt to gloss things over. "And you had flowers in your hair." For the first time since she's entered the room, her tone wavers, and I sense she knows more than she's telling me. She lifts her eyes and I see she's wondering if perhaps I'm the one who's holding back details. "I don't have all the notes here, but the flowers didn't grow anywhere near where they found you."

"What do you think happened?"

"We've had two detectives working on your case. The lack of detail, frankly, is disturbing. That's why I'm involved. Based on the circumstances—"

"Circumstances," I echo. That word again, a maddening allusion to things I ought to know but don't.

"Based on the circumstances," she continues, "I doubt that it was a random crime. However, that's always a possibility. You're telling me, with certainty, that you know nothing about your life prior to being here?"

"I promise," I tell her, and though it's as genuine as it can be, something about her is putting me on the defensive, and I know I sound sharp. "What can you do?"

"There are databases we can check. Missing persons is a starting point. It can take some time, once we begin requesting records from out of the area."

"The doctors all said I'd remember within hours," I say, lifting a pencil to my notepad, drawing a shadow that morphs into an angry-looking cloud. "Then it was days. Now, it's been two weeks."

"The hospital has relationships with several memory care facilities in the community," she says, not sounding overly concerned. "I spoke with the charge nurse, who estimated that you'd be discharged within another one to two weeks."

"So, what do I do?"

"When they clear you to leave the hospital, I'll meet with you at the police station. Hopefully by then, I'll have some returns from missing persons. We can show you photographs, compare what you remember by that time with whatever information I can gather." I want to ask her: and then what? But she's already folding her papers into an immaculately organized briefcase, checking the clock on the wall, then glancing with annoyance at her watch.

"Your clock is slow," she says. "I have a meeting in ten minutes. I apologize for hurrying out like this. I'll be in touch with you."

"What else can you tell me about the symbol?"

"Not much," she answers. "Sophia means wisdom, but in different traditions it's something like feminine, divine wisdom."

"A big idea," I said. "For a regular first name."

"It's not that common a name around here," Detective Radford answers. She reaches out to shake my hand. I grasp her hand firmly and release it.

After she leaves, I walk to the dry-erase board and wipe off the 'JANE DOE' with the tip of my finger. In its place, I write 'Sophia', then, after scrutinizing it, erase the last letter, change it to 'Sophie.' It's better than nothing.

I don't know how I got the necklace, but I'm not sure I want it out in plain sight, either. I decide to keep it under my pillow. Anjali told me that I may have given someone hell, but I certainly got more in return.

When night comes, I don't dream. I disappear, into a sea of red. I wake in the dark and stare out the frosted glass at the hallway, my heart pounding. Each time my eyes begin to close, I jolt awake, convinced I've heard the latch of the doorknob twist to open. Hospitals are always cold, or, maybe, it's the constant chill of fear. Either way, sitting awake in the dark, I hug my knees and whisper, "*Sophie,*" as if it's a life raft.

CHAPTER FIVE

Anjali arrives for her shift at seven in the morning, sharp. She opens her mouth to greet me, but her smile falters.

"You look like you've been awake all night," she scolds. "You've got to let them prescribe you something for sleep. Your body needs it as much as your mind does."

"I'm okay. Thanks." I hold out my arm for the blood pressure cuff. After checking all the usual items, Anjali walks across the room to update the dry-erase board. She sees the change I've made and turns back to me with a grin. "Sophie," she says. "That's new, right? Wait." Her eyes widen. "You remembered?"

"No," I answer, feeling as though I should apologize. "My necklace. The symbol—it has a name. Sophia."

"So, it's good luck."

"It could be bad luck as easily as good," I answer, smiling. "But it's pretty much the only thing that feels like mine."

"It suits you."

"Thanks."

"What's bothering you?"

"What do you mean?" I want to snap, to ask her what wouldn't be bothering me, but I gather she knows what she's talking about.

"You look more worried than usual," she says. "That detective came to see you yesterday, right?"

"They want me to stay in a long-term care facility," I mumble.

"Oh, when you leave here?"

"Yes."

"You know," she answers, "it isn't the worst idea. You'd have access to doctors, round-the-clock emergency response."

"Why would I need that?"

"What you're coping with right now, the memory loss, it's almost never permanent. It can take time for things to come back, and the timeline's unpredictable. The thing is…" She pauses to lean over, parting my hair, scanning the healing cut there, then nodding with approval. "When you do remember, that can be unpleasant. It can happen all at once, or it can happen in pieces. Ideally, you wouldn't be alone—that's what I'm trying to say."

The truth is, I don't want to be alone, either. I don't even like when the nurses leave my room. But something about the idea of living in a home fills me with dread.

"In thirty years, I must have done something. I must have people that I know, a life. Is nobody looking for me?" I ask her as if she would know, my tone pleading. "How was none of that permanent?" I'm rubbing my eyes, more from frustration than fatigue, pressing down until swirls of green fill the dark space there. Anjali's hand is firm on my knee.

"Breathe," she says. "That is the first thing. Always."

I move my hands from my face and comply, commanding my lungs to do their job. She holds my gaze. "In through your nose. Count to four. Out through your mouth. Count again."

She follows her own instructions, and I follow her lead. "Now what?"

"Keep doing it," she says. "Keep breathing. I'll order breakfast for you, if you're hungry."

"Yes, please," I answer.

"I got you something," Anjali says, her tone a bit hesitant. "Just because you said it was calming for you and, I mean, there's not much else here for you to do. Hope you don't think it's an overstep." She places a plastic shopping bag at the foot of my bed, then leaves the room before I have a chance to open it.

I reach for it, the plastic crinkling under my fingertips, then pull back as if it bit me. Anjali seems kind, but I don't know her. She says she doesn't know anything about how I got hurt. That might not be true. I glance at the doorway and remember her calming voice saying *keep breathing.* My curiosity wins and I open the bag. Inside, I find a leather-bound sketchbook, with soft vellum paper, pleasantly heavy. I rustle it out of the bag and find a pack of felt-tipped ink pens as well. I should run after Anjali and thank her, but I'm too excited, tearing into the markers like a child with a present. My mother taught me how to do this: a gift. There aren't many things I'm sure of, but this is one. I take the blue pen and open the sketchbook to its title page. There, on the blank lines, followed by exactly one hundred blank pages, I write in block letters 'WHAT SOPHIE KNOWS.' I open the red pen and fill the page beneath these words with the only thing I can bring myself to draw.

CHAPTER SIX

I find that a proper sketchbook in my hands sets me free. I fill it with sketches, lines, images, and, between the pictures, bullet points of any fact I can think of that I know for certain. Some days, I add several, some days, none. It's something to open when I can't find anywhere else to turn, when everything else is too shaky. By day, I sit in the chair in the corner to draw; when it gets late, I move to the bed, drawing with the sketchbook resting on my folded knees until my eyelids are too heavy to continue.

Asleep, I find the interior of my mind to be like a large, empty building. Among the echoes, I sense ghosts. I search for anything left behind from before, hoping for something indelible. I call my brother, without words, inviting an image, a voice, a memory, and still find nothing. I realize that this distance is part of him. His absence taunts me, then comforts me, and there's a sharpness to it, a sense of danger. This reaching for him is a part of me, same as teeth or limbs.

There was a little girl with a backpack, without her brother. She stood at a doorway with a woman behind her, someone kind but unknown, not comforting like a mother. "This is going to be your home now," she says.

"But what about Mom and Dad?" the child asks. She asks for her brother, too. But when she walks in the doorway to the new family waiting inside, she is alone.

When I wake up, I'm already fumbling for the sketchbook with one hand, reaching with the other to turn on the light. The memory of having a mother, of knowing her, can't have been a mistake. Seeing a night shift nurse in the hallway, I hope, without knowing why, that she'll stop in to talk with me. When she passes by, it feels like a punch in the stomach. Some tougher instinct reminds me, though, that survival demands strength, so I sit up straight and make my face smooth as glass, refusing to cry.

CHAPTER SEVEN

When several days have passed, a detective arrives to drive me to the police station. All week, Anjali has been talking about my upcoming discharge from the hospital as though it's some kind of emancipation. She even brought me some secondhand clothes that she got at a charity shop. I've managed to postpone any concrete plans for a long-term psych facility, though I suppose that may only leave me without a place to sleep. In the passenger seat of the officer's car, I blink my eyes in the bright sun.

I meet with Detective Radford and a man in her office, a room with shiny paneled walls that are lined with diplomas and awards. I see her sitting behind the desk, offering a practiced, friendly greeting.

"You're going by Sophie now. Is that correct?"

"Yes."

"Sit down, please," she says, and I do. "How are you feeling?"

"Not bad."

"You look well," she says, opening a folder, referring to a sheet of paper. "Your recovery seems to be going smoothly. With one exception, of course." I know what she's talking about, though I'd rather not dwell on it. For all the hours I've spent drawing and dreaming, my mind is still empty.

"You said we'd meet when you had some information," I say. The other detective begins to show me a series of photographs. Some are of missing persons, while others are of the families of missing persons. Some, he doesn't tell me who they are, and I gather they're wanted criminals. All the while, Selena sits across her desk, clicking idly at a computer screen, though I sense she's watching me for my reaction to the photos.

"We're waiting on results from a few nationwide databases," she says. "But this is everything from the state." I wonder if she sees my disappointment when I sigh; her tone seems to soften a little. "Sophie, wherever you're from, it's almost like nobody's looking for you." Though she's only being honest, the observation stings. I realize it's familiar to me, this sensation of being a girl that nobody would miss.

"I don't know what to tell you," I answer, trying not to let my hurt show.

"The smallest detail could be meaningful," she says. "Any seemingly random fact could help me find out where you're from, what happened to you. Sophie, listen: for you to have led a life where someone could hurt you like this, there'd be warning signs. Maybe you trusted someone, in spite of red flags. Maybe you were isolated from friends, family."

"I don't understand."

"Or maybe you crossed the wrong person—but what put you in their path?"

"It sounds like you think it's my fault," I interrupt. "Somehow or other."

"No, Sophie, absolutely not." Detective Radford cuts me off, but there's an intensity in her blue eyes that shows me she's listening to me. "This is one thing, maybe the only thing, we know for certain here: whoever harmed you, they made a choice to take those actions. And I intend to find out who that was." She says this as if it matters to her personally, and I eye the awards on the wall of her office.

"Thank you." My voice comes out gravelly, and I clear my throat and repeat myself. "Thanks. You're the first person who's said that to me."

"Your charge nurse told me you're leaving the hospital in the next day or two. What are their plans?"

"For me? None," I answer. "I don't know of any, at least."

"That won't do," she says. I don't know if it's me or if it's her, but this sounds like a threat. "It's alright," she says. "I don't mind helping you set something up." I hear a phone ring, not the one on her desktop, but a cell she takes from her pocket. "Would you excuse me?" she asks. "If you'll go back to the waiting room, I'll come downstairs and catch up with you when I've made a few calls. Amber is our secretary—let her know if you need anything while you're waiting."

I nod and leave her office, walking through the corridor and down the stairs into the waiting room. The door is propped open, letting in a warm breeze. I sink into a chair miserably, pull my knees up to my chin as if I'm a kid waiting for the principal to call my name. I'm grateful for the clothes the nurse brought me, but they're a bit too big, which makes me feel even more conspicuous. I scan the room, move into a corner chair where I can see everyone around me, as well as the door. The familiar sense of tension creeps over me, setting me on alert for every slight noise. Outside the door, from the sidewalk, I hear a man's voice.

"Found anyone? No, I haven't." His voice is a deep tenor, one that crackles with annoyance. "It should have been easy, but I guess that's my good luck at work."

My heart pounds a little. Found who? I slip my feet to the floor, lean forward to look around the doorway.

"It's not like I can run an ad in the paper: anyone could show up."

I cross my arms, fingertips wrapping tight around the opposite elbows. I don't know what that stranger might be talking about, or might not be. I don't even know who I ought to be hiding from.

"Sure," the voice continues. "I'll leave his bag at the desk."

When I hear footsteps come into the waiting room, I quickly go back to my chair, as if it could hide me, and point my chin to the side to conceal my face. This only turns the scar on my temple toward the doorway, a sure identifying mark. Still half cowering, I raise a hand to cover my hairline. I see him pause out of the corner of my eye, no doubt sending a confused look my way. Or one of recognition. I wait, but nothing happens. The man doesn't sit down, instead lingering impatiently near the door. There's sawdust on the shoulder of his T-shirt, mud on his boots, but there is an impatience about his stance that's almost bold. Maybe, I think, allowing myself a careful exhale, it was just a random phone conversation. I unfold into a normal sitting position, but keep my eyes on the floor. I watch his boots as he walks to the desk, greets the secretary, Amber.

"I heard you were having trouble hiring someone." The woman takes the bag that he hands her and places it behind the desk. "You want to put a notice on the bulletin board here?"

"No," he answers, adding a quiet "thank you," as if it's an afterthought. The secretary shrugs.

"Just offering," she says. "It can't be easy to find somebody who wants to live and work an hour away from town, up to their elbows in thorns all day, right next to a haunted house."

"It's not haunted." The man appears to take this as an affront. "Have a nice day." Without waiting for Amber to answer, he turns to leave. Moments later, I hear heels clicking, and Detective Radford walks into the waiting room.

"Sophie, I spoke with the charge nurse. She's going to arrange a spot for you by the end of the day."

"Is there any other option?" I ask, grasping at straws. "What if I could find somewhere else to stay?"

"Of course. You're not a prisoner," she says, though her smile fades. "But please don't do anything reckless. Detective Brown will drive you back to the hospital. I'll send him down."

"Thanks." She pauses to speak with Amber before she disappears down the hallway. Once she's gone, I sit up straight, making deliberate eye contact with the young woman behind the desk.

"Yes?" She puts her paperback down on the desk to address me. I gesture at the doorway.

"What was that about? The haunted house?"

"Dovemorn," she says, as if it were obvious. "You new here?" she asks, after I look confused at this response.

"Yeah."

"Historic estate outside of town, up that side of the mountain. Decrepit, really. That guy's the caretaker, or groundskeeper, or something. If you could see it, you'd agree it's haunted. Miles from anywhere. I'm pretty sure a lady died there, like, ages ago."

Just then, Brown arrives to drive me back to the hospital.

"You ready to go?" he asks.

"Yes."

"Probably feels like you're getting handed off between baby-sitters," he says, a hint of apology in his tone. I reflect that he probably feels like he's been instructed to babysit me. For myself, I don't mind. It's better than being a stranger in a new town, always on edge, without even a clue what I ought to be afraid of.

CHAPTER EIGHT

The next morning, I wake to a little pile of going-away gifts. The nurses and staff have collected a small assortment of necessities: a pair of shoes and some more secondhand clothes, toothbrush and hairbrush, even a backpack. I open the good luck card, poring over the brief notes and signatures. Anjali walks into the room behind me.

"I know you won't miss it here," she says. "But it's been nice getting to know you. We'll all be wishing the best for you."

"Thank you." I turn around and offer her an awkward hug, which she accepts. As I turn, I see the flowers on the bedside table. It's an elaborate arrangement, flowers in all shades of red: dahlias, roses, carnations.

"Did you send these?"

"No," Anjali says, beaming. "I'm not sure who did, actually. Oh!" Her pager begins to buzz. "Excuse me. I'll stop in again before you leave."

For a moment, I'm struck dumb, my feet glued to the floor. I can hear my heart pounding so loud that I almost can't hear my thoughts.

"Who delivered these?" I ask. But Anjali has already hurried away to answer her call.

Run, I'm thinking. *You have to run.* It's like moving through water. Hands shaking, I reach to touch the arrangement. There's no card, no message, just the address of the hospital and my room number.

They know where to find me.

But who are they?

In the bathroom, I change into a top, some blue jeans and a pair of sneakers that almost fit me. I carefully place all my gifts into the bag. Wherever I'm going, it'll be nice to have a few things of my own. I stop in the kitchen in the hallway and add a few bottles of water to my bag, as well as whatever food I can reach: granola bars, instant noodles. A nurse's aide walks into the room as I'm scanning the counter for more food.

"Miss, can I help you with something?" she asks.

"No." I inch past her toward the doorway.

"Are you alright?" She takes a step after me. "You're Sophie, right? From room sixteen?" I want to answer no. To tell her that if I don't know who I am or where I'm from, then she certainly doesn't. But I can't; something tells me I couldn't lie convincingly, not even if my life depended on it. And what if it does?

"You're transferring to the care center—is that right?" the aide asks. She's following me down the hallway now, which means it's a matter of moments before someone else overhears. "Sophie, I need to ask you to wait here, please." At the end of the corridor, the elevator is open.

"Hold the door!" I shout, mouthing a silent apology to the aide as I dash away. Slipping between the closing doors, I inch into the corner of the elevator. When we reach the lobby, bustling with people, I head straight for the mechanical glass doors, throw the backpack over my shoulder, and set off at a brisk walk.

*

Under different circumstances, Hazel Bluff would be charming. I walk the streets for an hour or so, attempting to get my bearings. The streets are lined with willow oaks, tall enough that I suspect they've been here as long as the Victorian buildings around them. The town is built on foothills, just in the shadow of the mountains beyond. Before long, violet-bruised clouds spill over the skyline, threatening bad weather. When the rain begins, I head back toward the hospital, trying to walk as though I know where I'm going.

Near a block of municipal buildings, I pass a tourist center with a sign that reads:

WELCOME: HISTORIC HAZEL BLUFF.

Inside, I browse posters with enlarged photographs, maps, trying to pass the time. As I walk past a poster that covers the 1840s to the 1860s, discussing Civil War history and emancipation, I hear the doorbell chime and duck behind a standing display. It's a family of four, husband and wife, two young children.

I continue browsing, hoping to stay inside until the rain stops. The next display covers the late nineteenth century into the early twentieth, and I see a reproduction of a painting, enlarged to poster size, of a stately, shadowed house overlooking an expansive garden. The heading reads: 'Dovemorn House: Bygone opulence; tragic history.' I scan the bullet points: Railroad fortune. Construction: artisans and imported marble. Edwardian gardens: art nouveau meets natural landscape. A marriage gone wrong.

I step closer still, to look at a contemporary photograph of the grounds, expecting to see a restored home offering tours. Instead, it's a grainy black-and-white image of the house and grounds, a ruined ghost of the building in the beautiful painting, the color-coordinated flower beds and structures giving way to decay and overgrown with weeds. The final bullet point reads: 'Restoration. Reopening this fall.' Behind me, the door chimes again, and I hear the patter of the rain outside. I inch to the side, dodging behind a glass display case. In the backlit glass, I see the reflection of a man's silhouette, a woman's figure behind his shoulder. They're conversing, perhaps deciding whether to come in. Maybe, like me, they're just trying to get out of the rain. I see the man, light-haired, square-shouldered; the woman, standing behind him, slips out of focus. He isn't the man I've glimpsed in my nightmares. That man had a scar across one eyebrow. A swell of memory hits me: the certainty that I would die. The man's silence, when I asked for help. But it isn't him. It can't be—yet, dodging further into the shadows, I realize I can't be sure.

Turning around the other side of the display, I rush for the back door and hurry outside. It's raining, but I keep right on walking. I take a bottle of water out of my backpack and drink it as I pace up and down in the alley behind the building. The last door on my right is for a local food pantry. It looks open and, as I'm peering in the doorway, a woman at a desk takes a look at my face and waves me inside. Trying to think practically, I browse a shelf of donated items. I find a few protein bars, some cans of food, apples and oranges, which I fit into the bag along with my sketchbook and clothes. Cans of soup, a box of cereal. Back outside, I keep moving and eventually pass by a library. Maybe a place to stay for a couple hours, I think. Maybe they have computers I could use to look up somewhere to go. I'm just inside the glass door when I see the couple from the welcome center again, walking past outside. I'm not sure whether I'm more panicked or frustrated with my paranoia, but I sense I can't stay inside. The library has a large lost-and-found items bin on the right side of the entryway. I glance inside and find a baseball cap and a jacket. I pull the cap over my eyes and put the jacket on before stepping back into the rain.

So I walk, slowly, regardless of the rain. Away from downtown. Through a neighborhood, past a park. It must be afternoon by now. The trees grow taller, and the hills a bit steeper. The houses on the road are further apart, and the speed limit's higher, just the occasional vehicle whirring by.

The sky cracks with thunder. There's no point in continuing. I'm just going to tire myself out. Standing still, at the side of what looks to be a highway, I'm forced to take stock of where I am. It's clear that I've only made things worse by walking away from somewhere that might have fed and housed me, but on the other hand, I can still feel the chill of that red bouquet in the hospital room. I can hear a vehicle approaching behind me from a quarter-mile off, even over the rain, a large engine, maybe a truck. I'm wavering. I don't know who it is. I don't know what I'm running from. At the last moment, I take a leap of faith, for the first time since I woke up in the hospital. I whirl around to face the oncoming lane, and throw my arm out, thumb up.

CHAPTER NINE

The truck pulls over and I breathe a sigh of relief when I see the driver. She's stocky, in her fifties, I think, with gray-speckled hair in two frizzy braids.

"What you doin' out here, hon?" she shouts, rolling down the window. I'm not sure how to answer, but I think my silence probably speaks for itself. She sighs, leans over to push the door open. "Which way you headed?" Now I know I need to speak. I think hard, picturing the map back in the tourist center. "South," I answer.

"Me too," she says. "Come on." As I climb up, mumbling some sort of clumsy thanks, she scolds me with a parental frown. "You know you shouldn't be out here, don't you? It's not safe."

"I…" I settle into the seat, put my backpack at my feet. "I wouldn't be here if I had a better option. If I explained it to you, you'd think I was crazy." She seems to accept this, with a gruff sigh and a shrug.

"I'm Peggy," she says. "I make candles in my garage. Delivering a few boxes to gift shops along the tourist trail."

"I'm Sophie," I answer. My silence, again, speaks for itself. When our path sweeps around a sharp curve, the edge of the road is marked only by a short guardrail. We're driving through fog so thick I can barely see. Peggy's truck slows to a crawl.

"Not bad, considering the storm we had earlier," she comments.

"Really? I've never seen anything like this."

"Where you from?" she asks. I shrug, thankful when she doesn't press the matter. "We're in the middle of the cloud cover, now," she says, the engine protesting as the road climbs sharply uphill. Another half-mile and the mist thins, opening to a vista of mountains that extends as far as I can see. The nearby peaks rise above the cloud bank like islands above water. I almost imagine I could leave my short catalog of memories, all my wounds and question marks, behind in the hospital room. I realize suddenly that Peggy is speaking to me.

"Sorry," I say. "Nice view out here. What'd you say?"

"Anywhere in particular you're trying to go?" she asks. "I might have friends who could help you."

"I'll think on it," I answer. "Thanks."

But I don't. I'm staring out the window, watching the spectacular views, the breathtaking valley and the crests and rises of the mountains unfolding beyond, not a city or a building in sight. As miles pass in a blur, the clouds in the sky patch and clear sporadically, the wind off the mountains bringing a change in weather every few minutes. When we pass a sign, I turn sharply, making sure I've read it correctly.

"Oh, that?" she says. "Dovemorn House. Just up the road. Bit of a local legend. There's not that much to see now. Just a falling-down mansion and a bunch of sad stories."

"I heard they were reopening," I mention. "That they might be hiring for help."

"Reopening?" She huffs a sigh of disbelief. "They'll have a lot of work to do if that's the case."

"It was on a sign in town," I answer. When I see a gravel drive that forks off to the right, I sit up and turn to face Peggy, who nods at me as if she knows I'm torn, as if I'm at the edge of something that, for some reason I can't pinpoint, feels momentous. Looking in the mirror, I pull off my hat, fumble for the hairbrush in my bag, then try to tidy my hair. This is an act of deception—I can tell because it makes me more uncomfortable than brushing my hair ought to—I'd like to look like someone who hasn't spent all day wandering town in the rain with nowhere to go, hair stuffed under a hat. I part it on the side to hide the scar at my temple and straighten my shirt.

"I think I'll hop out here, if that's okay?"

"You got it, Sophie," she answers. The brakes sigh and screech as the truck comes to a stop, and I take my backpack and swing my legs toward the door. "Good luck."

"Thanks, Peggy." I hesitate, then reach over and grab her hand, squeeze and let go before I jump to the ground. The lost-and-found ballcap is left on the seat, but I'm moving now, and don't want to go back for it. One leap of faith wasn't a bad thing. Maybe I could try another.

CHAPTER TEN

I walk a quarter-mile up the drive, which bends sharply uphill and around, and by the time I reach the tall iron gate I'm nearly out of breath. There's nobody in sight, and though the rain has stopped, there's a gentle mist that obscures the grounds from sight. The iron gate, wrapped with a length of chain secured with a massive padlock, connects on either side to a stone wall, too high to see over. On this side of the wall, a row of towering cedars casts a deep shadow, giving the impression almost of a moat. I step close to the gate to peer through the bars. I can see a few outbuildings, a scattering of overgrown thickets and thorns, a few stone structures that could be statues or fountains. But there's nothing like a doorbell or a knocker, no way to ask to be let in. I turn to the side, eyeing the nearest tree. I walk over, grab the lowest branch, and try to climb up. When the soles of my shoes slip on the damp bark, I kick them off, hanging from the branch. Barefoot, it's a quick climb. I find my balance on one of the large lower branches, holding to the others for support, before stepping lightly onto the top of the thick stone wall, and swinging myself down to the ground. A flock of creamy-gray birds shuffles and coos in my direction, but they don't take flight. This side of the gate feels different: it's quiet here. The heaviness of the stone at my back is a comfort, and, after a day of running, I lean against its cool solidity, a cushion of moss behind my shoulders, and feel a sigh of relief so sweet, rising from so deep in my body, I could almost cry.

But I won't. Not least because I hear the sound of tires crunching on the gravel drive. Remembering I left my hat behind in Peggy's truck, I figure she's come back to return it, and walk toward the gate to greet her. The gravel is sharp under my feet, and I walk gingerly, then look up from my bare feet to see not Peggy at all, but a man.

"What the—" He's as surprised to see me as I am to see him. "What are you doing here?" Before the scowl settles over his face, I see his eyes widen, just for a moment. I see I've frightened him.

"It's alright—I just—"

"You shouldn't be here." His hair's dark brown and wet from the rain. This is the man from the waiting room at the police station. His brow settles into an impassive line. "No trespassing."

"I didn't mean to trespass."

I draw another deep breath, taking in the sweet fragrance of the cedars, and lift my chin to address him. He's taller than I remembered, though I'm admittedly on the shorter side of average. "I heard that someone here was hiring. I came to see if a position was still available." He digs in his pocket for a ring of keys, then shuffles through it, flicking suspicious glances in my direction.

"That why you're here? On the wrong side of the gate?"

"I thought there might be an office," I answer, more clearly this time. "I was looking for the owner."

"The owner lives in California," he scoffs. "I'm the caretaker. And interviews are by appointment only." He finds the key he wants and opens the padlock, unwinding the chain. "Kids around here like to sneak in, get drunk, have pretend seances."

"I'm not a kid," I answer. He looks pointedly at my bare feet, his hands gripping the unlocked gate between us. "I climbed up the tree right there to get in. So if you have trespassers, that's probably why." If I had to guess, he's in his late thirties, but it's hard to tell. "My name's Sophie." Through the bars of the gate, I reach out to offer a handshake.

"Hi, Sophie." When he finally speaks to me, I could swear he rolls his eyes. "Could you stand aside so I can open this?" With a sense of surprise that quickly turns into annoyance, I step back. He opens the gates and walks straight past me. I catch up to him, walking across the gravel as though it doesn't hurt my feet.

"You're still here," he observes.

"Look, I'm really sorry for sneaking in. I didn't mean to be rude." I don't want to tell him that I've spent the last three weeks in a hospital room, that I was afraid the wrong eyes might find me if I stayed on the other side of the gate. "I'm new to the area."

"Oh, really?" he asks, looking over his shoulder at me as he walks. "Where are you from, that a gate means something other than keep out?"

"Just listen. Please." Turning so we're face to face, I take two quick steps forward so that I'm now standing in his way. "I said, my name is Sophie. Tell me about the job." When I offer a handshake for a second time, he grasps my hand, and I feel the brush of calluses on my palm.

"Nathaniel Wells," he says. A moment passes, and I clear my throat with expectation. I pull my hand back, suddenly afraid the criss-cross of scars there is more visible than I think. "And you need to make an appointment."

"I heard you the first time."

"Fine," he sighs. "Landscaping. Garden work. Maintenance." He takes off walking again, and when I hesitate, looks back at me as if to indicate I'm meant to follow him.

We pass what looks as though it might once have been a circular garden, with a low concrete wall dividing it into quarters, and a pathway carving through the middle. I try not to stare, though it's impossible to stand here, in the ruins of something once so magnificent, without feeling a little humbled. When Nathaniel speaks again, I use it as an excuse to slow down, inching my sore feet from the gravel path onto the softer grass. "How'd you hear about the job?"

"I was—in town." I weigh how much I can conceal without outright lying. "There's a sign at the welcome center that says the house is opening for tours in the fall. Someone said you were hiring for help. That you were having trouble finding someone to work here."

"Yeah?" he says. "Well, it's hard work. And it's nearly an hour to the closest town. There's living quarters, decent enough to stay in, but no air conditioning. No phone."

"Will you show me around?"

"No." He answers so promptly, and with such certainty, that I can see something about him enjoys saying it.

"I'm already here." I cross my arms and he rolls his eyes again. There are bits of wet grass and dirt in between my toes, and it takes all I've got to try to look serious.

"Fine," he says. "I'll show you around. But it's not an interview, the job is not on the table, and you wouldn't be interested in it, anyway."

"Fine."

Nathaniel sets off again, and I try to match his pace. We face an expanse of overgrown foliage and structures—walkways, trellises, statuary—that I assume to have been a garden. It would be beautiful, I think, if it were cleaned up. No—it's still beautiful. At the far end of the gardens, I can just make out the shape of a house, huddled in the mist like some kind of animal.

"Very brief background," he says. "The house was built between 1904 and 1907. Marble from Italy, brought over by steamship and pulled up the mountain by horses. Ten dozen craftsmen worked on it over three years. Stained-glass windows by Tiffany himself. It was built as a gift from Colonel Atwood to his wife."

"Wow," I breathe. I stare as the marble house comes into view, four layers of windows flanked by a tower on either side. The windows are dark and the roof is strewn with fallen leaves and branches. One of the porches on the first level looks dangerously slanted. "Imagine someone giving you that as a present. How'd it end up like this?"

"You could say their marriage went south. Nobody's lived here or maintained the place since the sixties. The owner hired me to chase off the occasional trespasser and then, six months ago, got the wild idea to open for tours. So, here we are."

"That's it?"

"I said I'd give you a brief background." Nathaniel pauses and, in the short silence, I pull my jacket closer. I can't tell if he's looking at my ill-fitting clothes or if the scar on my temple is showing. "The Edwardians loved outdoor living spaces," he says. "Walkways, courtyards, terraces. Most of the structure of the gardens is intact. What it needs is to be cleaned up, cleared out, and some of it replanted. It's just too much for one pair of hands. Maybe too much for two," he says, fixing me with a doubting look. "You live in town?" he asks. I nod my head, justifying the lie by telling myself it's been mainly true until today. "It's a long drive," he says.

"You said there was a place to stay here?" As I wait for his answer, I see him sneak a look across the pond.

"Yeah, but—"

"Can I see it?" I ask. A long, quiet moment passes.

"It's not in the best shape."

"That's fine." I follow him across the grounds and over a footbridge that arcs over a wide pond, edged with overgrown ornamental grass and wildflowers.

"Watch your hand there," he says, indicating a loose spot on the handrail. "I'm having it repaired, but it's not steady right now."

"Thanks." He leads me across the garden, along a wide granite pathway covered with a high trellis, where climbing roses with peach- and white-colored flowers are in bloom.

When we reach the other side of the mansion, we walk up a small incline to see a much smaller stone dwelling built into the hillside. There's a wooden door and a pair of windows either side. The upper part of the structure is perforated with little indents, almost as if someone meant to hide or plant something there. Rows on rows of them. I take a questioning step closer and place a hand on the stone wall. A dove startles and takes flight from one of the nests, fluttering past my shoulder. I gasp and stumble backward. For the first time, Nathaniel laughs.

"This was the dovecote. They used to keep doves here. There are no birds inside, but they still come to the nests."

"Keep doves?" I ask. "How do you catch them?"

"You don't catch doves." For a second, something akin to a smirk softens his expression before it settles into a frown again. "You give them a safe place to stay, and sometimes they do." He unlocks the door and pushes it open for me. Inside, it is quiet and shadowed. When Nathaniel turns on a light, I see what was once a small but graciously appointed study. By the windows at the front of the room, there's a sprawling desk and a carved wooden chair, and I can sense the quality of the hardwood under my feet, despite its scratches.

"Even for estates of this period, a structure like this was unusual," Nathaniel says. "But Zenaida—Mrs. Atwood—loved doves."

"Zenaida," I repeat, savoring the delightful-sounding name. The walls of the high-ceilinged room are hung with mirrors and paintings, I assume to carry light into the room from the front windows, all coated now with dust.

"*Zenaida* is also the Latin name of a type of dove," he says. "Mourning doves. The ones you see out there. So, in a way, he named the house for her."

"It's so pretty," I whisper, though there's something of sadness in my tone. "Why hasn't it been in use? It's such a lovely building." He gives a pointed look at the desk before speaking.

"Well, the family that was living in the house at that point didn't want it. I think they repurposed the building as an alternative to demolishing it," he answers. I lift my chin, look down the length of the wall at the carved chair rail, the stone fireplace in the corner adorned with carvings of autumnal fruits: apples, figs, pomegranates. It's not in the best of condition, but the detail is striking.

"Why?" With a hesitant, almost reverent hand, I step closer to the fireplace, trace the carvings at eye level. Nathaniel clears his throat in a way that tells me he's choosing his words carefully.

"The ghost stories started going around almost as soon as she disappeared," he says. "It's got historical value. But I think the truth is, nobody wanted to use it."

"What happened?" I remember the secretary, as well as Peggy, both saying that the house was haunted.

"I don't think anyone's really sure. She left a cryptic note, like a poem or a riddle, almost. Left it on the desk, right there. A cook thought she saw Zenaida walking into the woods one evening, but nobody is exactly certain when she was last seen," he adds. I can tell he's skimming over things. "They never found her body."

"Oh." I hug my arms, rubbing my hands to warm them in the sudden chill. "Not even now?"

"One thing you've got to understand about the woods," he says. "Even experienced hikers can get lost. The trees muffle sound."

"Maybe she got lost, or…" I trail off.

"Maybe," he agrees. "The note she left behind might contradict that."

"What did it say?" I trace a hand along the massive desk, coated with dust.

"I don't remember." This is so obviously a lie that I'm ready to call him out on it, to insist he tell me, but he keeps talking. "Not long after, a gardener found one of her gloves in the rose trellis, way up, like it wasn't there by accident. Several years later, a child found her wedding ring in the pool by the willow grove. A year after that, a hiking party found one of her shoes, out in the woods, ten miles in the other direction." Nathaniel sees the look on my face and seems to snap back to normal. "Sorry—I did say I'd give you a brief background."

I would have thought this kind of story would send me running. But the room has a feeling of invitation, almost, like an old friend asking me to stay and catch up. I'm relieved when Nathaniel opens the next door and points to a staircase. "Upstairs is the bedroom and bathroom. This part used to be the dovecote. They would come in through the holes in the wall and roost here. That's why there aren't windows on this side." Turning back into the study, he points toward the back of the room. "This was used as servants' quarters mid-century, and they added the kitchen and bedroom. It's not state of the art, but everything works. There's no laundry," Nathaniel adds. "No storage. It's fifty miles to the nearest gas station, let alone a town."

"It's fine." I follow as he walks outside and shuts the door behind him. "When can I start?" Nobody will find me here, I know it. I imagine that I could sleep without waking in fear. That I could spend all my days working outside, keep moving until I'm tired enough to rest. And something about the landscape has me enchanted. But when Nathaniel Wells answers me, he's shaking his head.

"I told you, the job's not on the table. I don't mean to be rude, Sophie, but I might have understated the situation: this is difficult, physical work. Landscaping, clearing brush—"

"I can do it," I snap. I understand I'm being scrutinized, and the challenge sparks my temper. This place wants me: I can feel it. This man knows nothing about that. "No wonder you haven't been able to hire anyone." *You're insufferable,* I add silently.

"I bet you'd quit inside a week," he says. I look down at my crossed arms and remember the nurse telling me that I gave someone hell.

"Yeah? How much?"

"Excuse me?"

"One week. Trial period. You don't even need to pay me."

"Fine," he agrees, as if daring me. "When can you start?"

"Anytime," I retort.

"Tomorrow, then," he says.

"Fine," I repeat, my voice rising a note. Nathaniel takes a step back, as if he's looking at me for the first time. It makes me nervous, and I stand here on edge, squeezing the necklace I carry in my pocket.

"Be here at eight," he says. "And don't feel bad if you change your mind."

"I won't change my mind." I brush past him, our shoulders almost colliding, and storm out into the open air. "No need to walk me out."

CHAPTER ELEVEN

I leave Nathaniel standing outside the dovecote and walk briskly past the flowering trees, across the footbridge, and through the ruins of the elaborate gardens. The rain picks up again as I walk barefoot down the gravel drive, out through the gate. I retrieve my shoes from the foot of the cedar tree and gratefully slide my feet into them. I look over my shoulder with a scowl, whispering a few choice words in Nathaniel's direction. Several yards from the gate, I find a dry spot to sit against the wall, under the branches of another tall cedar.

Wherever my brother is, I hope he'd be proud of how I'm looking out for myself. Thanks to the food pantry, I've got protein bars and a bottle of water for dinner. I open my sketchbook and uncap the brown marker, immediately begin a sketch of a dove, thinking as I sketch. Sleep is out of the question, but I'm certain I can find a place to wait out the night. As the rain continues at its steady pace, I put my sketchbook away. Though it's nearly summer, clouds darken the evening. I pull my knees up to my chin and try to make myself as comfortable as I can. From a distance, I hear the startling clatter of the chain links. Nathaniel can't see me from here, watching as he locks the gate for the evening. Walking into the fog, he paces along the length of the stone wall as though he's looking for something. When he turns around and walks back, toward where I'm sitting, I lean back and try to disappear between the trees. Over the noise of the rain, I don't hear his footsteps until he's almost right in front of me.

"Sophie, right?" he says.

I guess this ends right here. So much for a leap of faith.

"Hello." I sigh, any energy for arguing depleted. If I tell him the truth, that I'm unable to remember an injury that should have killed me, that I fled the hospital because I was afraid of shadows, he'll surely have the good sense to tell me to leave.

"Catch." Something drops into the grass at my side.

"What is it?"

"Keys. To the apartment."

"What?"

"You don't have anywhere to go, do you?"

I reach to the ground, my fingers searching in the wet grass until I find the keys. With the same guarded expression, almost grudging, he turns back toward the gate, waiting for me to follow him.

"How'd you know?"

"I thought about it." Offering no further detail, he chains and locks the gate behind us, then, a little way up the path, cuts off to the right.

"Any emergencies, my house is that way, past the willows," he says. "See you at eight."

"See you at eight."

In the near dark, the shapes in the garden look like phantoms. Despite the gloom, I catch sight of something glinting in the fading light. Someone's watching me. I know it in my very bones. But there's nowhere left to run, or to hide. Sinking onto my knees in the damp grass, I wait for whatever comes next. The horizon itself seems to bend and waver as I try to catch my breath.

Then, I see the massive stained-glass window. Spanning a length of the second and third floors, it must be ten feet high and made up of countless bits of colored glass. In the center is a portrait of a woman in a violet gown, one arm outstretched. Flowering vines surround her, and doves perch along her arms and on the greenery. This could only be Zenaida Atwood. I tilt my head, and I swear the opalescent colors shift, some trick of the light giving it a faint glow. As I turn away, I almost trip and fall. Recovering my balance, I throw an incredulous glance back at the lady in the window, half expecting her to wink at me. She saw me, I think. She saw every bit of me. Does she know I'm in her study? Does she mind? I tell myself that ghosts aren't real. That the world has enough fear in it without bringing the supernatural into the mix. I should know.

As I unlock the apartment, a handful of birds take flight from the nesting holes. Inside, the air is deliciously cool. I stand in the doorway and breathe in quietly. For the first time that I can remember, I'm standing in a place that, for now at least, is my own.

Tracing my fingertips in the layers of dust, I admire the desk, imagining how beautiful it must have been once. I arrange my sketchbook and markers, nod a silent request for permission in the direction of the stained-glass window, and take a seat. Then I notice the sound of the quiet. There's a lull in the air outside, something vast but intimate. I open the doorway and stare out at the deepening night. From the forest emanates a depth of sound: air on leaves, animals moving in dry brush, birds and crickets and tree frogs in their conversations. Beyond the yard, the skyline is dark.

With a sudden, faint cry, I rush back inside and slam the door, locking it behind me. That sound, those woods. I know it—or it knows me. I've been out there. I huddle over the desk and open my book, immediately putting pen to paper, drawing a shape, any shape. Doves, at first, and behind them a mass of a shape that suddenly looks back at me: a mountainside, with all its desolate lushness. No one walks past my door, no one rattles the lock. Nobody scratches at the window. As I sit here in the quiet, I take the necklace from my pocket and place it on the desk, like some kind of offering. After a few minutes have passed, I walk slowly through the apartment, putting away the contents of my bag: lining a cupboard with my supplies from the food pantry, enough dry goods, I think gratefully, for at least few days. Upstairs, after putting away my clothing and hair brush, I find a rather dusty set of linens in the closet, and shake them off before making up the twin bed. I remove my lost-and-found jacket, baring my arms to this new place, tracing over the patchwork of scars. Detective Radford all but promised me: *wherever you're from, it seems like nobody's looking for you.* Though it isn't cold, I shiver, pulling the jacket back on. Despite what the detective said, I can't look at this skin without thinking that somebody wants me gone.

CHAPTER TWELVE

I wake with the sunrise and, though the analog clock on the wall reads half past six, make up my mind to dress and go outside early. In contrast to the converted study, the bedroom built here into the dovecote is sparse and small. The walls are plaster, covering over the indents that would have allowed doves inside, though I find an occasional feather under my feet. There's only one window, and I cringe at the thought of the damage done to the stone exterior to put it there, though I'm grateful to be able to wake to the sunrise. Aside from the plain metal bed frame and a little table, the room is bare. I shower and run a brush through my hair, then dress, choosing a long-sleeved T-shirt that covers my arms. I make a cup of instant oatmeal and eat sitting at the desk, imagining a goodbye letter left here. It feels like sacrilege to sit here, but then, remembering the way that stained-glass figure seemed to study me, I wonder if she'd mind. I put a bottle of water in my back pocket and walk outside, locking the door behind me.

After yesterday's rain, the morning light casts a different light on the gardens. The structures and plants that remain of what was cultivated here seem to rest gladly alongside the tangles of thickets and wild greenery.

I hear the sound of a hammer and follow it across the garden to the east side of the house. In the distance to my left, a row of magnolia trees shines in the sun, and I breathe in the lemony fragrance. The main walkway leads through a lawn where I can make out plants and shrubs in rows, all overgrown, cobwebs sagging with dewdrops between the tall grasses. I see gladioli and tulips astray among the brambles, and suppose they may have been planted here in rows once. Beyond, toward the edge of the wide clearing, I see the pond, larger than it looked yesterday evening. The narrow bridge reaches over it in a rounded arch, a beautiful arc against the landscape. To the other side, I find the trellised walkway bordered with roses leading to the west side of the mansion.

Nathaniel is in boots, jeans, and a faded black T-shirt, sitting atop an unreliable-looking roof over one of the doorways, hammering what looks like shingles or nails into place. When he sees me, he sits with his knees stretched out in front of him on the rooftop, and opens a bottle of water, one forearm shading his eyes from the sun.

"Morning." After his readiness to argue yesterday, he seems on notice, but decidedly withdrawn.

"Morning." Yesterday I felt tension, the air between us thorny before we even spoke. Now, I wait for another barb, another invitation to leave, but he offers none, and I almost feel as if he's waiting for me to speak as well.

"I could show you around the place, if you like. Just need a few minutes to finish this roof."

"No, thanks." Although I'd love to see more of the property, I haven't forgotten about his assumption that I wasn't up to the job. I'd like to prove him wrong before I do anything else. "What are you working on today?"

"Patching this roof," he says, gesturing with the heavy end of the hammer. I flinch and he puts it down at his side. "Then, clearing out the herb garden over there." He indicates a circular garden bounded by a hedge. It's filled with vines and leaves, as if they'd been poured into it as into a basin. The vines also cover a curved bench that faces what I assume was once a fountain. Among the vines, I can see the overgrown and thick-stemmed descendants of an herb garden: rosemary here, lavender there, what might once have been mint. Nathaniel climbs down the roof on a ladder and follows me over, and I tense, remembering his words the previous afternoon: *It's difficult work. I might have understated.* This doesn't look difficult. He walks over and pulls up a vine that's rooted to the ground at several spots.

"This is English ivy. Popular plant, but it chokes out anything else it touches. The idea is to recreate how the garden would have looked in 1907. It turns out, if someone plants ivy in one spot and then deserts the place for decades, it takes over everything in its path."

"Easy enough," I answer.

"It's tougher than it looks. In some spots, it's thick. You leave it long enough, ivy can pull down a porch roof. That's what happened over there," he adds, pointing again with the hammer. "Herbicide would kill it, but it would probably take out everything around it, too."

"Okay." I take a few steps into the garden. The ivy reaches past my ankles, deeper in some spots. Nathaniel waits, as if I'm going to ask for further instruction. Instead, I put my water bottle on the vine-covered bench, turn back to him, and nod my head.

"It's going to be warm," he says.

"I have water." I remember I'm wearing long sleeves. Nathaniel doesn't know there's a network of injuries beneath those sleeves, that the skin over my shoulder still feels tight when I move, though it doesn't hurt anymore, not really.

"Gloves?"

"I'll be fine."

"Alright." Nathaniel still seems uncertain. "I'll be over there if you need me."

And, finally, he leaves me alone.

CHAPTER THIRTEEN

Without a moment's hesitation, I walk to the fountain, which looks as if it might have been functional half a century ago. It stands in the middle of the circle. I tell myself I'll finish all of it before midday. I grasp a strand of ivy and pull.

An hour later, I adjust this goal. The vines hold onto the earth with roots along their length, somehow even clinging to the pale granite of the fountain. Along the ground, they pull up clods of soil along with ants and earthworms. The truth is, I'm not afraid of hard work. Ever since waking up in the hospital, I've been living on a baseline of nervousness, an almost constant desire to run, walk, do something with this energy. Working myself to the point of exhaustion might be the only way to relieve it.

I first pull the vines from the fountain, from the top down, then work outward and around in a spiral. The discarded vines go into a pile at my side, and every few minutes I haul an armful to a heap at the base of the fountain. Soon, I've rolled my sleeves up past my elbows. When the sun is overhead, I move to a spot in the shade. Nathaniel's finished the roof, gone out of sight to work on some other task. As midday passes into later afternoon, I let the prickle of sweat and the heat of the hour become a distraction from the disquiet in my mind.

This side of the mansion faces west, and I see that the sunlight will fall beautifully on this wall as it sets. There's a roofed porch on the ground level, bordered by more unruly and overgrown plants.

One column looks close to collapsing. Up both sides of the wall and across the third level is a line of ornate windows, though the glass is cracked in places and dark with dust. A tendril of ivy is creeping out one window and wish I could be up there, pulling it away, too. All the while, my hands are moving, uprooting vines from the soil, and I sit with my knees folded under me. The dry leaves beneath my fingers rustle and I freeze. Just a few inches from my hands, a coiled snake rests. It's beautiful, almost, with a dainty crosshatch of brown and amber scales that wrap around its back. A copperhead. *Go on,* I think, looking into the black beads of its eyes. *Why aren't you moving?*

"Still here?"

I didn't even hear Nathaniel's footsteps. When I don't move, he takes a step closer. "Don't move," I say.

The snake is close enough to bite, close enough that there's more risk than safety in shying back. I hear Nathaniel's gasp as he notices it. I realize my arms are exposed and with them the pale patchwork of healed scrapes that line my arms. *He's looking at the snake,* I tell myself. *He's not looking at me.* In that moment, the copperhead slithers away into the ivy. I shove my sleeves down to my wrists and sit up straight. "I guess I should have told you to look out for snakes," he mumbles.

"Not a problem." I gaze after the creature as if I could call it back. My heart is racing, but I don't feel frightened. Instead, something like a thrill runs through my veins. *A dream, maybe*, I had said to the doctor. But was it? "All you have to do is be still, try not to startle them. They'll know if you're frightened."

"Right," he answers, watching me as if I've said something unearthly, rather than offering facts. "I'll finish up."

"I can do it," I answer. If I find a branch, clatter around the rest of the garden before I go plunging my hands in, any remaining snakes will clear the area. Besides, I made a bet I'd stay here at least a week, and I don't plan to lose it. Nathaniel glances at the stack of cleared vines, raises an eyebrow, and says nothing. For the first time today, I find myself smiling. He rests a hand on the fountain, and follows my gaze to the wall of the house, where the stained-glass portrait is playing tricks with the afternoon light.

"It's really something when the sun starts to go down, isn't it?"

I nod and get back to work, then feel a set of eyes on me. Nathaniel lifts a hand to touch his temple and tilts his chin. The unwelcome reminder is a shock. I open my mouth to answer, then realize I don't have the words to do so.

"Car accident," I whisper, with a shrug that dismisses the topic.

"You said you were new to the area," he says. "How long have you been here?" I don't want to lie, but I don't want to chat either.

"Long story."

"No need for small talk, right?"

"No, it's actually—" Just as I realize I'm on the edge of telling him something I maybe should keep to myself, he interrupts me.

"That's fine." He brushes his hands off, takes a step back in the other direction. "I'm the same way."

Though I'm wondering if I should explain further, I let his comment stand. I've impressed him, and that's enough for now.

"I'm finished for the day," he says. "Just so you're aware, there's a crew coming by in the morning to repair part of the trellis." I open my water bottle and take a sip, nodding. "And I'll probably drive into Hazel Bluff for groceries on Friday, so if you need to pick anything up, you can come along."

"Thanks." It's true that my food pantry supplies are going to run out at some point. I imagine I could also use this trip to check in with Detective Radford. Nathaniel's waiting for me to speak, and it doesn't escape me that this offer doubles as an excuse for me to pack up and leave. "I'll, ah, I'll go into town with you on Friday," I answer. If the detective has found any information on my brother, or, I suppose, on me, I'll be leaving. But I'm not sure how to explain this to him, so I change the subject. "Same thing tomorrow?"

"Yeah," he says. "I'll be out here early. Hey, one more thing."

"What's that?"

"How long were you sitting here by yourself, making eyes at that snake?" he asks.

"Oh, it was an hour or so," I answer. "We had a lot to catch up on." His eyes widen, and he opens his mouth as if to answer me, but says nothing. Despite my best efforts, I find myself smiling, holding back a laugh. "No—it wasn't more than a second or two."

"Just wondering," he answers, a hint of a smile tracing his mouth. "See you tomorrow."

For another hour, I stay outside, pulling at the vines. It's only because I want a reason to stay out until I see the full glow of the sunset on that window. As the time passes, I watch the ground for snakes, and it occurs to me to wonder why I know the first thing about a copperhead, or not to move too suddenly when it was watching me. My palms are stinging and my limbs are sore, but there's a comfort about it: the mundanity of a blister from a day's work. I sit back and see that I've cleared almost a third of the herb garden. For my first day, I'm satisfied.

As the sun begins to go down, I sit cross-legged on the ground and watch the colors change on the stained glass. Behind Zenaida's figure spans a gentle violet-blue mountain range, same as the landscape behind me, as though I'm sitting at the axis of a reflection and its original. *They found your shoe, your jewelry,* I think. Is the rest of her here, somewhere, disintegrating into this strange landscape, or did she disappear right into that other side of the glass? Mourning doves call and it sounds like they're saying, 'Go home, go home.' I pick up my water bottle and walk toward the dovecote.

CHAPTER FOURTEEN

The doves continue to call late into the night. I'm half in a trance as I draw, and when I pause to think, I rest my hands on the worn wood grain of Zenaida Atwood's desk. I wonder what dreadful sadness she must have felt, that it could make her want to leave this beautiful place.

Nathaniel said that nobody knew why Zenaida left. And, I recall, he didn't want to tell me what was in the letter she left behind. What makes anybody run away? Pointless question, I reflect. Everybody's got something to run from, or maybe toward. Suddenly, as if I'm watching a flower open, there's a sense of alignment, of a center point from which my fragments of memory unfold. My sudden anger when the detective said that nobody was looking for me, that memory of feeling unwanted. Holding my pen tightly, I see a blot of ink spreading from the felt tip. I remember running away, as a child. I left no such note, no riddle behind. I wanted to disappear into the city just like my mother had, so that nobody could find me, no social workers or foster parents.

I had run away from my first foster home, almost on a weekly basis, until they moved me to another family. The woman there was kind. When she brushed my hair, it never pulled or tugged. I ran away again, just the same, every chance that I got. I remember that the kind woman found me huddled in a bus stop, trying to get—somewhere, I'm not sure. She brought me home, fed me dinner. After I'd changed into

my pajamas and been put to bed, I crept back out into the hallway,
listening to the hushed voices in the kitchen.

"She's six, Jean," the man had said. "She had to take the bus and
change stops on the subway twice to get all the way to Brooklyn. I
don't understand why, or how she was able to do that."

The woman's response was hopeful, but muddled with sadness. "If
she keeps running off, they'll try to place her somewhere else. I don't
know what to do for her. She's incredibly sweet, just…"

I remember that I lingered there, weighing two unknowns.
When my brother and I were with our mom, there wasn't always
food. It wasn't always warm in the apartment. But my brother was
there, and I wasn't alone. His name comes back to me, too. Miles.
I could say Miles before I could say Mom.

I didn't know if I'd be able to find him when I ran away, or
whether there would be hot meals and kind voices when I did.
Even then, at six, I knew the choice I'd make. The next day at
school I snuck away during lunchtime. The social worker decided
to place me with another family.

When I blink my eyes open, I'm still hunched over the desk.
It's nearly one in the morning. I'm resting my hands on the solid
wood beneath me, as if a concrete sensation could ground me
here, instead of in the past. Though finely made, the desk has
not been repaired or refinished at all, and I trace its scratches and
scars, savoring the texture. Just under the rim of the desk, I feel
a deeper scratch than the rest, and peer down to look. I find the
letters ZA, followed by a date: August 1, 1910. I trace over it again
and again, breathing a deep sigh. Some of the dust from under
the desk goes into my nose and I cough.

Leaning over the desk, I look down to see I've sketched a child
with an apple in her hand, too young to appreciate that food and
safety aren't always easy to come by. In my book, I add an item
to the list of things that Sophie knows, and decide to make an
attempt at sleep.

CHAPTER FIFTEEN

After spending weeks indoors, it's a relief to be outside for entire days in sunlight. By night, I'm contending with bad dreams and imagined footsteps, scarcely sleeping. But daytime is easy: I let whatever task I'm given consume my energy, taking only a midday break. Though the warmth makes it easy to skip a meal, I soon learn that, if I wait too long to eat, I'm impatient and muddled. Once the circular garden is cleared, I'm tasked with a thicket of blackberry brambles that are crowding the roses by the walkway.

"They're related, you know," Nathaniel says, moving aside a blackberry cane with a deft arm that either avoids or ignores the thorns. He's all work, but when he talks about something he likes, his voice turns smooth and warm. "Blackberries and roses. Gardening's relaxing for most people, but there's a tragedy to it, if you think about it. Pulling up some plants, cultivating others."

"Suppose so." The leaves have a similar shape, almost the same. I try not to think about it. After Nathaniel walks away, I step closer to the brambles, and see almost no difference between the thick, green, swaying branches, the thorns on either swiping at my arms the same. The roses alternate peach blossoms with white, delicate tea roses that tangle with the blackberries. I watch Nathaniel, who's far off now, cutting a beam of wood with a handsaw. *Pulling up some, cultivating others.* I let my gaze flicker back to the thorns tangling in my sleeves. I don't know whether they're catching on my skin or if I'm imagining the same old pain, but it's so sharp that I blink my eyes.

All those times that I ran away, I was hoping to find my family. My mom and my brother. I could never find my brother, all those excursions out on my own, not only because I was a little child, but because he was always in trouble. With a counselor. In a group home. Now, as the thorns catch on my shoulder, while I try to hold one branch aside to get to the other, I feel a surge of anger, a dash of pain mixed with something older, simmering. I remember that my brother never did anything wrong. That he needed help, not punishment. The vines surround me, roses and blackberries both, so that whichever way I move, I'm stung with thorns, hacking uselessly at the vines. I'm tugging with one arm, hissing curses at the plants, when I sense a quiet presence behind me and turn to find Nathaniel, watching with one corner of his mouth turned up.

"Thought I'd check and see how it's going."

"It's going," I answer, dropping my arm, pulling the bramble along with it, waving my hand as if to shoo it away, only making it worse.

"Hold still." Nathaniel loosens the vine from where it's caught in my shirt. "With thickets like this, you don't want to fight it." He steps forward so that his shoulder is just in front of mine, then takes the shears from my hand, pointing to where the offending bramble branches off from another cane. I see where he cuts it, close to the ground.

"Thanks."

"If you fight it, you'll lose. Watch the vines and follow it in." He hands the shears back to me. "You good?"

"Yes," I answer. "Thanks."

At first I think it's going to get the better of me, but I begin to cut down the thickest canes with a big set of garden clippers. As the morning moves toward midday, I remove what I can by hand,

and clear the rest with a small lawn mower, all the while shoving this bitter feeling of unfairness back in my mind. When I'm sure Nathaniel is far-off, working on something else, I pluck a berry off a vine to taste. I keep busy until the sunset hits the stained-glass portrait of Zenaida Atwood, and I watch her with suspicion and a near adoration, coming almost to life with the shifting colors in the glass. Something in the back of my mind tells me that, somehow, she sees everything I keep secret, maybe even the parts I can't get to myself. As I walk back toward the dovecote, I turn back to the window, throwing a guilty look over my shoulder, my mind full of roses and blackberries and thorns.

Her presence, though, is warm, as if she were a sister or a friend. Suddenly, I'm reminding myself that I'm forbidden to cry, even now.

The berry brambles are thorny work, and take the better part of the week. But when the evening comes, I wash my stinging hands with a begrudging acceptance. Inside the apartment, there's the constant patter of dove wings and coos. When I sleep, I grasp for anything familiar, as if I'm in a dark room, pressing my hands against the walls, every other step colliding with an unknown shape.

The end of my first week here draws closer. A week without fearing that someone's trying to kill me. A week without running. At this point, there's only one reason I'd leave here, and that's my brother. Yet, I wait to see what the next day will bring with a mix of fear and hope. On Thursday morning, I clear the last of the blackberry vines. I've helped myself to berries throughout the morning, so I don't eat lunch right away. Instead, I sit inside by the window, curtains open, sketchbook in my lap. It's too warm today, even by my standards, and I've changed into a camisole. Before I find Nathaniel to ask for my next task, I'm planning to put on long sleeves. For now, I let my limbs rest, let the weight of my body sink against the chair.

With a sparkling crash, the window breaks, with an impact that echoes against the wall to my left. Glass shards sprinkle over my arm and shoulder and I duck on instinct. The chair tips forward and I slide onto the floor, catching myself on my forearms.

I open my eyes. Not a sound crosses my lips. As I draw a silent breath, I look from side to side. My heart beats loudly, but I'm searching for any noise or movement. Moments pass, and I see none. I'm trying to make myself small, to disappear against the stone floor.

They've found me.

Who's they?

It feels like reaching for shadows. If I could, I'd grab this specter that crosses my mind, interrogate it. In every recess, I imagine snakes slithering toward me. An image flashes across my mind, a man with fair hair and a scar across his eyebrow. My stomach twists.

The window's broken. It was too big and fast to be a bird, though a rock is possible. Then, just as I'm becoming aware of glass fragments embedded in the skin of my forearm, I see the football on the other side of the room.

"Hello?" A child's voice calls from outside. "Lady, are you okay in there?"

Wincing, I stand up. A little boy peers in through the broken pane, panting as if he's just chased his football from the other side of the county. A flop of chestnut-brown hair hangs close to his thick-framed glasses, which slip down the bridge of his nose.

"Hi," he says, tucking his glasses back into place. "Please, don't be mad at me. I meant to throw it over the pond, but it went the wrong way. I'm not supposed to throw the ball out here."

"No harm done," I answer. The boy heaves a sigh of relief and a lock of hair slips over his glasses again. There are no snakes, no danger here. Just this doe-eyed little boy with his halting apologies.

"Well—the window's broken, so a little harm. But I'm sure that can be fixed."

Through the broken window, I smile at the boy, wondering why he's still standing here.

"Are you okay?" I look again at the winsome, honey-brown eyes and realize he must be Nathaniel's child. No threat. But there's no disarm button for the panic lingering in my chest.

"Yeah." The boy shuffles his feet. "Can I have my ball?"

"Of course," I breathe. "Hang on a sec."

I retrieve the ball, making sure there aren't any stray bits of glass. Blood drips down my arm and off my fingertip. I think it hurts when I flex my arm, but it's distant; I'm tuning it out, feeling almost nothing at all. Still, there's no need to frighten the kid, so I throw a dish towel over my arm before venturing outside. The little boy is standing right outside the door.

"Here you go." I hand it over and he stares up at me with unabashed curiosity, the sort that only a child can get away with. He looks about six.

"Do you live here now?"

"For now," I answer.

"Why?"

"Well, I don't know. Because—"

"Is it true this was the doves' house? That mean you're a bird?" He cracks a smile, showing off a gap where he's lost a tooth. "My name's Lincoln."

"Hi, Lincoln." I crouch down a little so we're face to face. "My name's Sophie."

"I'm gonna call you Dove Girl," he says. I laugh.

"Sounds like you've made your mind up."

"Yeah." He answers with a shrug. "Sorry about your window, Dove Girl."

"I'm sure it'll be fine."

"Oh, I forgot!" Lincoln adjusts his glasses and turns a serious look up at me. "We're supposed to shake hands. It's good manners. I'm Lincoln Wells."

"Nice to meet you, too." I hold out my left hand, the one that's not wrapped in a towel. It crosses my mind that Nathaniel taught his son how to greet a stranger, but he took his time deciding to extend the same courtesy to me last week. Then again, I had climbed over the wall to get in, and I wasn't wearing any shoes. It seems entirely possible, though, that Lincoln picked up his good manners from someone else.

"Um, Sophie? You got hurt." His eyes flicker up to mine and latch on. "You said you were fine. Was it from the window?"

"No," I laugh, waving his concern away with my free hand. "Grown-ups get scratches all the time."

"You have to show my dad," he announces. "He'll be mad that I broke the window. But if somebody gets hurt, you have to ask for help. Besides, he knows how to fix stuff."

"No—it's nothing," I insist, aiming for an officious, adult inflection.

"Dad has a first aid kit." Lincoln leans closer, as if he's telling me a secret. "It's so cool. Come on!" Moving on to a new idea, he heaves the ball off in a random direction, and I wince again as he takes off running. "Come on," he repeats.

Exhaling a whine of annoyance, I follow him at a brisk walk. The last thing I want is for Nathaniel to think I need help. Or maybe the last thing I want is for him to see the healing scars along my right arm. If you look long enough, they seem like a deranged map, a map of places nobody would ever want to go or even hear about. Deciding to turn back, I raise my voice to tell Lincoln that I've got too much work to do. But when I see him take off across the footbridge over the pond, I speed up a little.

"Hey, slow down, okay?" My voice is more authoritative than I expected. He lingers on the bridge while I catch up, walking with him to the other end. "You a good swimmer? Because you'd better be, racing along like that with barely a railing to catch you."

"I can't swim," Lincoln answers, then brightens up. "Can you?"

"Oh, I——" The truth is, I have no idea, but before I can answer, he's on to the next subject.

"I'm a fast runner, though! And I don't fall. Well, not when my glasses stay on." I wonder, now, if the oversized glasses had anything to do with his football flying in the wrong direction. Beneath the bridge, the water is murky, greenish-dark.

Once we're on land, Lincoln takes off again at full speed, and I power-walk after him, past the west end of the grounds. A walkway leads through an opening in a flowering hedge and, beyond there, I see the caretaker's house. The yellow farmhouse is unadorned, but freshly painted.

"Dad!" Lincoln shouts with a startling volume. "Dad, come outside!" I start to follow him to the door, but he stops me, pointing to the paved driveway under our feet. I look down to see a network of hopscotch squares that wraps around the entire front of the house, an imaginary perimeter. "This is the gate. You can't walk through it," Lincoln says. "You have to follow the steps if you want to get in." He lowers his voice and his eyes widen behind his glasses. "It keeps the dragons out. Their feet are too big for the hopscotch squares."

He scatters a handful of pebbles, then speedily jumps from square to square, the soles of his sneakers scuffing on the pavement. "There!" Eyes twinkling, he looks at me hopefully. "Hurry! Dragons."

With a sigh, I obey, jumping on one foot, trying to hold my balance while I clutch the dish towel against my right arm. Lincoln cheers, and I feel the slightest bit less foolish. Until the front door swings open and I freeze, right where I stand, feeling more foolish than I even thought was possible.

CHAPTER SIXTEEN

As Nathaniel takes a step outside, his eyes sweeping across the front yard, I plant both feet on the ground. Lincoln stammers, almost as if he's afraid to disappoint his father.

"Nothing's wrong," I announce, before he can ask. "Football accident. The window at the apartment broke. Your son asked me to come with him to tell you." I realize, then, that it's more than hopscotch and my disheveled appearance out of place here. I'm a stranger, standing in his front yard, playing with his kid.

"What happened, Lincoln?" Nathaniel walks directly down the yard, placing himself in between me and the little boy.

"She got hurt," Lincoln says. "It was my fault—my ball went through the window. I…" He holds his glasses in place with both hands. "I threw it and it spun the wrong way."

"You know we don't throw balls near the house, right?"

"It could have happened to anyone," I murmur. "Footballs are famously unpredictable. You never know what they're going to do." A smile plays at Lincoln's mouth, so I keep it up. "And this football clearly went rogue."

"So the window broke, huh?" Nathaniel asks the boy, as if I haven't said a word. I'm afraid he's going to scold him. But the man who kneels to eye level with the child, brushing the hair out of his eyes, is almost unrecognizable. "Are you okay, buddy?"

"Yes. See? I'm fine." Lincoln holds out his arms for inspection and turns in a circle. I get the sense that he's done this before.

Lincoln points to me. "It's her," he says. "I think she fell over on the glass. I told her you're good at fixing stuff, though. You're not mad, are you?"

"Of course I'm not mad. We can fix windows." Nathaniel touches Lincoln's glasses. "These still too big for you?" he asks. "I thought Mom was going to get you another pair."

"She did," the boy answers. "I left them at home." I make a note that, to Lincoln, somewhere else is home.

"Let's go out this afternoon, then," Nathaniel says. "We'll get you a pair to keep here. Windows fix, okay? What if your glasses slipped and you fell?" His eyes track toward the pond and I see what he's thinking, see that he doesn't want to say it out loud.

"I don't want to go to the glasses store," Lincoln sighs.

"How about a movie after?" Nathaniel suggests.

"Yeah!" Lincoln punches at the air and grins, scampers toward the house. I'm left stammering as Nathaniel approaches me.

"Two of the panes broke." I cross my arms and speak in a matter-of-fact tone. "I don't think you'll need to replace the whole window." He stands an arm's length away and looks at me as if he's waiting for something. "I cleared out all the blackberries, so if you'll remind me of what was next on the list, I'll get out of here."

"So, what happened? Lincoln said you fell?" he asks. I try to laugh off a shock of embarrassment.

"I was sitting by the window when the ball came in. Ducked so fast I tipped the chair."

"Sorry." He holds out a hand. "Let me see."

"It's fine." I shrug my shoulders inward, feeling the healed cut down the middle of my chest. It makes me cold with fear to stand this close to anybody. I'm turning to leave, but then I notice the change in his expression: his chin lowers, his brow softens, as if something in my direction warranted a second look. When he extends his hand again, palm up, I inch forward and reluctantly unwrap the dish towel.

"Bend your arm," he says. I do, and, feeling a twinge, squeeze my lips together, breathing out through my nose.

"Hurts?"

"No."

"Yeah, it did." He casts a look my way that's more confused than anything else. "It's a piece of glass. You can come inside and wash it—"

"No, thanks," I interrupt.

"—if you want." Nathaniel pauses. He's only offering, and I realize I'm bordering on making this worse. I'd rather take this piece of glass in my arm with me than stand here in front of him. But I can see that it's going to make more of a scene to refuse any help.

"Okay." I follow him up the steps, gritting my teeth. The door opens into a foyer; there's a dining room to the right, a living room to the left. We walk through the dining room and, in the hallway that adjoins the kitchen, Nathaniel opens a large china cabinet, taller than I am. Each shelf is lined with supplies, too many to name, though I see a row of disinfectants—iodine, hydrogen peroxide, isopropyl, chlorhexidine. An assortment of bandages and plasters and gauze. Sterile scissors in plastic wrappers. Surgical tape.

"Lincoln mentioned you had a first aid kit." I don't need to voice the next half of that thought.

"Yeah, well, we're far from everything out here." He turns a furtive glance at me over his shoulder, then away. "It's good to be prepared."

"Right," I say, as if it's anything but strange. He scans the shelves, plucks out a few items. "That's a good point."

"I was in the military when I was younger," he says, still shuffling items in the cabinet. "I guess if you see enough injuries you can't fix, it makes you want to be ready for the ones you can."

"Makes sense."

"Anyway, Lincoln's nearsighted," he says. "Very nearsighted. But the doctors don't want to prescribe contact lenses until he's eight, so we've got a couple years left with glasses." I realize he's changing the subject, so, feeling just a hint of empathy, I follow along.

"It must be tough keeping up with the right size," I say, "while they're growing so fast." Nathaniel agrees with a curt nod of his chin and turns into the kitchen. With spotless countertops and appliances, it has the look of a place that's usually very clean, but that has acquired some sudden clutter, in the form of a lunchbox and children's toys scattered here and there. Nathaniel sees that the freezer door is ajar, pushes it shut with his foot. "Hey, Lincoln," he calls, the deep volume of his voice startling me. "You been in the freezer?"

"Maybe!" Lincoln shouts back, his voice sounding from upstairs.

"If you eat up the ice cream, you won't have any for after dinner," Nathaniel calls back. He tilts his head, indicating for me to stand by the sink next to him. "He's only here twice a month," he says. "I try to make it fun. Terrible parenting, right? Ice cream before dinner." He laughs, but I sense somehow that it isn't a joke.

"I can think of worse things," I offer, wondering if my mother would have let me eat ice cream before dinner.

"Yeah?" Nathaniel mutters, as if he almost expects me to challenge him. He pauses for a moment, and I see his thoughts reaching in several directions, upstairs toward his son, the first aid cabinet, my unlikely presence. And then, he seems to shrug it off, the hard line of his brow settling just a bit. "Me too," he says, "I guess."

He turns on the tap and dampens a paper towel. I take it from him, blot the cut off, then hold my arm under the running water. Nathaniel hands me a disinfectant, then another paper towel. I pat it dry, gritting my teeth again when I feel the bit of glass that's still there. He unwraps a sterile set of tweezers and hands them over.

"It's a pretty clean cut," he observes, reaching to turn off the water. I exhale, closing my eyes in a long blink, remembering my shoulders are exposed, showing the healing marks across my right side. I feel like there's a rock lodged in my throat. I pluck clumsily at the loose skin with my left hand. Maybe it hurts. I don't know.

"You want a hand?" he asks. I pass the tweezers over, quickly, noting that my hand shakes just a little, and stand still as he turns my arm in his hand. Something about the set of Nathaniel's expression softens when he focuses. He's younger than I had first guessed, even close to my age. Holding the tweezers, he draws close, then—it's gone. I watch patiently as he rinses my arm under the tap, as if I'm standing across the room, not right here next to him.

"There you go." He covers it with clean gauze. "Cover it until the bleeding stops, but take the bandage off when you sleep. It'll heal better if it can breathe."

"Thanks," I answer. He's still holding my arm, though, looking now at the blisters on my hand, a few on the pads of my fingers and on the slope between my index finger and thumb. Nathaniel moves back toward the cabinet, puts back some of the supplies, removes others: a box of Band-Aids, some antibiotic ointment. He hands me the Band-Aids and ointment.

"Thanks," I repeat, putting them in my pocket. I'm grateful when Lincoln clatters down the stairs.

"Hey, Dove Girl!" he shouts. "How's your arm?"

"It's good," I answer, smiling back at his contagious grin. "All patched up. See?" Lincoln never stops moving, his feet dancing a hopscotch pattern down the hall.

"When can we go, Dad?"

"Just a few minutes," Nathaniel says. "I'm going to walk Sophie back and take a look at the window." Lincoln leans around the corner as we walk out the door. "Watch out for dragons," he hisses. I return a conspiratorial smile and wave goodbye.

As we proceed down the walkway and back into the yard, Nathaniel looks back toward his son with a bemused smile. I notice a dimple in his left cheek. "He's usually pretty reserved. Seems to like you, though."

"Seems like a fun kid."

"He is."

We walk in silence past the flowering hedges and across the footbridge. The air is cooler over the water. On the narrow bridge, I walk a few steps ahead. As we cross the other side of the gardens, a flock of doves scatters, and the tips of their wings whistle as they take flight. I hurry into my apartment, leaving the door open behind me.

"Right here," I say, pointing to the window. "See—it's not bad."

"I'll call a repair company." Nathaniel looks over his shoulder back toward the house, as if he's checking on Lincoln from all the way over here. "If you wait a couple minutes, I'll get something to cover it until it's fixed."

"No need." I linger near the door. "It'll be fine for a few days."

"Okay." As Nathaniel turns toward the door, he passes by my sketchbook, which is resting open on the desk, red flowers fairly leaping off the page. "Wow," he says. "This is beautiful. Are those poppies?"

"I… don't know." While I realize I sound unfriendly, it's at least an honest response, and if it wards off further conversation, that's okay with me too. He looks once again at the drawing of the blue-clad woman reclining in the flowers.

"There's actually a couple of opium poppies growing here, in the grounds."

"Really?" I scrunch up my nose. "Opium poppies?"

"Yeah. If you look on the other side of the plum trees past the trellises, they're over that way—on the south side of the house. It's just a few plants. But that many?" He nods at my sketchbook. "Nobody would grow that many poppies for a flower garden."

"I don't even know what a poppy looks like," I stammer.

"Like these pictures," he says, indicating my drawings.

"Why were they on the original estate?"

"It wasn't uncommon back then. Medicinal purposes. Although," he adds, "Mrs. Atwood was known to have had an opium addiction. The day she disappeared, her maid found several empty bottles of laudanum in her room." I imagine the shifting colors in the stained glass and wonder what else they may conceal.

"You mentioned she left a note." I reach one hand toward my sketchbook, inching it away from him. "What did it say?"

"Not sure." His eyes flicker toward the desk, then back to my drawing. "I don't think anyone even saved it." It's plain that he's guarding this story. What I don't understand is why it means so much to him.

"I see," I answer, glancing between Nathaniel and the open doorway, hoping he'll take the hint and leave. "Anyway—I finished clearing out those blackberries. What else do you have for today?"

"Why don't you take the rest of the day off?" he asks. I don't love the idea. "You said you were in a car accident," he says. I tense. "Looks like you landed on your side?"

"Yeah, I don't really know." I answer with short, sharp syllables. He refuses to tell me about her letter, a woman's final words, left in the very room I live in, and in the next breath asks me about the story behind my own skin. Finally, I'm more annoyed than I am overwhelmed. "I don't know, and I don't remember asking you in to look at my drawings, either."

"Sorry, Sophie." He takes a step back, but not before I'm snatching the book away. Part of me can't bear to be so unfriendly, but I don't have the energy to explain. I want to thank him for the Band-Aids, but I can't even manage that. When I look up again, he's once again a stranger: his frown businesslike, eyes distant. "Won't happen again."

I wait to hear the door close, then sink into the chair, miserable. My stomach growls and I remember I've eaten nothing other than a few stray blackberries. "Idiot," I sigh, angry with myself for several reasons now. And now I'm supposed to sit in a car with him for an hour on the way into town tomorrow. Even the sketchbook seems to laugh at me, the words *What Sophie Knows* more ironic with each day I fail to remember anything meaningful. I flip open to the familiar drawing. There, the figure in the blue dress rests, bounded by an expanse of tall red flowers on all sides. If they're really poppies, it's enough to put someone to sleep forever.

CHAPTER SEVENTEEN

Despite instructions to take the afternoon off, I know I can't sit still until I'm properly tired out. I eat a small lunch and return to the blackberry patch, where I stab at the dirt with a spade, digging out the last bits of stubborn root. After a few hours, I walk to the little row of flowering plum trees, buzzing with honeybees, and then past a row of foxglove. It takes a few minutes, but I find it: the flowers from my vision, leaning this way and that, caught on a breeze I can barely detect. There are only a few blossoms, but I sink to my knees as if on instinct and rest my hands on the ground. Here, they're almost eye level with me, shimmering red with a kiss of black in the center. I wonder what it would feel like to float in an ocean of them, an entire field. *Nobody would grow that many poppies for a flower garden.*

One of the red blossoms is fading. The petals are delicate, and when they start to wilt, it's already almost over. I watch the poppies in front of me, and imagine, in a series of images almost like a film reel, the process that begins when they wilt. The petals fall back to expose a pale seedpod. I can almost see a woman who stands next to me, a willowy figure with a long, dark braid. Her graceful hands score the pods with a little blade, leaving a strange sap that darkens as it dries. It looks like blood. I blink my eyes. Some kind of fever dream. Pure hallucination. It has to be. And yet, I see that woman so clearly, I almost feel as though she could have been my sister.

The sun is setting, so I begin the walk back to the apartment. As I pass through the west yard, I feel eyes on my back, turn on my

heel and hold back a shout, a dare: *If you know me, come and get me.*
My eyes land on the stained glass again, and I feel certain Zenaida
Atwood is watching me with a narrowed eye. That's all it was, of
course, the eerie figure on the side of the house, shining from the
corner of my eye. I want to throw my hands up, to ask her what
she's looking at, but it seems that she already knows. I imagine a
ring at the bottom of a pool, scattered bones throughout a forest.
I study the figure in the glass and wish I could touch her, caress
her like those arms of ivy that adorn the window. *Why did you do
it? What happened?* As the sun slips below the trees, I hurry inside,
locking the door as if the window isn't broken to invite the night in.

This is one of the nights that I only go to bed because I know
morning will come early. I toss and turn. My arm is warm under the
gauze, and I imagine not bandages, but armor. It seems that other
people are a danger even when they're not: they're one thing, but
then, perhaps, something different, just when you're getting used to
the first idea. I tell myself I can make myself bulletproof, assemble
whatever I find in the world around me like an invisible exoskeleton.

You won't, though, will you? You've already tried that once. The
voice that I hear is gentle, and I look up to see a soft-limbed,
ethereal figure, with doves perched on her shoulders. I shrug off
her stare and she continues: *It's braver to live without armor.* She
waits for my response, and I know she's figured me out.

I grip the bed sheets, half waking with a jolt. Zenaida's image
wavers and resettles; only half-conscious, I search for her again
and find her. But someone stands behind her: it's a young girl,
with dingy hair, a large purple bow behind her ear. Something
smells like smoke. Something's beating against the rafters. The
doves have taken flight; her arms are empty. I look for the little
girl and see Zenaida instead.

You got hurt, she says.

No, I didn't, I snap, churlish. *It was a clean cut.*

What happened to you was not a clean cut.

You don't know what happened to me, I mumble.

It will heal better if it can breathe, she hums, dissipating into light.

As I sit up in bed, gasping for air, I hear the whisper of the sheets around me, and maybe, just maybe, something else. It's a gentle sound that flutters away into the dark. I sweep the hair off my face and touch my arm, where, sure enough, I've forgotten to take the bandage off. I pull it away, stretch out, and recline again, slipping back into a deeper rest.

The next morning, I find that a dove has flown in overnight. Its soft coos call me down the stairs, where I see it sitting on the table, right next to the broken window.

"You had me thinking a ghost came in," I say, sleepy but relieved. "Or something else." The dove shuffles its feet, slightly annoyed at my presence, but it doesn't seem frightened. As I heat water and prepare some oatmeal, I open the door to offer it an easier path out. Something drags under the door and I startle, not sure what I expect to see. I peer around the corner to find a set of gardening gloves, sturdy waxed cotton with leather panels on the palms. If Nathaniel meant this as an apology, it only makes me more ashamed for snapping at him.

The dove watches calmly as I heat water and stir the instant oatmeal. "It's nothing special," I tell it. Breakfast in hand, I walk to my only seat, the chair by the window. The bird takes a few preparatory steps and flutters out the way it came in. "Come back anytime," I say, unsure whether I'll be here to see the doves again after this afternoon. "This was your home before it was mine."

CHAPTER EIGHTEEN

When I walk outside, I see Nathaniel's truck parked off the main path, near the willow grove on the east side of the grounds. I walk over to meet him, my discomfort at yesterday's awkwardness soon overshadowed by my awe at yet another corner of this place that has, until now, escaped my notice. A semicircle of weeping willows shelters a shallow pool, made of stone, their draping leaves forming a curtain across the water. There's a set of stairs built into the stone, walking three steps down to the base of the pool. There are a few inches of water in there now, clogged with leaves and muck, but the steps bring an image of dinner guests removing their shoes to cool their feet in the water. Around the edges of the pool is a border of freshly tilled soil, and I see as I approach that Nathaniel is unloading plants from the bed of the truck. I approach, holding up my gloved hands in greeting. "Thank you," I whisper, almost just mouthing the words. He nods, expressionless.

"These are larkspur," he says, indicating the taller flowers, big spikes of blue, then points to the smaller ones. "Lily of the valley." That one, though, I already knew. "Plant the larkspur on the inside of the border, closer to the pond, the lily of the valleys on the outer edge." I nod my head in answer, pick up two large flowerpots, one in either arm, and then go back to pick up a hand trowel. I walk to the far opposite end of the pool to start planting, and each time Nathaniel finishes a row and moves down, I hurry to catch up, working in the opposite direction. I'm making good progress until I slip, dropping my trowel into the water. It disappears under the surface with a trail of tiny green bubbles. "Ugh," I sigh. I roll up my sleeve and reach in, using my left arm to keep yesterday's cut on my right arm dry, pursing my lips with disgust. It feels more like a mud puddle than water, and the green pond scum on the surface drags. I reach around under the water, feel something brush my hand. Nathaniel has paused what he's doing to glance at me, and I can't quite read his expression. Then it hits me. I remember him saying they found her wedding ring, in a pool, by the willows. I suck my breath in, pull my arm back.

"I think I have another one," he calls. But I stare into the surface of the water, focusing on something that might not really be there, and slowly dip my hand in. The trowel is right beneath my fingertips.

"Got it." As I sit up on my knees to resume planting, the surface of the water stills, and I feel almost that it's watching me, that I ought to thank it. Nathaniel looks at me with something like surprise and stands up, brushing the dirt from his hands.

"I'm going to meet one of the contractors. It should take an hour or so."

"I'll finish up here."

"I'm driving into town after that." He reaches a hand back, straightens his hair. I know what he's not saying: it's been a week. For some reason, I feel as though whoever brings it up first loses. "Come along if you want. I put a week's pay under your door."

"That wasn't the deal," I remind him, though I feel I ought to thank him. "You let me stay, first week free." Nathaniel shakes his head.

"Wasn't a fair deal. I shouldn't have agreed to it," he says. "Anyway: a week's up. Leave if you want. Stay if you want. Either way, I'm going in a couple hours."

"Okay." He watches me a moment longer before turning away, and I know he's waiting for my answer, but I don't have one yet.

*

The drive into Hazel Bluff is long and quiet. I squeeze against the passenger side door, looking out the window. I'm pretending to be at ease, though I sneak a glance at him every few minutes. He's blank-faced, staring out the windshield, one elbow propped on the open window. When we finally make it downtown, he parks on a side street.

"Meet back here in two hours?" he asks. "I've got a couple errands."

"Me too," I answer. "I'll see you then."

When Nathaniel has walked out of sight, I turn toward the police station, heart pattering with hope that I'll learn something meaningful. It occurs to me that if I leave, I'll never learn what happened to Zenaida Atwood. Why she swallowed all that laudanum and walked away to die somewhere, leaving pieces of herself behind. Then again, I think of my brother, what I know of him. Someone who was always there when I needed him. Someone who would never have let this happen to me. That's all I need to know. It's a short walk to the station, and, when I walk in, the secretary seems to remember me.

"Heard you left the hospital."

"Yes," I admit, then continue without offering any further explanation. "Is Detective Radford available?" She picks up the phone and dials, then murmurs quietly for a few seconds. When she hangs up the phone, her expression seems a bit different. "She's in her office," she answers. "I'll walk you up." Selena Radford sits behind her desk, and when the secretary knocks on the doorframe, she looks up, pushes aside a stack of papers.

"Sophie, come in," she says, angling her chair to face me. "Sit down," she says. "Amber, would you close the door, please?"

The door clicks shut behind her. The detective sighs before she speaks. "Are you alright?" she asks, finally.

"Yes."

"Considering the details of your case, it was concerning that you left the hospital against medical advice and went off the map for a week."

"I—" I pause. She's spoken the words so cleanly, with such precision, that it takes me a moment to realize she's telling me that she was worried. "I'm sorry. I was feeling—" I begin to tell her about the flower delivery, about the feeling I've had of always being watched, but the words sound crazy even before I consider speaking them. A bouquet of flowers for a patient who's been in the hospital long enough to get to know the staff is hardly a suspicious gesture.

"You were feeling…?"

"I was feeling a bit cooped up, I guess."

"Erratic behavior concerns me." She reaches into a drawer at her side for a folder before she looks up to face me again. "But I'm not your doctor. You have a place to stay?"

"Yes," I answer. "I do."

"Very good. So—" Holding a pen, she opens her notebook to a new page and scratches a few words. "Memories? You have a brother, who, you said, is named Miles. That's what we know. Anything more there?"

"That I miss him."

"Okay," she sighs. "What else?"

"Not that much, really. I'm sorry. I remembered my mother," I answered. "That she taught me how to draw."

"What did she look like?"

"I don't know." I lean forward a little, disappointed. "She was—big. I was little, and she was a grown-up. She looked big." She watches me, pen in hand, as if she hopes I'll say more. "And—I know this poses more questions than it answers, but—I'm fairly sure I was in foster care. I remember running away. More than once."

"Okay," she says, her voice finding a note of certainty. "Could be useful. And, just so that you're aware, your dental records didn't return anything. Missing persons—nothing. Even your fingerprints—nothing. But all that means is that you don't have a criminal record."

"I guess that's something." I shuffle my feet, searching for distraction. "Why isn't anybody looking for me?"

"If you have a recollection of running away, I…" Detective Radford begins a thought, but trails off.

"What?" I place a hand on the edge of her desk.

"It makes me wonder if there was something you were running from. An abusive home, maybe. I was going to mention human trafficking, kidnappings, but—" She pauses politely when she sees my reaction. "You don't fit the profile for someone who's been trafficked. You're healthy, no detectable addiction problems or anything like that. Better to know, right? I'll put in another records request."

Thinking of the poppy field in my drawings, I don't know how to answer her. I'm relieved when the phone rings. She takes a look at the caller ID and answers.

"Okay," she says. "I see. I'll be there as soon as I can. Sorry," she says, turning back to me as she rises from her chair. "I was supposed to be at the courthouse half an hour ago." With relief, I hop up and move to the door, hold it open behind me and let her walk past.

"We'll keep in touch," she says as she walks down the hall toward the stairwell. I think she's forgotten that I don't have a phone.

Back in the sunlight, I walk up the street slowly, trying not to drag my feet. I had felt so hopeful that there might be a detail that could be useful. Detective Radford seems so competent that her lack of answers makes me feel hopeless. As I walk past the library, I notice a large clock on the wall outside and see that nearly an hour has passed already. I remember the cash in my pocket and the empty cabinets in the dovecote apartment. I'm certain I had walked past a grocery store at some point last week, but now, unsure where it is, I wander for several blocks before finding it.

Inside the store, I'm overwhelmed by the noise and the selection of items—who needs fifty different types of breakfast cereal to choose from? I'm ill at ease, too, in the checkout line, looking over my shoulder to see who's behind me, then over the candy shelves to scan the adjacent lines. My eyes fall on a row of home and garden magazines. One magazine promises, in bold pink letters, to teach anyone the basics of classic cooking in the space of a ten-page article. I flip it open and see a column titled 'Five Basic Sauces': bechamel, velouté, hollandaise, espagnole, tomato. There's a chart with cartoon sketches of dishes made from each recipe. Bechamel has lines pointing to potatoes au gratin, lasagna, macaroni and cheese. I glance over my shopping cart and wonder what it would be like to cook something besides instant oatmeal and canned soup. Suddenly, I'm next up, and I drop the magazine on the checkout belt with the rest of my items. When I reach in my pocket for money, my fist closes on the necklace first. My hand trembles as I pay and take the receipt.

I planned poorly. It's a long walk back to the truck, and I'm not sure what time it is. It occurs to me as I'm walking that I never told Nathaniel whether I'd chosen to stay or not. Particularly now, as late as it is, it would likely appear I'd just decided not to come back, taken my one week's pay and moved on. My heart's sinking as I walk, arms full of grocery bags that I constantly readjust. As I pass the library again, I check the clock to see that it's been nearly three hours. I can't remember the name of the street we parked on, and I walk down Main, looking up each side street, even though I know I'd look just as lost as I am to anyone who's watching me. Finally, on what seems like the hundredth cross street, I see a black pickup. I turn and approach it, unsure whether it's the right one.

When I see Nathaniel sitting in the driver's seat, I catch his eye, and I could swear he smiles. I know I do.

"I figured you weren't coming back," he says, talking to me through the open window as I place my grocery bags in the bed of the truck.

"Then why are you still here?" I swing the door open and climb into the passenger seat.

"In fact, I don't know." He turns a sidelong glance my way, then down at his hands, as if it hadn't occurred to him to wonder. "That's usually your answer, isn't it?" I open my mouth, ready to snap, but instead find a quiet, tired laugh in my throat.

"Guess you lost your bet."

"What's that?"

"You said you'd bet I quit inside a week." I buckle my seatbelt and let myself exhale.

"Do you need anything else before we head back?"

"No," I answer, leaning back in the seat, trying not to let on how relieved I am. "I'm okay for now."

CHAPTER NINETEEN

Though the drive back is as quiet as the one there, the silence feels calm, almost comforting. Nathaniel doesn't ask where I went. I don't volunteer anything, either. Once or twice, watching the gold afternoon light on the blue-tinged mountaintops, I nearly drift off to sleep. I squeeze the necklace in my pocket to stay awake.

Though the strange charm carries an unidentifiable foreboding, I can't help but keep it with me. Good luck charm or otherwise, it's the only concrete item I have from before, something I can hold in my hand. Half-asleep, my thoughts begin to mingle with the sounds of the engine, the breeze in the open window. I remember Detective Radford describing the symbol as being about feminine wisdom. Divine knowledge. How spectacularly frustrating, that I know absolutely nothing about where I'm from, how I got here, other than that it nearly killed me. The rushing wind from the open windows begins to sound like the crackling of a campfire, and as my eyelids grow heavy, I imagine peering through shadows.

"You said something about Sophia?" I leaned forward to whisper to her, this woman who was a stranger to me, but smiled at me as if we were sisters. "If this is all about divine femininity, why do the women do all the cooking?"

"You've misunderstood—women are cherished," she answered. "The world's dangerous for everyone, but for women and little ones especially. You've been through enough to agree." She slipped her collar just to the side, revealing a tattoo, a symbol I'd never seen before. There were

other voices that began to chime in: "Femininity is wisdom," then, "Wisdom is part of God." The phrases were repeated, all around me, until my question was extinguished, rather than answered.

I blink my eyes, hearing a melody that calls me back from this bizarre daydream. In the driver's seat, Nathaniel is humming. The tune is familiar, but I can't quite place it. When he catches my eye, he falls silent, but his mouth curves in a momentary smile.

"Go ahead." I yawn and lean back in my seat. "Not bothering me a bit."

When Nathaniel parks his truck in the driveway outside the yellow house, I climb out and begin collecting my bags.

"Need a hand?"

"No, thanks. I carried them all the way across town," I answer, turning to walk away. "I've got the hang of it by now. Hey."

"What is it?" He pauses outside the front door.

"Thanks for waiting."

Before he goes inside, Nathaniel almost smiles, just shakes his head, a silent answer that says it was nothing, then the door closes behind him. I shuffle across the grounds, shifting bags between arms to balance the weight. When I've put away my groceries, there's still plenty of daylight, so I walk back outside, to the far east of the grounds, back to the willow grove. It's eerie, almost foreboding, the trees blocking a good deal of light. I walk around the perimeter of the stone pool inspecting the rows of flowers we planted this morning, checking to see if any of them have started to wilt.

A pair of doves scatter, their wingtips making a soft sound, almost like a flute, as they take flight into the evening. I feel that I'm not quite alone, somehow, and look up, expecting to see Nathaniel, but no one is there. The water glints with the remainder of the daylight, as if it's calling me down. I'm so certain someone else is here that I take a few quick steps backward, nearing the boxwoods that border the grove, and dip my shoulder, pressing myself between the close-cropped branches of one of the trees. I can see mosquitoes hovering over the pool and the yellow blink of an early firefly across the field. I can hear my own breath. The necklace slips from my pocket and drops to the ground. I curse out loud and fall to my knees, scrambling into the hedge to look for it. There are mosquitoes, ants, probably even more copperheads back here, but I don't care. In the dim light, I'm patting the ground with my fingertips, inching forward, the branches squeezing around my torso, when finally, I see the necklace, just off to my left.

The hedge seems to snuggle tighter around me as I move, each limb negotiating for space. It's a familiar feeling, I realize. I remember a time when I clambered into the branches of a similar boxwood, much smaller than I am now. Hoping desperately for it to hide me. Something courses through my veins, icy-cold and quick. I remember huddling into a hedge, and, just as I did then, I circle my arms around my knees, pulling them close. That day smelled like smoke. I squeeze my eyes shut. This isn't a memory I want. One of those days that changes everything after it, only I was too little to realize it at the time. But even a six-year-old knows what dread is, the way it feels in your stomach, tastes in your mouth. I didn't know, not with words, the kind of things that can befall a child nobody is looking out for, but I knew I was in danger. And I heard a voice that I knew, and I reached forward out of the hedge, and someone took my hand.

Miles.

And when I heard his voice, called his name, I knew I would be okay. That Miles would never let any harm come to me.

I crawl out of the hedge on hands and knees before the rest of the memories surge in around me. I hide from most of it, dodging everything but a chilling sense that I did something terribly wrong, the memory of smoke that crackled, made my eyes tear up. I'm safe here, for now. I look toward the house and, though I can't see the stained-glass window from here, its west wall perpendicular to where I stand, I can almost sense the light from the sunset reflecting off the glass, breathing its glimmering colors into the air. I wonder if Zenaida felt safe here, just as I do. Did she?

As I walk the perimeter of the ghostly pond in the darkening evening, I whisper my brother's name over and over and tell him I'll find him, no matter how.

CHAPTER TWENTY

As the days grow longer, I wake earlier, always with the sun. I work later, too, since I like to stay outdoors until I see the sun set on the stained-glass window. The flowers and plants in the gardens aren't bad company, but my free time poses more of a challenge. I spend any spare moments silently calling my brother's name: *Miles*. I chase him through what semblance of sleep I can find at night, though I see only a little girl with peach-colored hair, who searches for him the same as I do. When I'm not drawing, I read and reread the cooking magazine, teaching myself a few recipes: a basic banana bread, a batch of cookies, potatoes au gratin, macaroni and cheese. There's a comfort that comes with working in a kitchen. It reminds me of being around people.

One night, standing anxious watch over a loaf of bread that refuses to rise, I imagine a set of hands alongside mine, deft and practiced. They're accompanied by a low, sweet voice, the presence of a woman I'm certain was my friend. I almost turn on my heel in my kitchen right there, I'm so sure she's at my side. I can hear her voice: *I make tea from the seeds, after the harvest, so nothing's wasted.* She measured scoops of tiny seeds. Poppy seeds, I thought, out of a jar, and boiled them, adding flowers and leaves she'd foraged. She hummed a made-up song while she worked, singing the name of each ingredient: *poppy, sassafras, passionflower, honeysuckle.* It seemed as if she loved each one equally. Just a cup of it had me complacent, happily chattering about nothing. She warned me against brewing it too strong.

Suddenly, I'm on edge. I wish I had someone, anyone to talk to. I glance toward the window, then hurry over to draw the curtains. The bread still won't rise. I bake it anyway. It's barely edible, but I break it into crumbs, which I scatter outside the door for the doves in the morning.

Though the details of the gardens draw me in, every so often I find myself in awe of its immensity. On the east side of the grounds, a pergola sits just at the cusp of the mountainside, opening to a view of the hills beyond, its latticed roof covered with periwinkle-blue clematis flowers. It faces a stone-paved walkway, which curves below a series of terraced flower beds that reach up the hillside, pathways winding in between. Here, I spend a day wielding a large pair of shears, bringing a long row of boxwoods into shape. I sleep poorly, sunburned and haunted. All the next morning, I'm huddled over, the sun on my back, transplanting lavender plants into the soil, the blue of their fragrant blossoms echoing the deeper blue of the hydrangeas behind them. Blossoms in so many shades of blue, but none of them as clear or pale blue as Miles' eyes, which I see now, just as if I'd never forgotten them.

The midday sun feels too warm, so I sit in the shade of the pergola and pull my hair into braids that glint red under the mottled light. I lean close to the lavender, breathing in as deep as I can. Among the ghosts, I know these long hours outdoors preserve what I've got left of a sense of peace, of stability. Something stings in my throat. Smoke. I stand up, cast a look toward the manor. Nothing. Yet, from the south, a wisp of gray steals across the sky. A smudge of dark gray is just visible on the horizon of the blue, rolling hills. Somewhere, there's fire.

I remember that, after I'd run away from my previous foster homes too many times, the social worker dropped me off at a new house. The house was painted the color of the sky above, and it looked so welcoming

from the road. But the moment the door had closed behind me, I knew
something was wrong. There were supposed to be two grown-ups and
me, the only child. Instead, there was only one grown-up, a woman
with a pink dress and blank eyes. The woman told me my room was
at the end of the hall on the left, but I turned right by accident, and
opened a closet door. A little girl looked up at me. Her dress was dirty,
but she had a purple bow clipped into her hair.

"Why are you in here?" I asked. She answered with the kind of
silence that was worth more than words. Even children understand
that some things are unspeakable. "Is there another grown-up here?"

"There are lots," she answered, her voice flute-like but scratchy.

Hearing footsteps approaching, I closed the door and crossed the
hallway to my room.

Coughing on the mingled fragrances of lavender and smoke,
I don't realize I've closed my eyes until I open them to bright
sunlight. I'm grasping for anchors, reaching to touch the arms
of clematis that hang down, the blue of the lavender, the baubles
of petals on the hydrangea stems. I never have to go back there.
Because Miles helped me. I don't have to go there, even now, not
even in my thoughts. I cover my hands in lavender blossoms,
fastening myself to where I am now instead. I grasp for every shade
of lavender, hydrangea, clematis, trying to erase the blue of that
faraway suburban house. Listening for birds and rustling wind to
cover the voice of that girl in the closet. But the voice I hear this
time is real, and close by.

"Hey, Sophie?"

When I hear Nathaniel, I turn and listen. He's near the house,
and, climbing up the walkway and into the garden, I see him, on
the veranda that extends from the second floor.

"Morning." From where I am, I wave a gloved hand as I shout.

"Can you give me a hand here?"

As I make my way over, the breeze plays with the scent of smoke.
The eastern façade of Dovemorn House is bounded by a striking

colonnade, its marble walls in shadow. A curving staircase, looking as though it were carved from a single piece of marble, pirouettes from one end of the terrace, across its length, and down to the ground on the other side. Jasmine vines twist up the banister, and I follow them up the stairs. I've never been this near the house before. Reaching the top of the steps, I lift a hand to brush the hair from my forehead, and soil crumbles from my gloves, leaving me blinking. Hearing Nathaniel speak, I walk closer and see that he's holding one end of some large, wooden panel with intricate carvings. "What is this? Did you make this?"

"No," he answers, pushing his hair out of his eyes with his wrist; eyes that sparkle amber in the sunlight. "The owner had to hire someone to recreate the originals—they're shutters. See?" He heaves one end up and holds it in place next to a window. "Shouldn't be that hard to fit in, if I could just hold that side still." I take the opposite corner and hold it up. "Thanks," he says, turning his attention to a hinge and a set of screws he takes from his pocket. There are four windows, so eight shutters to fit. I take a moment to trace the carvings on each one as I hold it steady for Nathaniel. I think he's talking, but I can barely hear him, my thoughts trailing on the smoke, far away. The shards of memory click together: that little girl with the ginger-blonde curls is me, coughing, hiding from the smell of fire.

After I heard footsteps approaching, I'd retreated to my room. In my recollection, it looked more like a walk-in closet with a twin bed stuck in the corner, not a window in sight. The woman opened the door and told me I needed to change clothes. That I should look nice when her husband came home. She helped me change, putting me in a ruffled red dress, brushing out my hair so that the curls frizzed and hung down my back. I don't remember why, but she left the room, looking for something else. I knew it was a stroke of luck. As she walked up the stairs, I tiptoed into the kitchen and found the phone. The receiver was large in my little hands, but I knew Miles' number by heart. It didn't even occur to me to call the police. What would I have told them, and what could they have done? I knew that I could trust my brother.

"Miles," I whispered.

"Hey, you." His voice sounded like a hug. "How's the new place?"

"Miles," I repeated, the very sound of his name a comfort. "Something's wrong here. There's another—"

"Stop. Are you hurt?"

"No," I answered, and started over. "There's another kid. They said I was the only kid. She's—"

"Get outside," he said, his voice urgent and commanding. "Stay on the street."

"There's a little girl in there. Something is really wrong."

"Listen to me," he said. "Focus." He raised his voice. "Can you see a door right now, or a window?"

"Yes."

"Get the hell out of there. Hide and wait for me."

I turned back, though, and opened the closet door. The girl didn't turn to look at me this time. "Come with me," I said. "My brother's going to help us." When she didn't move, I pulled on her hand.

"Stop it," she cried. "You'll get me in trouble. Stop it." Her voice rose to a wail, and when I heard the woman's footsteps on the stairs, I ran for the front door, into the hedges and hid as best I could in their scratchy embrace.

Standing in the shadow of the porch, it's as though my very lungs reject the smoke, with all its memories. My hands slip on the shutter I'm holding.

"Are you okay?" Nathaniel asks, helping me to steady the shutter.

"It's just the smoke."

"It's the meadow, a couple miles up the road. They burn a part of it every summer."

"Why?" My voice must give away my dismay, because he gives me a searching look.

"It's a controlled burn," he says. "At some point, the forest would catch itself on fire, every so often. Makes room for shorter growth, gets more sunlight to the ground."

"Right," I answer, though I think it doesn't seem right at all. I can see a dot of paint just at the corner of his jaw, where the angle of bone meets the muscles of his neck. My hands twitch and I think if they weren't full, I'd be reaching to brush it away. I sigh and turn my focus to the task at hand, though the moment I look away from Nathaniel, my thoughts are wandering again.

After I made it outside, I hid in a row of boxwoods at the outer edge of the front yard. Only a few minutes had passed, and I looked up and down the street, hopeful that the social worker was still in sight. I could hear the woman's voice calling, a gentle-sounding voice. She spoke to a neighbor over the fence: "Our new foster daughter is here somewhere. She may be frightened. Can you help me look?"

I choked a sob into my hands and her body swiveled in my direction. Nobody would believe a kid who ran away from a perfectly good home five times. Even at six, I understood this. Just then, I heard a muffled noise from inside the house, a sound of glass breaking. The woman's voice rose in fear and she rushed back into the house. The noise that came next was the sound of fire. I know that now, but then, it was just a rushing growl, the fire pulling air from everywhere else around it. Thick, dark smoke rushed out through the smashed windowpanes in the front room, and I could see the curtains catch fire in a rush. The door hung open, and all I could see inside the house was fire and shadow. I knew enough about fire to know that I should get away from it, but I'd been told to wait by the only person I trusted. Who would come for me first—the fire? The woman who used a friendly voice when her neighbors were listening?

That was when I heard my brother. "Come out," he said. "There you are. It's okay." I reached for his hands and he picked me up. Looking over his shoulder, I saw little flames licking at the hems of his jeans. He reached with his free arm and patted them in an almost friendly manner, as if it was an animal he'd tamed. As we walked away, he seemed to wink over his shoulder at the blazing fire. Once we got to the sidewalk, he paused.

"Are you okay?"

"Yes," I answer. He hugged me again and picked me up. Over the sounds of the fire and shouting, I heard sirens.

"We can't go," I said. "There's another girl inside. She's locked in."

"We have to." Miles, still holding me, looked over my shoulder. Whatever he saw made him start to run.

"What did you do?" I asked.

"Just distracted them." He smiled as he answered me, kissed my cheek. "Don't you worry."

I knew I'd never forget the sadness in Miles' cold, pale eyes when he asked me to run away with him that day. The strange moment when we had finally gotten out of the neighborhood. Tears ran down my cheeks, and he set me on my feet, tugging down the red dress with a look of anger, then taking off his flannel overshirt and putting it over my shoulders.

"Miles, the girl was still there," I cried.

"Listen," he said. "I'm sorry. All I know is I had to get you out of there, okay?"

He told me that we could leave the city, go somewhere new, pick new names. Even now, I wish that we had. We rode the subway for hours.

"Miles," I whisper, nodding off next to him on the bench seat. "Why did Mom leave us?"

"She didn't leave us," Miles says, turning my chin up to look at him. "She died. That means she's not coming back. She didn't choose to leave you, okay?" I blink at my tears and he kisses my forehead. "Tell me what you remember about Mom," he said, coaxing.

"She always took me into the corner store for a cookie," I answered. "She was pretty. And she was an artist."

"That's right," Miles said. "You always tell yourself what you remember about her. Say it out loud so that you never forget. But you didn't say the most important thing about her."

"What's that?" I asked. Miles holds my shoulders, looks into my eyes.

"She loved you, more than you can imagine. You have to tell yourself that every night, especially if I'm not with you. Mom loved you and me more than you can ever know." I nestled against his shoulder and let myself drift off.

The police picked us up before dinnertime. Miles left in handcuffs. I didn't know why. I only knew he'd done something big to take care of me, and that he hadn't done anything wrong. The woman was not harmed, and there was no trace of any little girl, despite every police officer I asked, every adult I could think of to talk to. I think that was when I finally learned that I wasn't getting my mom back, not ever. That Miles was my only family.

"Sophie."

"No," I murmur, feeling as though I've lost something important, thinking of a little girl locked in a closet. "Oh, no, I—" The weight of it sinks around me. The shutter slips in my hands and I manage, barely, to catch it. A muttered profanity escapes my lips. Hands clenched, I look wildly around for a foothold, for anything I recognize, and find Nathaniel's deep brown eyes, touched with something like caution.

"You alright?"

"Yeah. Sorry." I see that spot of paint on his jawline again. He holds a metal hinge in place, a nail between his index and middle fingers, bites his lip in concentration as he taps it into place. I turn my face to the other side and pretend I'm looking through the window of the old house. Through the panes, I see walls of bookshelves that reach to the ceiling, furniture covered with dusty drop cloths.

"That's the library," Nathaniel says. "I always forget you've never seen the inside."

"Maybe it's better from the outside," I answer. "Some houses are."

"Not this one," he answers, and when I look at him, I see he's watching me, somewhere in between curiosity and amusement, as if he hopes I'll ask more.

"Is that so," I say, though it's more of a closing statement than a question. *I left her there. I didn't go back.* I feel half sick. "Sorry: I'm moving slowly today. I'm going to get back to what I was doing."

"Thanks for your help. Sophie?"

"Yes?"

"There's someone coming by to fix the window next Wednesday."

"Thanks," I manage to say, retreating quickly down the stairs, and hurry back to finish my work alone on the mountainside, surrounded by a dozen shades of blue.

CHAPTER TWENTY-ONE

For a few days, the lost little girl is all I can see or think about. Her too-thin face, the stringy hair, that purple bow. I recall what Detective Radford said to me about child trafficking, abuse, and try not to imagine what the little girl must have endured. I'd do anything to forget about it again, that I didn't try harder to get Miles to turn around, that I didn't do something more, something different, and that a little girl disappeared in a burning house. Over and over I sit down with my sketchbook, intending to commit my memory of that day to paper. I draw a house on fire, a boxwood hedge, a page inked in with solid gray, a cloud of smoke. But I can't bring myself to draw the little girl's face, those downcast eyes.

*

It's Wednesday when I finish planting the garden beds by the pergola, and lavender fans over the walkway, bringing butterflies and honeybees. I've worked later than usual, and it's just past sunset when I cross back to the west side of the house. The last iridescent streaks of daylight glint on the stained-glass window as I walk to the apartment. I'm wearing a long-sleeved T-shirt that's somewhere between green and marble-gray, almost the same color as Zenaida's gown. I'm so accustomed, now, to the sense I'm being watched, that I couldn't hazard a guess as to whether it's true or false. With a nod, I bid the window goodnight, and she seems to return a cautionary glance.

I stop when I reach the door. It's just barely open, the door on the frame but not latched.

Even though I live behind a ten-foot-high gate, and even though I'm never more than a half-mile away, I always lock the door. With a light push, it swings open.

It's dark, as I left it, and silent, though I sense immediately that something is wrong. Every cabinet door stands open, the refrigerator and the closet in the kitchen as well.

The instinct to run, to get away, rises swiftly through my body. But I'm frozen right where I am. I remember a set of cruel, expressionless eyes, a scar running through one eyebrow. I remember asking for my brother. Not knowing where he was.

They've found me.

With a rushing noise in my ears, I find I'm transported, that I'm no longer here.

My wrists are lashed behind my back, something that bites into my skin. I look for Miles. Finally, I see a face. But it isn't my brother. There's a man, broad-shouldered, sharp-eyed, with a scar that crosses one eyebrow. I recognize the sound of my voice, feel myself in duplicate. I'm here, but also there. Whole and well, as much I can be, but also—whatever that was. My knees fail as I remember the man's face, his blank expression. He pushes me back and my head hits something, hard. As everything goes dark, I realize he'll kill me, and beg, again, for my brother. Miles would never let this happen. The dark rushes in.

Just as it's dark now. I'm breathing. I'm not hurt, and I'm alone. My hands trace my head, look for blood, find none.

The sketchbook that I left upstairs by my bed is open on the counter. In the dim light, I see that it's open to the first drawing, the poppy field. I step forward, my footsteps shuffling across the hardwood. I feel all the scars on my body begin to smart, just as if they're brand new. *A blade on my chest and ties at my wrists.* At some imagined noise, I spin around in the dark and almost lose my footing. I turn back to the kitchen and see a half-full glass of water on the counter. I hurl it into the sink with a cry. There's no one here: I know it, and yet it seems impossible, I'm so certain of another presence around me. But then I see it, lying there on the sketchbook: the necklace that stays hidden under my pillow, sitting right there on top of the page. My mind spins with frantic commands: *Do something: turn on a light, go and look around. Try to think what Miles would do. Let them know you're not afraid.* But I can't, and the truth is I am afraid. It's all I can do to turn around and walk away.

I feel numb, lightheaded. I'm afraid to run, afraid I'll fall or somehow give myself away. I stop once on the footbridge and muster the nerve to look behind me. Nobody is following. But if I wait a moment longer, then what might I see? Though the sun has set, the stained-glass window seems to glint in the distance, as if reflecting some unearthly spark. I imagine Zenaida instructing me to keep walking, so, despite the fear that would root me to where I stand, I do, forcing one foot ahead of the other.

With a silent apology to Lincoln, I hurry across the hopscotch perimeter that guards the yellow farmhouse and walk up the front steps. I knock on the door without pausing to breathe. Somewhere in the distance, an owl calls, and I bite down on my lip to stay calm. The door opens.

"Hey, Sophie. What's—" His face changes. "What's the matter?"

"I think someone was in my apartment." I speak slowly at first, then begin to trip over my words. "There are things out of place. The door was open. And the cabinets. And the refrigerator. And—" I draw a furious breath and catch it, fighting against the phantom in my head for control. "I'm really sorry to bother you, but I thought I should tell you, in case there's someone sneaking around the house." I look up at him and realize I've given myself away. I ran here because I was frightened, and I'm pretty sure we both know it.

"Come inside," he says. When I cross the doorstep, he looks outside behind me, then pulls the door shut.

"Are you okay?" he asks. I nod my head, then fold my arms protectively across my chest. "What happened?"

"I always lock the door. There were things out of place." I try to explain, again, but I'm too jittery to speak; I lift my eyes to his hopelessly. "Something felt wrong." After I've spent—I count in my mind—five weeks here, shutting down conversation at every opportunity, I'm not expecting much by way of response. But then I see something I hadn't anticipated: Nathaniel is listening to me. The shape of his mouth changes, as if he's making up his mind about something.

"I'll go over and look around," he answers, his tone calm but alert. "You stay here, okay? Can I get you some water?" I don't like this offer. I dislike knowing that I must look like I need help, more than I like the idea of staying here by myself.

"No," I answer, shaking my head. "No, I want to go too." I want to tell him that I'm not scared. The truth might be a little different. It might be that I don't want to be alone.

"Okay," he says, moving back toward the door. I look over at the row of plum trees that leads through to the main garden, but he walks into the driveway and climbs into his truck. He leans over to open the passenger door, then reaches down to grab my hand. I pull myself up and sit next to him.

The driveway connects to the main circular drive behind a row of oak trees, and he circles back toward the dovecote. He puts it in park and turns to me with one foot out of the truck.

"Should I bother asking you to stay here?" he asks. My feet are already on the ground.

The gardens are silent and now, somehow, less menacing. But I'm quiet, my heartbeat pounding in my ears. We approach my doorway again and I slow down. Nathaniel goes ahead of me and opens the door, while I walk just behind him. I hesitate, crossing my arms against a wave of fear that I think could knock me over. But I have to face it: this darkness, somehow, is familiar. It knows me, even if I don't know it. Inside, I can see the shadows cast by the cabinets, the glow of the refrigerator light. I take a quick step across the threshold, heart beating so loudly I'm certain Nathaniel hears it, too.

"Hang on a second." He moves as if he's going to touch my arm, then pulls back, instead reaching for the desk chair and bringing it slightly closer to me. I sit down, feel the tremble in my limbs. "Just sit. I'll take a quick look." His voice softens, as if he's talking to me about plants in the garden. "Okay?"

"Okay." I notice again the shape of his jawline, the line of his neck. He holds my gaze until I've taken another breath, gripping the arm rests. I wait as he walks around, hear his footsteps through the kitchen, up the stairs, through the rooms and back down. He sits against the edge of the counter and turns to me. "That glass was broken?"

"Not when I came in, no." A bit more composed, I turn to look at him as I answer. Nathaniel takes a paper towel from the roll on the counter and quickly cleans the broken glass from the sink, dropping the pieces into the wastebasket.

"Nobody's here," he says. "Not right now, anyway."

With a hesitant relief, I stand and begin to straighten up, close my sketchbook, brush imaginary dust or fingerprints from the cover.

"There was somebody here, though," he continues.

"There was?" I ask. "You're sure?" Nathaniel points at the window and I see the broken panes have been replaced. I slump over the desk, so embarrassed it almost knocks the breath out of my lungs. "Oh, my God," I whisper. "I'm an idiot." He shakes his head.

"No—listen. Obviously, that doesn't explain your cabinets being open, or your things being out of place. That's not okay, even if it was just a nosy repairman and not some—phantom out of the woods, or something." He's trying to joke here, so I force a smile in response. Nathaniel takes his phone from his pocket and dials. "Tom?" he says, after a few seconds go by. "Nate Wells. I know, it's late. The window? It looks—" He steps up close to the glass, runs a hand over the windowpanes. "The window looks fine. Thanks. Yeah, who'd you send out here to install it?" Moments elapse between his responses. "They new? Well, did they bring anyone with them, a trainee, anything? Yeah, give me a call after you've asked him tomorrow. Thanks."

He begins to put the phone back in his pocket, then it rings in his hand. He looks at the caller ID and raises an eyebrow.

"Excuse me," he says, walking to the doorway. "You alright for a second?"

"Yes, go ahead."

Though I'm too decent to intentionally eavesdrop, I can't help but overhear. "Hi. Everything okay... Sure, but what kind of schedule mix-up did you have at eight PM on a Wednesday?" His tone changes just slightly and I get the feeling that he's standing up straight, on alert. "Of course," he says. "No, it's absolutely no problem. Bring him by. I'll have dinner ready. Okay, see you soon."

He walks back inside. "My ex had a scheduling mix-up," he says. "She's dropping my son off in an hour. He hasn't had dinner yet. So, I need to go get that together. Would you like to come with me?"

"I'll stay here," I answer, anxious to be alone with my embarrassment. "Listen—" I say, underscoring my words with a raised eyebrow. "Thank you. I appreciate you coming over here."

"Of course." Nathaniel takes another exacting look around the little room, a detailed sweep that lands, finally, on me. He's not going to ask me out loud, not after how I yelled at him the last time he was here, but I know he's asking if I'm okay.

"I can't believe it," I blurt. It's a relief to speak, so I continue. "Honestly, I've never been so embarrassed in my life." I shake my head in disbelief, flustered again.

"It's not that bad."

"When you walked outside and met me playing hopscotch with a busted arm, that was probably a pretty close second. But this is worse. You even told me there was a repair scheduled. You hired someone to work in the garden, not a resident crazy lady. I'm so sorry."

"No, don't apologize." Nathaniel hesitates. "You sure you're good?"

"I'll be fine," I tell him. "I'll try not to die of embarrassment before morning. Have fun with your son." As much as I'm trying to make some sort of joke at my discomfort, he's not laughing, regarding me instead with something like curiosity.

"Have dinner with us," he says. "We're not the greatest company, but it might be more fun than being alone with your thoughts."

"What's that supposed to mean?" I bristle, but, unshaken, he answers me plainly.

"Look, I've seen people scared for their lives before. I know what it looks like. As you said—" He pauses, making a clear show of words omitted. "As you said, you're fine now, so that's settled." Nathaniel checks the counters again for broken glass, glancing back at me every few moments. "I'm just saying, twenty minutes ago you were not fine."

"Maybe you're right," I sigh. I pray he doesn't ask me anything else, let a few moments elapse. "Okay, okay. Let's go."

I make a point to turn on the light before we leave, intending to spare myself the anxiety of returning alone to a darkened room later. And, as Nathaniel walks ahead of me to the truck, I lock the door firmly behind me, as though it could make me any less afraid of the dark within.

CHAPTER TWENTY-TWO

We walk into the kitchen, which, as I suspected the previous time I was here, is impeccably clean when Lincoln isn't around. "Now to try to throw something edible together," he said. "Of course, edible for an adult and edible for a six-year-old can be two completely different things."

"What does he like to eat?" I ask, glancing around the kitchen, trying to hide my curiosity.

"If you ask him what he wants, he'll always tell you: mac and cheese, broccoli, and berries." Nathaniel opens the fridge, giving a skeptical glance at its contents. I see broccoli and a carton of strawberries in the produce drawer. There's butter, milk, a block of cheese. Fresh greens. He opens a cabinet, takes out a box of instant macaroni and cheese as if displaying it for a television commercial. "There's this—and yet, as of a couple months ago, Lincoln tells me instant mac and cheese tastes like, and I quote, worms you'd use to catch fish." I laugh.

"Any alternatives?"

He looks in the freezer. "Couple of frozen meals, if I can't think of anything else. His favorite macaroni and cheese is the one my mother makes, the baked kind. Like, crunchy on top. Outside of that, even stuff from a restaurant, is a poor second choice." He wavers, then opens the freezer door again. "Frozen meal's probably a safe bet." He takes out a brightly colored cardboard box with a photo of a plate with compartments on it. "Need to preheat the oven to…"

I look at the cabinet door left open when he took the mac and cheese box out. There's a bag of flour behind it, jars of dry pasta. With a few ingredients, baked macaroni and cheese is easy to make. But there's no telling whether it's an overstep to suggest it, or if I cook it and screw it up, which would be even worse. I decide to risk it.

"Is that flour still good?"

"Huh?" He glances back at it, thrown off. "Yeah, I think so. Does flour go bad?"

"And the milk and butter? And the cheese?"

"I may live on my own," he says, "but I don't keep spoiled food around."

"Right," I answer, smiling. "It won't be as good as your mother's, but I can try to make baked macaroni and cheese. Probably take about forty-five minutes."

"You know how?"

"Yes," I answer, glad to be certain of something, a concrete if mostly useless skill to offer.

"You're on," he says, looking at the clock on the microwave. "She'll drop him off in about an hour. What do you need?"

"A pan for baking, a pan to boil the pasta, um, first of all…" I turn to the stove and pick up a saucepan. "This clean?" He nods. I reach for the fridge, feeling a bit of time pressure, and turn back to him. "Do you mind?"

"If you know what to do, you're in charge," he says, smiling, a bit surprised. I melt half of a stick of butter, low heat, then add flour, a little bit of salt, and give it a minute or two to warm. I preheat the oven, put a pan of water on to boil for the pasta, reach open a cabinet and take out a drinking glass which I use to eyeball what looks like the right amount of milk. The multitasking of cooking soaks up some of my nervous energy, enough that I almost don't notice how I'm making myself at home in his kitchen.

"You want me to do anything?" He stands leaning against the counter, looking unsure about what to do with his hands.

"Yeah—grate some cheese?" I open the fridge again and hand him the block of cheddar.

"How much?"

I pick a clean bowl from the drying rack and give it to him, pointing an inch or so below the rim. "About this much."

I add milk to the saucepan, stir it, and give it a moment to warm. Add a little more salt and then, spying a little cluster of spice bottles by the stove, I add the littlest bit of paprika, remembering that six-year-olds might not like strong flavors or unexpected spots of color in their food. I find that I'm enjoying remembering which little component needs to be ready when, draining the pasta over the sink with a spoon. "Could you pass me that?" I ask, extending a hand for the bowl of grated cheese. I pour it into the saucepan, stir again, then mix in the macaroni. The oven dings to indicate it's preheated, just as I pour the mixture into the baking pan. I pause, suddenly, give the dish a hopeful stare, then open the oven door and put it on the top rack. A wave of warm air mists my eyelashes as I open the oven. I stand back and brush flour from my hands, turn back to him and shrug my shoulders. "Half an hour," I say. "Maybe a little more or less. You know how to steam the broccoli?"

Nathaniel laughs out loud, his chin tossed back, slapping the counter behind him. I can't help but just watch for a moment, caught between the curve of his smile and the impertinent spark in his eyes. "What's so funny?"

"I don't know, really," he says. "That's usually your thing, isn't it?"

It takes a little more effort to hold my smile. "Yeah, I guess."

"It's not funny," he says, as if apologizing. "It's just—you're quiet, you just watch things, until you get your hands on a goal, and then—get out of the way," he says. "Just like last month, when you sat down and started pulling ivy up out of the ground. I don't think you even looked at me when you told me to grate the cheese."

I'm looking now, though, so stunned to see him at ease and laughing like this. "Well," I say, "hopefully it's edible. I guess there's the frozen meal for backup."

"It looks like you know what you're doing."

"I certainly hope so, after—" Embarrassed again, I wave in the direction of my apartment.

"Don't worry about it. I—" He stops himself mid-word, turning abruptly away.

"What is it?" I ask. I can see him looking in my direction, though he doesn't face me.

"Nothing," he answers. "Forgot what I was about to say." This is obviously untrue, but I let it go. I stand aside as he washes and cuts the broccoli from the fridge and sets it up to cook in a steaming basket. While it's heating, he takes the berries out and begins to wash and cut them up. The window above the kitchen sink shows a scattering of stars in the sky, a waning moon nestled among the dark silhouettes of branches. The window faces out toward the mountain range, but I'm studying the backyard, a hammock in one corner, children's toys here and there.

"Lincoln was almost one, in that picture. Ten months, I think."

"What?" He's been talking to me, while I stared out the window. "I'm so sorry. I was just—looking," I say. "Out there. What'd you say?"

"Nothing," he says, turning back to the strawberries. "Thought you were looking at that photo."

In the corner of the windowpane there's a snapshot taped up, and I recognize Nathaniel, and a toddler, almost a baby really, that must be Lincoln, just a big set of brown eyes above squishy cheeks, a tuft of brown hair. In the photo, Nathaniel, clean-shaven, his hair close-cropped, is laughing, almost recklessly happy.

"Yeah, that's Lincoln and me, right after I came home from my last deployment. It was the first time I'd met him," he says. "I was overseas when he was born."

"It's a nice photo." The man in the picture is handsome, even striking. Glancing at the photo, then back to Nathaniel, at those deep brown eyes, the angle of his cheekbones, I take an awkward step backward, wondering how I had failed to notice it until this very moment.

"That was five years ago—feels like longer." He pauses. "I guess it hardly even looks like me."

"Not that different." Stammering, I search the room for something else to focus on and begin to wash the dishes in the sink. Nathaniel turns to open the refrigerator, tossing the hair from his brow with a subtle nod of his chin.

"You said your son's here twice a month?"

"Yes. He lives with his mother, in town. We sort of called things off, a few years back. But she's a great parent. You know, organized, dependable. But also fun." I cross my arms, trying to act normal, and tune in to what he's saying. This is the kind of praise, I realize, that comes after loss. You don't say those things about someone you wanted to call an ex. "We've got sort of a standing agreement to revisit things after—well, it doesn't matter." There's an ease in the air; something's got him talking. Considering that, before today, the man's barely spoken ten words to me in one go, I find I can't help but listen.

With an alert glance flickering back my way, Nathaniel rinses the knife and puts it in the dishwasher, then sets a bowl of sliced strawberries in the fridge. "It always seemed that everybody in her life had crossed her some way or other, and she couldn't forgive a slight."

"Sounds lonely, a little."

"I was eighteen when we met, an enlisted kid from nowhere, who'd never had a coat that wasn't a hand-me-down. It seemed too good to be true."

"Me, too." I remember suddenly that I did, once, have a coat that Miles gave me. But it wasn't a hand-me-down. That winter that he turned eighteen. It was brand new, beautiful, nicer than anything I'd ever owned before.

"Military?"

"No," I say, feeling foolish. "Hand-me-downs."

"You have siblings?"

"I grew up in foster care," I answer. "I have a brother, but—" It's tricky, being around someone who listens when I talk. Seems like it would be easy to say too much. "You were telling me about Lincoln's mother."

"Suffice it to say, if something seems too good to be true, it usually is," he says. "We have our son in common—maybe that's all, these days. I wish I saw more of him, but she has reasons for keeping things the way they are." He's building toward something, something he wants to say, but I'm shocked when it finally surfaces. "I haven't always been a good parent." He speaks casually, rinsing his hands at the sink. "I'm not sure if I am right now. After I left the military, I had a hell of a few years."

"I'm sorry," I say. I can't imagine that he's anything less than a great father, though I've only seen him with Lincoln the once.

"I never hit him, nothing like that. But you can do as much harm passively, especially when you're talking about parenting. That was all before we left San Diego—split up and moved to the same town," he says, laughing at himself. "I wanted to be able to see him, though. This was the first job I found that gave me space to be alone, but kept me close to him. Predictable—quiet, you know," he says. "Until the owner decided we needed to have the place ready for tours this fall. And, here we are." Nathaniel pauses, his eyes flickering up to meet mine. There's something so bare, so uncertain, in his silence, that I'm about to reassure him: *whatever it is, it's alright,* without even knowing why. But before I can, he's speaking again. "You ever just wake up and look around, and your life seems like a project someone else walked away from? Except it's unfortunately yours, and it turns out you're the one that walked away from it to begin with? Since then, it's just been one foot in front of the other."

More than you know, I think. I trace his figure with a gentle look, the distant expression and guarded posture appearing in a new light.

"Sorry for rambling." He inches back, withdrawing.

"Like a project someone else walked away from," I repeat. "Actually, I do know what you mean." I check the stove and see that the mac and cheese is nearly ready, bubbles at the edges and nicely browned on top.

I close the oven door. Until now, I haven't told Nathaniel any more than he needed to know, and that was with good reason. But I see now that I can't stay here any longer without telling him the truth.

"You know," I say, deciding to hazard a smaller confession first. "When I snapped at you before, I hadn't eaten breakfast. Or lunch." He looks up from his hands with a sly grin.

"I was being nosy. You weren't wrong."

"I might have answered you a little differently."

"That an apology?"

"Yes," I answer. "There's something else, though."

"What is it?"

"I woke up a couple months ago in the hospital." I look around for something to hold, or some task that needs done, settle for grasping the edge of the countertop behind me.

"Car accident, right?"

"Yeah, the doctor said it looked like I fell out of a car. Slowly. Over a distance." My mouth goes dry and I feel anger mixed with fear, distant, like a faraway drum. "The trouble is, a car accident didn't tie my arms behind my back, and it doesn't explain knife wounds, either." Nathaniel's looking over at me and I know he's thinking about the marks on my skin. I'm growing familiar with this unpleasant magic, with how speaking things aloud conjures their ghost, calls it up around you. I lace my fingers and stretch my arms out, reminding myself they're free and whole. "It might explain the concussion, though."

Well aware of his eyes on me, I hurry to open the oven, grab a dish towel to wrap around my hand as I reach in and lift the dish out.

"I don't remember how it happened," I add. "Or anything, other than a few childhood memories. I couldn't even tell you my real name."

"Oh, Sophie—" Nathaniel whispers a string of swear words, then purses his lips like he doesn't know what else to say.

He lifts a hand and presses it to his temple, steals a look in my direction. I sweep my hair into place, trying to part it to cover where the stitches were. "A project someone walked away from, right?" I shake my head and sigh, then turn to face the stove.

"And so, when you saw someone had been in the apartment—"

"I might be a little prone to overreacting," I answer, facing the stove. "Sometimes, I think the memory of fear is worse than what you are actually afraid of. Because I can't always tell the difference. It's like my mind sends me signals about what's what—but it's obviously not reliable." I chew on my lip, thinking. I've said too much. There's something heady, almost intoxicating, about the way he listens to me, the way he wants to hear my thoughts. "I don't know what that even means, honestly."

"To the contrary." He looks at me with a new attention. "I've tried and failed to put it that concisely many times. The memory of fear is a totally different animal. One that follows you." A moment goes by while I wait for him to say more. "I'm sorry."

"No need to be," I answer, with a hint of an edge. "Here's what I do know: I remember I have family, somewhere. I have an older brother. I know he's always looked out for me. I know that if I can find him, everything will be alright again." I look over the food, then brush imaginary crumbs from the countertop. "I'm sorry I didn't tell you sooner. If you're concerned to have me around, I understand."

He looks square at me. "I'm not," he says. "I'm not sure exactly why, but I'm not. And I've kept some bad company. I'd know if I ought to be worried about you. I mean it—I'm exceedingly cautious about who can be anywhere near my kid."

"That might be the nicest thing I've heard since I woke up," I say. When I hear a car on the drive, I decide to leave, suspecting this isn't my place. "I'll head out and give you some time with your son."

"No way." He smiles. "You said you'd stay for dinner—and besides, you're the one who cooked."

I hear a knock at the door, and Nathaniel goes to answer it. The door squeaks on its hinges, and through the door I hear their muffled voices. Though I stay back in the kitchen, I'm fighting an impulse to sneak around and peer out the doorway, to see this woman he speaks so highly of. I'm still on the fence between leaving and staying, when Lincoln tears in through the hallway, bumping into edges and absorbing the shock in a way that seems impossible, jumping up to give his dad a hug.

"Smells good," he says, looking around the kitchen brightly. "Hey! The Dove Girl's here," he says, tugging on my sleeve. I give him a high five which he accepts with a jump. "How's your arm?"

"It's all better," I say. "Thanks."

"Is dinner ready?" he asks me. I look at Nathaniel smiling, and I don't need to answer.

CHAPTER TWENTY-THREE

Without intending to, I find myself taking plates from the cabinet and serving food, carrying it to the table as if I weren't a stranger here. I'm not very hungry, but I get a small serving of everything so as not to be rude. While I wouldn't admit it, I'm more than a little nervous about how the food will be received. Nathaniel picks up a fork and Lincoln scolds him, makes him set it down, and recites a simple grace. "God is great, God is good, and we thank him for our food. Amen! Okay," he says. "Now we can eat." Lincoln takes a bite of the mac and cheese, and I'm trying not to let on that I'm watching him. He swallows it, loads up another forkful, then pauses with it halfway to his mouth.

"Dad," he says. "Was Grandma here and you didn't tell me?"

Nathaniel grins at me, glass of water in his hand. "Cheers," he mouths. "No, buddy," he says. "Sophie made it."

"It tastes just like Grandma's," Lincoln announces, as if this is a higher compliment than "good." He cleans the entire plate. I don't jump in too much as they talk; I don't want to barge in on their limited time together, which I can see means so much to both of them. Lincoln is excited for an impromptu sleepover and makes plans for building a fort in his bedroom while watching a movie. He makes a series of demands for treats: popcorn, ice cream, waffles for breakfast. I see Nathaniel smiling at each indulgence, and remember the guilt that crossed his face when he talked about his past.

"My dad makes the best waffles," Lincoln tells me.

"Is that so?" I smile politely.

"Dove Girl, do you like waffles?" Lincoln asks. Before I can come up with a suitable answer, he's on to the next subject, and I'm thankful for the capriciousness of childhood. After eating second helpings of everything, Lincoln jumps up from his chair. "Oh—sorry," he says, wiping at a smudge on his glasses and only making it worse. "May I be excused?"

"Of course," Nathaniel says.

"Can we play football before dessert?" he asks, jumping from one foot to the next. "Please—please, Dad?"

When Nathaniel hesitates, I stand up. "I'll take the dishes out," I offer. "Go on."

They go outside together and I smile. In the yellow glow of the porch light I can see them playing in the yard behind the house while I rinse and wash the dishes. I move on to cleaning up the dishes I used for cooking, standing over the sink, determined not to stare out the window. The love glows on Nathaniel when he talks to Lincoln. My eyes flutter up to rest on the photograph above the sink.

As much as I'm enjoying being here, it feels like a risk. Something different. And besides, it's been days since I had more than a fifteen-minute conversation with anybody besides the birds outside my apartment or a stained-glass window. I busy myself with cleaning up from dinner. After I've washed and dried the dishes, I wipe the countertops and straighten up the dining-room table. I hear the door open and footsteps coming inside, then Lincoln's at my side, pulling open the freezer.

"Can I have ice cream?" he says. "Please, Sophie, please?"

"It's up to your dad," I say.

"Dad said I could," Lincoln says. Nathaniel catches up to him, grass stains on his jeans from playing in the yard.

"I did not say you could," he laughs. "But you can."

"I'm gonna start a movie." Lincoln retreats into the living room.

"How long have you been here, now?" Nathaniel asks.

"Five weeks."

"And you still haven't been inside the haunted house."

"Oh, is it? Honestly, it's hard not to wonder." *Especially when the damned lady in the window talks to you every night.* Looking for something to do, I start to put away the dishes I've washed.

"Why don't I show you around sometime? Something tells me you'll like it."

"Yeah, I'd like that."

"Next week is busy," he says, "but one day the week after. Friday?"

"Next Friday," I agree, smiling.

Nathaniel takes out a bowl and a spoon. Since I'm next to the freezer, I hand him the carton of vanilla.

"Ice cream?"

"No, thanks." I realize I ran out of reasons to be here several minutes ago. As I begin to close the freezer door, I see the ice cube tray is empty, so I pick it up. Turning to the sink to refill it, I almost bump into Nathaniel. While he's serving ice cream, I fill the tray with water, balancing it on my hand, and turn back to the freezer, carefully replacing it. I want to say something before I leave, but I haven't worked out what it is, or how.

"Right behind you," he says, reaching past me to put the ice cream away.

"I'm just refilling the ice tray," I murmur. "Then I'll—" I close the freezer and turn around. Our shoulders touch, and we're standing so close that my forehead brushes his chin. I stumble, torn between stepping away and standing right where I am. Nathaniel steadies me with a hand on my waist, and I laugh, resting my other hand on his chest. It happens so suddenly, so easily. My pulse rushes, and I can feel his heart right under my hand. Then, I sense a question between us, a tilt of his chin. He touches my hair, his hand impossibly light against my cheek.

"Dad!" Lincoln yells from the next room. "Can Sophie stay for ice cream?"

We back away from each other. "I should be getting back," I say.

"Right." He scratches his jaw, straightens his shirt nervously. I reach forward and squeeze his hand.

"I'll see you tomorrow, okay?"

I walk through the living room on my way out, where Lincoln is waiting for his ice cream on the sofa. "Where you going, Sophie?" he asks.

"I'm out past my bedtime," I say, which is almost true, though it's not yet nine. "It was nice having dinner with you."

"Okay. 'Night, Dove Girl," he says, unconcerned.

I barely make it out the door before my face bursts into a bewildered smile. After just a few steps, I pause, lingering in the dark. I hear evening animals making their soft noises, crickets and tree frogs singing. My hand rises to touch my temple, where his hand brushed my hair.

It's then I hear the door open.

"Sophie, wait."

Though it's almost too dark to see, I note the intent with which he walks, and it quickens my breath. This time, he doesn't hesitate, and I step forward to meet him. He sweeps me into a kiss, a hand holding my cheek, the other tangled in my hair. When I stumble on the grass, he catches me around the waist, pulling me closer. To feel my hands on these shoulders, this face, I realize now that every time I studied him from afar, it wasn't just idle curiosity. I let my hand trace down his cheek to rest on the angle between neck and shoulder. One of us should say something. No, I think: both of us should. This is a bad idea, for more than one reason. I draw back, as if from a fire, and see that he does the same.

"Here," he says, "look." He holds my shoulders, turns me to face out across the gardens. "If you stand just here and look over that way—you can see your apartment from here."

I see it, a little square lit up in the dark.

"If anything—if anything else happens," he says, "if you feel like it's not safe, turn a light on and I'll be able to see it."

"Thanks."

"You sure you're okay?"

"Yes. It was a repair guy. That's it. I'm fine."

He squeezes my shoulders and I turn to press my cheek to his, willing myself not to wrap my arms around him again.

"Goodnight," I whisper.

"'Night, Sophie."

CHAPTER TWENTY-FOUR

I walk with long steps across the yard, down the path and over the footbridge. I pause, there, in the center of it, and gaze down into the dark water. I sigh and run a finger over my lips. Just then, something changes. I hear a difference, that's all I can think to call it. The starlight seems to shift. It's impossible to say why, but, for a moment, I'm certain I'm being watched. The memory of fear, I remember him saying, is a different animal entirely. One that follows you. I'm certain that it's not Zenaida, because I feel her there, too, her glass-and-lead eyes watching me as if she wishes she could say something. I remember she knows this forest, this darkness, better than I ever could. For a moment I imagine that she knows what's out there, and I can almost hear a voice telling me to pick up my pace. Then I remind myself that these signals I'm getting, my subconscious and when it wants me to be afraid, they're jumbled. Crossed wires. I keep walking.

The railing is still unfinished, and I walk carefully over the footbridge to the other side. From what I understand, replacing the old, rusted railings is a custom job, and not a small one. I look toward the house, then make a beeline for the west end of the yard until I can feel Zenaida's comforting eyes on me. It's normal, I remember, that I should feel something like paranoia, considering I can't remember anything. Add to that that I am walking home in the dark, alone. But I have a sense that I don't normally scare easily. By and large, I tell myself, walking quickly, the world is a safe place. Out here, especially so. As I approach the dovecote, a single dove peers out of a nesting hole, as if welcoming me home. I reach into the pocket of my jeans, my hand closing on the necklace, then find my key. Before I unlock the door, I take a moment to watch the dove in its perch. I remember the first time I stood here, how Nathaniel almost laughed at me, and told me, *you don't catch doves. You give them a safe place to stay, and, sometimes, they do.* Unlocking the door feels like touching home plate. I sigh with relief—gratefulness, touched with something else, something wistful, and repeat his words aloud: "A safe place to stay."

I fall into the chair at the desk, though my attention is still on the other side of the property. It occurs to me, briefly, to wonder what Nathaniel meant when he said whatever was between him and his ex didn't matter. I reach for my sketchbook, open the box of pens and choose a bright carnation pink. That coat Miles gave me, the year I was twelve. I can see it now. It was more beautiful than anything I'd ever owned.

There wasn't a vast amount of beauty in my first twelve years. I should have been grateful to have hand-me-downs, and I was, but in my heart, I longed for things that were pretty. At twelve, I was awkward. Everything that had been admired in me as a child turned into a flaw: my wavy hair, neither red nor blonde. My freckles. Even my eyes, neither blue nor green, infuriated me. I did my best to keep to myself, escape notice, which naturally made me a target for bullies. I never knew when I would see Miles, but if he showed up to visit me, it was sure to be after school, while I waited for the bus. If he wasn't there by six, he always told me, go home. Don't stay out late, especially not alone. That Friday in December, after the last school bell rang, I waited outside for his visit, instead of walking to the bus, not knowing whether I would see Miles or not. I paced up and down the block, then sat on a bench facing an empty basketball court surrounded by a chain-link fence. The afternoon was turning gray, and my hands were cold in my pockets, but I knew he'd come.

Almost an hour had passed, the streets easing into a warning quiet, when Miles appeared.

"Hey!" I jumped to my feet, ran to meet him. He hugged me close, and I saw that he wore only a T-shirt and jeans, but no jacket, though it was cold enough that I could see my breath in front of me.

"I missed you," he said, hugging me again. "God, you get taller every time I see you. Everything okay?"

"Yes," I said. "I'm taking swimming lessons at the YMCA." I saw him absorbing my answer, but also the sound of my voice. I straightened my shoulders and tried to sound grown up. "Aren't you cold?"

"How's school?" he asked, not answering my question. I went to hug him again, mostly because he looked cold. He was pale, thin as a knife's blade, but his arms were warm to the touch.

"It's okay."

"Okay?" he asked. Miles looked like Jack Frost from the stories I'd read in library books, at ease in the cold, eyes sparking with pale blue.

"Yeah, school's good. I made honor roll." As I hugged my secondhand jacket close, I saw that Miles had let his hair grow, and that it was blond under the streetlights, glinting almost silver. "How are you?" I asked. "It seems like it's been a long time since I've seen you." I was ashamed, suddenly, for not knowing more about his life. "How's…"

"Everything's fine," he said. A shadow crossed his eyes and, somehow, I understood that he wasn't telling me everything. "You don't worry about me. That's the rule."

"You don't have to lie to me," I insisted. "I'm not a kid anymore." Miles scoffed gently, smiling at me. Ahead of us, I saw the doors of the school building swing open and a group of boys in sport uniforms spill out. I took a small step backward. Peter Adelman stood in the middle of the group. As always, he was laughing.

"Hey, I got you a Christmas present," Miles said, before he paused. "Who's that?"

I shrugged my shoulders with a dismissive smile. "You got me a present?"

"Yeah, I——" Miles reached over his shoulder and slipped off his backpack. Peter and his friends started to walk in our direction. I was shuffling my feet, trying to stand behind my brother. My heart sank when I heard Peter's voice.

"Hey, guys, look who it is."

I crossed my fingers in my pocket, hoping he would just keep walking past us. "Ben, Ben," he said, laughing a handsome laugh. "Take her book. See what she's reading today." One of his cohort ran to approach me. I held a textbook out at arm's length, praying he'd take it and move on. I had missed a month of lunch money the last time it happened, but it beat the alternative. Another boy took my backpack, opened the zipper, and shook its contents onto the ground. Miles grabbed the boy's arm in one hand and my backpack in the other.

"Fix it," he said.

"What's your problem, man?" the boy laughed.

"Oh, I've got a couple. You don't want to know," Miles laughed, with a warning in his voice that was casual but edgy. "Right now, you're one of them." In an instant, with a light but commanding touch, he'd shepherded Peter and all of his friends into a line.

"What's going on?" Miles said. "Who's this?"

"Friends," I squeaked.

"Friends don't hurt you," he murmured, a wiry arm around my shoulders, as if none of them were there. "You know that, right?"

"It's okay," I whispered to my brother. "It's fine. He's just playing." I paused, then made another an admission. "The gym teacher says he has a crush on me."

"Who's this guy, anyway?" Peter sneered. "Trash Girl, you didn't tell me you had a boyfriend." I was trying not to cry, but I was fighting a losing battle, and I allowed myself a long blink, hoping to hold it in. Peter was always the most brash of his group. But in the quiet that followed his words, I could tell he sensed his mistake. Without an ounce of hesitation, Miles drew close to Peter, tapped on his chest with a light touch.

"It's this kid, isn't it?" he said, looking back to me. "If he told the rest of them to jump off a bridge, they'd do it. That right?" I opened my eyes to look at him, nodded quietly. "Okay." Miles clapped his hands, as if he was a schoolteacher or a coach. "The rest of you, go home, now. You're children," he said, dwelling on the last word for a moment too long. "You shouldn't even be out here by yourselves. Go home." Peter made as if to follow his friends, and Miles stopped him with a hand on his shoulder, a light touch again, though Peter nearly jumped out of his skin. "No," he said. "You stay a minute."

I felt a high-pitched whimper in my throat, as if I were a frightened baby, not a twelve-year-old girl. I didn't want to talk to Peter. I didn't want Miles to make him apologize. I spent all my time in those days avoiding interaction. As Peter's friends disappeared down the sidewalk, Miles took a step closer to him, and Peter took a corresponding step backward, as if Miles were the one moving him, as if he were a puppet. I was reminded of a word from a vocabulary lesson: compulsion; compelling. When Peter backed up to the chain-link fence, running out of space, Miles stared him down, watching him fidget. I saw what he was doing: he was letting Peter feel scared, just for a few moments. I wasn't scared, because I knew Miles wasn't dangerous. I wondered if Peter had ever felt frightened before, the way I had plenty of times.

"Miles, please," I whined. "It's fine, really."

"Nope." His tone was gentle but determined, and he turned away as if he'd forgotten Peter was there altogether, wrapping me in a hug. "It's not fine. Listen: it is not fine." When he looked back to Peter, his eyes were cold, icy-blue. "Tell me when this started, and why. I'll know if you're lying."

"I don't know." Peter's eyes darted to either side. His hand gripped his bag so tightly I could see the bones in his knuckles. "We were just playing around."

"You were just playing around?" Miles repeated.

"Yeah," Peter answered, "I was going to give the book back. It was meant to be funny."

"*Stop,*" *Miles said, waving his hand.*

"*What?*"

"*I told you I'd know if you were lying. That was a lie,*" *Miles said, suddenly appearing taller, a little meaner.* "*You're messing with her because you think you can get away with it. Because you think it's funny. I cannot fix whatever's broken about you to make you do that, but my sister?*" *He leaned close to Peter's face.* "*You do not touch her. You do not look at her. You do not talk to her. Now, tell me the truth.*"

"*I copied off her test in science in September,*" *he says, quavering.* "*We had the same answers, and the teacher made us both go to detention until someone owned it. She should have just said it was her,*" *he huffed.* "*It's bullshit. It was no big deal.*" *Miles was nodding his head again as he absorbed the information.*

"*That true?*" *he asked, turning to me.* "*You wouldn't lie for him, and he started following you around? Taking your schoolbooks?*" *I nodded my head.* "*He doesn't need your test answers. Look at his shoes. He can afford to fail a test. His parents can get him a tutor, hell, they can probably come in here and boss the principal around just like he's trying to do to you.*" *Miles gave Peter a look that said he was disappointed more than angry.* "*What are you gonna do, when this happens again?*" *he asked me.*

"*I—I don't know.*" *I bit my lip.* "*Tell the teacher the truth.*" *Peter scoffed at me.*

"*Like they'll believe you,*" *Peter laughed.*

"*The problem is, he's right,*" *Miles said, turning back to me.* "*They won't believe you over him. And the world is full of people like this. If they can take from you, they will. It only gets worse from here. You need to be ready to push back.*"

"*I can't do that.*"

"*You have to.*" *Now those cold eyes snapped to me.* "*You can, and you have to. Now, tell me what you're going to do the next time something like this happens.*"

"*Tell a grown-up.*"

"*Wrong,*" he snapped, *and I could hear pain in his voice. "You're twelve years old now. Listen to you! Grown-ups aren't going to protect you. If anyone knows that, it should be you. You sound like a baby. What,*" he said, slowing down. "*You gonna cry?*"

"*No,*" I said, but I was crying, I couldn't hold it in. He shook his head, sighing angrily.

"*Can I go now?*" Peter asked anxiously.

"*No,*" Miles answered. When Peter flinched, he scoffed in response. "*Don't worry,*" Miles said, annoyed. "*I'm not going to hurt a little boy, okay? Would that be fair?*" He turned to me, put an arm around my shoulder to bring me close. "*You are, though.*"

"*I can't hit anybody,*" I said, blinking at tears. "*I don't know how.*" He clapped my shoulder.

"*See, now we're talking. This is a learning opportunity, right here. Now, listen, okay?*" His voice was tender, soft again, pointing to Peter as if he was a chalkboard. "*When I hit someone, I like to hit them in the mouth. It hurts. It's embarrassing, messy. But they can still see me. I want them to look at me.*" He leaned close to Peter's face as if to guarantee his audience. "*You hit someone right in the stomach here, under his ribs, it'll knock his breath out. You have to do it hard, or there's no point. Come on: try it.*" He touched Peter's shoulder again. "*Stand up straight, kid.*" Miles looked into my eyes and nodded. I closed my eyes and threw a fist, which landed and bounced off Peter's ribs. It was grotesque, frightening. My stomach turned a bit. But I saw Peter cough, shrugging it off, and something about him made me angry at him, wished I'd gotten it right. "*That's it,*" Miles nodded. "*Now, listen. You're strong, okay? But you're little. If you're going to hit someone, it's not going to be for fun, and you need to move fast. Go for the nose, as fast and hard as you can. Even if you don't break it, he'll see stars, and it'll hurt like hell. Gives you a second to take the next move. Go.*"

That time I didn't close my eyes and I didn't miss. Peter's nose clicked under my fist, drawing blood almost instantly. As he spit out swear words along with blood, I felt sorry for him, but also relieved.

I blinked my eyes and watched him trying to collect himself. I was sitting behind my fear now, as if it were a steering wheel, rather than something chasing me.

"You alright?" I asked. I stepped between Miles and Peter, pulling Peter to his feet.

"I'm sorry," he whined. Part of me was anxious to reassure him, but I silenced it.

"Go home, Peter," I said.

"What am I going to tell my parents?" he asked, wiping blood and snot from his chin. In the silence that followed, I recognized it: an opportunity. I looked calmly into his eyes.

"Tell them the truth. You started a fight with the wrong girl."

"Try that crap with my sister again," Miles whispered, pulling his face close. "I'll be watching." Peter was sniveling as Miles patted his shoulder and lightly pushed him away.

As soon as Peter was gone, I felt tears drying on my cheeks, ice-cold in the chilly breeze. Miles hugged me tight.

"I'm sorry," he said. "I might not always be here. Don't you know I worry about you?"

"You'll always be here," I snapped back.

"I'm never leaving you," he answered. "But I might not always be here, when something like that happens, to jump in and help you. You have to stop coming at things like they're going to be fair." He brushed my cheeks dry. "The world is not fair. It's the opposite of fair. Look, I have to go. If I'm not at the shelter before seven, they'll lock me out." Miles opened his bag and took out a package wrapped in wrinkled tissue paper. I opened it, my hands still shaky. It was a winter coat, carnation-pink wool, name brand. Nicer than anything I'd ever owned.

"Thank you."

"Try it on," he said. I did, and it felt warm and smooth. Miles looked happy. "You're really pretty, you know? You look like Mom."

"You think?" I couldn't remember what she looked like, but I hoped he was right.

"Listen—" he said, trailing off, suddenly awkward. "It doesn't matter if that kid has a crush on you. If he's trying to get your attention by being mean, it's still mean. You understand?"

"Yes," I said, although in truth I wasn't sure. "What's the shelter like?"

"It's—"

"Don't lie to me," I said. "Come and stay at the group home?"

"I can't," he said. "You know nobody else is allowed. You'd get kicked out if you snuck anybody in."

"It's not fair," I said, then caught myself. "I wish it had never happened," I said, my throat squeezing in on itself. "You don't have anywhere good to stay and it's my fault, Miles."

"What?"

"That girl in the closet. The fire. What if I had just had the sense to run, instead of calling you?"

"I would do it twenty times over again to make sure nothing bad happened to you. Never tell yourself that. I look at you, and it's worth it."

"Why?"

"Because you're my little sister." The peaceful, enigmatic smile slipped back over his features. "Because you're mine. Listen, I really have to go. Wish me luck finding a job."

I hugged him as many times as he let me before he finally left, and then I found my way to the bus stop. Reaching for my bus fare, I found a little stack of twenties in the pocket of the pink coat. I didn't want to know where Miles got it, and I'd already forgiven him for anything he might have done. Peter Adelman never spoke to me or got near me again, and the one time one of his idiot friends did, he called them off so fast I couldn't even reach them. There were others, but I wasn't scared of them. I did well in school, in swim lessons, too. I didn't usually have to punch anyone, but Miles had taught me something. I was no longer surprised when things weren't fair. I remembered that Miles went back to jail; eighteen now, he went away for longer, and *not in juvenile detention. I don't recall the details, but whatever it was, I'm certain he was innocent. I know that he's good. When I heard, I'd held the pink coat against my chest and cried, though I knew if he were there he'd have told me not to.*

That lesson must have sunk in at some point, because now, despite the weight of sadness in my chest, my eyes are dry. I sit awake late into the night, sketching that beautiful pink coat over and over. I remember the weight of the wool, the smoothness of its striped satin lining. The only coat I'd ever had that wasn't a hand-me-down. I look out my window across the yard, listening to the soft call of the doves that make this place home. I wonder if Nathaniel's sleeping over there. I begin to assemble the little bits and pieces I've learned about him. He told me he's seen people afraid for their lives. I assume it's something to do with being in the army. He talked to me about fear, about the memory of fear, like I was saying something that mattered to him. But somehow, the thing about him that grabs me now, is that once, he was another kid, like me, who'd never had a new coat before.

CHAPTER TWENTY-FIVE

In the days that follow, Nathaniel and I exchange few words, and carefully, as if we're not quite sure what they might mean once spoken. A handful of days have passed when I meet him in the morning, near the edge of the pond, the footbridge reaching in a graceful arc above its still water. Yesterday, when he explained the work we needed to do here, he was wearing a gray T-shirt, with sleeves that hugged his upper arms. I can't remember exactly what he said about the gardening.

"Where do we start with this?" I ask.

"Here—I have a picture of how it used to look." He pulls up a photo on his phone and hands it to me, a snapshot of a page from a book or an old newspaper. In the old image, the pond is carefully tended, its perimeter planted with irises and ornamental grasses, the water dotted with lily pads. The ironwork on the original footbridge is beautiful, curling spirals like vines.

"It's not that different," I observe. The shape is still there, if blurred with wild greenery. "I'll trim the grass around the edges, pull up the taller weeds."

"Don't get too far in," he says. "It's deeper than it looks." The surface of the water is opaque, pulling light down without reflecting it back.

"Right." I place the phone in his hand and let my eyes trace up his forearm, toward his shoulder as I step away. "How deep is it?" I ask. He shrugs one shoulder. The one nearer to me. His forearm brushes mine.

"One time I was carrying a sixteen-foot ladder over that bridge—set it down across the railing for a second, and knocked it off. It fell almost straight down before it hit the bottom." I wince, looking at the green-hued depths.

"How'd you get it back?"

"Rigged up a fishing line with a coat hanger," he answers, his face breaking into a grin. I smile with delight, not even sure why. We both stop short, eyes locked, taking small steps back from each other.

"I have to go meet the blacksmith who's working on the new handrail," he says. "I'll be back in a couple hours."

"Okay," I answer, turning toward the pond, sizing up what my day will be like. "I'll be here."

"Okay, Sophie."

I step close to the edge of the pond, testing with my feet to see how near I can get before the ground starts to give way. I look over my shoulder and see that he's still there. "You'd better get going," I say. "Looks like rain." But instead of turning to what I ought to be doing, I stare back, the distance between us giving me a sense of daring.

"It won't rain until afternoon," he answers without taking his eyes from mine. "Look out for snakes this time, will you?"

"Sure," I answer with a smile. I purse my lips and turn away, feeling a warmth in my chest. If there are snakes here, by the water, they could be water moccasins as easily as copperheads. They're meaner than copperheads, and have a more dangerous bite, too. When Nathaniel turns to leave, I look up as he walks away, taking note of how he occupies his space, the character of his steps. I find a branch and shake it through the grass before I decide where to start, hoping to startle any snakes away. Though I can't say why, I can picture a water moccasin, thick, oily-dark body, almost translucent white belly, the way the mouth lays open when they're warning, the shock of white that lines the gums. That means *get back*.

And, while I'm tugging stems out of the marshy ground, soaked up to my calves, then taking down the shorter growth with a small hand mower, I'm watching for them. Imagining what I might see. Something in me here isn't afraid, not like it ought to be. As I work, I almost feel I'm searching for them. I reach down to wrap my hand around a thick, clustered stem of grass and see something dark and slick by my wrist, and imagine it could curl up around my arm, that I could hold it, look into its eyes. When I wait for it to move, I see that it's only a root. Something skitters through my mind like a bug and I pull back, bringing up the grass stem with clods of mud. *They shall take up serpents.*

I notice that the sky is dark. Nathaniel's prediction for afternoon rain might be a little optimistic. What I'm not ready for, though, is how quickly the wind brings in a change in the weather, and I stand by the water, watching clouds in every shade of bruised violet steal across the sky. *They shall take up serpents.* Silently, I mouth the words, feeling a tremble up my arms. Though the doctor told me I had no snakebites, I can't help looking for them again, checking over every inch of visible skin. I'm drawn in, tracing over the healed cuts on my right arm, when I hear a crack of thunder and realize it's raining, a mist of droplets at first that gives way to a downpour. I hurry across the lawn and find a spot under the eaves of an archway on the south side of the house. The windows behind me reach floor to ceiling, to the next story, though I can barely make out what's inside—some large, wide-open, shadowy space. In the corner, I think I see a wide, spiraling staircase. There's a snap of thunder, the rush of rain, and I turn back around to watch the storm, sitting cross-legged on the patterned granite tile.

They shall take up serpents.

With so much lightning and thunder right overhead, I think the storm clouds must have snagged themselves right on this mountain and become stuck there.

And if they drink any deadly thing, it shall not hurt them.

I rest my face in my rain-slick hands, squeezing the damp hair away from my forehead. I didn't need to come over here. I was already soaked through. I wanted to sit. Something in me was looking for shelter. Isn't that what I always do?

They shall lay hands on the sick, and they shall recover.

Sure enough, I know these words, the flavor of something biblical about them. But why, and why does the voice that speaks them in my memory sound so familiar? Though any name other than Miles eludes me, I remember seeing a man bitten by a copperhead. Remember that he didn't go for help, even when his leg swelled to double in size. I remember sitting through the night, coaxing him to drink tea, keeping a cool cloth on his forehead. I don't remember if he lived.

Like a riddle, I sit there mouthing the words into my hands, staring at the falling rain. It crosses my mind to wonder, the same as Detective Radford had: is it possible that I'm dangerous? *You gave someone hell.* The nurse's words echo across my mind. But I got twice as much, and if I was harmed, or injured, as in the verse that comes to my memory now, I did the better part of recovering on my own. *It isn't done yet.* I hear the whisper, and I recognize it from my dreams: Zenaida Atwood with her riddles. *What isn't? Recovering.* But, I want to hiss, I'm doing it on my own, all the same. And I imagine her staring back, as always, as though she knows exactly what I'm hiding from, gracing me only with riddles and fragments. I'm still mouthing the words into my knit hands, chin resting on my thumbs, when I sense somebody's nearby. I start to scramble to my feet, then see Nathaniel as he takes a seat a few feet away from me.

"Hey." He looks at me for a moment, brushes raindrops from his forehead with the back of his wrist, then nods out at the weather. "You were right." I manage a smile and a nod.

"Did you get the railing?" I ask, eager for something else to talk about.

"No," he answers. "It wasn't finished. He says he needs another week. Just be careful, if you use the bridge, until it's done."

"Right," I answer, staring out toward the pond.

"No snakes?" he asks.

"No." This time I can't force a smile, just sigh into my hands, bringing them back toward my face. I can feel Nathaniel watching, waiting for me to speak. "What would happen," I murmur, then turn to him with a hard set in my jaw, "what do you think will happen, if nothing ever comes back to me? Would I have a way to get a birth certificate? What about a driver's license?" I'm curious now, but it's not idle curiosity.

"I'm not sure," he answers. "But—"

"What is it?"

"Nothing—but it seems like you wouldn't be wondering about that, if…" He's studying me openly now, brow darkening as his eyes trace over the marks on my arms, the scar on my temple.

"If what?" I press when he hesitates, inch closer, as if I'm making a demand. When Nathaniel speaks again, his voice has dropped almost to a whisper.

"If you wanted to remember." His eyes soften as he looks at me, and his hand moves close to mine, close enough that I could stretch out my fingertips and touch his. "Maybe you don't want to go back."

"Well, I—" This hadn't occurred to me, and I'm stunned into silence, anger and frustration like a swarm of bees between my ears. I scoot back again, away from the warmth in his eyes. I could fall right into that space, but it would mean admitting I'm afraid. I imagine a man with a scar across his eyebrow. More poppies than you could hope to count. "Of course I do. That's what I want the most. It just—" Nathaniel stops me with a gentle shake of his chin.

"That's alright." He gives an unassuming shrug, though I can tell he's choosing his words with care. "I don't know you. I'm just saying, if you didn't want to go home—if there was something you didn't want to go back to—there's help for that, too."

"I didn't say that." My voice comes out in a low, warning breath. "I'm sure there's nothing wrong. I just need to find my brother." He places a hand on my wrist, leans forward so that I can look at him without moving from my hunched posture.

"Sophie."

"Nathaniel," I say, rolling my eyes a little. He's undeterred.

"When you get hurt this badly, something's wrong. You know that—I see it. What else is going on here?"

"They said it might have been random."

"But maybe not, right?"

"Ugh!" Though I wave a hand at him, as if to shoo him back, he stays right here, close enough I could grab hold of his arm and pull myself close to him. Lean on his chest and let it be okay, even for a fraction of a second. With another sigh of annoyance, I scoot further back an inch or two.

"When I find Miles, everything will be fine," I insist. "That's all I know."

"If you're hiding things from yourself—telling yourself you're fine, things are fine, when you know inside that they're not? That kind of a disconnect is not going to help you."

"What do you know about it, anyway?" I'm trying to push him away, but I whisper the words into my hands, barely louder than the sound of the rain around us. He crosses one knee over the other, stretching his legs out, and turns his face toward mine.

"Is that a question you're asking me? Or are you telling me to shut up?" When he speaks softly like this, I can hear a touch of his accent, the *g* disappearing from his present participles. "I'm just saying, pay some mind to what you're feeling." Maybe I would, I think, but I don't know how. I'm too ashamed to admit it out loud, but this anger, this fear, is too big to stand up to.

"Crying relieves stress. It's a scientific fact."

"I'm not stressed."

"And being angry? It—"

"I am not angry!"

"I'd be angry, if I were you." Though he speaks gently, I sense he's nudging me toward something. "I'd be angry if somebody beat me to a pulp and left me for dead. Your anger is coming from the part of you that knows what happened to you was wrong."

"Yeah, well, life's not fair," I say, anger flickering in my throat like a candle. "Life's never been fair."

"It's almost like you're protecting someone," he says, looking at me curiously.

"Trust me." Now I find some certainty behind my words. "When I find my brother, he's going to find whoever hurt me, and he's going to make them pay. There is no *protecting* about it." I shoot a furious glare at him, then close my eyes. This wall, this brittle strength, is part of me, I can feel it. I wonder if I've ever been able to let myself swear or cry or feel angry, to drop this exhausting optimism. I can't do it now, that's for sure.

"The thing I don't get," I say, "is that nobody's looking for me. Not even Miles. Why?"

"It's only been a few weeks," he says. "You could have a husband, a family." He steals a glance at my lips as he speaks, and I see this isn't the first time the thought has occurred to him.

"Come on." I purse my lips, shaking my head a little. That alternate reality seems too much to even imagine. A time when there was a different me, one without these scars. Maybe before, they were better hidden. "You think so?"

"Don't you?"

I don't answer him right away, but something tells me I've always been alone.

"What's inside, here?" I ask, changing the subject.

"Ballroom."

"Ah." I peek into the dark window, partly covered on the inside with heavy velvet curtains the length of the walls, and see a massive piano in the corner and imagine, for a moment, the sound of stringed instruments. What it might have been like to arrive here in the winter, for a party, by carriage. "She have a lot of dances?"

"No," Nathaniel answers. "No, she pretty much kept to herself. I don't know why, but I think she liked the quiet." But I think he does know why. I see that he's thought about it a great deal. A person choosing to be alone with this big house, with all its shadows, isn't just someone who wants to be alone, but someone who, maybe, needs to be. There's a reason Nathaniel doesn't talk to me about Mrs. Atwood unless I push him to. There's something they share.

"Of course," I agree, studying him intently now, as if I've figured something out. I see a patch of clear sky on the horizon and point to it wordlessly.

"Weather changes fast up here," he says.

"I see." As I turn to look at him, I rest my head on my knees. I don't bother smiling. He'd know it was fake. "I'm going back to that pond."

"You can take a break sometimes, you know."

"Some people need quiet," I remind him. "Some people need to keep busy. Everyone has things that keep them sane."

"Okay, Sophie," he says. "Meet you on Friday?"

"Friday? Oh," I remember. "You were going to show me the house. I didn't forget—I just thought—" I begin to stumble over my words, standing up in a hurry. Once again, I think, one or both of us ought to be drawing back, drawing a line between us. And instead we're sharing this foolish smile. "Friday afternoon, right?"

"Sure," he says. "I'll meet you here."

CHAPTER TWENTY-SIX

I've spent, now, the better part of two months studying this house from the outside. Watching pieces come together: the roof Nathaniel repaired, the windowpanes replaced here and there. Even so, I haven't given myself time to wonder what the interior might be like. He's joked about it being haunted, but, as I follow Nathaniel through the massive front doors, into the cavernous entry hall, I'm struck with a lingering feeling of sorrow. It feels more mournful than ghostly. The room rises all the way up, a series of skylights and rounded windows letting sunlight in. The walls are carved with wooden paneling and adorned with paintings. There's a fireplace taller than I am.

Nathaniel points out the carvings of cherubs with doves that line the fireplace. There's something slightly spooky about the gravity of the room, and I realize that it's not perfectly square.

"How much of this restoration did you do yourself?"

"Most of it was hiring people, keeping everything organized. Budgeting." He turns around to face me, smiling. "A lot of it was cleaning. The house itself was surprisingly intact. It seems like even the high schoolers who snuck in here to get high had a sense it was worth taking care of."

In the center of the entry hall, a grand staircase leads up to the second-floor landing, where the steps branch to either side.

"It's like a maze," I breathe. Around the landing on the second floor, a columned walkway looms in shadow, which appears to connect to the third floor, and from there to the fourth, at points that follow no logical sequence. It seems, almost, designed to disorient. I follow slowly up, tracing the amber-tinted marble of the banister. At the top of the stairs is Zenaida's stained-glass portrait. I feel as though she smiles at me, and I tiptoe toward my left to stand in awe in the patchwork of tinted sunlight falling through the glass.

"It's impressive," I say, "even more so up close."

"I see you studying it, sometimes."

"I like it," I admit. "It isn't just the window, but the way it's located on the house, on the land."

"Catches the sunset."

I smile and nod.

I follow down a set of stairs that curves into a flourish, down into the ballroom, that I saw from the outside only a few days before. While Nathaniel stands on the stairs, I slip past him and walk down into the near dark. There is just enough light from the windows on the opposite wall to make out geometric patterns in the tile flooring. I trace them with my feet: it's blue and white stone, an abstract interpretation of a night sky, stars under my toes. I turn back to where he waits on the stairs. I always have this impulse, when I see something beautiful, to turn to the nearest person as if to say, *have you seen this?* Of course he has. He's seen it a thousand times. Yet he looks in my direction, as if he's studying something intently. I feel my pulse start to hammer in my veins and grasp for something to talk about, something to fill this silence that begins to feel dangerous. "Tell me again," I ask, "when was the house built?"

"It was finished in 1907." I take a step forward, and, as if reading my cue, he proceeds up the stairs, while I follow him back to the first floor.

"The tourist center in town has a display," I say, feeling as though the space commands me to whisper. "It says it was their summer home."

"There's a little bit more to it than that," he answers, as I walk behind him again, across the towering entryway, toward the opposite wing. Here, just above ground level, there's what used to be a conservatory. I can imagine that it was once like stepping into a rainforest, a greenhouse, but with the windows dusty and lined with cracks, an army of unnamable vines creeping through the windows, it feels like standing in the midst of a huge spiderweb. I recognize an ivy leaf, but none of the others.

"This is going to be a custom repair job," he says. "I had to have architects and historians come consult on it. I cannot begin to tell you," he continues, with just the hint of a mischievous smile, "what an absolute pain in the ass this house has been." In the way his eyes light up, I see that he loves it. "It's not even done yet, and I can honestly say I preferred it in ruins."

"Will there be plants in here?"

"Orchids, mostly," he says. I try to picture it, to imagine the opulence of a room filled with rare, tropical flowers. In one corner, near a fountain, there's a tap extending from the wall: brass, I think, stepping over to swipe a finger in the dust.

"Gold plumbing fixtures," he says. "In the bathrooms, too. At the time, finished indoor plumbing was cutting-edge. Not to mention the cost."

"Jay Gatsby would've been right at home," I say.

"Mrs. Atwood wasn't much of a Gatsby," he answers.

Neither, I think, *are you.* "Maybe that's why she spent so much time outdoors," I offer.

"And in her study. With the doves." Nathaniel holds the door as I walk back into the entry hall, then moves past me to approach one of the two grand staircases leading up either side of the room. His hand brushes the back of my shoulder, as if he's saying, *come this way*, and, I think, it ought to be a perfectly innocent gesture, but I'm following him now like I'm on a string. "You said it was a gift," I reflect. "Do you mean, you don't think she liked it?"

"I'm not certain she did," he answers. His hand trails the banister, that striking red marble, and I can almost feel the warmth of his fingertips where mine trace after his. "Colonel Atwood promised to build her a house here as a wedding gift. But by the time he built it, they'd been married six years. Living apart for three." I walk through a ladies' parlor. The walls are marked with pale, square-shaped blotches, as if it was once adorned with large paintings. Now, only one remains. A Pre-Raphaelite, siren-like woman stands in the frame, feet in a stream, hair bedraggled. It's lovely, in its way, but all I can think is that, between her dress and that long hair, she must feel awfully weighed down. The parlor is divided by a spacious corridor from a salon, where I imagine men in suits with cigars drinking hard liquor.

"What happened?" I ask. He doesn't answer me for a few seconds, and, as we walk from the salon into the library, I sense he's dodging something I've asked a bit too directly.

"Whatever I can guess is from census records, newspapers, family letters."

"Okay," I say. "So? What's your account?"

"Early in their marriage, there was a stillbirth. I think that was where the opium came in. Laudanum prescription, probably."

"Oh, the poor girl." I cross my arms tight, wishing I could throw my arms around her. "Was she very sick after?"

"Don't know," he says. "He got rid of all her diaries. But it's just as likely they prescribed it for hysteria." I wince, taking into consideration in a new light the size, the shadows of this estate.

"My guess is, they grew apart, in the sense that her husband left her to herself too much. There were rumors of affairs," he says, pulling back a curtain to allow some sunlight onto the dozens of bookshelves. "Her family said she wrote letters, detailing that he was distant, unkind. They spent holidays together, society events, but that was it. Whatever it was—"

"She was young."

"And not from money. Even for that time period, they weren't on an equal footing," he says, finishing my thought. "It's almost like fulfilling what he promised her was a play to get back what he'd already lost."

"How long did she live here?"

"She moved here for the summer in 1907, as soon as it was ready," he says. "And never left. Until she disappeared. There aren't any clear records, but it was the end of July, or early August—"

"August 1, 1910."

"Why'd you say that?"

"It's on the desk," I tell him. "You've seen it."

"No." Now he's intrigued.

"Under the desk, on the right side. Her initials, and the date. August 1, 1910. You haven't seen that?"

"No," he says. "No, honestly, we didn't do a lot of renovations in there. It didn't seem right."

"It still doesn't seem right, sometimes," I add, "staying in there. Then, other times, I think she wouldn't mind me there." I walk away from him, eyeing the dust-coated spines of books. Feeling oddly at home, I drop into a cloth-covered armchair, a cloud of dust around me like spirits. "You know I have to ask you," I say, laughing, waving a hand in front of my face and trying not to cough.

"Ask me what?"

"What did the letter say? You said it was a riddle. That she left it on the desk."

"Oh," he says, as if he'd hoped I wouldn't ask. "Well, the original went to the colonel, who, I think, willed his papers to—"

"Nope," I interrupt, watching as he pretends to browse the shelves. "Tell me. I know you know."

"Fine, fine." He takes his phone from his pocket. "I have a scan of it." He swipes the screen a few times, then offers it to me. I walk back across the room to take it, dust on my clothing like ash or

feathers. I tap the screen to enlarge the image. I always imagine
Victorian handwriting spidery, scrawling, romantic. But Zenaida's
hand is precise, the tidy letters gently sloped.

> *To the finder of this brief missive: I leave in your care my*
> *only possession: a century's worth of sorrow, condensed into*
> *twenty-six short years. I am but a wraith, a muse who has*
> *outlived her purpose. Whether it should follow me down*
> *what remains of my path, or rest here, allowing me to walk*
> *away freed of it, I now go to find out.*

I read the words several times over, dwelling on the note
where its meaning hides and then emerges, twisted: *care, posses-*
sion, a century. In my mind, I go to find out. I imagine the desk
underneath my hands, the way I've casually littered it with my
pens and my shabby, lonesome breakfasts. I push the phone back
into Nathaniel's hand, my lips moving in disbelief.

"You mean to tell me, you—"

"What?"

"Don't play dumb." I turn on my heel and walk back the way
we came. At least, I thought I was. But the room I thought was
the salon is a stairwell, not a familiar one, and I follow it anyway,
up, then through a landing that opens on to a balcony overlooking
the grand staircase, and I see the window. I'm leaning with both
hands, scrutinizing it, when Nathaniel catches up to me.

"I have been spending my days in a room that more or less has
a curse on it, and you didn't think to tell me?"

"You don't believe in ghosts, right?"

"I'll plead the fifth on that one," I answer with a small smile.
"But sometimes I think you do."

"Come on," he says, turning back into the stairwell. One
more flight up and we're on the third floor. In the once-opulent
bedrooms, what furniture remains is covered with drop cloths and

moth-eaten. I count more than one bird's nest, and in the hallway, there's a long-deserted servant's cart. The master bedroom sits at the corner where two corridors meet.

"After Zenaida disappeared, the house belonged to her husband. She didn't own anything legally, of course."

"You're changing the subject," I say, watching his eyes sparkle as he dodges my gaze.

"The colonel left it to her family. It was an unusual gesture. Guilt, maybe. They sold it—made quite a scandal. It was considered rude, but they needed the money. They were poorer than the servants who worked here." He's lingering outside a stately doorway, red and white marble inlaid with tile carvings. "They sold it to a Canadian family—who moved out a couple years later. It was left vacant for a while—someone inherited it, lived here briefly in the fifties, then sold it again. So, it fell into disrepair."

"Lovely history," I say. "Back to how you let me sleep in a cursed room without so much as a heads-up."

"Then tell me you don't like it." There's laughter in his eyes, that brazen gleam. I can't tell whether I want to slap him or kiss him, but it's definitely some of both. But when he opens the doorway to the master bedroom, I forget what we're talking about entirely.

It's quite breathtaking, windows on two walls looking out at the mountains, a massive, carved bedframe. With so many details, I can't decide where to look first: the crystal strands dripping from chandeliers, the beaded lacework of the canopy over the bed, the dust-coated paintings on the wall. Near the bay window, I find what appears to be a cabinet door built into the wall and thoughtlessly reach to open it, like a child in a toyshop.

"Oh, look out. There are—"

When the door swings open in my hand, I'm looking into what appears to be a narrow but bottomless fall, giving rise to echoing chatters and scuffles. I leap back, catch my heel on the edge of the carpet, which no doubt cost more than any house I've ever lived in, and fall backward on the bed, scrambling on my elbows away from the noise.

"What the—" I'm fighting to compose myself, gesturing at the open cabinet, as Nathaniel crosses the room instantly. He rests an arm on the carved bed frame.

"Breathe, Sophie." I see that he's smiling.

"What is that?"

"That's the dumb waiter," he says. "There may or may not be a family of squirrels living in there." He pauses, reaches out to offer me his hand. Slowly, I reach out to take it, then, hearing another scuffle from inside the dumb waiter, melt into laughter.

"You sure you don't believe in ghosts?" he asks.

"Don't make fun of me," I gasp, still laughing.

"I'm not." A hush falls between us; his smile fades into an earnest gaze that almost makes me blush. Finally, he pulls me to my feet, brushes a bit of dust from my shoulder.

"Thanks," I murmur, my heart beating loudly in my ears. I throw another suspicious glance at the dumb waiter. There are curtains that hang from floor to ceiling, and, as my eyes track up to the ceiling, I see that it's painted with images of mourning doves and vines.

"Wow," I breathe.

"That, up there," he says, gesturing at the ceiling, "was the biggest pain in the ass to clean out of everything in this place."

"How did you do it?"

"Scaffolding," he says, "and a special brush, some water. A certain type of finish to prevent any more damage to the colors."

The ceiling must be twenty-five feet up. I follow the carvings that run around the doorway, the marble inlaid with colored glass and tile. Above the door, I see the outline of a pair of doves, carved in glass; one in a dusky sapphire, the other a bare outline, the original carving apparently missing.

"How will you fix this part?" I ask. "What a shame, that someone would take it. Do you think it was a trespasser? Or maybe someone who lived here after?"

"See, I'm not sure that was garden-variety vandalism," he says. "One dove, alone," he says, "is a symbol of—"

"Peace?"

He nods again. "Two, love. They pair off for life." He pauses. "When Zenaida's family was given the estate, they found it this way. Someone would have had to go up a ladder, take a knife, or... something, and chip or pry one of those carvings out. I'm not sure it ought to be repaired."

"What happened to her?" I ask, not so much to him as to the room in general. "A ring in a pool? A shoe in the woods? That note—"

"I haven't studied it too closely," he says, "and I haven't thought about it too much, because I don't think she wanted anybody to know exactly where she went, what happened. I think she wanted to just—I don't know." I imagine what this must mean, imagine the serene, willowy Zenaida from the stained-glass window pulling down love's symbol to make herself a place of peace.

"Disappear," I answer. "You think?" Nathaniel falls silent but his eyes light up with sparks of amber.

I follow down a hallway to another wing, where a large wooden staircase spirals down from a dizzying height. "Something about it is so disorienting," I whisper, holding the railing tight as I walk.

"You noticed," he says. "There's almost no right angles in the entire building, all fifty-two rooms. I don't know if it was intentional or not. But it always feels a little off-kilter."

Just as I think I'm going to need a flashlight if it gets any darker, he walks across a landing and throws open a pair of doors. Daylight streams in and I see a stone patio, and gladly walk out into the sun.

"Who knows exactly what went wrong between them, at this point," he says, though I can tell he's thought on it. "But this

house, even if it was an impressive gift, didn't do much to help."
He sits on the granite tile; we're now looking over the gardens,
and I can see the neat shapes of the flower beds and hedges that
we've worked on.

"Imagine someone caring for you this much," I say, my thoughts
wandering aloud. "Not the cost of building it—it's not that I think
he loved her more because of what he spent. But just the size of
it. Fifty-two rooms, right?" He nods. "And all the gardens. The
rows of trees. All of it filled with detail, all for one person. The
birds on the ceiling, the carvings."

"It's a lot."

"Imagine someone wanting that much to fix things, to ask
forgiveness." It's impossible not to think of the wistful tone he took
when he described Lincoln's mother. Those allusions to some possible future plans, the uncertainty in his voice when he mentioned
them. "Of course, anyone could put in that much thought. But
the difference with this place is, you can see it. You could walk
into it and get lost in the shadows." It makes me wonder, now that
I've said it, how many people would build requiems, monuments
like this, to love lost.

"Maybe he wasn't trying to win her back," he says. "Maybe it
was just what he owed her. Something that was promised."

"I guess it's hard to know for sure."

"It was one conversation," Nathaniel tells me, staring far away,
as if he's putting distance between himself and his words. "When
we moved here, three years ago. This idea that we'd wait until
things were better, try to stay together. She's dated. I could tell
you I have, but it would be a lie. I thought things were better. I
guess she still thinks I'm—"

"What?"

"Nothing," he murmurs. "A risk, I guess."

Despite how he's downplayed the work he's done, I can see that
he knows every detail of this house, with a familiarity that makes

it more than a job. It's not a story to him, but living history. He's lonely here, has been for some time. His own house is so sparse and quiet; I sense that he hasn't let himself really move in. This is a kind of penance, I can see it now, and wonder terribly what must have happened. Without trying to hide it, I study his profile, the measured stare he casts over the yard. "It makes you wonder, I guess," I say, "did he think this was going to win her back? Or was it already over?"

His gaze lands on mine. Maybe I've pushed it too far. But he nods, answering calmly. "You mean the structure is here, stayed here," he says. "Even once its reason for existing, that hope, was gone. That's why we don't build mansions for people we love." He cracks a smile, though his laugh is restrained. "As if just anybody could. And here I am, just a guy who could never make anything like this." I place my hand next to his, not touching, but right there, an offering, like these glimpses of his life he offers me. "Nathaniel, nobody in their right mind would ask you to." Though I'm hoping he'll take my hand, he doesn't, but he traces his fingertip over the back of my hand.

We're startled at the sound of a car in the drive. It's not a delivery truck or a contractor, instead an immaculately clean SUV, dark blue with tinted windows.

His eyes flicker up to meet mine, betraying a ripple of worry. "That's her." When he speaks the word *her,* I don't have to wonder who he means.

"Everything okay?"

"I don't know. She didn't call." He stands up, watching as the car comes to a halt. Nathaniel walks toward the granite railing, as if trying to draw closer to her, and for a moment I'm frightened for him, afraid he'll walk right over the edge. It's an untimely reminder, though one I guess I needed. A reminder that this woman could show up at any moment and he'd move toward her instead, and why shouldn't he? But then, I realize, I'd do the same, if my brother appeared. I'd drop everything, turn away from anybody else, and go right to him. If anything, I'm worse odds than Nathaniel. Yet, I can't help but take a curious step forward, peering over the railing. I just want to see what she looks like: the mother of his child, his first love, his first loss.

From this distance, the woman who steps out of the car is statu-esque, every detail in crisp focus. Her hair is sable brown, styled in a low ponytail, not a hair out of place. She wears sunglasses, a red blouse, crisp black jeans and black pumps. She's somehow effort-lessly casual and yet perfectly assembled, ready for battle. When I recognize her, I gasp and inch backward, until I'm close against the marble wall, feeling the shadows of the house around me.

"Hey, Selena," Nathaniel calls. "Everything okay?"

CHAPTER TWENTY-SEVEN

"Lincoln got a puppy." Selena extends one arm in a sweeping, ta-da gesture. The car door swings open and Lincoln bounds out, followed by a little black dog. He runs and it follows at his ankles, a black, shiny little coat, yipping and bouncing after the boy. "He insisted on coming by to show you."

"Dad, look," Lincoln calls. "I got a dog!"

"Be right there," he answers.

My head's spinning. Lingering in the shadows at the back of the porch, I look from Nathaniel to Selena, then back to him.

"Would you like to come say hello?" he asks, brushing past me toward the stairs, the jasmine blossoms fragrant in the breeze. "I'm sure Lincoln will be excited to see you."

"No, thanks." There aren't a lot of things I know for certain. But I know I saw Nathaniel in the waiting room, that day at the police station. I know Selena Radford hasn't trusted me from the start. I know I've felt like someone's been watching me. What if it's him? Instead of following him down the exterior stairs, I take a step into the darkened doorway of the house. I'm not sure whether I'm hoping to go out by a different doorway, or just to get away from him.

"Sophie, where are you going?"

"I'm leaving," I answer. "I have to get out of here. You—"

"What's wrong?" He draws closer to me and I take another step backward, into the darkened corridor.

"You know her?" My voice drops to a whisper, though Selena is fifty feet away, too far to hear. "How? What's going on?"

"Know her?" He looks over his shoulder in Selena's direction, then back to me, confused. "That's my ex, Selena. Why?"

"No, that's the detective working my case." I take another step into the darkened hallway and realize I don't know which way to turn, stumble over a stair I hadn't seen.

"That's my ex," he repeats. "She's a police detective."

"She has you keeping tabs on me." When I speak, I feel my throat squeezing in on my words, the hiccup of a sob following my speech. "She's told you to watch me. I thought I was safe here."

"No, Sophie—"

"Stop talking." Searching his eyes for insincerity, I step closer, so that our toes are almost touching. "Tell me the truth." Nathaniel pauses and I see the uncertainty in his expression give way to a decision. He places both hands on my cheeks and tilts my chin up to kiss me, drawing in a deep breath as our lips press.

"I am not lying to you," he whispers, voice low with emphasis. The tip of his thumb brushes a tear from the corner of my eye. "Sophie, if you're safe anywhere, it's here."

I can't help but think that's a big *if*. But in this moment, to my surprise, I think I believe him. It feels like fresh air in my lungs and solid ground under my feet. I don't know how, but I know he's not lying to me. I breathe in, count to four; out, count to four.

"Come with me," he says. "Lincoln will be thrilled to see you."

Nathaniel walks back into the sunlight, down the stairs and toward Selena and Lincoln, while I linger, making my way slowly behind him.

"He had to show you," Selena says. "I picked her out as a surprise a few weeks ago, but his softball team won yesterday, so it seemed like a good time."

"Didn't know there was a game," Nathaniel murmurs, obviously feeling a bit out of the loop.

"Hi, Dad!" Lincoln races to meet him. "Look—I got a puppy."

Nathaniel kneels to meet the dog, scratching its ears as it leaps around, a little blur on the grass. I'm lingering on the steps, hiding behind the jasmine, trying to size up my next move. "What's her name, pal?" Nathaniel asks.

"Roxy," Lincoln answers. He pushes his glasses up the bridge of his nose, and I wonder if he lost the pair that fit him, or if he broke them already. He runs back to the car, finds a tennis ball, and throws it sharply across the yard. Roxy shoots after it. He runs past me and swivels his head just long enough to shout: "Hey, Dove Girl's here!" As I return Lincoln's greeting, Selena Radford's eyes land on mine, and I walk straight toward her.

"Selena," Nathaniel says, "this is Sophie. She—"

"We've met," she says, cutting him off. "Nathaniel, would you give us a moment?" Nathaniel hesitates, but when Lincoln calls him again, they run off across the lawn.

"Detective Radford," I murmur.

"What are you doing here? Explain to me why you're here." Her polite smile holds firm, but her voice is icy. She waits for me to speak. I stand up straight. I can't blame her, not wanting me here around her son, whatever Nathaniel is to her. I stick my hands in the pockets of my jeans, look down at her perfect shoes.

"I work here," I say shortly. "You—you know him?" I nod in Nathaniel's direction.

"You might say so," she answers, and I sense I've made a mistake. "Sophie—if that's your name—if you have anything to tell me, I'd like for you to say it right now."

"What about you—do you have something to tell me?" I gesture after Nathaniel. "Did you ask him to keep an eye on me, or something?"

"No," she answers. "Not in the least. I had no idea you were here." She waves Nathaniel back over to us, Lincoln following, obliviously gleeful.

"Both of you," she says. "Is either of you hiding anything from me?"

"No," I answer, throwing a suspicious glance in his direction. "Not me, anyway." Nathaniel's bewildered.

"What's going on?"

"How much has she told you about herself?" Selena asks Nathaniel. "The accident? Her memories?"

"She's told me." He answers without hesitating.

"It's quite the coincidence," she answers. I'm the one hiding something, now—that I saw him that day at the police station. That I made my way out here, even if I didn't really mean to.

"If you have her living here, you must think she's trustworthy," Selena continues. "But your judgment of character has hardly been a great reference in the past."

Nathaniel flinches as though she's struck him. For a moment, they're both silent.

"Sorry," she murmurs.

"Don't be." His expression is distant. "You're not wrong." Watching with more than a little curiosity, I'm grateful when Lincoln interrupts.

"Sophie, see my dog? Her name is Roxy."

"I see," I answer. "She's lovely." He scoops up the puppy and I can't help but adore her, stroking the silky forehead and fine little ears. "Mom," Lincoln says, "did you meet Sophie?"

"He's been talking about you nonstop," Selena murmurs. "But Nathaniel, you didn't even tell me you'd hired someone."

"Well, I—" He clears his throat. "It never came up."

"I'm glad it's out in the open now," she says, though she doesn't sound pleased. "And Sophie, I know where to find you, should anything come up." For a moment, she lets the silence settle, and I'm struck with how beautiful she is. She might have stepped out of a magazine. Next to her, I look like a farmhand, freckles and scratches from working outdoors, dirt under my fingernails.

"Have you—" I want to ask her if she's found anything.

"Nothing." She shakes her head. She raises an eyebrow, looks at Nathaniel, then at me. "Be careful," she demands, and I'm not sure which one of us she's speaking to. I'm still wondering what she means, exactly, when Lincoln runs off after the puppy.

"Come on, Sophie!" Lincoln shouts, tearing off across the yard as he follows the puppy.

"Go on—he wants you to play with him," she observes, as though granting me her permission to be here, then raises her voice. "Lincoln, sweetie, five more minutes."

I catch up to Lincoln and Roxy as he throws the tennis ball for her. The puppy hasn't quite got the concept of fetch yet and I run to retrieve the ball, then toss it back to Lincoln with an easy, gentle throw. But Roxy's taken off now in her own direction, exploring for the joy of it, it seems. She runs across the yard, her nose in the flowers, tunneling through a bed of gladioli that rustle around her, a bit indignant.

"Come on, Roxy," Lincoln calls. "Time to go. She doesn't know her name yet," he says, as if apologizing to me, then runs after her. He's running further than I expected and I look back toward Nathaniel, half hoping he'll call Lincoln back or catch up with us. He's leaning against a tree, arms crossed, his eyes downcast. Selena's a few yards away from him, watching me with her hands in her pockets, but the distance between them may as well be miles.

"Hey, Lincoln, slow down a little," I call. "She'll stop running if you stop chasing her. She's playing with you."

But he's not listening to me, laughing as he follows the dog through the circular garden toward the footbridge. "Slow down," I warn. "Do not run up there."

He does, though, because he's a little kid following his brand-new puppy. I remember Lincoln assuring me that he never falls. The dog skids to a halt and leaps around his knees, and he claps and calls her a good puppy, slowing down so fast that he stumbles.

I see it in slow motion: the little boy's shoulders going sideways, the weight of his body following, a hand grasping for and just missing the railing, the gaps between the temporary railings too wide. In a painstaking half-twirl, his weight shifts, one foot stuck at the ankle, then twisting loose, and he falls, calling for his dad. I remember him telling me he can't swim. Lincoln goes straight down, bobs back up, just his mouth and nose at the surface, and I can see the water move without breaking where his arms flail. There's no noise, no scream, no splash.

CHAPTER TWENTY-EIGHT

I run after him, up onto the bridge, and jump over the side. In the moment before I slip into the water, I draw a breath and hold it. The murky water is sour in my nostrils. I sense motion, get my bearing, and zip down to grab Lincoln. He's panicking, reaching for me with a frantic energy that will pull us both down, so I wrap an arm around him, bracing it around his torso before I kick upward. He's a blur of motion that's only tugging him down faster, but luckily for both of us, he doesn't weigh that much, and I pull him upward and over, toward the shore. I'm in constant motion, my body taking over, and yet I wonder whether, while I'm down here, if I stayed to look, would I find anything else? Something left behind? As I'm pulling us back toward the air, I realize part of me has wanted to look deeper into this water since the first time I laid eyes on it.

I lift Lincoln up so that he surfaces before I do, then turn my chin to face him, attempting to hold him still. "Easy," I say, my voice short and clear, kicking my feet and keeping us afloat with one arm. This is an order, one I know he can't obey, but I say it anyway, holding him tight as I kick toward shore. It feels like forever, but it's not more than three or four yards, and finally, I feel the sludge of the ground beneath the toes of my shoes. I push aside a few water lilies, as the green-brown muck from the shallow edge clings to the legs of my jeans. This is the sort of murky pond you'd expect a corpse to walk out of on a dark night, and I suspect that's probably how I look. Nonetheless, I breathe in deeply and look at the boy in my arms with relief. I take a few squishing steps up to dry land and set him on the bank, then sit on my knees, so we're eye level. He's coughing, spluttering. That's good. I know drowning can be quiet.

I pat his back, hard. "You're okay." I say it like it's a fact, and it is. "Everything is fine."

Lincoln's arms move just as fast, but this time he's wiping the water and pond weed from his face and hair, blinking. He leans forward, and for a moment, I'm afraid he's unconscious. Then I feel his little arms hugging me, hacking again, loudly.

"Thanks." His voice is hoarse. I rest a hand on his shoulder, then stand up. "Sophie, where's my dog?"

Shit. I glance at the water. It's young, but a Labrador, right? It should be able to hold its own. The surface is still; there's no sign of the dog.

We hear a yelp and look up. Roxy is panting, looking with apprehension over the side of the bridge. I try to stifle a laugh. "She's right there, Lincoln. She's fine, too."

"Can you stand up?" I ask, helping him to his feet. Water squelches in both our shoes as we walk up the incline. He trips in the grass and I lift him up. As we walk up the bank, I see Nathaniel standing just at the water's edge, Selena just behind him. He's gone pale, and there's a wide-eyed, stark fear in his eyes I've never seen the likes of before.

"I don't know what happened," I stammer. "He was so fast. I tried to catch up before he went up the bridge, but—"

"Sweetheart," Selena says, almost crying. "Lincoln, you—" I can see that she wants to reprimand him, that it's her fear speaking.

"What, Mom?"

She shakes her head and smiles weakly. "Sweetheart, you just run so fast."

"Hey, Dad," Lincoln bleats. "Did you see that?"

Nathaniel is tight-lipped, silent. Selena doesn't appear to have noticed him, not even now that Lincoln calls to him. I can see his chest rise and fall with his breath. But I see his face soften as he realizes he's okay. I think I see the life come back into him when he begins to move: patting Lincoln's back, pressing water out of his hair. The dog joins us, yapping at Selena's ankles until she picks it up.

"Did I see it," he echoes, attempting a laugh that sounds hollow, weak. "Yeah. From way too far away. I'm so sorry, buddy," he says. "That was all my fault."

"No, I mean, did you see Sophie?" Lincoln says, excited now. He wiggles free of me and jumps to the ground, shoes squishing as he walks. "I want her to teach me how to swim. She was so fast! That was way cool."

"Yes, Lincoln," he says, a ghost of a smile finally crossing his lips. He raises his eyes to mine. "That was way cool."

"We should get going," Selena murmurs, still stunned. "Nathaniel, can you help him get some dry clothes on?"

"Yeah, of course. Come on, Linc." They walk away toward the house and I'm left standing alone with Selena again. She studies me openly. I wring water from my hair with both hands, wiping bits of leaves and mulch from my shirt, then realize I'm not wearing a bra, and hastily cross my arms.

"I didn't think he'd run onto the bridge," I say. "I caught up as fast as I could. I'm so sorry."

"It isn't your fault," she says. "I'm grateful to you."

"No need."

"That was quick thinking," she said. "And you acted quickly, too. Drowning can happen fast. Thank you."

"I'd better go clean up," I answer, starting to move away from her. The truth is, I'm not very sure about Selena's or Nathaniel's intentions right now. Lincoln and the puppy are the only two I'm sure I trust here; I didn't jump into the water to help either of his parents.

"Listen." She's studying me again. "Before you go—"

"Yes?"

"Don't let yourself forget: this is a temporary job. You're here until you find out where you really live." She's speaking to me, but she's glancing in Nathaniel's direction, as if she'd like to say something else, but can't find the words.

"There's nothing I want more than to find my brother," I answer. Her suspicion might not be unfounded, I can admit that, but it's exhausting even so. I'm hardly in the mood to be questioned any longer with water and pond muck dripping from my hair and clothes. "It was nice to see you."

"Goodbye, Sophie."

I let myself into the apartment and close the door. Out the window, I see Nathaniel walking with Lincoln, now in some dry clothes but with his hair still damp. He gives him a high five and then a big hug, a kiss on the cheek. Even from here, I can see that he's still jumpy, moving as if numb. Selena nods as she says something to him; she doesn't touch him before she gets in the car. He waves at the car. The sun lights up his dark hair, the ripple of muscles in his arm. I turn from the window in an instant. Selena's vague warning now makes sense. She was warning me to stay away from him. Whatever is broken between them isn't my business. I tell myself that I'm alone here, just as I was in the woods where they found me. I have no foothold, no place to ask him not to drop everything when she appears; my presence, aside from hired help, is nothing more than a disruption.

Upstairs, I undress and shower, scrubbing myself all over, trying to wash the pond off. As the hot water hits my skin, I remember the feeling of the pond water around me, the cold, the sensation of jumping in. I can recall, now, the weekly swim lessons that I attended through school. How my focus turned to studying, while Miles grew harder to find, his visits more occasional. Any number of bad things could have happened to him in the time we've been apart. What if he met someone in prison who hurt him? What if he's in trouble again for something that wasn't his fault? I dry my hair and comb through it with my fingertips and find a clean camisole and a pair of shorts. As I'm getting dressed, I turn an unforgiving glance at the mirror. All the marks are still there. I shouldn't let the passage of time numb me, fool me into pretending that there's any story other than the truth. I'm reminded of the painting in the parlor, Ophelia or some other drowned woman. I turn away from my reflection, mouthing the words: *You do not belong here.*

I pick up my drawing book and pencils, flipping over the pages as I walk down the stairs. Poppies, a symbol I still don't know the meaning of. Sketches of doves, of Zenaida, then poppies again. On one page, an idle sketch of Nathaniel and Lincoln. Then, several pages of Miles. *What Sophie Knows,* I think. Plainly not enough. I find I can't sit at the desk now I know what was in the note Zenaida left here. *I leave in your care… I'm sorry,* I think. *I don't want your century's worth of sorrow, any more than you did.* I carry the sketchbook and pencils outside to draw a bit and let my hair dry in the sun. The energy inside feels too close, almost as though I'm not alone.

But I'm not alone. Nathaniel's sitting out there, with his elbows propped on his knees, his forehead leaning on one hand. All my thoughts of self-preservation vanish as I sit down next to him.

CHAPTER TWENTY-NINE

Nathaniel doesn't speak, so I wait a few moments. "It was my fault," he says, finally.

Lincoln's a fast little boy and it wasn't my fault that he fell. I know that. But it would be better if it were my fault than for Nathaniel to feel this way; I could forgive myself for a mistake. "I saw him running that way and I didn't catch up fast enough."

Nathaniel shakes his head. "I was so far away." He speaks in a low, breathy voice, mumbling through his hands. "I knew I needed to move, and I couldn't."

"You did move," I say. "You were there by the time I got him out of the water."

"I didn't know you could swim." Now, he turns to focus on me.

"I wasn't a hundred percent sure either," I say, moving past it. "It's nothing, really. Lincoln is fine, okay?" He knows that, though, and I see that there's more at work here. I hesitate, then let myself reach over to rest a hand on the back of his neck, sweeping softly over his shoulder blades. "Your boy's fine," I repeat, letting my voice drop low and soft, resisting the inclination to slip my hand under the collar of his shirt. With an honest curiosity, I lean over to look into his eyes. "Hey, look at me. What about you?"

"Huh?"

"Are you okay?" I ask. He nods his head, too quickly, and I watch him waiting for his real answer.

"Yeah, I'm fine," he says, talking through his teeth. My palm comes to rest just beneath his shoulder blades, and suddenly I feel him flinch, drawing slightly away from me.

I pull my hand back, closing it into a fist, as if I could keep something of him, though I know I can't.

"Can I say something?" When I speak, he turns to face me. "I don't know you—I know that. But there's something that's plain to me, as an—" I pause and choose my next words carefully. They ring hollow. "As an objective observer."

"What's that?"

"You, and Selena? It's out of balance. Something isn't fair. Whatever this is—" I try to indicate this weight he carries. "It has reins, and she is steering it. I'm not saying her reasons are wrong, I don't know those, but it isn't quite right, either."

He sighs, and I see that he knows this, somehow. He's punishing himself, then. "If you knew, you wouldn't say that."

"Try it. I bet I would." I shrug. "You can tell me. I might remember where my real home is and be gone in the morning."

"What was it like?" he asks. "Jumping in after him, I mean."

"It happened fast, honestly. I didn't really think about it. But that pond water—yuck!" I tilt my head, wondering if he understands, then see a sly smile. "Don't change the subject." He stretches his hands out, cracking knuckles.

"So, back up, I guess, fifteen years. I grew up an hour or so from here. Enlisted the year after high school. Didn't know what else to do with myself, and, honestly, I thought I could get my education paid for. It was quiet, the first few years, then, you know, 2001 happened."

"Right."

"After I came back, I couldn't keep a job, couldn't sleep. I was distracted, at best. And when I looked at Lincoln, all I could see was—" He shakes his head and closes his eyes. "My best friend was worse off. I drank too much, but for him it was pills. I was sure I could help him. You know, he was the person I could call, when I was too bad off to talk to Selena. We looked out for each other." He sits with this for a moment and I can sense that it's difficult. "After he died, we moved here. Separately. I asked Selena to take custody of Lincoln. So, now, here I am: thirty-four, my family's split up, and I have no college degree. Just a bunch of frayed nerves and bad attitude."

"It's difficult to let go of what you thought your life was," I murmur. "What it was supposed to be."

"You think?"

"I don't know, really."

There's more, that's clear, but I'm not going to press him. Whatever happened, he obviously feels responsible.

"I'm sorry." Wherever his mind's gone, it's dark. I see shadows in his eyes as he sighs and answers me again.

"I do not deserve it."

"Yes, you do," I say. "Of course you do."

"No, I don't." He's morose, but this disagreeing has come naturally to us since our first meeting, and I see it begins to call him back from wherever he's gone.

"Do so," I say, like a kid, poking his arm, daring him to argue back at me. The connection is tenuous, but it's as natural as it has always been.

"Do not—ugh! You are infuriating." He looks to me, exasperated, the heat of an argument warming his confidence, then, suddenly, he breaks into a smile and takes a long, steady breath. "Thank you. Did I say that? For jumping in after him."

"Don't think anything of it," I say. "But I don't think we're getting the glasses back. Unless, you know, you really want me to go looking for them." Smiling across at him, I realize that it's true, I probably would jump back in that filthy water if he said he needed them.

"What would it be like," he asks me, as if an idea has suddenly occurred to him, "if we weren't here? What if we were somewhere different?"

"I don't know."

"We should get out of here." He waves his hand at the looming dark of the mansion, the familiar landscape. "Forget all this. Let's go somewhere."

"Where to?"

"Let's go to the beach," he says. "Samara Island is just a couple hours away. I'll drive—we'll be back by dinnertime." Lit up by an idea, his charm is hard to deny. I want to go as soon as he suggests it, but I also want to hear him ask me again.

"Are you sure?"

"I'm sure." He tilts his chin and when he smiles, his eyes are warm and daring. "You'll love it. Come with me," he says. I can't contain my smile. "Let's just not work today. I won't tell the boss."

"You promise?"

"Sure," he laughs.

"Okay," I answer. "Let's go."

And, just like that, we do. I even leave my sketchbook behind, right there on the windowsill. I follow him to his truck. Nathaniel opens the door, takes a pair of sunglasses from the pocket of his jeans, and leans close enough to put them on me. And, just this quickly, I leave Hazel Bluff for the first time since I can remember.

*

Samara Inlet, Nathaniel tells me, is a little town on a peninsula just across the sound. He describes it like he knows it well, and I remember that he grew up around here, although he lived elsewhere for years. I wonder what it's like to feel back home, to be somewhere that you have missed. Is there such a place for me? As the road merges onto a highway, the trees begin to thin out and there's a wash of warm, yellow sunlight. It seems to clear away the cobwebs, chase out the ghosts from this haunted house I live in.

"Hey," I ask. "The name. Samara. Why—"

"So, the sound is sort of hourglass-shaped. They named it after a maple seed. Samara. You know, the seeds that fall and spin—maple copters, right? Some of the kids called them helicopters."

"Whirlybirds," I answer. "That's what I always called them." He looks away, half smiling, one hand rising to his chin, as if he's thinking. I stretch and yawn, sleepiness making me bolder than I ought to be. "What were you thinking, earlier? When you were laughing at me, after those squirrels scared the daylights out of me?"

"Thinking? Not a single thing. I was looking at you." His answer isn't bold, but honest. I let the sunglasses slip away from my eyes. "You're beautiful when you're laughing."

CHAPTER THIRTY

The lull of the engine is even and loud. I fall asleep and dream of water, of being somewhere I know. I wake as I feel the car slow down and hear the tick of the turn signal. The sun in the window now is bright; we're somewhere with almost no trees. Behind the dark lenses of the borrowed sunglasses, I watch Nathaniel driving. He looks at ease. Then, somehow, he knows I'm watching him and turns a gentle glance my way. I look back and smile without feeling any need to speak. We are nowhere, nowhere that I know, and time seems to have come unstuck. We're only here, and now, and that seems to be all that matters. I haven't been asleep long, but it seems long enough to have washed away everything else. One more turn and there's sand dunes by the side of the road. The truck slows to a crawl and we drive through the small town, which is just a gathering of the necessary businesses in the midst of a patchwork of vacation homes. He parks the truck outside a general store.

"That's as far as we can drive."

"How much further is it?"

He points out the windshield. "The ferry comes every hour." A nearby sign informs us that it's booked for vehicles, but still has plenty of room for pedestrians.

I can't wait to get out of the car and feel this different ground under my feet. The breeze is hot and dry, and I can smell the ocean. I try not to show how excited I am, but I can't help it: I'm happy to be here, thankful that he would guess it would make me so happy to go somewhere new. And I think he can feel it, too. My hand swings close to his as we walk onto the ferry and find an empty spot along the railings of the pedestrian deck. I watch the land recede behind us. It's not a long way, but the boat moves slowly, and the cooler breeze on the water is pleasant. I lean over the railing and point at a lighthouse on the approaching island, with a black-and-white diagonal stripe.

"Look."

"It's pretty, isn't it? Been there for ages. They actually moved the lighthouse, when the dunes shifted."

I imagine the lighthouse by night. Wonder how the ocean beyond would look from way up there. "Is it open?"

"I think so," he says. The ferry docks and we slowly file off. The captain warns over a loudspeaker that the last ferry leaves at seven PM sharp. There's a sign welcoming us to Samara Island, a tourist area, lined with brochures and phone numbers. It's as if we've gone back in time, almost. I count three streetlights, four shops, and one small hotel. The rest is just an expanse of sand and dunes and grasses, with the gentle roar of the ocean beyond. At the end of the road, the lighthouse is visible in the middle of a wide lawn of scratchy grass and beach plants.

"It's open," he says, pointing. "But you know there's no elevator."

"How many steps is it?" I grin.

We buy two tickets and head up. It's warm inside the lighthouse, all its heavy bricks soaking up sunlight all day long. The pamphlet informs me that it's six hundred and twelve steps up. We walk slowly, in no rush. Groups of tourists step past us, and each time, we move closer to the wall to let them by.

"I used to come here with my family," he says, "when I was young."

"What's your family like?"

"Loud," he says, laughing. "And there's a bunch of them. Five kids, including me. With my parents, that makes seven. We had three dogs and four cats."

My smile must show that I'm charmed, because he continues, "That was meant to be a warning." But he's smiling, too. Taking the stairs slowly enough to keep talking, he tells me about Lincoln's aunts and uncles, that he's lucky to have so many of them nearby. "They were there," he says, "when—I wasn't all the way there, they were always there. Bugging me. In a way that helped. Hey." He looks up the center of the spiral staircase, which narrows. "Almost there. Tired yet?"

"No way," I say, grinning. "Bet I can get there first."

Breaking every safety rule in the pamphlet, I take the stairs two at a time, skipping up past him, holding the railing as I begin to feel dizzy. Finally, I make it to the top landing and push the door open, walking out into the blinding sun.

I cross the patio and stand with my hands on the rail, look out over the beach, blinking at the bright light. He's only a few moments behind me.

"Told you I'd beat you here."

"I wasn't really trying," he says. "Let you win that one."

"Whatever you say." I smile. We stand with shoulders touching and catch our breath as he points out where they used to stay at the little hotel, and the fishing tackle store. The spot in the surf where you can see a wrecked ship when the tide is low. I wonder if the lighthouse was off that night.

"It was before they built it," he answers.

"Makes sense."

I think about shipwrecks, about men drowning at sea. And legends of mermaids. I imagine that tourists must be tiresome to people who live and work here, but to me, a beach is magical. A meeting point of water and land. A bit of hazard. Nathaniel's studying the water, too, the way it shifts in color under the occasional cloud, patches of deeper green-blue.

"It isn't that deep," he says, as if answering my thoughts. "It's the tides that are dangerous. They sneak up on people who don't think about what they're doing."

His tone is serious, and I have to turn to look at him. A group of tourists joins us, chattering and pointing, but giving us our space.

"My buddy—Spencer—he spent months trying to get clean."

I give him space to speak, relaxing my arms, staring out into the distance, listening intently.

"He got into trouble a lot, buying shit from the wrong people, running out of money. And then he'd call when he was at the bottom, didn't want to live anymore. I had points like that, too, so I thought I could help. We helped each other," he explains. "That was how it was. I let him stay in the spare room at our house once. He promised he wasn't using anymore, said he was suicidal and needed company. I insisted," he remembers.

Now, I take off the sunglasses, turn to look at him.

"Selena said she noticed things missing, but I figured she was exaggerating. She didn't like him, anyway. But I found her watch and some cash in the pocket of his jeans when he left some laundry in the drier. So—I thought I could handle it, right? I told him he needed to leave. Gave him until the end of the day. Found some contacts, intervention programs. I told him I was still his friend." He swallows. I wait for the rest to surface.

"So, three in the afternoon, we're sitting there, I'm holding Lincoln—two years old, almost three—this guy's like his uncle. Takes his gun out. Points it at me. He was angry," he remembers, "I could barely recognize his face. And then shoots himself in the head. And I'm just—sitting there, and it happened so fast, I couldn't even cover my kid's ears." He exhales through his nose, squeezes the railing. "If I'd been in my right mind, I would never have let him stay with us. I thought if I could help him, I could help myself. My reasons were wrong," he says, as if it's a scientific conclusion. "I failed my best friend, and myself. And, worse, my son."

"So, when Selena said you weren't a great judge of character—"

"That would be why," he says.

"It was a bit unfair of her, wasn't it?" I ask. "Time has passed. And you clearly don't make light of what happened."

"It was her home. Her son." His gaze lingers over the horizon, but I know his thoughts are somewhere further away. "I don't blame her for not being able to let it go."

Things click into place. I see his protectiveness, his fear and guilt, all part of the same picture now, all these moving pieces. "Lincoln doesn't remember," he murmurs, "but being scared that badly changes you, it shapes you, whether you have it in your actual memory or not." He says this like he knows it for a fact. I find my hand grasping his, and he wraps his fingers around mine. "In a way, that was a wake-up for me, although that was just the beginning of the hard part. Getting better, I mean."

"How?"

"Hard work," he says. "Therapy. No good answer. When I couldn't find any reason, I would ask myself what would break if I were gone. I just had to think of Lincoln. I couldn't find a way to kill myself that didn't hurt him too. You owe your children your full presence."

"Right."

"You know," he says. "One foot in front of the other. That was four years ago." His eyes flicker up to catch mine, his face open. "Today, this feels like the first time I've stood still since." He laughs ruefully. "Sorry. You probably don't want to hear all this."

"You're wrong." I shake my head. "I do. I'd like to hear it. Whatever you want to tell me." He doesn't know how admirable he is, how strong he has to be to have done all that. "And besides, you can tell me anything. I'm nobody, from nowhere, right?"

"No," he says, looking at me with curiosity. "You're someone, alright."

"What does that mean?"

"You have a life somewhere, something to go back to. Where maybe there's not room for any of this."

Our quiet voices seem to encircle us, to create a boundary between us and the others up here, marking us in a different world; though the noise of other visitors is audible, it seems at a greater distance.

"Sometimes I wish—" I drop my voice to a whisper, as if that makes it any less dangerous to voice thoughts like this. "I wish things were different."

I hear a group of voices from a few yards off, at the other side of the patio. There's a gathering of kids, college-aged, maybe even in high school.

"Hey, man," one of them calls. Their voices are friendly, jovial. "Kiss her already."

"You kids mind your own business," he shouts back, scolding. But he does. His hand finds my shoulder, the other wrapped in mine, and his lips brush mine, patient and deliberate, calling my heart right into my throat, before our lips press. This isn't a spontaneous spark, like in the kitchen two weeks ago; it's like a fire, kindled.

We pull back, standing side by side.

"The water looks nice," I whisper.

"It does."

He's still tracing my hair, caressing my shoulders, then resting his hand on the middle of my upper back. I see him glance at the skin there, but I don't flinch or turn.

"Let's go," I say. "I want to see the beach."

CHAPTER THIRTY-ONE

As we walk down the stairs again and toward the waterfront, something feels different. Nathaniel's bearing is lighter, somehow. It seems a barrier that was between us has lifted; now, we're walking together, his arm around my shoulders. We stop in one of the beachfront shops for supplies. I buy a towel and pick out a swimsuit, blue with crisscrossed straps in the back. I change in the fitting room, slipping my clothes back on over the swimsuit, and I'm ready to go.

Nathaniel lifts his arm from around my shoulders. I sit to take my sandals off, to feel the hot sand between my toes. Nathaniel reaches down and offers me his hands; I pull myself to standing and swing against him, then we walk into the water. Side by side, we wait until each wave recedes, letting the tug of the tide pull us along a foot or two, until we're standing shoulder-deep, just past the breakers. We're an arm's length apart, drifting a little further away, then joining hands again. He's head and shoulders above the surface of the water, ducks under, then back up, brushing water from his face. I can feel the day slipping by into afternoon, the sunlight's angle changing. I remember that the last ferry will leave at seven, and wonder what time it is now.

"Sophie?" he asks. Glancing back to the sand to check that my clothes and towel are where I left them, something catches my eye. I see a woman with dark, loose hair, standing there looking out at the water, almost as if she's looking right at me.

"Sophie, hey." His voice sounds far away. The woman isn't dressed for the beach. She's wearing boots and a gauzy, black button-up dress. Her chin tilts and I feel certain that she's looking right at me, with deep-set eyes the color of honey. My feet reach for the sand under the water; seaweed or a fish brushes my ankle. I reach out for Nathaniel's arm and squeeze hard, digging my heels into the sand. He hugs me and I lean in, feel the warmth of his skin against mine.

"Sorry. I was—" Distracted. I look back at the shore, glimpsing through a family walking past, obscuring my view.

"Everything alright?" he asks. When I look toward the shore again, the woman is gone.

"I think so."

I kick my feet and hold his hand, lifting myself up as a wave passes around us.

I'm keeping my feet planted on the bottom now, though more than ever I can feel the necessity of going back to shore. Still holding his arm, I cast a meaningful glance up at the sun, creeping closer to the horizon in the west. Nathaniel seems to understand what I'm thinking, and we begin to walk back toward shore. Though it's a warm evening, a salty breeze has kicked up over the water, so that my skin feels exposed and cold when I surface, the heavy blanket of the water warm by contrast, though it's several degrees colder than the air above. Nathaniel doesn't seem cold, or if he is, he doesn't show it, walking into the air without flinching. I feel braver just for standing next to him. Standing next to my towel, I nudge my bag with my toes, see that it's still there, everything apparently as I left it. I scan the beach, all the way up to one side and down the other, and see no trace of any woman in a black dress. Shaking my head, I sit on the towel and stretch my legs out in front of me. Nathaniel sits at my side.

"Do you know the time?"

He looks at his phone. "Six."

I'm squeezing water from my hair, tugging it into a braid. I scoot close to him, casting an anxious glance around the beach, looking for the woman, but she's nowhere to be seen. A stranger, I think. That's all.

Nathaniel finds a shell in the sand and pushes it toward me. I lean my head on my knees and study him openly, his gorgeous shoulders, the shape of his torso, one leg extended, the other crossed over it. Backlit with the beginning of a sunset. Sand in his hair. This day and this place, us here together, this feels both imaginary and more than real. But the one thing I know for sure is that it's temporary. This is a moment that will never come again. We're both trying to get back to our own places, places that might not have room for us, or even exist, anymore. But this day, which I know I'll always remember, belonged to us alone.

When he checks his phone again, we both rise. I shake the sand off of my clothes and pull them on over my almost-dry swimsuit. I notice that my shorts feel light, and pat the pockets. My necklace is missing. I check the sand under my towel, throw a few handfuls aside.

"I dropped something."

"What was it?" he asks.

"A—a necklace. I—"

"Were you wearing a necklace?" he asks. I shake my head. He doesn't miss a thing.

"No," I answer. "Long story. I keep it with me. Kind of a good luck charm. I think." I could have lost it anywhere, changing, walking, washed away in the sand. "It's okay. Probably fell out of my pocket in the car."

If we don't leave soon, we'll miss the last ferry, and we both know it. With an uncertain distance between us, we walk away from the water, toward the street.

"Oh," I say, passing a restaurant. "That smells amazing." I remember I haven't eaten since lunch.

"Yeah, I'm starved," he says, as if just realizing it himself. We both glance at the patio, the smell of food calling. We look at each other furtively, but keep walking. I feel the back of his hand graze mine as we walk. The ferry is waiting; I can see people lined up to board. We pass the hotel, just two stories of rooms, with windows facing the sea. The sign outside the office says: 'Vacancy.'

"That's adorable," I sigh. I wish I could wipe his memory clean, too. Maybe here there would be room for us to stay. "Imagine waking up to that view. I bet it's quiet here."

"And there's a breakfast spot," he says, pointing. "Right on the marina, up there. Biscuits and eggs, stuff like that. Nothing fancy, but it's the best you've ever tasted." He yawns.

"Tired?"

"A bit," he nods. "It'll be a late night getting in."

"Too tired to drive?"

"I don't think so. Not unless you are."

"No, I don't think so."

We share a regretful smile, fingertips brushing but not clasping, and walk on board the ferry.

CHAPTER THIRTY-TWO

The pedestrian deck on the ferry is sparsely populated. I'm guessing that everybody else either left earlier in the day or is staying the night. There's a bench along the railing where we sit, our backs to the water. The clock reads a quarter to seven. I stretch my legs out, letting my feet rest on their heels, toes swinging back and forth.

"Fifteen minutes till departure," the loudspeaker calls. "Boat leaves at seven sharp." I excuse myself to find the restroom. It's down one flight of stairs, isolated from the rest of the passenger area. I take a wrong turn into the car park area. A figure catches my eye, and, sensing I should keep walking, I do, but turn my head when I see a second figure, a child. No: it's not a child, I see; a young teenager, though, perhaps fourteen, a boy. A woman faces him and slips something into his palm. Money changes hands. I pass by quickly. *He's a kid,* I think, disgusted. But the woman's low voice follows me like a tune stuck in my head as I make my way to the bathrooms.

I use the bathroom and take a look in the mirror as I wash my hands, noting the freckles across my nose, the sand in my damp braid. The other stall door whines on its hinges as it opens. I startle, not realizing there was anyone else here.

"Sorry," I say, stepping aside to allow room at the mirror. "I—"

Then she appears behind me. Taller than she looked from a distance, her black hair almost oil-dark, and her voice is sweet and low.

I know her. The woman from my daydreams, those spidery hands scoring poppy seedpods. Turning the leftover seeds into an intoxicating tea, singing as she worked.

"You followed me in here," I say bravely. "Why?"

"I found something of yours." She talks to me like we know each other, stepping toward me, her hand open. In her palm she holds my pendant. "Sophia, right?" she smiles. I hesitate and she steps forward again, my feet walking backward. I bump into the sink, extend an arm to hold her away. She presses the pendant into my open palm.

"I saw you," she says, "way out in the surf. How much do you know about drowning?" I turn around and eye the door. Her reflection appears on my other side, between it and me.

"People drown because they think they're somewhere safe, and they inch further and further out, and the next time a strong current comes in, it's too late." I step closer to the door, chin jutting out. "Did you know—most people who drown at sea do so facing the shore?"

"Yeah, well, I'm a pretty good swimmer." My throat is tight with fear.

"That's sweet." The woman smiles as if she's teasing me. "But who's looking out for your brother?"

"What did you say?" I step up close, just inches away from her. She breezes past me, lingering in the doorway.

"I said we have to look out for each other." As she closes the door behind her, I make out a symbol inked on her arm, one that matches the one in my hand.

I blink and she's gone. The tiles echo with her voice; I'm holding the necklace so tight in my fist that it hurts as though it's red-hot. I pace furiously, press both fists to my temples, then hug my arms around my chest, half-wishing I could squeeze all my breath out, float away into the air, anonymous.

They've found me.

Who's they?

And what am I going to do?

Where do I go now? Jump into the sea and swim until I tire out, turn to face the shore as I drown?

I hear the bell ring again, followed by the loudspeaker: ten minutes until departure. I hear the jolt of machinery, the bridge that lets the cars on pulling up into the ferry. I know I'm paranoid. Objectively, I know it. But I'm almost certain now that someone's following me. Both can be true. When I close my eyes, I'm fighting visions of venomous snakes, of poppies and lost children, a desolate silence that threatens to drown out everything hopeful I could imagine. A phrase crosses my mind: *a century's worth of sorrow.* I shove it down, angry, telling Zenaida to stay back there, in the mountains, as I rush for the door.

Breaking into a run as I dodge through the car park, I know I ought to be fearing for my life. I leap up the stairs to the pedestrian deck, telling myself I'm lucky to be alive, that tempting fate like this is nothing but reckless. Maybe disaster waits for me on the other side of this water. But all I can picture is the way Nathaniel's eyes light up, and how he laughs.

I don't slow down until Nathaniel's right in front of me, waiting where I left him. I grab his hands in mine and pull him to his feet, skidding on my heels to slow down, throw my arms around him as if this is anything but hopeless.

"Sophie?" His arms close around me, uncertain, a hand tracing my back in a gesture of comfort. I pull back to look desperately into his eyes. Nathaniel takes my hands into his, wraps his fingers over my clenched fist. "What is it?" he asks. I release my hand, see the silver charm staring back at me. "I found my necklace," I squeak, then throw myself around him again in a careless hug. "I don't want to go back," I whisper against his shoulder. "I don't want to leave. I want to stay here." I lift my chin up and look into his eyes. "With you." When he hesitates, I'm looking at the clock.

"What do you want?" I stand close to him, but allow enough distance for honesty.

"I don't want you to get hurt." He catches my hands in his, drops his eyes. I squeeze his hands and step closer.

"Do you want to know what I want?" I whisper. We lock eyes and his hand traces my cheek. "I want to remember you. And I know—today doesn't change anything. Not for me, not for you."

"We already know that isn't true," he says, drawing me closer.

Before the bell rings again, we're holding hands, each pulling the other along, back toward the exit ramp. The attendant opens the gate for us and we hurry down the ramp. "Forget something?" he asks.

"You could say so," I answer. "Have a nice evening."

CHAPTER THIRTY-THREE

When the ferry disappears, the island is quiet, deserted to its solitary evening. There is no sound of cars or buses, no haunting whisper of the forest, just distant music and the ocean waves. We order dinner at the restaurant we passed on the way out, and I think food has never tasted this good. Slowly, the comfort of food in my belly, the calm that hangs in the air here, begin to soothe my nerves. That dark-haired woman, the mark on her arm, that can wait. We're out of reach.

"Buy you a drink?"

"Sure."

"What would you like?" he asks. I turn to look at the bar, making it an excuse to put my chin on his shoulder. I answer from habit, without a thought.

"Gin and tonic, with lemon," I answer. "What's so funny?"

"Nothing," he says, smiling at me. "Timeless, understated. But not quite what you expect."

"Oh, is this the game?" I laugh back. "What's your order?"

"I don't drink," he answers, shrugging it off. "When I did, it was bourbon, in abundance. If you make anything of that." And I do, I think. Southern boy. Simple tastes. A classic choice. Yet, that's not the sum of who he is, not anymore. In the little half-nervous glances he gives me, I see that he's got more to say, and wait, my silence an open space, drawing him out. "Panic attacks and alcohol are not friends," he adds. "Well. Maybe they are. But not friends of mine." He leaves me with this, goes to the bar for my drink, returns to find me turning the silver charm over in my palm again.

"So, what is it?" he asks. I place it on the tabletop in front of him.

"They said I was wearing it," I answer curtly. He nods, touches it with a fingertip, but doesn't pick it up. "A woman came up to me in the bathroom. She said she found it on the beach."

"That a good thing?"

"I guess," I answer. I can't hide my fear, my frustration. "Something about it gave me a weird feeling. I'm a mess." I try to hide my despair with a gentle laugh. "I'm nothing but crossed wires. Even if I ever find my brother, find a way to get home—I'll never be the same again."

"How much do you remember?"

"I remember being little." I take a sip of my drink. "I remember Miles, my brother. Other than that? Nothing that matters."

"Focus on what you do know," he says, as if it's a dare.

"Okay," I answer, as if stepping to the plate. "I know I don't cry. Haven't, this whole time. Not going to."

"Okay," he says, uncertain.

"I make friends easily," I say. "As in acquaintances. Not close friends. I don't know if I've ever had a real friend, someone I could talk to about anything." Nathaniel smiles back at me and I realize, suddenly, that I am talking to him, about anything. "And I know I don't run from things," I continue. "If something needs saying, or facing, I don't avoid it."

"Those aren't things that change," he answers. "You already know what matters."

The lights dim and there's music playing, a modern, pared-back cover of a fifties pop song, the kind that everybody knows. I look at his arms and want to touch them, to feel his hands on my waist. When he stands up to go pay the check, I follow, standing at the counter behind him as he pays the tab.

"Nathaniel, wait."

"What's up?" he asks. Habit shows on his features; he's asking me what's wrong, is everything okay. I smile back, an indolent feeling softening my limbs.

"Nothing," I murmur, smiling almost with disbelief. "It's just us." I slip my hand into his, duck into his arm so that he's holding me, turn half a step. I let my eyes focus on his, forget everything around us. There's not another ferry until morning. Whatever ghosts wait for me do so on the other side of the shore. For tonight, just one night, we're safe to be just us. He smiles back, and I think he understands, an arm wrapping around my waist as we dance close and slowly.

"You don't want to go back, do you?" *Back to the mainland, sure*, I think, *not tonight*. But that isn't what he means. I don't want to go back to whatever else there is for me, not right now. I guess he can see it. My silence, I think, answers for itself.

Before long, a rainstorm blows in without warning. Without discussion, we walk to the hotel and pay for a room. My hair didn't have a chance to dry before it's soaked again. He unlocks the door; it's a spacious room with a dresser, armchairs by the wide window, and a bed as wide as it is long. This is more than just a bad idea. I know it from how my heart races while I unbutton his wet shirt, tugging it off of his arms. I take a towel from the stack folded on the dresser and dry his shoulders. It's not just a bad idea, because it's also dangerous. Neither one of us can afford to get hurt; both of us are balancing too much already. As much as I promise myself this doesn't matter, something beneath my skin is telling me a different story. It matters a great deal.

For a moment afterward, I'm almost shy, resting on my side, my cheek on a pillow. I let my hair fall over my face, watching him silently. But when I see him smile at me, I realize I don't want to lose a moment of closeness. Drawing close to him, pulling the cover up to his shoulder, I fit myself close against his chest. He wraps both arms around me, squeezing me tight.

"I have to tell you something," I whisper, leaning close to trace his cheekbone, the line of his jaw, that I've studied from a distance so many times, punctuating my words now and again with a kiss.

"What is it?"

"I saw you," I answer, my hand tracing now to his collarbone, a soft line that begins at his shoulder and draws in toward his neck. "I saw you in Hazel Bluff, at the police station."

"When?"

"The day before I came to Dovemorn." I pause. "Why were you there?"

"That day? I was dropping off Lincoln's backpack. He left it in the truck."

As he speaks, I run my hand through his hair. "I heard you talking on the phone about trying to hire somebody."

"That why you came out there?"

"Yes," I answer. "I didn't know I meant to at first, but I wandered around a bit and then hitchhiked out that way. I left the hospital alone."

"Why?" he asks, turning his cheek so that my hair falls over his eyes.

"I was scared."

"Are you still?"

"Yes." There's no point lying about it. Besides, I think he'd know if I were. I let myself fall forward onto his chest, tuck my forehead under his chin. His hands slip down my shoulders, rest on the small of my back.

"Want to know something funny?"

"Yeah, I do."

"I've been at Dovemorn almost three years," he murmurs, his lips pressed to my forehead.

"I know."

"But I never gave a second thought to the rumors about it being haunted. Until I walked up to the gate that day, and saw you staring back at me from the other side. Barefoot in the fog." I melt into laughter, relaxing against his warmth. "It seemed for all the world like you were expecting me. I thought I'd better ask you in, hear you out, or you'd put some kind of curse on me, like in a fairy tale."

"That's the only theory anyone's come up with so far," I whisper, snuggling close, letting my eyes grow heavy, drawing in for a kiss. "Maybe I'm a ghost."

"If you're a ghost, then you never have to leave me," he says, stroking my hair. "You can haunt me forever."

I wake to a bright moon in the dark, shining through the window. The digital clock reads close to midnight. I stand up, the air conditioner making the room pleasantly chilly, and linger at the window before I close the curtains. The view of the water is lovely, but I'm more interested in studying the man that sleeps next to me. I climb back into bed and inch near him. When my cold knees brush his legs, he stirs.

"Sorry," I whisper. "Freezing in here."

He pulls me closer, murmuring something in his sleep.

"What was that?"

"Don't go," he says.

I lay my head in the crook of his shoulder and close my eyes. Earlier tonight, he asked me what I wanted. I wish I could wake him now and tell him exactly what's on my mind. I want so much more than a few brief hours, but if this is all I get, I'll treasure it all the more. I float into half-sleep, lingering there, as if afraid to fall into the depths of what I might dream. I feel danger. I dream that I look for Zenaida and she isn't there, the stained-glass mountains replaced with a poppy field. Again, the man with the scar across his eyebrow. This time, I study him, see his yellow-blond hair, the oddly slack, relaxed set of his mouth. I remember thinking that pain has color. Sometimes red. Sometimes murky, like a bruise; sometimes bright and flashing like lightning. I remember all these colors and shades at once. And that I cried for Miles, that I couldn't find him.

Finally, the spell breaks and I move. Under my clammy arms, the sheets are cool and fresh. In the light of dawn, everything around me appears in shades of gray. Nathaniel sleeps sprawled out on his stomach, squeezing the pillow beneath his head with both arms, chin resting on the swell of his shoulder. The man's so organized, so independent and spartan by day, that I smile to see that he sleeps in this beautiful disarray, limbs asymmetrical, a carelessly relaxed set to his face. He half-smiles in his sleep, and I remember his hand holding my cheek, looking into his eyes, finding the same, almost shy smile there. I purse my lips, study-ing the canvas of his back, a jagged diagonal line of a scar, just beneath the shoulder blades. The skin around it is peppered with pale marks of scar tissue, spreading out over his left side. He has told me, I realize, from the very first; it's only that I never put it together until now.

I rest a hand on his back as he yawns and stretches.

"Morning." He blinks, then opens his eyes without lifting his head. "How'd you sleep?" I lower my eyes. I don't want to tell him that I didn't sleep—that I don't, not really. I bend down to kiss his perfect shoulder blade, tracing his spine.

"Not much, huh?" He rolls over, leaning on one elbow. I lift my eyes to his. Somehow, I realize it, now that he's right here with me: I'm tired, so very tired, but not the kind of tired that sleep alone can fix.

"How'd you know?" I ask. He pulls me close, and I lay down with my head on his chest.

"I don't know," he answers. His arms tighten around me. Outside, I hear the bell of the ferry ring. It sounds far-off. I lay there still for a moment, until it makes me too sad, to feel this close, to feel what I can't keep. "You know I'd take all of this off your hands," he says, "if I knew a way to."

"If there were a way to, I wouldn't let you," I answer, placing a kiss on his shoulder.

"I know how tough you are," he says. "But it's heavy. I see that, too."

"Yeah, well, it doesn't make it any easier to point it out like that," I answer, almost gruffly, a warning in my tone, though I snuggle in next to him.

The sun rises orange and beautiful and warm. As much as I wish we could stay right here forever, I also know I need to go back. I need to find that ghost that teased me, I need to grab hold of it and hang on and find out what I need to know. Most of all, I need to find my brother.

"I feel like I've got a lot of work to do," I answer. "You know what I mean?"

"We'll get dressed and head out," he answers. "Should be back by ten."

"Do we have time to stop for breakfast before the ferry comes?"

"Definitely," he says with a grin. "Like I said, the diner has the best breakfast. You'll remember it for the rest of your life."

"Yes." I rise to my feet and kiss him, feeling both energized and grounded. "Yes, I think I will."

CHAPTER THIRTY-FOUR

We return from Samara with our secret between us, warm and fragile, and we protect it with silence. As we quietly eat breakfast, elbows touching at the counter, and as he drives us back, I know I ought to feel sad. I ought to be turning back to everything else I have to worry about. But somehow, going back to Dovemorn with him feels like going home.

"What are you working on today?" I ask.

"Probably catch up on what I was supposed to get done yesterday," he answers, smiling out the windshield.

"What's that?" I ask. After he parks the truck, he walks me back across the grounds, expending a few well-chosen swear words on the railing over the pond. "Got some plants to put in," he answers, "near the patio on the southern face of the house."

"Give me an hour or so to get dressed," I say, approaching the door of my apartment. "I'll meet you out there."

"Sure." We pause at the doorway and I jump up to kiss him.

"You know I can't ask you in," I whisper, my face near his neck, breathing him in. "It was her room, only hers. It wouldn't be right." When he smiles back at me, I can tell he agrees.

"I'll see you in an hour."

I walk back into my familiar rooms with a new reverence, revisiting the new things I learned about its original owner. A stillbirth. Laudanum. Wanting to get away so badly that she didn't even want her body found. As I walk toward the stairs, I trace the desk with an affectionate hand. I don't know if I can take on a hundred years' worth of sadness, or whatever it was that she called it, but I like that I can stand in her space with a fuller idea of what she went through. While I shower and dress, I'm humming, something almost without a melody. When I return to the table, my hair still drying, I line up my pens and sketchbook with a different respect, a fuller knowledge. I draw idly, as I always do, my mind wandering, biting down on my lip, a foolish smile that returns to me again and again. I sketch a beach at sunset, the way the changing light turns the water from diamond-sparkling into pearls, a creamy orange kissed with sky blue. The warm sand behind it. A droplet of water falls from my hair onto the page, casting a shadow that blends with the ink below. If I let my eyes fall out of focus, it turns into the shape of a woman in a dark dress, waiting for me on the shore. I find my hand tracing her words at the foot of the page: *Most people who drown at sea do so facing the shore.* I close the book and hurry outside into the light.

On the windowsill, I see two doves, pecking at the ground. They move aside, though they don't fly away when I walk up, seeing it's just me. Approaching the door, something catches my eye, and I pause.

A flower rests on the windowsill. Red. A poppy. They wilt quickly, so I know it's freshly picked. I glance around, but nobody's there. It's a strange gesture, I think; but then, Nathaniel hasn't got any reason to know that my dreams of poppies are something less than blissful. I put it behind my ear, smiling, and walk to meet him.

"Thanks for the flower," I call, waving my hand as I approach.

"Say what?"

"There was a flower outside my window." My hand jumps to my ear, brushing the bright, wilting blossom.

"It wasn't me," he says.

It's my turn to wonder, now. But I'm in no shape for critical thought, here. I could blame the wind, a bird, one of the contractors or repair crews. In moments, I've forgotten all about it. "So what's—um—"

"I'm putting in some flowers in the marble planters by the…" He waves his hand toward the other side of the gardens. "By the south entrance. Maybe, ah." I try not to smile. I've never seen him trip over a word.

"Maybe I could help."

"Yeah," he says, as if the idea just occurred to him. "That would be great."

So I help to move trays of flowers and wheelbarrows full of soil. I plant gardenia in the center of the large planters, then creeping jenny that spills over the edges of the planter, and continue to the next container. It takes both arms to carry the gardenia, its roots bundled in brown paper. The white blossoms smell like midnight, honey-sweet and tender. I pause to breathe in the scent of the flowers, and my hair tangles on a leaf. I shake my head to free it, and Nathaniel laughs.

"What?" I laugh.

He doesn't need to speak. We're back at his house by midday. His bedroom is sparse and comfortable, a four-poster bed with a gray quilt. There's not a photograph or a decoration in sight. I pull the blanket around my shoulders and sit up, glancing out the window.

"It's nice in here," I say, sitting up in bed, holding the sheet around my chest. I can reach the window from the bed, open the blinds just a touch. I can see the plum trees, the manor house off to the side, the pond and bridge all in miniature. And beyond, my own little window. I turn my attention back inside. "It's simple. You can breathe in here." Nathaniel stretches out next to me and I trace a hand down his chest. I'm studying him, lost in the depths of his eyes, when he reaches out and places a hand over the scar that runs down my chest. I feel a chill raise the hairs on my arms.

"Don't," I whisper. "It still—it doesn't hurt. It's just—" My hands flutter. I don't know how to explain it. I find a way to cram that cold menace of fear back into its cage.

"Sorry. That was thoughtless."

"It's okay."

He looks into my eyes and I know that he believes me. The shape of his pupils shifts, and something in his heartbeat seems to change pace.

"I want so much to tell you that nothing will ever hurt you again," he whispers, an edge in his voice that's bold, almost reckless. "I'd do anything to be able to promise you that."

"The scars are all I can see sometimes," I say. "I'm afraid they're all anybody will ever see."

"They do get better with time." He rolls onto his stomach, pointing a finger at the line on his ribcage. "I've got a piece of metal in here that's never going to come out. Car bomb." He twists to show me a patch of scarring on his side. "We were outside a school building," he continues. "There were little kids there," he says. "Families. It was morning."

"I'm sorry."

"I thought I was fine, at first, days after. Then, one day, I wasn't: everything set me off. And the times in between, I was waiting for the panic to hit me."

"How long ago?" I ask. He thinks for a moment before answering me.

"Eight years. I would say I've been functional for the last two. Listen," he says again. "They do get better, over time. I'm never gonna be the same person I was, but..." He trails off.

"How are you different now?"

"Older," he answers with a dry laugh. "I used to be fun, if you can believe that. Selena was the smart one, I was the fun one. Now, it's things like—being over-prepared. Control is a stress response." I picture the first aid cabinet. "A bit of an ass, maybe."

"Well, I like you." I settle into his arms with a teasing smile. "Not on a scale of ten compared to how you used to be. Not in spite of anything. I like you the way you are."

"Same to you, Sophie."

We spend most of the afternoon there, and, wrapped in his arms, I fall asleep with the gold afternoon sun peeking in through the blinds. In sleep, I can feel it, still, the scar between my breasts. Until he placed his hand there, I had, somehow, almost forgotten. Now in sleep, I remember with terrible clarity that I'm standing in the shadow of something unknown. I see poppies, and when I look closer, snakes slither between the stems, some slick like oil, some rattling as they go. I call for my brother, and, when I look up, the man with the scar on his eyebrow is there, instead. I sense that I left Miles to this nightmare, somehow. That he didn't make it out with me. I wake Nathaniel with kisses, with an embrace that's almost feverish, as if I hope I can burn away to nothing before I have to go back to whatever chased me away before.

CHAPTER THIRTY-FIVE

Several days later, on a Tuesday morning, Nathaniel's phone rings. I'm standing next to him when he answers it, and I can hear Selena's voice on the line as she asks if she can talk to me.

"Hi, Selena."

"That was quick," she observes. "I've found something I'd like you to see. In person would be best. When can you come in?"

I hold the phone away from my cheek and whisper to Nathaniel: "Is there a time you could drive me into town?" He nods, knowing how much this means to me.

"Today."

"This afternoon?" I ask Selena.

"Great. How about two PM?"

"Sure," I answer. "I'll see you then."

Fear and anticipation muddle my thoughts in equal measure, and I want to ask her what she's found, but I sense she wouldn't tell me over the phone anyway. I'm a fidgety mess until it's time to leave, planting a row of fragrant spearmint in the herb garden. Before we go, I tuck my sketchbook into my bag, something of a comfort object.

As Nathaniel drives into Hazel Bluff, I'm checking over my shoulder, half expecting to see a car following us. Does the woman from the ferry know where to find me? In the middle of the day the streets are busier than I usually see them, and we circle the block outside the police station several times before Nathaniel taps the clock.

"It's two now. Why don't you go inside? I'll find parking and come wait for you."

"You'll wait for me?" I'm not sure why, but I had hoped not to have to talk with Selena alone.

"Yeah. That okay?" he asks, slowing down on the street in front of the doors.

"Why don't you come up, when you've parked?" Whatever it is Selena has to tell me, I'd rather not hear it alone.

"Sure." One hand on the steering wheel, he reaches his other hand to cup my cheek. "Hope she's found something helpful."

"Yeah?"

"Of course I do," he answers, pulling me forward to kiss him. "I think you could turn out to be a criminal and I wouldn't care."

"You don't mean that." Though I see he's mostly joking, I feel my eyes widen, a wave of possibility wash over us. Another thing I've never considered until now, though, at least not seriously, is that there could be something left for the two of us when this strange in-between ends. I squeeze his hand, then open the door and jump to the ground. A chicory plant bursts from a crack in the sidewalk, its ragged button-sized flowers fanning out like a firework. It has no idea it's not supposed to grow here. I glance back at Nathaniel and feel a sense of foreboding. I walk inside and greet Amber at the reception desk. I know where Selena's office is, now. I wonder, as I'm climbing the stairs, whether I ought to call her Detective Radford, or use her first name. She appears to be waiting, the door standing open a few inches, and invites me in when she hears my footsteps.

"Come on in, Sophie. Sit down."

"Hi." I sit in the chair that waits by her desk.

"How was your weekend?"

"Okay," I answer. "Thanks. Yours?"

"It was fine. Thank you." Pleasantries out of the way, she turns to her desk. "Any news?"

"Not really."

"Lincoln says you're an artist," she murmurs, by way of small talk, her eyes on her computer screen. "What do you draw?"

I take my sketchbook out and show her my drawings. I tell her about swimming lessons, about Miles, about the fragments of memories I've recovered. Selena doesn't seem interested in my feelings or my pictures. I'm not sure whether I want to annoy her or break through her coldness, but neither works. She does, though, take note of the few recovered memories I tell her about.

"Have you written that down?"

"No, but—"

"Write it down," she says. "Everything you can remember."

"Why won't you tell me what makes this so significant?"

"Everything's significant," she answers. "Especially anything that might tell us what happened to you."

"Fine," I mutter. "I'll start writing things down. Next time I have a free moment. Promise."

"I may have found something," she says.

"What did you find?" I ask. Selena turns her monitor to face me and clicks the mouse until it lights up. She pulls up photos of a house, one that I recognize. The façade is painted blue. The next shot is one of the house blackened by fire, wrapped in caution tape. I clear my throat and fidget in my chair.

"Sophie, this house was in Queens. The fire happened in 1986. You would have been close to six years old then." As Selena speaks, I find a scuff on the ground, trace the toe of my shoe over it and back again. "There were allegations it was a child trafficking site, but nothing," she adds, "was ever substantiated.

"No foster children on record, though," she says. "If anyone ever sent a foster child there, it would have had to be—an emergency placement, or something that wasn't done with proper paperwork."

The house looked so welcoming, I remember, from outside. But once I walked in, I recall, I knew right away that something was wrong.

"Sophie?" she repeats. I cough, blinking. It seems, suddenly, that the smell of smoke is everywhere, and, though I remember that I don't cry, ever, I want to throw open the closet and look for that little girl with her purple hair bow, pull her out to safety. Selena can't know. Nobody can know. That little girl died, and it was my fault.

"Sorry," I say. "It doesn't look familiar."

"I see," she answers, clearly unconvinced. I want to plead with her: anything but this. Find anything but this. I have nothing to hide from, except that purple hair bow. "So, moving on. There is some information I wanted to share, that I thought might help you jog your memory."

"Oh? But you haven't until now?" I ask. She purses her lips and exhales a sigh through her nose.

"It's not as straightforward as you might assume," she answers. "Sophie, how much do you know about how you were found?"

"I know what you've told me," I answer her. "And what they told me in the hospital."

"You deserve to have all the information you need to find your way back to—wherever you're from." She says this with something less than kind in her tone. Selena, clearly, would like for this to happen sooner rather than later. I remind myself that that's how I'm supposed to feel, too. I hear footsteps, a tap at the door. Without waiting, Nathaniel opens it and looks in at me.

"Hey," he says, his voice low, familiar. He walks over to me and rests a hand on my shoulder. Without meaning to, my hand rises to meet his, our fingers twining and releasing in a silent hello. "Everything okay?"

"Yes," I answer. "I, ah—" I trail off, catching Selena's eye. Recognition flashes across her features. Nathaniel hasn't greeted her yet. She looks from him, to me, and then back to him.

"No need to knock," she says crisply, fixing him with an expressionless stare.

"Nice to see you," he answers, his voice smooth. Yet, I think he notices what she's seeing, attempts a retreat. "Sorry. I'll wait downstairs."

"No," Selena says, without deliberating. "No need, in fact. Why don't you sit down, too?" She indicates an additional chair in the corner and he pulls it near to mine, which she also notices. "Sophie, the problem is that this isn't just relevant to you. You've made it relevant to Nathaniel, and to my son, and therefore to me." She isn't wrong.

"Made what relevant?"

"Whatever brought you here," she answers. "As I was saying: how much do you know about how you were found?"

"Not that much, I guess. By the road, in the mountains. One of the nurses said—" I glance at Nathaniel, then away. "She said I had defensive wounds. And that my wrists had been tied." I realize there's a lot of room for what I don't know. That I haven't been asking enough questions, or the right ones. That I've been hiding, as much as I've told myself I haven't.

Selena opens a folder and angles it toward me. I lean over and look closely at a handful of photos in plastic sleeving. It's evident that, whatever it is, Selena's already seen them, and Nathaniel may as well. I see a figure, pale against the forest, sprawled on the ground, one arm fanned out, dried blood obscuring the face.

"But this is—"

I exhale and turn to the next one. There's a series of evidence photos documenting, I assume, the woman's injuries. My body realizes it before I do, a cold, rushing sensation in my veins. These are photos of me. She must have taken them from an evidence file.

I see the blue dress that has haunted my dreams. It's stained with blood, both dried and fresh. The woman in these pictures is displayed on an exam bed like a mannequin, her features blank, as if nobody lives there. I feel a rush of cold, ice cold that starts at my fingertips, fills my body, quickly turning into numbness. Her limbs are splayed as if she's dead. I wince with embarrassment, to wonder how many people have seen these. I flip back to the one of the forest. There are red flowers in her hair. I know what they are, but I don't want to even think the word.

Nathaniel scoots his chair closer to me, looking over my shoulder, then moves in a flash to turn them over. He takes the pictures from my hand and throws them face down on the table.

"Damnit, Selena." His voice is low and sharp, eyes dangerous. "Sophie, let's go." He reaches out for my hand, but I'm paralyzed.

I take the pictures back, holding them now, looking closer. I feel ill. There is something here that I haven't seen, that I didn't expect. I take stock of the injuries at the wrists, the slashes and the rope marks. The deep, ugly scrapes on the arm and shoulder. The matted hair and dirty face. The blue dress is torn past the breastbone, where red spreads from a jagged cut. Across the chest, on each arm, words are written in dark ink. My arms flutter over my midsection, then across the photo. I want to cover her, to put these images out of sight. But I can't not look.

My eyes flicker up to Selena.

"This—this is me?"

I'm still hoping she'll say no, that I'm mistaken, that something else is going on. But, of course, I know the answer before she speaks it.

"Yes."

CHAPTER THIRTY-SIX

"The hell were you thinking?"

I hear Nathaniel and Selena's tense exchange as if from far away. "I thought it might help—"

"No, you didn't," he says. "That is not the way to bring this up. Not without a warning. Not without a discussion first. What's really going on?"

"I could ask you the same thing."

I slump back in the chair, staring at the picture. Across the woman's chest, someone's written words, in oddly tidy handwriting. *Narc, snitch* on either arm. Under the collarbones, *traitor.* I feel as if my chest is closing in.

"Whatever happened, she was involved enough with someone dangerous that they found it worthwhile to punish her. She was close enough to do damage. Groups like this—"

"Stop it." He cuts her off with a wave of his hand.

"I thought it would help, to have all the facts on the table," Selena says.

Flowers. Tucked into my hair and behind my ears. Who would do this? Who would decorate someone when they're in danger, when they're in need of help? And what did I do to end up like this?

"You always say you want the facts out in the open." Nathaniel touches my shoulder, tries to pull the photographs away, but I snatch them back. "But then what you do is, you use them to hurt people."

He pushes his chair back and stands up, puts both hands on my shoulders. "Sophie, let's go."

Selena continues. "We knew she was a victim—of something. But this changes things. She's clearly involved with something dangerous. How do you know she isn't hiding something?"

"Because I know," he says. "This is not an act. This isn't some attempt at subterfuge, okay? Not everything is an effort to take control away from you."

Selena gasps, but her face remains smooth.

I manage an impression of calm and sit with my chin in my hands, looking at the pictures. I don't know if it's obvious that I feel a ticking bomb in my chest, that if I don't move soon, I'm afraid I'll implode.

"I was trying to help you," Selena's saying. "We're still family."

"You must have some weird ideas about family."

I'm numb all over. It's clear this argument was a long time in the making. I don't want to interrupt, and besides, I'm not sure I could even speak coherently.

"You can't just ignore problems until they go away," she insists. That's a point to Selena: he's like me, he dislikes even the idea of being too much of a coward to face something. This is meant to hurt, and it does.

"Facing things before you're ready does more harm than good," he snaps. "After what we went through together, I'm pretty sure you know that. This isn't about stability. It's about you being in charge."

That's a point to Nathaniel. Being the sensible mother and co-parent is her brand, and he's exposed a flaw in it.

"Watch it," she breathes, shock audible in her tone. She clearly isn't used to him pushing back. "Or it's over."

Nathaniel shakes his head. He's calm, but I see an inkling of sadness in his eyes. "It's been over, Selena," he says, his voice low but certain. "You've known that much longer than I have." I close my eyes and draw a breath that feels hot in my lungs, force myself to look at the photographs a few moments more.

She's a betrayer. She's a snitch. A liar.

My arms burn. Everything hurts. Then, a different set of words flashes across my mind: *a century's worth of sorrow.* I can't hold all of this. All these histories collapsing around me.

"I'm so sorry." My voice feels unsteady. I clear my throat. "I'm going to let you two talk." I put the photographs back in the folder in a neat stack, then collect my bag and sketchbook. I want to tell the woman in the pictures that I'm sorry. That I'm still too weak to reckon with whatever happened to her. I slide my chair back in order to stand up, then to the side in order to get to the doorway.

"Sophie, please don't go," Selena says. I lean forward a bit and push the folder toward her. "You're—"

"Erratic behavior concerns you," I snap. "I know. You've told me. There's nothing else to talk about right now." I turn out of the doorway and move, and there's something soothing in taking steps, so I keep going, hugging my arms against the cold that seems to seep out from my bones. I take a wrong turn, go down a back stairway, catching my weight along the banister when I finally get to the bottom floor. I lean hard against the handrail. My lungs, my chest, are doing something strange and I feel far away from my body. I hear Nathaniel's footsteps on the stairs, but the sound is distant.

"There you are." He puts his hand over mine, warm fingers against my cold ones on the railing. "Sophie, I'm sorry. I'm so sorry that happened." His hand rests on my back, as if he wants me to know that he, too, sees these breaths that want to gallop in and out of my throat, as much as I fight to hold steady. Standing in place is only making it worse. There's a door a few feet off, leading into the alley behind the building.

"I need some air," I say. "I'm gonna take a walk, okay?"

"Okay," he answers. "Let's go together."

"I'm going by myself." My voice sounds like a stranger's. "Just a few minutes. Just around the block. I need to be alone."

"I think you know that's not a good idea," he says.

The steadiness of his voice beckons me to stay here, where I am, within myself. The problem is, that's the place I'm afraid of the most. I walk outside, cut through the alley and back to the sidewalk, pulling a flower off the chicory plant as I pass it. It makes me angry, its very lack of awareness, knowing nothing but to grow, to blossom.

CHAPTER THIRTY-SEVEN

As I move through the door, I know I ought to head back around the block. But I turn the other way, walking half in a daze. I find pieces fitting together. There's connective tissue between images that wasn't there before. I look at the streets around me and realize that, although this is a small town, something about being in cities feels like home. I remember New York. My brother. I remember my favorite blue raincoat and boots, walking to the subway in the rain to go to work.

I wait at a stoplight, my mind ticking. I don't like standing still, and so turn again rather than wait for the light to change. Soon, I'm in a different part of town, a rather run-down residential neighborhood. I pass a bus stop, where a man sits reading a magazine, proceed to the next corner, and then cross the street, turning back the other way. Walk straight back, except when the road dead-ends, and I cut one block over, hoping to follow the same direction I had intended to.

Though the streets are oddly deserted, there's one other pedestrian. I take a look and my pulse starts. I'm almost certain it's the man from the bus stop. He's my age, or even a bit younger, in a shabby flannel shirt and jeans. He slows a bit, but doesn't stop. I keep walking, and now I make several turns, barely paying attention to where I'm going, trying to assure myself that I'm not being followed. But he's still there.

I stumble and look down to see that my shoe's untied. My feet are sore. I'm used to working outside, but not to walking this much in a day. With a momentary break, the man has already caught up.

"Who are you?" I call. With a combination of calm and dread, I look at him. There's no point, right now, in trying to run. I know him, the beady, glittering eyes, close-cropped, the scar through his eyebrow, the unmoving set of his mouth. That tattoo I see, peeking out from his collar, the same as the one on the woman's arm, the same as the pendant in my pocket. The very sight of him calls up memories, a pulse of fear numbing all my thoughts. But I can't remember his name.

"You're—" I trail off, nervous hands brushing loose strands of hair away from my eyes.

"Really—you don't remember my name?" When he laughs, his smile is devoid of any warmth. "You're hurting my feelings here, Dora."

Dora. The sound of the name brings a thrill of longed-for recognition, closely followed by dread, my now all too familiar impulse to start running, from anything and everything. From this name, that, until now, I thought I wanted to remember.

"I'm not going with you," I answer. "Not until I see Miles. I have to know he's okay."

"I know where he is."

"Then tell me," I growl, stepping up closer to him.

He laughs and steps back. "You'll have to trust me. Come and see him. If he'll have anything to do with you."

Confusion and fear blot out my anger. *What happened?* I want to ask him, but I don't trust him enough to say this.

"We've been watching," he says, but I realize I already knew this. "To make sure you're safe. Saw you got the flower I left you."

"The—" My hand rises to my ear as if to brush away the poppy I'd found a few days ago. "And it was you, sneaking around the apartment that night?"

"Wouldn't you like to know?" He moves closer to me and I step backward. "No," he says, "that wasn't me, honest. It was Iris."

"Who the hell's that?" I snap, but I'm picturing a willowy, dark-haired woman with amber eyes, and I fear I already know. "And what was she even looking for?"

The man laughs, and his arm darts forward, his hand closing on my arm. "For you, Dora."

"Let me go."

But I feel his grip on me tighten as he leans over me. "Are you really telling me you forgot about me?"

"Let *go*."

"I'm Sawyer."

At the sound of the name, I throw one shoulder forward, a fruitless attempt to shove him away from me. I see a car idling at the end of the block and look at his face with a depth of anger I didn't know I held. He isn't letting go of my wrist. Half a block in the opposite direction, I see a bus passing. It rests at a stop sign, then wheezes forward. I stomp my heel on Sawyer's toes as hard as I can, and though something tells me he's immune to pain, his surprise gives me an opportunity to wrest my arm free, then bolt after the bus.

I just make it to the bus and hurriedly pay the fare and take a seat. I'll get to Miles somehow. I have to. But is he safe? I feel closer to him than I have this entire time. What did I do to let him down? I stay on the bus until it winds around to a different part of the town, until I'm sure there's no car following. At one stop, I see a park, benches, plenty of sun. I walk off, find an empty bench, and sit down.

I need something to do with my hands. I open my sketchbook, thumbing coolly through the pages. I dwell on the first few drawings. The woman in the poppies. This is wrong: none of them were right. I had half the story. My hands shake. I uncap a black pen and scribble over her arms, holding the pen to the paper and

letting the ink bleed where her eyes should be. I know her name.
He knew it, too, the man whose image has haunted me. When the
ink runs out, I open the red pen and add markings on her body.
As I write across her chest, I blink and see him. I see my brother.
I remember his face, not as a child but as an adult, as he is now.
He's there in the picture, too, just beyond the edge of the page.
Miles. He was there. I can only imagine what they've done to him,
these horrible people who hurt me. Everywhere, there's a lingering
sense of fear, of dread. I imagine an engine overheating, systems
locking where they ought to function. And, again, the startling
memory of pain and fear. My chest aches with it, tight as a drum.
I want to get up and run, but I can't. It must be dinnertime, now;
the park is nearly empty. I wonder if I'm being watched. If I am,
it doesn't matter. I'm out of energy. I'm out of fight.

Unable to do anything else, I sit and begin to write. Selena
told me to write things down. That anything could be significant,
and I try to follow her instruction. I write it down as if I'm telling
myself this story for the first time. I remember my life from before
as a series of unanswered questions: a co-worker wondering, *why
is your brother calling for an advance on your paycheck again?* An
ex-boyfriend leaving me with the words, *I don't see any point in
continuing this relationship if you can't share your past with me.* I
credit the swim team for keeping me sane through high school. It
was the only place I was always good at something. I couldn't let
up through college or graduate school, working to cover what my
scholarships didn't. Among the other art students, I was a bit of a
bore, determined to be the most organized, the best at every class,
surrounded by kids from comfortable families who paid hundreds
of dollars for clothes that looked chic and ill-fitting. I took a job
at the design firm where I had worked as an intern, and stayed
there after I graduated, glad for a chance to build something like
a home, a life that felt steady. I saved everything I could, always
ready for bad luck to strike. On the surface, it probably looked

steady. Until one day in March, when Miles called, unbeknownst to me, to ask the payroll department to wire him an advance on my next check. When they declined, there was an argument. He was in trouble with the law, they told me that, as if it should be a surprise. But Miles never keeps a secret from me. He was wanted because he was overdue on court costs, which were compounded by late fees. It's an unfair system.

I don't know why I let it get to me. The tone my boss took when he asked me about Miles was so cold, so cruel. Like he was a piece of trash that somebody tracked inside. Nobody's ever given him a fair shot. That evening, I asked Miles to let me come and visit him. He told me he was living on a farm in the mountains, somewhere in South Carolina. That he was going to church, living clean and didn't want to screw it up. I was certain that if I could talk to him in his comfort zone, I could convince him to move back, maybe to stay with me, or to get his own place. I could help him get things evened out. A lawyer, money, whatever he might need. He was so talented and warm and magnetic. He agreed to pick me up. I bought a plane ticket, paid a few months' advance rent on my apartment, and left. I had no close friends, no pets. It was that simple. Nobody to miss me.

The felt-tipped pen in my hand begins to scuff along the page, the ink getting low. I put it away and glance over the account I've written. How Dora, a graphic designer from Brooklyn, came to leave her job, her apartment. How she moved to live with her brother in the mountains. How, for the first time in her life, living with him and his friends, she didn't feel alone. But there's still a piece missing. I'm missing the part where Dora became a nameless woman at the side of the road. Where Dora became Sophie. I replay what I've remembered, searching for new detail, and finding none. When I run out of memories to write down, the name Dora repeats in my mind with the impression of an alarm sounding, and I write it over and over until I've filled an entire page.

CHAPTER THIRTY-EIGHT

I blink, and the park comes back into focus. The thudding sensation of my heart pulls me back into my body. I don't know how long I've been sitting here, but my legs are numb, the sky turning colors. Dora echoes in my ears. I sit here and wonder: what does time consist of, the way it can pass and mean nothing at all? I remember the flowers. I remember my brother's smile. I know that I must have done something terrible for this to happen to me. I think of the little girl lost in the fire, of how my brother saved me, how I've let him go again. My name, again. I hear it. I'm afraid if I get up I'll be sick or pass out. It seems possible I might keel over sitting right here. I'm twice removed, then, from trying to get somewhere. I bring my focus back to the sketchbook, which is the only thing keeping me calm.

Who is Dora? After the brief page of journaling, this one stands in contrast. The words are printed over and over, a row that repeats itself dozens of times down the length of the page. In a brief moment of objectivity, I recognize that this work, these scribbles, are not the handiwork of someone in their right mind.

The warmth of the afternoon is mellowing into a breezy, gentle evening. I can hear every noise. The rustle of each blade of grass. The sound of every bird. Somewhere a car door opens and smacks closed. I'm not sure what's in my memory and what's here around me. There are footsteps. I close my eyes and brace for whatever comes next. He's followed me, or someone who was with him.

If I can get moving, I'm sure this insane energy thudding in my chest will carry me away, but—

Nathaniel sits down next to me. Without a question or a word, he wraps me in a hug.

"How'd you know I was here?"

"I didn't," he answers. "I've looked everywhere I could think of. It's been hours, Sophie."

"Something's wrong," I say. My voice sounds distorted and squeaky, like I'm hearing the echo rather than my own words. I risk a glance up at him and gesture vaguely at my chest. "I can't breathe. I can't—get a grip on where I am."

"I'm here with you." He meets my panic with steadiness, an almost casual pace in his words, though he squeezes me tight. "You're going to be okay."

"You say that like you know it," I mutter, hoping he's right.

"I do know it," he says. "Your eyes, your breathing. I know that when I see it. If you've been there, you recognize it."

"I'm scared."

"Scared is good," he says.

"It's not," I say. "It's bad."

"It's real," he counters. "It's an appropriate response, in certain scenarios. It takes care of you. Sometimes, if you're afraid, you listen to it, you get out alive. Like you did before, right?"

I force a slow, shaking breath. "Your body, your mind, they're trying to keep you safe. It's crossed wires. Feels like absolute hell." He touches my hand. "Sophie, I know it does."

"What do I do?"

He doesn't look at me, but shifts his arm closer, the two of us huddled together. "Wait it out," he says, his voice calm and steady. "Talk to someone. Remind yourself of things you know. Get some kind of footing in the things around you."

"You're right in front of me." I squeeze his hand tighter. "Tell me about yourself."

As I wait for him to speak, I pick out things in front of me and name them: tall, bright-colored gladioli, a row of geese on the pond, trying to remind myself of the here and now. But I'm also looking around to see if anyone's following me.

"I was born in—" I cut him off, shaking my head.

"What do you feel like when you wake up in the morning?"

"Usually? As little as possible," he says with a regretful shrug. "Routine helped me when I was getting better. The last few years, I perfected it. Waking up at the same time. Having the same schedule every day. Wherever you don't have routine, when you're making it up as you go, that's usually when things happen to you, instead of the other way around—I've been working to avoid that, right? I've tried to minimize any occasion to have any extra feelings, whatsoever."

"Okay."

"And I thought I was fine, as I was," he continues. "Everything was predictable. Things were functional. But I feel like I'm seeing, now, maybe that was all they were. Functional."

"How?"

"You're—fearless." He draws an uncomfortable breath and focuses on me, leans into my hair, his lips close to my ear. "You said it yourself: you face things that need facing."

"I'm not," I answer. "Look at me. I'm a wreck."

"Next to me, you are. You're out here, taking things on, when the world already tried to take you out once. Seeing you, being around you, it felt like waking up. I thought I was fine as I was, but I see now that I wasn't."

I turn my face to his, our noses almost brushing. He looks at me helplessly and I raise a hand to his cheek, letting my lips meet his.

"I didn't mean to tell you all that," he mutters.

"I'm glad you did."

We each draw a quiet breath, our cheeks almost touching, the air full of everything we'd both like to say, if only we could. "I wish you could see yourself the way I do," I say. I see skepticism settle over his eyes, like a chilly breeze. "I've got no reason to lie," I add. "You know I don't have the option of sticking around. As much as I might wish I did."

"What if that weren't true?"

"Nathaniel. Look at me. You saw the photos. I can't be around you." My voice thins to a whisper, and I hold out my hands, empty, as if to show him I have nothing to fix this. "Your son. Your home. I don't want to bring anything dangerous near you. I'm so afraid I have already."

"If you have already, then that's done," he answers. "Sophie, if you got mixed up with something dangerous, I feel certain it wasn't coming from you. You don't give up on yourself—I bet you don't give up on other people easily, either. That can also be dangerous." He says this as if he knows it's true, and I remember that he does.

"I should leave." I'm shaking my head, the sound of my words muffled with dread, talking into my cupped hands.

"Where would you go?"

"I don't know," I bleat. "If I can't find my brother? Maybe it doesn't matter where I go. Just—" My eyes dart upward, and I imagine my eyes reflected in the sky, scattered into pieces. Just disappear. Nathaniel takes my hand and squeezes hard.

"I'm in this with you now, okay?"

How can I say yes, when I don't know what I'm exposing him to? When I don't know what might change? And how can I promise to stay, when I still don't know what I might be leaving behind? I can't, but I settle into his arms, tuck my forehead under his chin, close my eyes and feel his chest rise and fall with each breath until mine are steady, too.

"Can we go home?" I whisper.

"You got it."

CHAPTER THIRTY-NINE

The drive back to Dovemorn is soothing, the hum of the engine and blinking lights of fireflies easing me into life again. When we're back, I'm so pleased to feel the familiar ground under my feet that I ask him to walk with me. I want to tell him I'll miss it here. I want to tell him I don't want to leave. Without really intending to, I'm walking back toward the dovecote, my feet on their familiar path. He walks quietly next to me, and it must be a dozen times I begin to speak, half a word or even just a breath, before I finally land on what I want to say, as we're passing by the willow grove. I decide to start at the beginning.

"I never knew what happened to my mother. Only that she was gone. I was five then. Miles was eleven." As I speak, I can feel him listening to me. "I was in a foster home. I ran away all the time. I was little, and I wanted to see my brother, or my mom, and thought I could just walk into the city and find them."

"Did you?"

"No," I answer, my eyes falling on the walkway with its climbing roses. "Because I kept running off, they thought maybe a different home would be better. That one—" I have to skim over this. There are secrets I'll keep close to my heart forever if I have the choice to. "Didn't work out either."

"How come?" he asks. *Because when I called my brother to come and get me, he set the house on fire, even though that girl was still locked up inside. Because whatever unspeakable things happened to*

her almost happened to me, too. For the first time in my life, I wish
I could ask Miles why he had to start a fire. Why he couldn't just
find me in the boxwoods and sneak me away. I shake my head
without looking at Nathaniel.

"It wasn't a good fit. I wasn't happy unless I was near Miles,
and he was always hard to find."

"How so?"

"It took longer to place him in a home. He was older, sadder.
I remember that he got into trouble with the police when he was
twelve. It was my fault: he was looking out for me, and—" That's
all I can say.

"What happened?" he asks. I shake my head again.

"Doesn't matter. When he was in juvenile detention, I almost
never got to see him. But it was like he could always find me when
I needed him. I can tell you that he saved my life. And when I
was twelve, he gave me a brand-new coat for my birthday. He
never had anything to spare, but he'd always show up with a gift."

"I can tell how much he means to you."

"Miles always struggled. If you could meet him—he's kind,
and he sees people, really looks at you and understands you. I
know you'd like him. I think most people don't understand him.
Anyway, once you've got any kind of criminal record, it doesn't
matter whether you're guilty or not. I'd send him money sometimes.
There were times I suspected he had an addiction. I know he was
homeless once. I paid a month's rent and deposit on a place for
him—it was vacant three weeks later." I look up and we're standing
at the door of the apartment.

"Would you like to come in?" I unlock the door and let
Nathaniel walk in ahead of me, turning lights on as I go. Everything
is just as I left it. "Look," I remember, directing him to the desk.
"The carving. It's right here."

I drop to my knees on the floor, take his hand in mine, trace his
fingers over the letters. He kneels next to me and studies it, then,

turning his eyes to me as if I might be an apparition, slowly leans forward to kiss me. My limbs are heavy, every inch of my body and mind exhausted from a day running, wired with adrenaline. He sits in the chair and I drop into his lap, lean onto his shoulder. "What are we doing tomorrow?"

"There are repair people coming tomorrow to work inside the house," he says, trailing a gentle hand through my hair. "Honestly, I put it off as long as I could. Don't want to see it all fixed up, I guess. But summer's over halfway done."

"Right," I agree, turning to look at him. "The time's gone quickly. Nathaniel, will you stay until I'm asleep?"

"I'll stay as long as you want me to." He reaches one arm over to pull the curtains across, then dims the light. "I was so sure that, the moment you began to remember things, you'd be gone." Settling closer into his arms, I choose not to answer him. I felt the same way. Part of me still does. "You said you lived in Brooklyn," he says. "How'd you get here?"

"Well, Miles started to get better. He moved to the mountains and built a farm," I answer. "I think he even goes to church now. I didn't hear from him for almost a year, then, suddenly, he called me. He sounded happy. And then, he asked me to come and stay with him. He said leaving the city was good for him, that I should too."

"And did you?"

"I bought a plane ticket. Charleston."

"Just like that, really?" His fingers tousle my hair and I lean back against his shoulder.

"Yes," I answer, as if it should be obvious. "I remember I—" I remember wiring a lot of money. Emptying a bank account. Fragments scatter across my mind. "He lives on a homestead, up in the mountains. Beautiful—everything homemade, off the grid. I can see pieces of it. Hours from anything. I can't remember where, not for the life of me."

"Homestead?"

"They have a farm," I answer. "I remember it seemed isolated. Almost like they're self-reliant. They were so nice," I answer, as though remembering a good dream. "They treated me like family. People he's met here and there, I think, some from prison, some through friends."

"What do they do for money?"

"Why are you asking so many questions?" I sit up, so that I'm not leaning against him. "I thought you'd be glad I could remember anything." Sensing his concern, I press harder.

"Sophie, something sounds off about it. There are gaps, have to be. Things you can't remember, maybe."

"What do you mean?" I sit up straight, leaning away from him. "I was happy there. I know that for sure." I stand up and pace across the room, turn an angry stare at the carvings above the fireplace. "It's late." I turn my back to the fireplace and cross my arms.

"I'm sorry I brought it up."

"It's not your fault that things are what they are," I say, though I feel nothing now, only numb. "You don't have anything to apologize for. But—" I look up at him and shake my head. "It's late, that's all. I need to think." He nods, rises from the armchair and walks to the door. I sense the distance I'm laying down here before I see it in his eyes. How he wants to tell me that I don't have to be alone, but he doesn't want to reach too hard. For a moment I imagine what it would be like for things to be different. I cross to the doorstep and hug him tight.

"'Night, Sophie."

I shake my head mutely, lips pressed together. I'm so afraid that we'll have to stand by and watch this vanish. I don't know how to fight for it.

"Dora," I whisper. I pull in a breath through my nose, feeling the weight of finality around me. But he squeezes me back, presses a kiss to my temple.

"Do you think that's going to scare me off? Is that what's getting you down?"

"Maybe."

"You have enough to worry about, okay?" Nathaniel murmurs. "I can take one thing off that list. You don't have to worry about this. About us." He holds me back a few inches, looking into my eyes. "Things are gonna change. I'm not saying it'll be simple. I'm saying, I know you. It doesn't matter what your name is, or where you're from." I hold him so tight I hope he can't feel the sobs that catch in my chest.

"I need to sleep. I need to think."

"Sweet dreams, Dora," he whispers. "Get some rest."

"Thanks," I manage, pulling back from him. "You, too."

I don't tell Nathaniel about the loneliness that haunted Dora, that still follows me. I remember, now, that I always take the safe choice. That I don't let anybody in, ever. Miles warned me not to. I've remembered this too late.

After he leaves, I move back to the window and look out across the yard. It's a cloudy night; almost nothing is visible. I look through the dark to see the light on in Nathaniel's window, a figure there silhouetted against the yellow glow. He looks out for a moment then steps away, and the light goes off. I remember the first time we kissed, how he ran after me in the dark. How he held my shoulder and pointed with the other hand: if you look across right there, you can see my window. If you don't feel safe, turn on the light. I'll see it.

Maybe I was never safe here. I leave the light off, walk upstairs to go to bed.

Zenaida stands over me in a dream. *You're where you need to be,* she says, her lips unmoving, though she speaks. "Please, don't confuse me: no more riddles," I insist, feeling weak. I stir, imagine I hear noises in the dark. *Stay,* she whispers, and I dream that her hand weighs down my shoulder. She's never reached out to touch me before. I sigh and turn over in bed.

In the morning, I can feel right away that there's something off. Everything is in place, and I walk through the apartment wondering what it is. I've overslept, almost until eight, and the sun is bright in the sky, giving me an oppressive sense that I've slept through something important. Just outside the door, I trip over a dead dove. It looks as though it was sleeping. I wonder if it flew against the wall or tangled with an owl or a hawk. I nestle it into the grass outside the doorway, out of the way of footsteps. I'll find a place to bury it later. *How do you catch them?* I think. *You don't catch doves. You just give them a safe place to stay, and, sometimes, they do.*

The recollection of the previous day washes over me. The photographs, the bloodied woman in the forest. That was Dora. That was me. I look down at my hands, smoothing the dove's wing into place. A chill runs down the back of my neck. I brush its creamy-gray forehead and the head tilts back, its neck neatly snapped. It hasn't got a feather out of place.

CHAPTER FORTY

This morning, for the first time, I don't ask for any tasks, and Nathaniel doesn't ask me for any help. When a crew of contractors and repair workers arrives to work inside the house, I watch from the bench in the circular garden as Nathaniel walks over to greet them. They've brought tools, charts, and papers. I try to picture this place as a tourist attraction, imagining the house polished and magnificent. After a few minutes, he catches my eye and waves, then walks over.

"Morning." He sits next to me on the bench. "This is one of my favorite places to think."

"Then you've got good taste," I answer, watching the morning light on the stained glass. The gates are open, and the estate seems more awake than usual. I don't think anything of it when I see another truck pull in at the gates. "You expecting anyone else?"

"Yeah," he shrugs. "Not till later, though. They're probably with the crew working on the house now."

"I guess it's a big job," I answer. Neither of us loves to see this work done, but without it, we'd never have met. And, though it seems like sacrilege to expose the house's secrets, this wasn't Zenaida's home, not really. She's out here, in the flowers, in the curve of the mountainside. The willow pool, where she dropped a ring. The study, where she left her final note. The glove, nestled among the roses. The body, never found, almost as if it concerned her as little as the house itself did. I turn an admiring look around the familiar shadows and gardens; these lovely, jewel-green shadows and the mottled light. The truck that I pointed out still waits near the gate.

"Why don't we go see what they're here for," I suggest. Nathaniel agrees and offers me his hand as I get to my feet. A woman sits behind the driver's seat in the truck, an old beige pickup with a cracked rear window.

"Morning," he calls, lifting a hand in greeting. She must not hear him; she doesn't answer at first, though I think she smiles. The truck is sitting in the shade of the row of cedars, making it difficult to see through the windshield. I stand back a few steps, keeping the sun on my face. When the driver doesn't return Nathaniel's greeting, he adds: "Are you here for the repairs?"

"No, we're not," a man's voice says. A voice I know by heart. I move forward so I can see the man seated next to her on the passenger side. The pale blue eyes that make the morning sky look murky by contrast. "We're looking for the lady of the house, actually." He opens the door, long legs stretching to the ground, and turns to face me with that always half-joking smile. "Is this her?"

"Miles." I breathe his name, then, with all the force of a magnet pulled toward the sun, rush past Nathaniel and into his arms.

CHAPTER FORTY-ONE

"Miles," I say, stammering, my words falling over each other in my rush. "Where have you been? I was so worried about you, Miles," I whisper, close to tears. "Something happened, didn't it? I got hurt. I didn't even know how to look for you." The dark-haired woman climbs down from the driver's seat and stands between us.

"Oh, you didn't?" She laces an arm through Miles' elbow. Miles doesn't speak, just smiles at me with those placid eyes. "Convenient, Dora. I'm teasing," she adds. Her voice is a breathy alto, warm but with an edge, and she tilts her head as she introduces herself. "I'm Iris. Don't you remember me?"

"No," I answer. "No, I don't."

"It's almost like this is the last place anyone would think to look for you," Iris observes. She's the woman from the ferry. The one who watched me from the beach. If she's here with him, that must mean Miles is still in danger. I fight back an impulse to jump in between her and my brother.

"Miles," I repeat, leaning around her. "Somebody's been following me. I—I think. I've been so frightened. I thought I'd never see you again." As overexcited as I am, I can tell I'm borderline incoherent, that I'm almost babbling. The woman turns to me, now, and, before I can react, she wraps me in a cool hug. She smells sweet and smoky, like incense.

"Dora," she whispers. "Give him time. You really hurt him."

"I—" I draw back, horrified. "What happened?" She looks at me knowingly, catlike amber eyes, shaking her head.

"You don't have to pretend."

"I hit my head," I plead. "I haven't been able to remember anything. Tell me." I look between the two of them and receive no response. I realize my pulse is racing, that it deafens the joy I ought to be feeling.

"We only came to say hello," she says. "We'll be going in a minute. When I saw you before, you were so worried about your brother. And, see? Here he is. Alive and well."

"Don't leave." I find Miles' eyes, shadowy blue beneath the trees. "Don't go. I was so scared. I—"

"It's okay, Sophie." It's then I feel Nathaniel's hand brush my shoulder, reminding me of where I am. I feel the grass under my feet, look into his eyes for a moment, before I'm off again, chattering in this high-pitched tone I almost can't check.

"It's my brother," I say. "This is Miles." I look to my brother now, who seems to be staring into the distance behind Nathaniel's shoulder.

"Are you alright?" Nathaniel takes a small step to my side, and I realize he's placed himself between me and my brother. I feel confused, as if there's a context I don't understand, almost like a child, and my stare bounces between the three of them.

"Dora," Iris says. "He asked you if you're alright."

"Of—of course I am," I stammer.

"Actually," Nathaniel says, still staring at Miles, "I was asking you." Miles looks at Nathaniel as if he's just noticed that he's here and, finally, opens his mouth.

"Hey, nice to see you," Miles says, his voice kind. Nathaniel's arm tightens on my waist, and he reaches with his free hand to offer Miles a handshake.

"Nathaniel Wells."

"I'm Miles." He has this effortless friendliness. He always has. Even when he scolded those children, made me punch a boy in the nose.

"Miles what?"

"You're asking a lot of questions for someone who's kept my sister hidden here."

"He was not," I interrupt. "I hid here myself. Miles, I told you—someone's following me." Miles quiets me with a nod and a comforting look.

"How are we not supposed to have questions?" Iris speaks as though everything is an inside joke. "She's his little sister. Someone tried to kill her. And then? She disappears. Try to imagine how scared he was. We've been looking for her for weeks."

"Right," I whisper.

"I think you should leave," Nathaniel says. "You showed up. You said hello. I think you should go."

"Nathaniel, no," I interrupt. "I—"

"It's okay." Miles' tone is conciliatory. "We'll go. That's fine." My eyes water and I turn furiously to Nathaniel.

"All the times I've told you how desperate I was to find him. How much I missed him. What are you—" Just as I'm about to raise my voice, burst into tears, he pulls me close into a hug, whispers in my ear.

"Sophie, can we talk?"

"Sophie," Iris echoes, smiling at Miles. "Isn't that lovely?"

"Please," I say, looking from Miles to Iris, back to Miles. "I don't want you to leave me alone again."

"Come with us," Iris offers. She reaches out a soft, warm hand, as though I'm a frightened puppy. "Hey, you still have that necklace, don't you?" I reach into my pocket. "You never lost it," Iris whispers, drawing close to me. She checks the twine, then reaches up to tie it around my neck. Numb, I stand still, feeling the comforting brush of her hands on my skin. "You were never alone." Somehow, this reaches through my cloud of numbness, strikes right at my heart. "Say you'll come with us. Miles, that'd be okay with you, wouldn't it?" I look at him, ready to beg, and he smiles that wry, gentle smile, nods his head.

"You kidding? I'd do anything to have Dora back. Whatever happened in the past, that's all behind us." I look into his eyes for a moment. Does he mean the fire? All the times I've let him down? Whatever horrible, final thing I must have done this last time?

"Back where?" I ask.

"Silly," Iris says. "Back home. Did you forget that you have a home? A family?"

I don't know why I'm not weeping with happiness to hear this. It's overwhelming, I tell myself, plain and simple. So much has led to this moment.

"How'd you find her here?" Nathaniel asks.

"She's my sister," Miles answers. "I'd do anything to find her."

"Then how'd she get hurt?" Nathaniel asks. "How'd you lose her?"

"Stop it," I whisper.

"It's okay to be angry, you know," Miles offers. "The world's an indifferent place. That can be frightening. Humans are breakable. Hard not to internalize that." Miles reads people. He always has. "It can be hard to find a place you feel safe," Miles adds, casting a glance in the direction of Nathaniel's house. "I know how that is. Honest, I do." Nathaniel flinches. "Dora, you got anything to pack? Can I help you with anything?" Miles asks. I don't know why, but I can't answer. I search for words and come up empty-handed. Nathaniel's hand in mine calls me back into my body.

"Hey," he whispers, his voice low. "Let's just walk a little bit. You always feel better when you're moving." He gives a dismissive nod as we turn away from Miles and Iris. I look back over my shoulder, afraid they'll disappear again if I walk away. The sun is warm on my arms, and when we cross the yard, pass the herb garden and the long rows of flowers, it almost hurts my eyes. I pull to the side, into the shade, stand outside the door of my apartment.

"What is it?" I ask, my voice weak. "Why are you acting like this?"

"Inside," he says, looking back toward the gate, as he pushes open the door of the apartment. I follow him in, almost dizzy with the transition from light to shadow.

"I never thought I'd see him again," I say, still talking too quickly. I look out the window to check that the truck is still there. "I was so scared. But he's okay," I mumble, grasping Nathaniel's hand as if I could ask him to join me here, where I'm happy. "He's healthy."

"Okay," Nathaniel says, "but are you sure he's in his right mind? I could swear he's high on something."

"That's just how he acts," I insist. "He's almost psychic. He can look at you and know exactly what hurts inside your mind. Do you really think they'll let me go back with them?"

"Something's not right." He shakes his head, reaches toward me. I move away. "Those things you told me yesterday. Living on a farm? Off the grid? With people your brother, who you admit is troubled, met in prison?" His gaze is so apprehensive, so full of things he doesn't say, that I turn away again.

"What are you saying?"

"Do you remember when I told you, if things weren't okay where you came from, that I would understand? That we could find a way to help you?"

"You think I'm lying to you?" When his hand moves toward mine, I push it away, take a furious step backward. "You still don't trust me."

"That's not what this is about," he says. "I'm asking you if you're being honest with yourself."

"Stop it!" I say angrily, and decide to start packing. I climb the stairs two at a time, glancing around the little bedroom. My head is spinning. Nathaniel climbs the stairs after me.

"You know I'm happy for you," he says. "I've seen every day how much you missed Miles. How scared you were for him. But I don't think you need to leave with him."

"Why wouldn't I?"

"I wish you'd ask yourself that," he says.

"Say what you mean," I snap. "He was worried about me. Didn't you hear?"

"He's barely spoken two words to you!" Nathaniel cries. "You're acting like a kid on Christmas morning, but Miles didn't move an inch when he saw you."

"How can you be so unkind?" I cry, pulling away from him as if he's hit me. "I feel like I don't even know you!"

"Sophie, listen!" His voice rises a note and I leap backward, frightened, more on edge than I'd realized. "Wake up, okay? Something really bad happened to you. We know that. Do we know that going with your brother isn't going to put you back in danger?"

"My brother would never hurt me. That's the one thing I've always known." I know it, the way I know any fact, just like one and one are two. I need something to be certain here.

"I'm not saying, don't talk to him," he answers. "I'm not saying, don't find a time to see him again. I'm saying I think you should wait." He takes a step toward me and, though I don't push him away, I don't respond. He touches my elbow and stands close, talking in a low, calming voice. I can see in his eyes that he's almost pleading. "You're not happy. You're scared. This is not a time when your wires are crossed." I rush back down the stairs, unable to be still, and Nathaniel follows me into the study.

"Haven't you wondered what it would be like for us, if circumstances were different?"

"Of course I have," I say, leaning against the edge of the desk. "Why?"

"Well, if things were different, I'd ask you—stay with me." His eyes jump to mine and then away, as if he's guarding something, hesitating to speak these words. "Give this a chance. A real one. Not haunting, not wishing, not fairy tales. You and me, Sophie." I step closer, and he rests his hands on my waist. "You're all I want."

"I'm scared," I whisper, tears filling my eyes.

"I know," he answers, squeezing me closer. "I'll never let anyone hurt you. I—"

"We can't know that."

"I know how I feel for you." He traces my temple, hand lingering on my cheek. "That's not a question mark."

"Nathaniel, try to understand…"

"I do understand," he says. "All I'm asking is that you don't leave with them. Something's wrong."

"But I asked them to take me with them."

"Did you?" He tilts his head. "It looked like they walked you right into that. Listen: just tell them you want to stay here, for now. If that Miles out there is the person you've been telling me about all this time, he'll understand."

"I've heard enough," I shout, pulling out of his arms. "Let me go. You don't even know me. This is none of your business." His eyes widen and, for a moment, he's stunned into silence. I'm backing away, covering my mouth with both hands, my eyes watering to see how I've hurt him.

"Sophie, I—"

"I'm not Sophie." I can hear the meanness in my tone, the desperation to push him away. "That was never me."

"Fine," he says. "Then go." By way of an answer, he picks up my sketchbook and hands it to me. I take it and drop it on the desk.

"If you don't trust my brother, you don't trust me," I say, as I walk toward the door. I remind myself that Miles deserves this:

for me to choose him, protect him, over the outside world, over everything he says is always trying to pull us apart. There's a patient knock at the door and I hear my brother's voice.

"Dora?" he asks. "Is everything okay?" Another knock, then he pushes it open, looks around the edge. "Whoa, whoa, hey." Miles steps across the doorway and holds an arm out to me; I walk to his side. "Nathaniel, right?" he says. "Can I ask what the problem is?"

"Yeah, you can ask," Nathaniel says, as if he thinks Miles already knows.

"Why do I feel like you're telling my sister to stay here, with you? Why do I feel like you're asking her for something she doesn't owe you?"

There is a long pause.

"Look," Miles goes on, softly. "You don't think she deserves a win? You don't think she's been through enough?"

I try not to cry, and Miles squeezes me tight, pulling me toward the open door. I hesitate. I realize Nathaniel was right. Miles hasn't spoken directly to me.

"Tell me what you wanna do," Miles says, as if he's read my thoughts. "Nobody's pushing you either way. Right?" he adds, with a pointed look at Nathaniel.

"Um. Well, I—" I study the desk I've come to love, remember the etched characters in its shadows. I see Nathaniel's chest rise as he breathes in, waiting for me to speak.

"Yes?" Miles prompts.

"I'm not sure."

"Can I help?" Miles offers. I nod my head eagerly. "I've known you your whole life. I know your tells. You know what I mean?"

"I don't know," I say.

"This look on your face, Dora," Miles says, glancing between me and Nathaniel as he talks. "You know what this look reminds me of? The day I came and got you from that blue house. You just looked at me and reached your hands out. I didn't know until later, that—"

"Stop it, Miles!" I cry. Even if I walk away from Nathaniel forever right now, I can't bear for him to know this about me. "Fine: you're right. Please, don't say anything else."

"What's wrong?" Nathaniel turns to me, his voice softening. But I can't answer him. I can't even look at him. As Miles' eyes track between me and Nathaniel, I feel for some reason that I've given up a secret, without knowing why or what.

"So, does that mean you'd like to come with us?" Miles asks me.

"Yes." Numbness settles over me. I realize that this is what I know, bone-deep. The safe choice. The known quantity. I look back at Nathaniel, shaking my head.

"That settles it," Miles says. We walk back outside into the sunlight. I turn my head and see Nathaniel standing in the doorway, watching me leave, his eyes dark.

I turn away and look up at Zenaida in the window and the dappled light falling across her cheeks. *What's wrong?* I wonder, wishing I could shake a fist at her. *Aren't you happy for me?* Somehow I don't think she's happy for me at all.

CHAPTER FORTY-TWO

Iris takes my arm and leads me to the truck. I sit in the middle, between her and Miles. They say nothing to comfort me, nothing to acknowledge what I'm leaving behind. *Of course,* I think, *they probably don't know.*

"What have I always told you?" Miles turns the key in the ignition and the engine grumbles to a start. "The outside world is always trying to separate us. Always will be." I lean forward to look past Iris, out the window at the old dovecote, the gray expanse of the house rising behind it.

Miles doesn't ask me, but I begin to speak anyway as we drive, telling him everything: waking up confused and scared. Selena and Nathaniel, and the flashes of memory that taunted me until I finally began to put some things together. When I tell him about the pictures, about Selena, his eyes narrow. The words on my arms, the blood everywhere. His broad hand smacks the dashboard, the steering wheel jolting.

"Whoever did that to you," he says, "we're gonna find them, and they're going to be sorry. Look at me, Dora. Tell me they're going to be sorry." I cry with relief.

"They'll be sorry, all right," I echo. Miles throws an arm around me, one hand on the wheel, and squeezes my shoulders. He seems to know how I've longed to hear those words.

"There was something else, though," I say, looking from Iris to Miles. "Like I was telling you. Someone's been following me.

Leaving things here and there. Is everyone safe, back at home? Is everything okay there?"

"Everyone's fine." Miles whispers his answer without explanation, without looking at me. "Never been better. Especially now we have you back." No shock, but no explanation. Iris is oddly quiet, as well.

"He's nice," I venture, wishing I could tell Miles about Nathaniel. "He was just looking out for me." I hear Iris' soft laughter, the sound of wind in tall grasses.

"I'm just glad you're safe," Miles says. "You said his ex was still around?"

"Well, yes," I answer. "They have a son, so—"

"Trust me," he says, turning to look at me, though his foot is still on the gas. "She's the one who matters to him. You were there, Dora, that's all."

"You really think so?" I falter. Dismay squeezes my chest, followed by a rush of relief that I'm here with Miles again.

"You've got a heart of gold, but you're naive," Miles answers. "You've never been a great judge of character. You know that."

"Yeah." As I slouch down into the seat, Miles turns his attention back to the road, and I can tell he doesn't want me to talk anymore. I remember Iris telling me to give him time. That I did something wrong.

Fragments of memory align, falling into place, first raindrops, then a torrent. I've always listened when Miles speaks to me: when he told me to leave the blue house behind, I did. When he told me, year after year, that nobody was worth my trust, that nobody cared about me but him, I believed him. When he told me to send him all my savings, that I had no need for money, because I could come and stay with him, I bought a plane ticket.

What reason could he have, then, to hold anything back from me, when he knows I love him unconditionally? I tilt my chin up to give Miles a long, hesitant look, as if I'm seeing him for the first time.

CHAPTER FORTY-THREE

As we're driving, it occurs to me that, even if Selena's intentions were unkind in showing me those photographs, they may have had their intended effect. She had said that she wanted to help me remember. That day, I remembered nearly everything, all at once. And it was clear enough that she wanted me away from Nathaniel. I wonder if she'd be pleased. Still, though, I can't remember any signs of trouble, any clue as to how I was hurt, separated from my brother. But I'm sure he'll tell me. At least, I hope. He drives silently, paying me no mind, leaving me retracing my recollections.

Last spring, when he called me after months of radio silence, I had been overjoyed to hear from him. In the first week of April, it was still gray and cold. The lingering snow mirrored the color of the sky. Miles called in the evening, after I got home from work, from a number I didn't recognize. I hadn't heard from him in months, and the sound of his voice brought tears to my eyes.

Miles told me that he had changed. New home, new friends, new job: "new man," he said. He told me how good it was to get out of the city, and when I realized I'd spent my life in Brooklyn, that I'd barely even had the odd weekend away, something clicked. Miles needed money, which I'd never held against him. I told him the modest amount I had in savings, and he told me I had a home with him, that nobody needed money where he lived. That the air in the mountains was sweet and clean, that he woke to the sound of birds singing instead of traffic. He made it sound like heaven.

The next day, I told my boss I needed some time off, that I didn't know how much. I paid out the lease on the room I rented and I left. I remember how they picked me up at the airport. I remember the truck, too, the same one I'm sitting in now. He sold my phone for cash at a pawn shop outside Charleston. I was surprised, since I'd already wired all my savings. Soon enough, though, I was distracted, wrapped up in Miles' charm, entranced with the sweeping landscape as he drove us further and further from civilization. Just as I am being driven now. In the seat next to me, he sings with Iris, a song they both seem to know well, and I sit, bewitched, between them.

The first night I was there, everyone gathered around to meet me, as if being Miles' sister was enough to make me special. We sat outside in a clearing, around a glimmering campfire. Miles turned to the bench adjacent to ours, where a dark-haired woman with smoky eyes sat cross-legged. She leaned over on a slender arm and gave him a kiss.

"This is Iris," he told me.

"Dora, I feel like I already know you," she said. "I'm happy you're here with us. Oh, and this is Beckett." Iris nodded at a man sitting on Miles' other side, then reached over to tap his knee when he didn't respond. "Always daydreaming, this one."

"Oh! Sorry. Nice to meet you." As Beckett shook my hand, his sudden smile seemed pasted over an expression of regret or worry. I felt almost that he studied me a bit too carefully, though it may have been more true that I was the one studying him, wondering why anyone here would be anything less than happy. Soon enough, the smell of food cooking distracted me.

"Iris," Miles said, "would you get the girls to bring some dinner out?"

"Of course." She stood up and rattled off a few names, her voice musical and sweet: Rose, Morgan, Ellie. The one she called Rose drew up close to her side, and as they walked away, I could see her glancing at me as she whispered with Iris.

"There are twenty-seven of us," Miles told me. "Including two little babies, both less than a year old." I couldn't help but smile, basking in his glow. I couldn't remember ever having seen him this happy. It was as though he was, finally, himself. Iris and the others returned balancing plates of food, one carrying a large pitcher and carved wooden mugs. Others appeared to sit, and they paused one by one in front of us, as if in a receiving line, each face lit with what seemed very much like genuine happiness. A bulky man who looked to be made of solid muscle appeared from the shadows at Miles' side, greeting me with a cold stare. There was a scar through his left eyebrow.

"Dora, this is Sawyer," Miles said. I sensed that he was important, but that Miles didn't know exactly how to introduce him. "He's also been with me here since the beginning. Associate, co-worker?" he asked. "What do you think, man?" He laughed uneasily, but Sawyer did not.

"Investor? I don't know. Nice to see you, Dora." Sawyer spoke with a Midwestern accent, devoid of the usual friendly ease of that region. For a moment, a sense of unease collected around me again, until Miles resumed the rest of his introductions. Iris returned, placed a wooden cup in my hand. I lifted the cup, but Iris shook her head.

"Don't do that." Miles' voice was automatic, authoritative. "We've got to say a few things first." I placed my cup back down and looked around at the others. In the firelight, I could see several of them had matching tattoos on their hands and arms. The dark was settling in around us when Miles stepped close to the fire and lit his cigarette. It seemed like magic that the flame didn't touch his hair, that he flipped its length just out of the way with an impossible precision.

"Who's thankful today?" Miles asked, his voice cajoling and kind. A few voices rose. "Who's spoken with God today?"

Someone handed Miles a guitar and, at some cue that I didn't recognize, cups were raised. Just like fire, which I remember him patting like a tamed animal, music had always laid down at Miles' feet. I watched Iris and followed suit, sipping my iced tea. Iris slid close to me, but her eyes followed my brother. "Miles says that in most families like ours, only the leader would talk to God. But he lets all of us talk to him."

"Families?"

"What?" Iris laughed softly, looking at me through her long lashes. "You think we're a cult or something? Come on. We're farmers, Dora."

People volunteered bits of news and offered their thanks. There was a baby that took his first step. A man who received a message that he could forgive his late father for abandoning him. A pair of women told Miles that they found a patch of huckleberries growing wild in the forest, that there was more fruit than they could carry home. I felt warm and soft, strangely unworried. Miles was plucking at the guitar, playing soft chords and notes that seemed to wander in an upward spiral.

"And who," he asked, studying the fretboard, "who has anything to testify to?" Beckett pushed a crate toward Miles' feet, and he leaned over to look inside, all the while strumming the guitar. "And those who follow will be able to do these things as proof. They will speak my name to force out devils. They will speak in new languages. They will carry serpents and drink poison without being harmed." As he spoke, voices murmured along with him. "Those who believe," he repeated, alone. He set down his guitar. My teacup was empty, and I felt sleepy, but somehow, also, alert. "Baby, sit further back," Miles said to Iris, who complied, moving to the back row. He reached into the crate. When he drew his arm out, he held two snakes, both rattlers. Miles reached into another crate, and a smaller snake, mosaic-patterned in shades of brown, curled around his wrist. His pale skin gleamed in the firelight, and the snakes seemed to gleam, too, as if otherworldly. I watched people step forward, one or two at a time, and when they held the snakes, they seemed touched with magic, or something else.

By the time the snakes were returned to their cages, my veins were thrilling with energy, as if the fear I ought to have felt had turned to diamonds, lighting up my veins. I was calm, and awake, and exhilarated. Miles clicked his tongue and Iris reappeared at his side.

"You okay, Dora?"

"I—" I didn't want to tell her the truth, that it was the coolest thing I'd ever seen. I realized, then, that I felt funny, a bit light-headed. "Is there something in this tea? Is this safe?" Iris ignored my first question and skipped to the second.

"The snakes won't hurt you if your heart is clean," she answered, that evasive smile still hanging on her face. "Clean from sin, clean from drugs, from all the poison that's—out there." She gestured with a look of disgust, and somehow I knew what she meant. Iris rose to her feet and began handing plates of food around.

"The world outside is nothing but sin," Miles said. "These are God's final people. We're the last safe place."

I didn't question him, but my expression must have announced some curiosity. "This is all for you, Dora," he said. "Don't you see? All the things you went through? God used your suffering to lead me to the truth. Now, at last, we have a real family. A real home."

He wasn't talking only to me, but to a handful of people around us. He struck some chord, though, and I felt like a scared little kid again. I realized I had never felt that I had a family beyond Miles. For some reason, my mind seemed to skip over all of its usual steps, taking a shortcut straight to the middle, where it was soft and hurt.

"Dora, what is it?" Iris slipped close to me.

I felt too full of emotion to talk. "You missed your brother," she said. "You didn't realize how lonely you were. That's it, isn't it?" I nodded.

"I'm tired," I said.

"Is there a room ready for her?" Miles asked. Someone answered yes, and I followed him inside the big building.

We passed a cabinet, full of plates and tools. On the top shelf, I saw dark metal and the handle of a pistol. Car keys hung on a set of hooks here, too. My room was on the second floor, with an open window to let in the breeze.

"Here." Miles took a necklace out of his pocket and showed me the Sophia symbol. I leaned over to study it, but he gestured me closer and tied the twine behind my neck.

*

For weeks, I hung around the encampment, helping in the kitchen, watching young children while they played outside. I'm natural with children. I like them. But I was curious about where everyone went when they left in the morning. Finally, Miles agreed to take me. I figured they were farming. Dawn over the skyline was starry and violet-peach. I imagined that I had become a soft-focus version of myself, soaking in the quiet air and the simple food. I was seated in the back of a pickup, rattling over a trail through the forest.

"Beautiful sunrise," I whispered.

"It's the same color as your hair," Iris answered, twirling a lock of my hair around her finger.

"It is the same," Sawyer agreed. He lacked Iris' imagination, but at least he spoke his mind. I hadn't managed to find any fondness for Sawyer, but I could see that he was close to Miles, and that meant something. Between us, Beckett sat silently.

"Look at those clouds," Iris said. "There's no place as beautiful as this. We're far away enough from the world that everything is clean."

Though I was anxious to see where we were headed, I followed Iris' lead, leaning back against the side of the truck as we drove. When Miles went over a bump in the road, I grabbed her arm by accident and she laughed, but not unkindly. The forest woke up as the truck came through, and I heard birdsong greeting us as the sunrise began to turn to day. I saw the trees thinning ahead, which seemed strange to me, at this elevation, on these mountains.

"Perfect weather," Sawyer observed.

The truck rattled to a halt and I slid against Beckett's leg. He inched back, apologizing. I turned back to Sawyer. "Perfect for…?"

But then I turned and gasped. The sun had risen, pure gold, not a cloud in the sky. Before us the forest opened to give way to a field of poppies that swayed in the breeze, as if to an unheard melody. Something chilled in my blood, then I realized: there's only one reason I didn't suspect something like this, and that's because I didn't want to. Iris jumped over the side of the truck and walked right up to the edge of the field, like it was a body of water. She plucked a petal from the ground and handed it to me, like a coin or a blessing. "What do you think?" Miles asked. I drew in a deep breath, feeling the morning casting a spell.

"I think it's beautiful."

"We're just farmers, Dora." Miles smiled and opened his hands. "It's natural. See—how could anything bad come from this? You know why it's illegal?" Though I could think of a few reasons, I waited for him to speak. "Because the pharmaceutical industry doesn't want any competition. That's it," he said. "Victimless crime. We would never hurt anyone, ever." I saw Sawyer watching from a few yards off. Miles seemed to nod to him. "Everybody helps," he said. "This is a family, remember?"

"You aren't worried about not being able to come back? Live closer, work somewhere?"

"Dora, the world is never going to take me back." His eyes darkened. He carried his pain just below the surface. I recognized this and began to backpedal right away. Miles is like a hurricane. There's the charm, and then the storm. "I never got a fair chance. Not one time. Not after—"

"It was my fault," I said. "Not yours. I know that. I—you showed up for me, and..." All I could see were blank eyes beneath a purple hair bow.

He accepted my response, eyes flashing. "Everyone helps," he said. "You're here, you help."

"Okay."

So I was surprised, a little, when Miles didn't join us. He drove the truck back through the woods, saying he'd come pick us up before dinnertime.

For years, I had dreamed that I could one day see Miles this happy, this healthy. The poppies dancing in the fragrant breeze were more convincing than any words could have been, hypnotic and blood red. Maybe he was right. Maybe nothing could go wrong here.

CHAPTER FORTY-FOUR

The truck jolts and I wake with a start. Swearing softly, Miles throws an arm out to catch me; I realize I'm not wearing a seatbelt.

"Flat tire?" Iris asks.

"Don't think so," he answers. "The wheel's stuck in the ditch. Let's get out and take a look."

"Miles?" I blink, rub the sleep from my eyes.

"What?"

I'm looking at him, and he turns back to me as he climbs to the ground, as if he just noticed that I'm here. The poppies. The snakes. That sinking sense I had that he didn't want me to ask any more questions. *My brother would never hurt me,* I tell myself. *My brother would never let any harm come to me.* That's the only thing, in my entire life, that I've always known was true.

"Miles," I whisper again. His mouth hardens into a thin line, as if he's reading my thoughts. Maybe he is. I'm reminded of how unafraid he is of fire and of wild animals. He points at me and I cower back into the seat.

"Stay," he says. "Stay put right where you are." And I do.

"Hey, Dora," he shouts a few moments later. "Put it in neutral." I slide the gearshift as he and Iris begin to push the truck out of the ditch. "Now hit the gas," he says. "Easy, though." I do, just a bit, and it's free. For a moment, I wonder what would happen if I stomped on it, left them both here in the road. But before I know it, they're back in the cab, sitting on either side of me.

"Isn't it heavy?" I ask, looking for anything to chatter about.

"Older trucks like these?" he says. "Not really. You'd be surprised. Iris could probably push this thing on her own if she had to," he laughs. "Not so sure about you, though."

I remember this long, twisting drive, around mountainsides, always upward, into the depths of nowhere. It's disorienting, until I realize that it's the land itself that twists: we're on the same road the whole time. Until, finally, Miles pulls over, stepping on the brakes. Iris hops out of the truck to pull back tree branches that conceal the turnoff to a smaller road.

The first time I arrived here, a small crowd of friendly faces waited to greet me. But this time, the camp is quiet, just a handful of people sitting quietly around the fire. In the main building, I see a few faces at the windows, a few curtains hurriedly pulled aside. The sun is setting as Miles parks the pickup in a row of three or four dodgy-looking old cars. "Hey, everyone," he shouts, clapping his hand against the hood of the truck. "Dora's back! Let's get some dinner going."

There's a weak chorus of voices. "Everyone welcome my sister back," Miles says. "We missed you," he continues. I see Beckett looking at me, almost miserably. Iris goes inside and returns with a pitcher of tea. She fills a glass and hands it to me. I nod and thank her, then, when she's turned away, quietly pour it onto the ground. Someone carries out a platter piled with loaves of bread, a pot of soup and a stack of bowls. Bowls are filled and passed around. I know what comes next, though, before anyone is allowed to eat. In the light of the crackling fire, I watch Miles open one of the crates, and lift out a water moccasin. His voice projects calm even as he lets the snake near his face, closing his eyes, as he talks about faith and following God's word. Maybe it's the pangs in my empty stomach, but this time, I think I see it clearly. I doubt that Miles cares about holiness, or faith, or what I've heard him call divine femininity. Everyone is watching him, believing him, holding their breath with amazement. Maybe he's convinced himself he's here to sell opium or live according to some unforgiving reading of the Bible, but I'm pretty sure he's here for the adoring audience.

The snakes' crates are open, an invitation to anyone else who chooses to take part, and I peer in to see a copperhead. In the firelight, it's almost iridescent, this mottled brown creature that blends so easily into the underbrush by day. It seems years ago, that day the copperhead in the ivy watched me with its furtive curiosity. I smile when I remember Nathaniel asking me: *how long had you been sitting there by yourself, making eyes at that snake?* Before I know it, I'm reaching forward, curling a hand under the snake's belly when it moves, lifting it up. They'll know if you're afraid. But I'm not. A flash of memory chills my blood. I've been here before. These creatures aren't strangers to me. I open my hand and let the copperhead slither back into its crate.

Miles stops talking abruptly. In the silence, I sense I've committed some faux pas.

"What do you think you're doing?" He stands in front of me and I look past him into the fire.

"Just looking."

"You weren't just looking." He pulls me to my feet. "You are not to touch those creatures." I glance around at the wide-eyed faces and see that everyone's watching me. Then, I notice that everybody except for me is holding a plate of food, waiting to eat.

"God's command is for the faithful to take up serpents. Not you: you're nobody. Do you have anything to say for yourself?"

That isn't what you said before, I think. But this isn't the time to argue, so I nod my head and stare at my feet. "I'm hungry," I answer. Someone barely manages to conceal their laughter.

"Dora," Miles sighs, squeezing an exasperated sigh in his throat. "You know I'm glad to have you home. But you're not acting like yourself. You've been through a lot."

Something clicks. His voice is soft, but his eyes are cold. This is the charm. "You need rest. You're exhausted." Charm, and then the storm. I falter. My mind is blurry. Someone grabs my elbows and drags me away before I can stand up. I don't have to wonder who it is. I know it's Sawyer. I know the scar that runs through his eyebrow, the cold silence behind his eyes. As he pulls me toward the house, I don't resist, but his grip is like a vise all the same. Inside in the open room beyond the kitchen, he wordlessly holds my arms behind my back. Miles follows soon after, composed as ever, but his eyes still cold as ice. Sawyer squeezes my elbows and I wince, remembering with a jolt of fear that the last time I saw him I stomped on his foot.

"I didn't want to talk about this tonight," Miles says. "But it looks like it would make more sense to get everything out in the open. Don't you think?" I don't answer. "About what happened before? I never thought you would let me down again. I never saw it coming."

He takes a seat on a sofa, lights a cigarette. I half think that if my arms were free I'd take one. "You first," he says. "Tell me everything you remember. And I'll know if you're lying."

CHAPTER FORTY-FIVE

My mind spins, like a wheel loose on its axle. What I remember chills my blood. There's no point in glancing around the room, looking for a window or a door, but I do it anyway, out of plain habit.

"Talk, Dora." Miles' voice is sharper now.

Even when I couldn't remember my name, there were things I knew about myself. That I face things, instead of putting them off. That I'm not a liar. Dread tightens my throat, just as Sawyer is pinning my elbows behind me. I wonder if I can pretend those things aren't true. If I can convince my brother just like he's convinced all these people around him.

"Okay," I say finally. "I'll tell you everything I can remember. I've missed you so much," I add, looking up at him hopefully.

"Go on."

"I remember coming here for the first time. And meeting Iris. I remember the meal we had that first night." I try to stay on track, even though I'm starving. Thick-crusted bread with butter, roasted vegetables with coarse salt and pepper. I tell myself I'll get something to eat soon enough. "Miles—please, don't be angry. Is this about you growing poppies? Because I remember that." I try to deliver this as though it's shocking. "I remember the flowers. When the sun's rising on that hill, it looks like they go on forever." Miles is silent, and, after a moment, I continue. "I won't tell anyone," I answer. Try to remember what he told me, the first time I was there. "It's a victimless crime. You're basically just farmers. It's not that bad. You're still my brother."

"Let her sit down." Miles waves at Sawyer and he releases me. I stretch my arms out, stand with hesitation in front of him. I draw in a loud, shaky breath. Make my eyes large, trying to look sincere.

"What happened to me?"

"I told you to tell me everything you remember." His tone's dangerous.

"I'm dizzy," I whine. Miles has always thought I was a stupid little girl. "What's in the tea? I had three cups." I try to look tired as he laughs, his face softening. This time, I knew to avoid the tea Iris handed around, but I'm hoping Miles didn't notice that.

"Don't worry about that," he said. "Nothing that'll hurt you."

"I remember the harvest," I say. "And then nothing. The doctor said my concussion was severe." *Mild concussion,* I remember. *Not consistent with memory loss.* "That it was lucky I didn't have more brain damage." Miles seems satisfied. He leans over, taps the ash from his cigarette into a tray on the coffee table.

"You want to know what happened?" he asks me. I nod my head. "You ran away from us, Dora. Ran off into the woods. Listen. There are—we have enemies. Rivals. It's sad, since, you know, all I want is to be a farmer. One of them must have found you."

"Ran away?" I scrunch my face in confusion.

"You said you wanted to go to the police," he says. "You put me at risk. This is my family. I'll always do everything I can to protect you, but you run off like that, you're putting it in God's hands, and I answer to God. I don't tell him what to do. You know that, don't you?" Slowly, I nod my head. Miles is lying to me.

"In a way, Dora, I'm proud of you," he adds. "Running off like that. It takes guts. I didn't think you had that. But you aren't going to do it again." He leans in a little as he speaks to me, and just as I begin to feel scared, he hugs me. "I'm so happy to have you back," he says. "I missed you. I really did."

"I missed you too," I say, feeling a chill run down my spine, even though the words are true. "Every day that I was gone." Miles gets up and turns to the door, leaving half his cigarette in the ashtray. Now, he looks at Sawyer, not at me. "She is not to leave her room."

Without a word, Sawyer leads me down the hall and opens the door to a small room. It isn't the one where I slept when I was here before. This one doesn't have a window. I hear the door close behind me and lock from the outside.

From the very beginning, there's been one thing, throughout all of this, that I've known for certain fact. That my brother would never hurt me.

Now, hours too late, I remember everything. And I know that isn't true.

CHAPTER FORTY-SIX

Though I called it home, I hadn't been there more than a couple months. But I felt, as I think everyone did, that we were outside of time, outside of all its consequences. The sun rose and fell in a circle, rather than days passing in a line. That first day in the poppy field, Iris explained to me how you could make opium, or even stronger things, from the red flowers around us. I tried not to think about that. I liked the blossoms, the sweet air on my skin. Wherever a flower had wilted, she scored the pale seedpod, let it seep its resin, and left it. Later, she would return to scrape off the dried resin, which, to me, looked a lot like blood.

Miles didn't come back until late, long after we had returned to the camp. Sullen and looming, he waited for Sawyer to follow him. They stood alone in the trees behind the clearing; I drifted outward from the benches, pretending to be looking at plants on the ground. I could tell myself I didn't intend to eavesdrop, but I was worried about him. They whispered about a body. About Tulsa. *The cops know I'm in the state,* Miles said. *I don't know what to do.*

The ground seemed to spin beneath me as I realized where I really was, what kind of danger I was in. I didn't even have a phone to call for help. I sensed, though, that there had to be a phone somewhere in the house. I walked quietly back down the long, dim hallway. Suddenly, the entire place felt incredibly disorienting. In the storage closet near the kitchen, I glanced over at the shelves. There were a few sets of car keys and some jars of poppy seeds, but no phone. Up at the top shelf, the pistol was resting. Just to the side, I saw the edge of a phone. Wishing I were taller, I hopped on the tips of my toes to reach it and closed my hand around it. As I grabbed the phone, my fingertips knocked the gun aside, just an inch. I realized that I could disappear out here. Anybody could. I walked back down the hall, pushed the door to go back outside, but it was locked. I felt a hand on my elbow and turned to find my brother.

I remembered him as a child.

I remembered him taking care of me when nobody else did.

I could still see him in there. I believed that he wasn't lost.

"What are you doing in here, Dora?"

I threw my arms around him and squeezed. "Can we talk?"

Miles gave me a look and pulled me outside.

"What's up?"

"Miles, is there, maybe, something you haven't told me?" A cloud crossed his face. I grasped his hand and held on tight.

"I believe you, no matter what. I love you. Miles, did you—"

He pulled his hand away, stood up tall with a blank face. I tried to be brave but I could hear my voice growing breathy. I reminded myself that I was always safe as long as I was with my brother.

"You shouldn't be in here by yourself." His hand closed tight on my arm, steering me outside.

"We need to leave."

"You want to leave me? Is that it?"

"No, Miles." I reached for a hug again but he pushed me back a step, his lips twisting in a smile of disappointment. "I want us to leave," I said. "I can help you."

"You can't help me."

"You can stop this."

"No, I can't," he said, a flicker of childlike fear behind his eyes. "I don't know how to. Dora, we killed a man. I was with Sawyer, I don't even know how—anyway, I'm in this now," he repeats, whispering. He motioned at the house, at the campfire. "I don't know how I'd get out of it, even if I wanted to." I wanted to cry, but I saw that he needed me to be strong.

"We're going to leave and get help. Whatever happened, I know it wasn't the real you. I know it wasn't your fault. I'm going to call the police and get us out of here."

He saw the phone in my hand and reached for it; having anticipated this, I stepped back. I talked quickly. "You have to tell them everything that happened. Tell them you want help."

Miles swung a fist at me. I must have anticipated this, too, because I swerved out of the way. Still, there was an alarm going off, deep in my brain, beyond where words are formed. *Miles wouldn't hit me. Miles wouldn't hurt me. Something's wrong.* But I still tried to get through to him.

"I know I let you down before. It's not going to be like that this time. But we have to go. I can't lose you."

My words hung in the air for a moment and I looked at him with pleading eyes. In that moment, I thought he was about to agree, to ask me to help him.

But he swung at me again, lightning fast, and I felt an impact just behind my ear at the base of my head. I turned aside and dropped to my knees. The facts as I knew them were colliding with a physical reality that was very different. The cost of getting it wrong was so much steeper than I had anticipated. The lights of the fire faded in and out, and everything seemed to vibrate. Miles picked up the phone from where I'd dropped it on the ground. He hauled me to my feet and I could feel that his thin arms were solid muscle.

When I regained my senses, I was by the fire again, curious faces regarding me, Miles holding me steady with an arm around my shoulders. Only his closest friends were there: Sawyer, Beckett, Iris.

"This was a mistake," Miles said.

"I can see how it looks that way," Iris answered, her voice soft. She reaches across me to touch his cheek. "You gonna let her go?"

"How can I?"

"You gonna kill her?"

"I don't want to," he said. "She's mine. She's the only person that's mine."

"I'm yours," Iris reminded him. "We all are."

"It's different," he said. "I never thought she'd do this, ever."

"You're really hurt," she mused, stroking his hair. "I hate to see you so sad."

I coughed. A soft mist descended, quieting the light of the fire until it was almost out. "Anyone want to hear a story?" Miles asked. I heard a murmured chorus of assent from the others. "Dora was little when our mother left us. She was three. I was almost nine. Let me tell you, it's a lot harder for an ugly nine-year-old little boy to get a home than it is a precious toddler with strawberry-blonde hair." He smiled a self-deprecating smile. Charm, I see. "But the foster system's rough. Overloaded. Our social worker was kind, but she didn't have the resources or time to really make sure we were okay. We got split up after we left our first home. Hard enough as it is, right?" he says. "But it doesn't end there. Dora, do you remember what happened?" With a reproachful sigh, I waited for him to speak, eyes on the ground.

"At the second home Dora went to, there was something wrong. She called me and I could hear it in her voice. Child trafficking, pedophiles, who knows. I could tell she was scared. And here I was, twelve, angry, alone. Dora's all I have. And someone wants to harm her? I wanted to go right to her and take her somewhere safe and burn that house down." He caught Iris' gaze over the embers. "That's exactly what I did. Dora didn't tell me until later there was a little girl hidden in the house. Maybe God wanted to end her suffering. Who knows? That was the first time I was locked up. Been in the system ever since." He sighed, stroked his chin as if he was lost in memory. This is the charm, I remembered. With Miles, the charm always comes before the storm. "Dora was the one who left the girl there to burn, but she let me take the blame for everything. She went on to go to college, to get a good job. And you know what? She was going to turn me in again tonight. Turn in all of us." He turned to Sawyer and I saw something like fear on his face. "If anything, she's lucky the people you work for aren't here."

In the quiet that followed, Miles and Sawyer pulled me to my feet. I saw Beckett and Iris catching up, exchanging a glance that was difficult to read. Near Miles' pickup truck, we paused. He stood back, seeming far away from me, then reached an arm up to brush my hair out of my eyes. I saw the pocketknife flip open in his hand, began to flail, pushing him away in a panic. I felt its blade on my hands and arms.

"Would you hold still?" Miles rolled his eyes. "You think I want to use this on you? Please." I don't think he intended what happened next. Even now, I think he only meant to scare me. I saw Miles look away for a moment, and some desperate optimism threw me forward, an attempt to bolt on wobbly legs, and I fell right against the blade of the knife, felt it drag along my chest as I fell to my knees. I looked up at him in shock, and his face barely changed, one eyebrow flicking with annoyance. He shook his head, sighed to Sawyer: "Do something about her." Turning briefly to Sawyer, I saw him nod his chin; Sawyer twisted me around by my shoulder and tied both hands behind my back. "We're gonna let you spend the night outside," Miles said. "Let you think about what you did."

"I want to go home," I pleaded. "Miles, please." But his face was blank. The charm had run out. I spent a moment staring into his eyes, looking for the brother I knew, before he pulled me close and delivered another explosive punch to the side of my face. He threw me against the truck and I felt the window crack under my forehead before my knees failed and everything went dark.

CHAPTER FORTY-SEVEN

I woke up in the truck. Everything was blurry, my head throbbing. I was slumped against the door. Sawyer was driving and Miles sat on my left. Somehow, I already knew where we were going. With a sickening effort, I reached for the door handle and pulled. I could blame it on a desire to escape, or claim that it was bravery, but the truth was I wanted everything to stop, at any cost. When the door opened, I slouched outward, Miles swearing and grabbing hold of my knees. I tried to catch hold of a branch, a vine, anything I could grab onto and get free from the truck. But my hands closed only on thorns, brambles that pulled over my hands as I felt my shoulder and arm dragging along the ground like a length of gravelly sandpaper. Head throbbing, arms stinging, I gave up, my weight slack. Miles waited, though, before pulling me back up. His eyes were cold with anger. I felt the truck stop, the impact reverberating through my limbs. Though my vision was blurred, I could see the flowers, swimming by night like so many fish in the sea. Someone lifted me up, carried me to the field, threw me on the ground. Miles sat on his knees at my side, exhaling as though pained with disappointment. Blinking frantically, I watched the image of my brother double. Iris, also in duplicate, appeared to sit next to him in the poppies. I heard murmured voices from behind them, which I assumed to belong to Sawyer and Beckett, though I couldn't see that far.

Resting on my side, not a thought of moving, all I could manage was to blink my eyes until I could almost see. "Miles."

I could barely hear my own voice. There was no stopping these spells of anger Miles had, these storms. "Miles, think of Mom," I whispered. He leaned back on his heels to look at me, anger dancing in his eyes.

"Mom?" He laughed. "Mom was a whore and a junkie."

"No, she wasn't!" I cried. He slapped me for disagreeing, my teeth rattling. "Like you'd remember. They took us away from her when you were three. She used to go out at night, or have men come over, and she'd leave you screaming in your crib, covered in piss."

"I don't believe you. She died. You told me."

"She didn't die," he sneered. "CPS took us away from her, and she disappeared, never to be seen again. Hell, the way you cried and whined, she was probably relieved they took you off her hands. Who do you think brought you a cup of milk at night, tried to take care of you? It wasn't her, that's for sure. I did the best I could to take care of you. And this is how you thank me?" Iris knelt next to him. She held a permanent marker in her hand, though it never occurred to me to wonder why.

"Tell me how you're feeling," she said, holding Miles in her honey-and-smoke stare.

"She's a betrayer," Miles said. Iris wrote something on my right arm. "She's a snitch. A liar."

"There," Iris whispered. "Listen, baby. Everyone's afraid you're capable of this. Be the man they love, not the one they're afraid you are. Let this end."

"It was enough," Beckett added. "Before we left camp. You could have stopped there."

"I wanted to help you," I said, tasting blood. "That was my only intention."

"Is that so?" When Miles rose to his feet, I stared out at the flowers. "Sawyer, get the boxes." I heard footsteps as Sawyer walked to the truck, returned to us. When Sawyer sat next to me in the grass, I tried to catch his eye, to plead for help. But what I found on his face was something different, some cold amusement that let me know it wouldn't be of any use to beg.

"If there's no sin in your heart," Miles said, "you have nothing to fear." Sawyer lined up the crates at my side, opened each door. As I looked into the enclosures, all my thoughts evaporated on the breeze. I studied the glinting eyes, the fascination of the slithering bodies. The gentle rattles as the diamondbacks crept out of their cage. Miles didn't realize it, but, in a way, this was a gift. It forced me to be still, to realize the truth. He meant for me to die. I turned a weak stare into his eyes, wishing he'd just kill me. I didn't have any fight left. Every sense I could have once named was saturated to the point of uselessness.

What happened next left everybody speechless, even Miles. Despite how Sawyer rustled their cages, despite me being right in their way, every last snake slithered over or around or past me. When they disappeared into the poppies, I felt myself breathe and realized that I wasn't dead. At least, not yet. Iris stole close and tucked flowers behind my ears, into my hair, and I could hear her crying.

Finally, I heard Miles' voice. "That settles it, then. Everyone? Let's go." Footsteps approached me, then I heard my brother speak again. "Leave her! I said she stays the night. Beckett, you stay and watch. Do what you want with her. See if I care."

As soon as the truck was out of earshot, Beckett sank to the ground beside me and untied my wrists with shaking hands. "Shit, Dora," he whispered, "shit. He's never been that bad. You need a doctor."

"Help," I murmured. Though I knew he was there, I couldn't track him, my eyes flipping wildly from one side to the other.

"I can't," he said. "I don't have a car. No way to get one. Besides, I couldn't lie to Miles. I know I couldn't. He'd kill me. But you've got to get out of here," he said, speaking so quickly I could barely understand him. "You have to try." He pulled me to a sit and I struggled to stay upright. "If you go straight that way, follow the path until you pass the laurels. Go into the thicket and downhill. There's a road. Someone will find you."

I reached to touch the burning pain in my shoulder and he stopped my hand. "Get out of here," he said. "They'll be back at dawn." I stumbled into the woods, only a few steps, then fell. Then I got up again. When I made it to the laurel hell, I ducked in and collapsed. What I didn't expect was that, even here, it was painful to sit still with my own thoughts. A number of possible truths, explanations, came into my mind. One, that Miles wasn't the brother I thought he was. This was impossible. Second, that I should give up here, hope I could die quickly. That, I found, I didn't know how to do. A third option, though, came to the surface, and I reached for it. I let Dora go, and left her there in the laurels.

It might have been hours later, or days. I woke to strange sounds: doves singing, and something else, something loud that set my head pulsing with pain. Sirens.

CHAPTER FORTY-EIGHT

I sit up straight, leaning against the wall, and slowly rest my head in my hands. All the work I put into healing, into finding myself, all the optimism, was all for this. So I could leave the only good thing I'd found and run right back here. I press my temples and exhale. I could try to survive here as a prisoner. But one misstep, and I'm dead. That much is plain. And would I even want to stay here, to earn back his favor? There was a point in time, perhaps not that long ago, when, if I'd been offered a chance to give up my independent life in order to live close to Miles, to be forgiven and finally be his family, I might have answered yes.

Though there's no clock, I sense the hours passing, night creeping by. The house around me goes silent. I wonder how long it will take until the police find Miles and his crew. And then, if I'm still alive, will I be counted as innocent? I hear my voice saying, *I'm no one, from nowhere.* And a voice that answers: *You're somebody, alright.* Nathaniel was the one who was certain of me. That I had something worth remembering. That I could figure things out, as he would always say, one foot in front of the other.

In the morning, I can hear Miles' voice as he comes in and says good morning to everyone. There are footsteps on the stairs, coming closer, then, a hard knock on the door.

"Wake up." It's Sawyer's voice. But I haven't slept. The door opens and Miles is there, Sawyer behind him.

"How are you feeling this morning?" Miles asks.

"I'm okay." I'm afraid he'll read my eyes, so I don't look directly at him.

"You're going to stay in here for a while," he says. "For a few days. But once you're done, as long as you don't try to leave us, you'll be free as you want."

He speaks as though his words have some logic. I gauge his temperament. "I'm hungry. Can I have some food?" Having something to refuse will make him feel bigger, I think.

"No," he says, "not yet."

He closes the door and turns the lock.

As hours tick by, I replay it all in my mind, over and over. I force myself to recount every detail of what happened, until it doesn't shock me anymore. Anger, I remember Nathaniel saying, comes from the part of you that knows what happened was wrong. Since the day I woke up, I've been haunted by fear, anger. But what if those feelings aren't my enemies? By evening, I've stopped wondering if anyone is going to bring me dinner. I welcome my anger home, let it fill my empty stomach. If I had my sketchbook, I'd draw a picture of Miles and write *liar* right across his mouth. I'd finish the list of *What Sophie Knows*. I know my name is Dora. That my brother tried to kill me once, which means he's capable of doing it again. And that I have to find a way out of here first.

CHAPTER FORTY-NINE

Every night, someone stays outside my door. It's usually Sawyer, but Iris comes every few hours to walk me to the bathroom. I keep a close track of sunrise and sunset, but despite my best efforts, I lose count of the days. Either eight, I think, or nine. One day, in the morning, Iris walks me to the bathroom so I can take a shower. She hands me a clean dress. Light gray cotton with buttons and a pin-tucked blouse, a drawstring waist, slightly puffed short sleeves. I look like Wednesday Addams, or a farm wife at a funeral. Or a girl in a cult up in the mountains, I think, braiding my wet hair. I've only had water to drink. The occasional piece of fruit. My eyes look too big and I can see shadows under my collarbones.

"We're the same size," she observes. "Thought so." I try to laugh, but it sounds more like a cough.

"Yeah, I guess we are," I answer. "Are you hungry all the time, too? Or do you get used to it?"

"Poor girl," she answers.

"Don't 'poor girl' me," I answer, glaring at her reflection. "Tell my brother to give me a decent meal. He'll listen to you."

"I'll try," Iris answers. "I don't want you to go hungry. But you really hurt his feelings." Arguing with her would be useless, but she cares about me, in her way. I hope that I can turn that to my advantage.

She walks me back to my room, where Sawyer is still outside the door. He locks it behind me. By now I know the sound of his footsteps, the unfriendliness in his silence. I sit against the wall opposite the door, half-tired with hunger. At some point during the afternoon, I hear footsteps down the hall and startle awake.

"Hey," someone says. "Heard you needed a switch."

"My back's killing me." The door creaks as Sawyer stands up. "Been sitting here for over a week now. Honestly? I'm bored." I hear him laugh softly. "Not like she's going anywhere."

"How long has he had her locked in here?" I recognize Beckett's voice.

"I don't know," Sawyer answers. "What's the date? It's like time doesn't even pass up here."

"It's July 30."

"Nine days," he answers. "She's safer in here than out." Sawyer's voice drops. I inch closer to the door. "Let me tell you something about Miles. He likes having people around him. None better than his own sister. Unless she's a problem. If he feels like she's a problem, he won't hesitate. But he knows everybody's stirred up now. He doesn't want to make a show of it."

"Right."

"He'll probably wait a few days, off her quietly, tell everyone she ran away."

"Okay, man. That much is clear."

I hear footsteps. Then silence.

I wait a few minutes, until I'm sure nobody else is around. Then, I creep up near the door, tap against it with a fingertip.

"Beckett."

"Hi, Dora."

"Thank you."

"For what?"

"You know what," I whisper.

"I don't know what you're talking about," he insists.

"You know you have to let me out," I say. I remember how his hands shook as he untied my wrists. I know there's fear in him. I will my voice to find it, to find something soft. "You know what's going to happen to me if you don't. It's just a question of when."

Silence. I know I'm taking a risk, but every minute is valuable to me. "You can tell them I hit you. Or that I broke down the door."

"How do you think it looked, when I lost you before? He'd kill me if it happened again."

"Does he even know you're here? It sounds like you're filling in for someone else."

Silence, again. I feel quiet adrenaline steeling my veins. "Just unlock the door and walk away," I whisper. "Just go outside."

"Quiet!" he hisses. "I'm thinking." I draw back, hold my breath. But I hear the fear in his voice, and I know I've convinced him. "You can't get away now, anyway. It's broad daylight."

"I'm not going to," I answer. "Just give me ten minutes."

A moment later, I hear the key turn in the lock. The door relaxes on its hinges. I hear footsteps moving away.

I listen long enough to make sure I'm the only one here. There's nobody in the sitting room or in the kitchen. I drop low to the ground, below the windows, and make my way to the closet. The gun's not here. Neither is the phone. I grab a keyring with several car keys on it, wrap my fist around it, letting the metallic edges press into my palm. The hallway is still empty, so I turn, more than a little lightheaded, toward the kitchen.

By the time I'm standing in front of a cabinet, I forget where I am, why I'm here. That's right: food. Anything I can pocket quickly, eat quietly. A large pitcher of iced tea cools on the counter and I waver, nearly knocking it over. I grip the edge of the counter, forgetting at first the car keys in my hand, then sinking to the ground to pick them up. As I lean over my knees, I listen for any noise. It's easier, to sit here, and rather than standing up, I open the cabinet at my eye level. To my recollection, Iris doesn't store anything down here that's ready to eat. I reach into the cabinet and brush my hands over bags of flour, rice, then a glass jar. My hand closes on it. I remember Iris boiling the poppy seeds from the field, pouring the concentrated liquid into iced tea, winking at me as she claimed it was the passionflower leaves that gave the tea its calming effect.

Footsteps outside startle me, outside, I think—*on the steps,* I think. But still too close. With shaking hands, I open the lid of the jar and empty it into the pitcher of iced tea on the counter, then hide the jar behind a sack of flour. All the standing and kneeling almost knocks me out. As I'm hurrying back toward the hallway, I spot a basket of fruit on the counter, but I'm too nervous to try my luck by going back. Returning to my room, I pull the door shut behind me, then collapse onto the mattress.

I hear Beckett return. He says nothing as he resumes his seat. I hear the latch click shut, and the deadbolt slides as he locks the door. Soon after, more voices follow. I thank my luck that the walls are thin, that I can hear almost everything. I try to hide the car keys in the bodice of the dress, but when I rise to my feet, they slip past the drawstring and tumble to the floor with a clink that makes me gasp. "It's almost dinnertime," someone says. "Does he want her to come out tonight?" Hands clumsy with hunger and nerves, I pull the drawstring waistline of the dress as tight as I can, then place the keys once again next to my skin.

There's a murmur, then footsteps come my way. I recline on the mattress, lying on my side, an impression of listlessness. The door unlocks, then Iris and Rose look in.

"Oh, poor thing," Rose says.

"It's not for much longer," Iris assures her. "Aren't you hungry, Dora?"

"I'm starving," I say, though, in truth, adrenaline has killed my appetite. "And I'm lonely." I walk outside with them, arms linked with Iris again as though we're friends. We sit around the fire. Miles pretends I'm not there as he speaks, playing the same beautiful chords he always does on the guitar. He opens a crate and brings out a water moccasin, letting it dangle from his hand and climb up his bicep. His eyes are as clear and blank as the reptile's. He pauses to stare at me, and I'm half-afraid he can see right through my clothes to the keys hidden in my dress. But he continues, saying nothing, paying me no more notice.

There's rice and beans for dinner, and some kind of salad made from foraged greens that I can't quite bring myself to eat.

"There's not enough bitter in the typical American palate," Iris says. "We're not used to the flavor. But it's so important for your health." I want to tell her that she doesn't know me. That my palate has had plenty of bitterness. I bite my tongue instead. When the tea is served with the meal, I watch everyone around me with their glasses. I pretend to drink mine, too. Nobody makes any comment on the taste, and the appearance is the same. That's the wild card here: I don't know anything about how long it will take to work. Or how long it will work for. Only that, hopefully, it gives me a little bit of extra luck later on tonight. I eat slowly, taking small bites, torn between hunger and a fear I'll make myself sick if I eat too quickly.

There's the usual chatter, the wide-eyed compliments to the land and vague sentiments of gratefulness. They almost sound sincere. As high as they probably are, the sincerity might be genuine. It's dark when Iris begins to yawn. She's small, though, and I look up and down the rows of benches. I see the men yawning, too. What if someone falls asleep, and it's obvious what I've done? I begin to worry. What if I overdose all of them and they pass out right here? At least I'd have a way out, but most of these people have done nothing to me. Nothing except stand by while I almost got killed, I think. I can empathize with the need to follow someone who seems strong. I know what it's like to need a place to fit in.

The conversation winds on into the evening, but it seems stunted, and there are more yawns than usual. Miles is the first to stand up, and once he does, everyone else follows suit. He pauses by my seat, and I turn my chin up to stare back at him.

"I'm glad you're back, Dora," he says, speaking slowly.

"You, too," I stammer.

"What?"

"I mean, thanks." I shrug and force a weak smile. "I'm a bit lightheaded, honestly."

"You'll be fine." He pats my shoulder and I hold my elbows tightly against my sides, the keys under my dress pressing into my ribs. "Relax, okay? You're still family. This is still your home." I nod, holding his gaze until he turns away.

"Miles, I'm going to bed, love," Iris says. He kisses her cheek, then walks away toward the house. Iris stretches, then links her arm through mine. "Who's watching you tonight?"

"I don't know," I say. "Sawyer was there earlier."

"Let's walk you back," she says. Rising to my feet, I cross my arms tightly, feeling the keys pressing against my ribs. As we walk back toward the house she catches Sawyer by the arm. He has a half-eaten plate of food in one hand and a glass of tea in the other. "Here, you're watching her, right? Trade you." She takes his plate. He drains the glass, then hands it over, and nods for me to walk ahead of him.

"'Night, Iris," I say. *And, with any luck, goodbye.*

"You need the bathroom or anything?" Sawyer asks.

"Sure," I answer. I'm trying my luck. The door of my room locks from the outside, and I still don't know exactly how I'm going to get out, once he locks me in. I take my time in the bathroom, flushing twice to dispel any suspicion, looking at the cold blue of my eyes in the mirror. These aren't criminal masterminds. They're a bunch of misfits, who wound up here because they were bad at everything else. I know it because, on the inside, I'm the same.

I open the door and look back down the hall. Sawyer is asleep, sitting with his back leaning against the wall. I tiptoe toward the living room, reaching for the door. But as I turn the corner, the car keys slip from my waistband and fall to the floor with a metallic crack.

Freezing in my steps, I hold my breath. Sawyer can't be more than twenty feet behind me. For a moment, I wait. Another moment passes and I dare to think I'm safe, that the noise hasn't disturbed him. I reach to pick up the keys, steal further into the dark. In the shadowed living room, I stop for a moment to look at a stack of crates, listen to the faint rattle inside of a snake rousing itself. It's then that I hear his footsteps behind me.

"Where are you going, Dora?" Sawyer speaks in a low, dangerous voice. I remember that look on his face when I turned to him for help. He might be the one person in this place who really does warrant fear.

"I—"

"You cannot possibly be this stupid."

"What happened in Tulsa?" My question stuns him. He inches forward and I step back, trying to keep the space between us.

"Kid showed up to buy. He didn't bring enough cash. Tried to take what he couldn't afford." Sawyer shrugs his shoulders, annoyed that I've asked. "Why?"

"My brother's not a killer." Inching away still, I hold his blank gaze in the dark, see him grin with amusement. Something frightful sparks through my limbs. The memory of fear can paralyze you, but, in this moment, it gives me daring.

"Sure, and you're not a stupid little girl like he says you are. Get over here." When he grabs for me, I stumble sideways, knocking against one of the crates as I try to keep my balance. Fist closed tight around the car keys, I catch myself on my closed fist, push up and scramble to my feet, knuckles smarting. I dodge him as I stand, and reach out to grab the handle of the rattler's crate. He pauses momentarily and glances down at it, and I sense a difference in his stance. Fear. I jostle the rattler's crate in my hands at him and watch him startle.

"You're a fool, Dora," he says, shaking his head.

Holding the crate by the handle, I turn and run back toward my room. Sawyer's following me, and he's fast, but I'm smaller, which is, for once, an advantage. At the doorway, I step around him, and his momentum carries him into the windowless bedroom. Before he gets up, I smack him over the head with the crate, hard enough to knock him to the ground. I hear the rattler inside the crate hiss at the disturbance and, without stopping to think, slide the door open and throw it at Sawyer. He flattens against the floor, trying to hold still.

"Bitch," he hisses. "If there's no sin in your heart—"

"I only took one Bible study class," I whisper, "but I remember there being a line about not putting your God to the test."

The rattler slips out of its container and strikes at his shoulder. He wheezes in pain. I know their venom works fast, but I don't know how fast.

"Make a single noise," I say, "and I'll go get the rest of them." He swears at me, but he doesn't move, panting on the ground. I close the door and twist the lock, then run outside as quietly as I can.

As I sneak across the yard, a porch light flickers. I stand behind a dress hanging from a clothesline, hold my breath for as long as I can, then release it in a slow, still exhale. I make my way across to the row of battered old cars, crouched and listening, like an animal. The sky is black with clouds, every star concealed, a warm, foreboding wind weaving around the trees. It lulls everyone to sleep, bundling up and spiriting away any noise I make before it can rouse someone. It feels as though the mountain is telling me to go now, that it has my back.

I glance over the row of vehicles. I realize I only have one set of keys. What if those keys aren't even for one of these cars? What if it's one of the cars that's blocked in—how much noise will it take to maneuver out? Each car is at least twenty years old. One, a van, has a flat tire. The key doesn't unlock the door. The SUV behind it is parked so close that I'm afraid of the maneuvering it would take to get it out. The door is locked, but I reach in the open window and try the ignition: nothing. I look at the next car hopefully, a little four-door sedan, one that looks reliable, easy to drive. But the key won't open the door. With a hateful sigh, I look at Miles' truck. It has a starburst crack on one of the rear windows, courtesy of my head. The key unlocks the door. This truck just seems like a bad omen. And besides that, it's loud. But if it's my only option, it's better than none at all. I climb into the seat and slide the key into the ignition. Then I think better of it. I step to the ground then reach over the seat, shift the gear to neutral, and push. First against the doorframe, then, stepping back, against the fender. The tires creak, twigs snapping beneath them, and it starts to move. The drive is on a slight incline and for a few steps, I run alongside the truck and then, finally, grab hold of the seat and pull myself up.

I steer it down the drive in the dark as best I can. I know it's a few miles until the little drive crosses the road. If I can only make it to Dovemorn, I can ask Nathaniel to let me use the phone. It's half the distance it would be into town. My eyes adjust to the dark, a little at a time. After a minute or two downhill, I start the engine. When the reflectors of the main road finally come into view, I step on the gas and, daring to let myself hope, turn on the headlights.

CHAPTER FIFTY

Though it's a long way, I drive as fast as I can. This time, I know which way I need to go. I drive erratically, too fast, minding only the areas where the road hugs the mountainside, bounded by toothpick-like rows of guardrail. The truth is that I'm hoping against hope I'll get pulled over, which would be the fastest way to get some help. Luck isn't on my side for that, though. These roads are all but deserted.

I see a sign for Hazel Bluff and know that I must be close to Dovemorn. I pass the overlook which, it seems to me, was only minutes past the house. The truck coughs, then the engine growls and slows. I swear at it, shouting at the top of my lungs with all the fury latent in my mind. The gas pedal gives under my foot. It grumbles to a halt. For the first time, I notice that the gas meter is on empty. I throw the truck back in neutral, half sobbing with frustration, and do my best to push it off the road, though it lodges in a thicket. Sticking to the narrow row of grass that separates road and thicket, I take off running.

My body moves fast. I feel strong. Except for the fact that I'm running in the dark and that I keep slipping. Stopping to catch my breath, with my hands braced on my knees, I startle a herd of deer, their ghostly eyes looking at me from deeper within the forest. I say a quiet thanks that it wasn't something more dangerous and keep moving. As I turn back to face the road, I slip on the dew-damp grass, fall on top of my knee. As I land, my knee twists under me, and, exhausted, I collapse on it. I realize that I'm scared. I'm tired. I could lie down right here, let myself sleep.

Why do these woods call to me the way they do? Maybe this is why I've been so frightened of them, why I've always locked the door every chance I get. Because part of me has always wanted to disappear. In this half-conscious state, I hear a voice that's familiar, the music of doves and riddles, ringing from somewhere in between my ears. *Get yourself up. Keep moving. You're not done.*

I haul myself to my feet, test putting weight on my knee. It hurts, but it'll carry me.

When I see the familiar sloped drive, I begin to allow myself a fraction of hopefulness. I run uphill to the big gate and find the low-branched oak tree, then quickly scramble over the stone fence, dropping to the ground on the other side with less grace than I had hoped. I don't stop to look at the dovecote or the perfectly manicured gardens. I run straight to the footbridge, which is the fastest way across the grounds. In the middle of it, I pause to look at the stained-glass window, which shimmers in the dark. I can feel a whisper of gladness from its direction. The water murmurs beneath me and I keep moving, seeing a light on in the window. My footsteps are heavy and exhausted as I approach the familiar house, and I realize my legs are on fire with exertion, my knee screaming with pain from where I fell on it.

I knock at the door. Several quiet, urgent taps.

Then, at last, leaning exhausted against the doorframe with my forehead on my arm, I wait.

Only once I hear footsteps on the stairs inside do I realize that this is a long shot, to say the least. If he even answers, he might close the door in my face. He wouldn't be in the wrong. Holding my breath, I tap at the door again with a trembling hand.

The latch turns and the door swings open. I open my mouth to speak, to apologize, to beg him to let me in, but no sound comes out. Nathaniel rubs his eyes, as if trying to dispel a vision, then lunges forward and wraps me in a hug that lifts me off my feet and over the doorstep.

CHAPTER FIFTY-ONE

"I must be dreaming." He's squeezing me tight, his hands pressing into my back, not wanting to set me down. "Sophie—Dora. Sorry—" He pulls away just enough that we can look at each other.

"It doesn't matter," I say, pulling him close again and kissing him. He pushes the door closed with one arm.

"Are you alright?"

"Yes."

"Were you followed?"

"I don't think so." I look behind me nervously. "The truck's a few miles up the road, hidden off to the side."

"Come with me," Nathaniel says, moving toward the kitchen. I make it half of one staggering step, then collapse on the floor, wheezing as my knees hit the hardwood. "Jesus Christ," he swears, pulling me up against him. He brushes the damp hair from my clammy forehead, then holds my face in his hands, tracing the circles under my eyes with his thumbs, his eyes snapping with anger. "What did they do to you?"

"Nothing," I stammer. I don't have the energy to protest when he lifts me up and carries me into the kitchen. I'm not sure I would fight back even if I did. Nathaniel helps me to sit on the counter next to the sink.

The clock on the microwave reads 12:30. I see a child's pair of shoes by the doorway and a bit of a mess in the kitchen. He wraps both of my hands in his, and when he sees the scrapes on my knuckles, he lifts his eyes to mine.

"You're not hurt? Are you sure?"

"Yes." My eyes start to water, my voice catching when I speak.

"Tell me." He traces under my eyes with his fingers and runs a thumb down my cheek. It's not a command, but an invitation. Everything that I've locked away begins to spill out, and I can't hold myself together any longer.

"My mom didn't want me," I say. Nathaniel pulls me against his chest. "She left me to cry. When I went into foster care she disappeared. Miles took care of me," I whisper, "I could say Miles before I could say mom."

"Tell me," he repeats, a hand on my hair. "I'm listening to you."

"But my brother's sick," I tell him, covering my face with shame. "He's dangerous. I couldn't see it until it was too late. All I saw were the good parts."

"You needed someone," he says. "You must have been so lonely."

"He was the only person I trusted. When he told me he was off drugs, living in the country, I thought he'd finally gotten better. He asked me to come and stay with him. I emptied my bank accounts and left."

"Why?"

"Because," I answer, "he does love me. Part of him does." I still need this to be true, whether it is or not. I dissolve into tears. "A couple dozen people live up there with him. He's—you've met him. He's compelling. He's got everyone wrapped up in this cult thing. Snakes," I tell him, remembering, covering my mouth as I cry. "Symbols. But it's all—theatrics. No meaning. Just control."

"For what?"

"They're making opium. The poppies, you know? I can't believe I didn't see it. Miles has always been—" I begin to see it, now. He was always quick to act, and always quick to protect me.

Even when it meant the threat of violence, or more. Maybe this has always been in him. I see my naivety, how badly I wanted to feel I had family. Every time he told me nobody cared about me except for him.

"Dora," he murmurs. "I was so afraid I'd never see you again."

"You were right—about everything. What happened before— after I heard about the murder. When I tried to leave, he lost his mind." I lean forward, all my weight against Nathaniel's chest, trying to blot out the memories of pain. "I only got out the first time because one of them helped me." I cry, like a child, and let him hold me, knocking a final surge of pride out of the way. "I thought he'd never hurt me."

"I was so worried," he says, turning his gaze to me as he presses my hands in his. "I kept thinking if I hadn't pushed you so hard, maybe you would have agreed to stay."

"Nothing was going to stop me from following him." I wipe my cheeks dry. "I'm sorry. Sorry I left. That I'm not somebody else."

"You're here," he says. "That's all I want. You think I want somebody else?"

"I'm sorry I didn't turn out to be someone easier to know," I say. He holds me at arm's length now, shaking his head as if I know better.

"I don't need easy, Dora. I'm not afraid of difficult. I've been there." He pulls me close again. "I'm here for you. Just tell me what you need."

"I need to use the phone. I need the police." I hear something outside, a low noise that might just be the wind. Nathaniel looks at me. He heard it, too. Then, we hear a solid, lazy knock at the door. Without waiting for an answer, Miles opens it and walks into the hallway.

CHAPTER FIFTY-TWO

Miles wears a denim jacket over a worn vintage T-shirt with a band logo. He looks at ease, handsome. He's smiling, standing there in the hallway as if he's walked in on something amusing.

"Good to see you, Nathaniel," he says, then: "Dora."

"Hey, Miles."

I can practically feel the tension radiating in Nathaniel's chest, just behind my shoulder. "He's dangerous," he says in a low, almost inaudible whisper. "Whatever happens, do not leave with him. You understand me?"

"I—"

"No matter what," he says.

"You know I can hear you, right?" Miles laughs. Nathaniel's arm tightens around me, as if by holding me close enough he could prevent whatever is about to happen.

Part of me, looking at Miles, still says: *this is my brother.* That there is a line he won't cross, that we're not in real danger. But I feel my heart pounding and I know I have to listen to it. Nathaniel and I both exhale, waiting for Miles to speak. He notices this, I think, and it pleases him. He looks to the side of the hallway, into the living room. We follow him in, and I'm limping a bit because of my knee, one hand on Nathaniel's shoulder. I start to sit by Nathaniel but Miles waves me to sit at his side.

"You want some water or anything?" Nathaniel asks, an arm gesturing toward the kitchen door as if he's reaching for it.

"Nice," Miles laughs softly. "Nice try." His voice lowers. "Sit down."

There's a second or two of silence; Miles stretches, leaning back on the cushions next to me. I wonder if I should speak, and then decide against it. Miles looks at my face. "What, you wanted to say something?"

I stammer and he jumps in again: "Huh? Speak up. I feel like you have something to say to me." His voice is drawling, rhythmic.

"I'm sorry I took your car."

"Shoot, I don't care about that." He laughs. "Whatever belongs to me belongs to you. I've always given you whatever I could."

He seems so calm, so earnest. *This is the charm*, I think. *The charm and then the storm.*

"So—really, that was it?"

He looks at me as if we share an inside joke, a brightness so contagious I have to stop myself from smiling, though I don't even know what he's getting at. "Dora, come on. They're all sleeping pretty deep right now. I heard the car going down the drive and I wondered, why is nobody checking on her? I looked around. Checked for you in every room. Thought you might have tried to use Beckett to get out. Like you did before."

"I didn't." I stare at him coldly. "He offered me help."

Miles is laughing now, his energy building. He proceeds as if he hasn't heard me. "In each and every bedroom I checked I found everyone out cold. You drugged them stupid, didn't you? And poor Sawyer. I didn't like him much, but when his boss finds out—you've made some trouble for me, that's undeniable." He lets out a bark of laughter and his hand twists his long hair away from his eyes. In a flash, Miles leans forward and backhands me across the mouth.

I lean back, my face buzzing, pain bright in my mouth. I'm disoriented, but my senses serve me well. I see it: a flash of metal in the inside pocket of the jacket he wears. Nathaniel rises to his feet.

"Nathaniel, sit down now." I swallow the rush of pain and make my voice strong and certain, the syllables spaced with meaning. His eyes catch mine and I think he knows what I'm telling him. His mouth is a thin, tight line as he sinks back into the chair, fingers gripping the armrests. I blink and raise my eyes to look at my brother.

I always hit them on the mouth, he said once. *You do it right, it'll bleed like a nose hit, but they can still look at you.* The words come back to me now. Miles shakes his head with annoyance and looks to Nathaniel.

"Stole my car, drugged all my friends. When Sawyer's bosses find out what happened to him, they'll want someone to pay for it. She threw a rattlesnake at him, man. You had no idea what landed in your house, did you? This girl's a better thief, a better sneak, than anything you'd imagine. Better than I imagined, and I thought I knew her." He pulls my hand away from my mouth and looks me in the face. There's red on my fingers. "And I thought she was different now. Guess I was wrong: some things never change." He draws back a hand and I start. Miles isn't looking at me, though. He's looking at Nathaniel. Taunting him. *Don't hurt him,* I'm thinking, naming every deity I know and some I don't. Names from books, echoed lines of prayers, all sound like strangers. I think only of the lady in the window and offer her a silent plea. *Please, don't hurt him.* I thought I was afraid before. I can see, now, why people have to cut their fear loose in times like this. Because it will paralyze you. Miles is still talking. "She'll turn on you when you least expect it. You'll realize she was never there for you at all. Just wanted what you could offer her. In your case, a place to hide." Nathaniel doesn't believe him, I know, but it stings nonetheless. "She's always been that way. Even when she was a little kid. Dora, you wanna tell him, or should I?" I shake my head to decline. I can't find the words.

"When she was just six, she called me. Said there was something wrong, something dangerous, about her new home. I came to get her."

"You didn't need to burn the house down," I whisper. He hits me again, knuckles glancing off my cheekbone.

"You probably locked that girl in the closet and left her on purpose," he snarls. "You knew I'd light the house on fire. It was hardly the first time. What happened to her was your fault. You were a liar at six."

"Yeah," I whisper, but I'm watching Nathaniel and not my brother. "It was my fault."

"Do you know what it was like? Getting arrested at twelve years old? Can you imagine that?"

"I'm sorry, Miles," I say. "I could have lied for you. I didn't. What you did was to help me. Every time."

Miles looks at me with tears in his eyes. "You got to go to school, learn to swim. Went to college. And you visited me every so often, like hearing how well you were doing was going to make everything better."

"You're my brother," I whisper, sensing weakness. "I've always wanted to help you. I didn't know how."

"You never told him the first thing about yourself, did you?" I realize that Miles is jealous, somehow, that what Nathaniel sees matters to him.

"He's right," I say, holding Nathaniel's gaze. "That was one of the first memories that came back to me. I hid it from you." When I talk, I can taste blood on my lip. "I didn't want you to know that I messed up my brother's life. I'm sorry—I lied to you." I hear the tremble in my voice. Nathaniel leans over, wraps his hands around mine.

"Sophie," Nathaniel says, shaking his head gently. "It's okay— you were a child." Miles grabs my wrist away from him and hits my hand against the sofa.

"She's not your Sophie, man. That person's not even real." With his other hand, he takes the gun out of his jacket and rests it on his knee. Nathaniel watches with a mechanical expression.

Suddenly, there's a flicker in his eye, and I see his expression take on a look of dread like I've never seen before.

"Dad? I can't sleep."

"Stay in bed, okay, buddy?" Nathaniel's eyes go wide and blank. I hear footsteps on the stairs.

"Dove Girl, you came back." Lincoln's dressed in pajamas, his shaggy brown hair in his eyes. I cover my bleeding lip with one hand as Lincoln looks around the corner of the landing from the bottom stair. "Dad? What's going on?"

CHAPTER FIFTY-THREE

"Hey, kid," Nathaniel says. I have some small idea of the amount of control this takes, to make his voice sound as if everything is okay. "Go on up. I'll be there to tuck you in real soon."

"No, no," Miles says. "Come sit down."

"Hi," Lincoln says, his voice drawing out into a question. "Who are you?"

"I'm Miles," he says, with a grin, then turns to Nathaniel. "You've got to let them sit up late every once in a while, let them live a little. Maybe not as much as I did at his age." He laughs. I'm trying not to move, but my head is shaking with denial. My brother is gone. This isn't him. Lincoln looks at me and rubs his eyes with one small hand.

"Dad," he says, stepping into the room, halfway between Miles and Nathaniel. "I couldn't sleep. I tried to call Mom but she didn't answer."

"You can always come to me when you can't sleep, kiddo."

"Yeah, but you told me just now to stay upstairs." Lincoln frowns. Nathaniel bites on his lip, hard. I can see the strain in his eyebrows. "I was scared. Look." He reaches into the pocket of his flannel pajama pants. "I got your phone. Mom called back but I missed it. Here." He holds his hand out, trying to give the phone to his father. I see his little hand hovering over the green dial button.

"Hey, little man, give me that." Miles snaps his fingers quickly to get Lincoln's attention. Lincoln turns to face Miles, who has the gun still resting on his knee. Lincoln shakes his head, then reaches to give the phone to his dad. "Do not press that button, kid," Miles hisses. He fumbles for the gun and I see his finger on the trigger.

I throw myself across Miles' chest, wrapping both my arms around him in an embrace. My body covers his arms and the gun and I hug him tight against me, bracing for an impact that doesn't come.

"I'm so sorry, Miles. I'm sorry. Thank you for finding me." I feel the anger in his shoulders ease, somehow. "I'm sorry I didn't think it through. Thank you so much for coming after me." His hand rests on my back. "I know I can't make it up to you, but you're my big brother. Please." I lean my forehead against Miles' chest, tuck my chin down. From the corner of my eye I can see Nathaniel pull Lincoln into his arms, then behind him.

"You called Mom, buddy?" he whispers.

"Yeah. She didn't answer. Maybe she'll call back."

His eyes land on mine. I exhale slowly. This is the only way. I think he knows it.

"Miles, please," I whisper again. "Please, just get me out of here."

"You don't deserve to come back with me."

"I know." My voice is thick with tears, but not for my brother.

Miles sighs and finally returns my hug. He holds me at arm's length, with his strong hands on my shoulders. He looks at my eyes, and then nods his head. "Let's go." Holding the gun, he waves it at me in a gesture that means *stand up*. I get to my feet, carefully staying in between him and Nathaniel, so close to Miles that the barrel is almost against my face. Miles reaches an open hand out and I see Nathaniel place the phone in his palm. Miles puts it in the pocket inside his jacket. "You want to say anything to these two, say it now."

I start to turn, to face him, and Miles shakes his head, a hand on my chin. Staring past him into the wall, I begin to speak in a low voice. "Lincoln, stay cool, okay? Say hi to Roxy for me."

I pause and draw a breath. I will him to hear me, to remember. "Nathaniel…" The things I want to say to him, the time I want to share with him, could go on forever. It hits me suddenly that I'm not going to see him again.

"Make it quick," my brother says.

"You have to forgive yourself for the past. You're a good man. Anyone would be lucky to know you. I know I was."

Miles takes me by the elbow and we walk outside.

CHAPTER FIFTY-FOUR

Miles walks me across the gardens, and he offers his arm when he sees I'm stumbling. I don't take it, doing the best I can to manage on my own. I know better than to try to get away, but as we walk across the footbridge, there's part of me that imagines jumping in. Miles drops Nathaniel's phone into the water.

Following my brother across the grounds, I pray Nathaniel knows better than to try to follow us. Miles is looking for any excuse now to start firing. But Nathaniel knows that, I think. If my brother, my own flesh and blood, would do this, there's nothing else he can take away from me. I look over my shoulder, hoping to take a last glance at Zenaida Atwood, that she'll offer me some parting words. I grit my teeth and make a promise to myself: that I may be leaving, but I'll haunt this place forever. Maybe I'll finally get to ask her what that letter meant. But in the dark, it's nearly impossible to see the figure in the glass. Instead of the voice I've come to know, only my own thoughts echo in my mind: *My own flesh and blood. Nothing else to take away.* Another riddle, when I was hoping for solace.

The gate is locked, and I see Miles must have climbed over the same tree I once did to get in.

"Go on," he says.

"My knee."

"Go," he repeats. I make a show of doing the best I can to scramble up the wall, reaching an arm toward the branch, but fall down twice before he finally lifts me in his arms so I can reach the tree branch. Once we're both outside the wall, he turns his back to me as he opens the door of the car. My hands close tight, fingernails digging into my palms. Miles clicks his tongue, shaking his head at me.

"Sorry about your mouth," he says. I notice that it's still bleeding. "I needed you to hear me. You get lost in things, sometimes. I'm the one who cares about you, here."

"I know," I answer. "It's okay."

"Come on." He indicates the passenger seat and I sit down. Miles closes the door behind me, then goes to the driver's side and sits down. "You know I can't let you go again."

"I know," I repeat. Miles and I exchange a look. He's searching my eyes for something, resistance, I guess, which he doesn't find. I'm looking through him. The person I know, the person I thought I knew, is no longer there. All I have to do is get him away from here. *Nothing else to take away.* Maybe it wasn't an empty riddle. I realize that I have nothing else to lose.

He starts the car and peels out onto the road. I watch silently out the window, hoping to see sirens behind us, somehow knowing that I won't. We round a sharp curve and I grip the seat tightly. These roads are perilous enough in broad daylight.

"Why'd you do it?" He sounds wounded. "Why couldn't you just stay?"

"Miles, my life has always been about you," I answer. "Even when I couldn't find you—especially then. Maybe I'd like to make my own choices, for once."

"Since when?" His eyes cut over to mine. "You didn't hit your head that hard."

We're getting close to Miles' camp. I've faced my own death before. At this point, I'm not sure it even shocks me. But the knowledge of losing Nathaniel and, worse, that I put Lincoln in danger, that I leave him with a loss, strikes at me hard. I cry into my hands, then silence myself, not wanting to make Miles angrier. It's dark, but I can sense the shape of the road. I know where we're going.

"What is it now?" he asks. "Why aren't you happy? I want you to be happy."

My eyes water. "I love him."

"He doesn't love you," Miles answers. "Anyways, he wouldn't for very long."

It occurs to me now that love isn't words. Professions of love shouldn't be a balance for your actions, or in spite of them, and I don't know whether this is something I'm remembering, or if I've finally learned it.

"How do you know that?" I demand.

"Because you're a liar," he says. "You lied to me. You ruined my life."

"No, I'm not," I say, almost as if we're normal siblings having an argument. "You are—you lied to me." I point at my lip, gesture to my head. "You said you'd never hurt me."

In the near dark, his eyes are flashing, the pale blue of light on a blade, and I can see that he wants to hit me again. But he has one hand on the steering wheel, the other one on the gun, and I guess he doesn't want to let either go. I slouch against the door and turn my glare toward the darkness around us.

"Dora?" His voice is calmer now. "Come on, don't stay mad." When I don't answer, he falls silent. By dark, the twists and turns of the narrow road are hypnotizing. I want my brother back, the one who would surprise me with a present or a visit when I needed it most. I remember the pink coat he gave me when I was twelve. Back then, I clung to every word he spoke. *Now, listen. You're strong, okay? But you're little. If you're going to hit someone, it's not going to be for fun, and you need to move fast.* Every time the road curves around the mountainside, it's as if time doubles back and I blink to find I'm still here, still in this impossible reality. I breathe in, count to four; out, count to four.

Miles is talking again now, his tone almost apologetic. "We've both made some mistakes. We're together—that's what matters. Right?" Though he jostles my shoulder gently, I make no move to respond. "Oh—sorry. Didn't realize you were sleeping." But I'm wide awake. *Go for the nose, as fast and hard as you can. Even if you don't break it, he'll see stars, and it'll hurt like hell. Gives you a second to take the next move. Go.*

To my left, Miles relaxes into a yawn. I pull back my arm, curl my hand into a fist, and hit his nose as hard as I can. In the second that follows, the tires screeching around a curve, I hold tight to the handle by the window and pull the emergency brake.

CHAPTER FIFTY-FIVE

The brakes lock and the rear tires swing wildly, sending us into a skid. With a double impact, the car hits the embankment, then jackknifes to the other side, coming to rest at a right angle across the road. Something hurts, but I know I don't have time to waste, and thankfully, my body doesn't protest as I climb out the door and keep moving, the sound of the car hissing and spitting behind me and Miles swearing.

The night is black. Earlier, when I needed cover, this was an ally. Now, I need to be able to see to get away. I run blindly until I'm out of breath, and the thorns and scratches are my helpers, keeping me awake and letting me know which way not to walk. The forest is dense, beautiful, but up ahead I see a darker denseness and remember what they called the laurel hells, those wide tangles of rhododendron, thickets you could get lost in for days. There's no walking through it upright. No walking through it at all in the dark. I scramble up the embankment and into its dark branches. I can hear the crashing of dried leaves and brush around me, but bank on the hope that, for now, Miles is distracted enough by the noise of the wrecked car. When I hear quiet from the direction of the road, I sink to my hands and knees, crawling as quietly as I can. My hands reach out in front of me using branches to pull over or under, trying to find my way. My forehead hits a branch and everything spins with pain.

When I open my eyes, the dark seems diluted. My eyes have adjusted to the night. There must be a moon, somewhere, underneath these clouds. Then I hear him.

"Dora?" A voice not distant, but not close. "Dora, where are you?" I don't move.

"You know I'm gonna find you," he yells, his voice tinged with an almost friendly brotherly annoyance. "Don't make this hard." The sound draws closer and I see that he has a lighter, keeps snapping it in front of his face, giving him an advantage. I duck, but my hair tangles in the leaves, and I hear the bush above me rustle. *Shit.* I hold my breath and sit as still as I can, trying to find balance. I hear the brush rustling nearby and hope it's an animal. I slip forward, reach out to catch myself with my arms, and find both my wrists in a viselike grip.

I pull on my arms, but there's no space behind me, nowhere to pull to. I wrench my elbows weakly, slip one arm loose.

"Stop it already, Dora!"

"You stop it!"

I slap at him with my free hand then shove my weight to my feet and try to turn. Miles grasps my hand again, at the same time I stand up and crash full force into a branch with my shoulder. I can almost feel the bones straining in the socket and I sink back down. My brother laces an arm around my shoulders and sits down, holding me tight so that I'm leaning against him.

"Now would you finally shut up?" he says. "I've got a headache. Can we just relax?" I hold my breath and lurch forward, then feel the barrel of the gun against the back of my neck. "You do not give up, do you? I didn't know that about you."

I begin to feel the impact of the car stopping. All the discomfort I've tuned out rushes into focus. I feel the crack in my lip and the grain of dried blood.

"Dora," Miles breathes, his voice a bit softer. "What am I gonna do? We can't go back. I can't bring you back there again. Nobody would look at me the same."

"They already don't."

"All the more reason," he answers, as if we're having a regular conversation. "And I can't go anywhere else. I'll just wind up in jail."

"They could help," I say. "If you tell the truth. I can still help you. Get you a good lawyer." I feel the gun pressing into my skin and fall silent.

"I'm never going in again." He's dead serious. "You can't imagine what it's like." Maybe he's right. Maybe I can't understand.

"How did this happen? How did I let you down this badly?"

"You didn't," Miles says. "You're the only person who was mine. Even when we were little, it was like—you were the only good thing in the world. If I could protect you, that was all that mattered. When you had nice things, a safe place to stay, it was like it was okay that I didn't have them. But then, you started doing things on your own." Though his tone turns conversational, his grip on me stays tight. "All I knew was for us to be a team. I would have done anything to take care of you."

"But this is on a completely different scale."

"Not really," he says. "Once things started happening, they had their own momentum."

"I wish I could go back and change it," I say. "If I hadn't called you that day—"

"No," he says, shaking his head, no venom or muscle in his tone. "You did the right thing, Dora."

"But you said—"

"You were six years old," he says, then repeats: "Six. Of course it was not your fault. Can't you see that's goddamn crazy? Look at me, okay?" Though we're sitting in the dark, I try to comply, turning around a little so I can face him, though he doesn't let me move much. "It wasn't your fault that girl died. Say it." I start, then find myself crying again. After a couple tries, I manage it.

"It wasn't my fault."

"The whole thing," Miles says. "I want to know you believe it, before—"

"It wasn't my fault the little girl died." I'm leaning against his shoulder now. Trying to understand why it has to be like this: why does Miles have to love me, too? How am I supposed to understand this? "Before what?" I ask, suddenly combing over his last sentence. "Why now? Why tell me that now?"

Oh. My breath catches. He doesn't answer.

"I can't bring you back there with me," he says. "I can't have you running around again. It was only my good luck you didn't remember anything this last time. Dora, there's too much on the line, for—"

"You don't want to lose the people you have around you. I know—you're like me, a little," I tell him. "You don't want to be alone. Miles, I can help you."

"No, you can't!" he says. "Stop saying that."

"Well—well then—" I'm stammering, grasping for anything I can think to say. "I'll go away. Just let me go. I'll walk as far as I can. Hitchhike—go to a different town."

"Now you're lying," Miles laughs. "If I leave you here, you're walking back to the road and going to him. Ten out of ten chance. You're going to the police, coming up here and ruining everything for me, because you think you can help somehow."

"You don't know that," I plead, though I know he's right.

"I do," he says. "Because you don't give up on people. If you did, we wouldn't be here."

"Well—then—just wait," I say, beginning to cry, feeling cold all over. "You don't have to right now. We can sit here for a while, can't we?"

"You'll have to be still," he says. "So I can make sure it doesn't hurt."

"Doesn't hurt? Miles—"

He sighs, hard. "Don't make me say it. This is the only thing I can do."

"It's not too late."

"Yes, it is, Dora."

"Stop," I cry. Having nothing to lose, my hands fumble in the dark, pushing at anything I can find, closing my hand around his on the gun. I twist over, trying to get distance between us, and he grabs me again, his arm across my midsection.

I hear the shot, then silence ringing.

CHAPTER FIFTY-SIX

It's so loud. Just the echo of the noise makes me feel we're under-water. I close my eyes and imagine myself swimming toward the surface. I think of Nathaniel and feel an inkling of gratefulness: that I met him, that I knew him, that I got Miles away from him and his little boy. Is it true, that I'll get to see my entire life before I die? In my mind, I'm craning, trying to look into the dark, just hoping I can see him there. But there's nothing. No voice. Nothing flashes before my eyes.

I'm still here. And when I look up, I see the clouds are clearing, a distant half-moon scattering paltry gray light through the dense leaf cover. My ribs are on fire and there's blood soaking this stupid dress Iris put on me. I twist my neck to look down, wondering why I can still see. I guess I always wondered what it would be like to be shot. I thought it would feel cold. Not like this, not searing, spreading pain, like the mother of all scraped knees, but right on my side.

Scraped knees. I can't see, so, whimpering with pain, I reach down and feel with my fingertips. I touch the torn fabric of the dress, press my fingers around the edges of the wound. Blood slips between my fingers, but it feels like a surface wound. I press on my ribs, and I can't tell, but I don't think anything beneath the surface is seriously damaged. But the pain from my side reaches into my arms, and every breath and movement hurts. I draw a breath, deep and hard as I can, then let it out in a ragged whimper, nauseous with pain. It takes everything I have to stay awake. My nerves are ringing, my pulse rushing. Some time passes. I don't know how much. I wait to pass out. For some more serious injury to become apparent. I can't remember what I was supposed to do. Where I was trying to go. Still, I know there was something. I didn't want to stay here. I draw a painful breath and try to move, but fall backward again.

Something soft catches my weight. Miles. I feel more blood, warm on my back, lots of it. I turn to face him and he's staring at me, eyes wide with surprise, glinting in the moonlight.

"Miles, what happened?" My voice is ragged, a hoarse whisper. I touch his cheek with my good hand. I don't need to wait for his answer. A dark spot is growing on the T-shirt under his jacket, seeping through the denim.

He coughs, staring into my eyes. Fingers shaking, I reach for the gun, pull it from his fingers, and throw it into the brush, away from us. I turn back to my brother, shuffling closer so that I'm next to him. I look at his back, lift the jacket up, find his lighter in the pocket. When I light it, I can see a wide stain growing on the back of his lower ribcage, the color of engine oil in the dark. I reach to touch him, put a hand on the wound. Blood pulses out between my fingers.

"Give me your jacket," I say. "We need to tie something over it." I tug on his sleeve.

Miles shakes his head, gritting his teeth. "Not going to help," he says.

"It will," I insist. "Come on. Miles, please. Tie it up. We'll get back to the car. Do you have a phone?"

He shakes his head. "No."

"No what?"

"No phone." He exhales sharply, unevenly. "That car's going nowhere. Just no. Give up, Dora."

"I'll walk. I can do it."

"Sit." He raises his voice, and I can tell how much it hurts him. "You're bleeding. You'll hurt yourself worse if you don't sit still."

But I know, if I can get him to a hospital, and quickly, if he makes it, he'll have to get help. I can visit him every day. I'll take care of him, be the dependable, focused sister he should have had. "We can do it," I announce, realizing as if from far away how naive I sound. "I'll—I'll help you get to the road." I try to stand up in the dark, feeling my way around branches, swearing with pain and exhaustion at every step until, not two yards off, I fall. "You had to throw Nathaniel's phone away!" I can't mention his name without weeping again. "That's the one thing that could have helped us!"

"I don't want help, Dora."

"What about me? What if I don't want to watch you die out here?" I yell. I realize he'd already considered that. My vote didn't count, at least not enough. I'm crying as I speak, watching the bloodstain spread on his clothes. Miles has always been a hero to me, and I think it's in this moment I realize for the first time that he's also human. I sink down next to Miles and snuggle under his arm. He's groaning a little bit with each breath, and, within a few minutes, when I snap the lighter, I see blood around his mouth when he coughs.

"It's okay," he says.

"No."

"No what?" He leans his head against mine.

"It's not okay," I say. "None of it's okay."

"This is the best way it could have happened," he says. "Wish I'd thought of it myself. I'd have done it cleaner. Don't—" He swears, his voice thick with pain. "Don't you see? I can't come back from this. I don't want to go back into the mess I've made. I don't want to live, having hurt you. I would have," he coughs again. "But I'm glad I won't. The only good part of me would have been gone."

I would have, he said. He can't stop himself, I realize. He really can't. To him, this is like breathing.

"I didn't mean to make it worse for you," I whisper. I can feel blood in different stages of drying, on my side, on my back.

"You didn't," he said. "You were the only person who always loved me." His voice catches and I can almost feel his pain just to look at him.

"Don't you have anything to help?"

"What?" he says, practically biting the air off as he speaks.

"Something for your pain," I ask. He shakes his head and I'm swearing again, squeezing my arms around my ribs, though they hurt just as much. "You, of all people, don't have anything for your pain. Damn it, Miles."

If he dies now, nobody will ever know the good Miles, the kind, funny brother, the one that I know. The scattered moonlight seems only to make the night feel colder; I'd almost prefer that I couldn't see at all. My legs go numb from sitting still. Miles' breath sounds wet in his lungs and I reach up to hold a hand against his clammy cheek. My hands and arms shake, and then I realize I'm trembling all over, and it must be making him hurt worse.

"You're shaking."

"No." My teeth chatter. "It's warm. It's summer."

"Shock," he says. "Take my jacket."

"No," I repeat, harder, my eyes burning.

"Dora, it's not going to do me any good. You've got to keep yourself together until dawn. This road isn't so deserted that they won't find you. It happened once before, right?"

Miles tries to remove his jacket, but gasps with pain.

"Stop," I whisper. "Fine: you win. I'll put it on. Just be still." I pull the jacket from his arms and slip it over my shoulders. This seems to wear him out, and he doesn't talk for a few minutes. I'm afraid he's gone. I feel myself slipping into numbness, too. I want to go with him. Miles whispers, coughs, then forces a couple words out.

"Are you there, Dora?"

I barely recognize his voice. The layers in his tone, of knowing, of teasing, of making you wonder what he really meant, all are gone. He sounds young.

"Yes, I'm here."

"I'm scared."

"I know." I reach in the dark and find his hands. He draws a dreadful, shaking breath. "You're loved," I whisper. "You're so loved."

I'd say it even if it weren't true. It is true, though. I'm not sure what that says about me. Evidently, this ability to love my brother unconditionally turned out to be a fatal flaw.

"You remember Mom?" he asks.

"A little bit."

I want him to stop talking so it will hurt less, but I don't want him to be gone from me. "You know she loved you, right?"

"You said she left me to cry."

"She loved you," he says. "Dad was never there. He left her alone with two babies and an addiction. She didn't have a shot, but she loved us."

"How do you know?"

"I was there," he says. "I was old enough to remember."

I feel this wash over my numbness, tuck it away for later. For now, I turn to Miles. He slips away for longer, now, minutes at a time. We huddle together like two children, and the night seems to hold off the sunrise forever, indifferent to our attempts at bravery. I talk, though, in spells, sometimes to him, sometimes to distract me from the pain in my side. I tell him about our family.

Mom, first. Mom and her colored pencils. Mom's hands on my small hands. The smell of her hair and the softness of her body.

I tell Miles that I've seen, with my own eyes, a mother and father who would give everything they had for their little boy, that their love makes up his whole world. That I dared to hope I could fit into that world. That I think I almost made it.

Mostly, though, what I know about family is Miles. My magical, sometimes-there big brother, who was always brave and funny, even when he scared me, who made it so that I had a chance at a solid life when nobody else cared about me. That's the one here with me now, and the one I'd like to remember.

I tell it all to him, like it's a bedtime story, and when I've told him everything I remember, he's asleep.

CHAPTER FIFTY-SEVEN

I wake to dove song and wish I could cover my ears. I don't want to hear anything. Dawn is coming, and I can sense it hasn't been more than a few hours; the blood on my dress is still damp. I slouch, trying to snuggle closer to Miles. I've always loved the dawn. Early mornings. To wake up just before the sunrise and meet the day with it. Now I wish I could block it out, along with the doves that won't stop singing. Mourning doves, named for the sorrowful tone of their call. The rising and falling note, the final note echoed.

I remember sitting at Zenaida Atwood's desk, wondering what a young woman could find so desolate in a summer dawn that she wanted to walk away and disappear into it, to let the woods swallow her whole. *I leave in your care my only possession: a century's worth of sorrow, condensed into twenty-six short years. I am but a wraith, a muse who has outlived her purpose.* And, letting myself sink back into weariness, I realize I understand her now. This depth of numbness, of solitude that seems to go out as far as I can see. The wilderness of the forest, all the numerous ways it can make you disappear, couldn't hold a candle to this life-sucking dark, all somehow contained within my own chest. Miles has always been my purpose. Last night, before I wrecked his car, I'd told him there might be things I wanted, but that my life had always been about him. Now I can't even imagine what that kind of life might mean.

But the doves keep singing, soft coos calling down through the trees. Doves, and some other distant noise, are keeping me awake. I'd shout at them to shut up, but the air itself hurts in my throat, any motion in my ribs sending pain shooting through my body.

It's still dark here in the laurels, but through the waxy leaves I can see flashing blue lights, pulsating, almost nauseating.

I hear sirens first. I can't see much of anything, but bursts of distorted light disorient me. The crunch of heavy footsteps and voices. They're going in the wrong direction. I close my eyes and, once again, everything fades.

I wake later, in the light of dawn, to the beam of a flashlight scattering through the leaves, sending shards of light falling around me. Still clinging to Miles, I breathe out a swear word, my voice rasping noiselessly.

"Something's up there," a voice shouts. The crashing noise of footsteps draws closer. I try to ignore the words, but I hear that there's at least a couple people, that their bodies form a web around me, that they're getting closer.

They're shouting my name, mine and my brother's. Several yards off one of them stops and shines a light directly at us. I hear bits of conversation. Someone's wanted for involvement in two murders. They've just learned he's in the area. Probably accomplices. Maybe that's me.

"Dora Bailey, hands where I can see them!"

It doesn't occur to me to wonder how they know my name. I hold my eyes shut, my body slack, as the light lingers on my face. I can hear more sirens, more voices. Tires screaming to a halt.

"Miles Bailey, we have you surrounded."

Another voice, off to the side, yells at me, too, to put my hands up. I squeeze my brother close to me and hope that if any shots are fired they hit me instead. I'm overwhelmed, now, trying to keep count of how many voices there are, how many footfalls in dry leaves, how many cars I've heard, how many commands.

"Catch me up. What do we have?" Footfalls and a commanding, female voice. "What's going on?"

"Two suspects, ten o'clock. Neither of them responding."

"You sure they're conscious?" the woman asks.

"He saw movement."

"First of all, the woman's not a suspect. Weapons down." There's an exasperated sigh.

"Coffee?"

"No. And put the coffee down. Tell me you don't have one hand on your weapon and the other holding a cup of coffee. Go back to the car or give me your badge."

I recognize the voice now, crack an eye open to see Selena. She turns her eyes in my direction, searching, scanning. Her strength draws my eyes like a moth.

"No," she says, her voice changing tone, turning away from me. "Absolutely not. I let you come along, the deal was you stay in the car." I tune out again, let my limbs go as slack as I can, but my body is stiff as the branches around me. There's a bit of a commotion and I hear Selena's voice rising again. I've seen Selena in action before, but she's in her element now. She is so formidable that I forget how pretty she is, because it's irrelevant. She seems cut from marble that moves without losing any of its solidity, aware of every branch that moves, every breath drawn around her.

"Back in the car," she clips. "You said he was armed. Sit—"

"Selena. Let me go." Nathaniel's calm voice belies the laser focus I recognize in his tone. There are footsteps, again, and I hear Selena yell at the other policemen to lower their guns. Nathaniel walks with ease through the brambles and vines, up to the edge of the thicket. It seems to let him pass. *You don't fight a thicket like this,* he had said. *You follow it in.* I see that Selena's a few yards back, no doubt waiting for Miles to pull a gun. Nathaniel ducks under the arm of a rhododendron and steps over another branch that reaches low across the ground. I hear his ragged breath, the noise of his knees as he sinks to the ground.

He's close enough to touch Miles, whose arm slips off my shoulders, his weight falling slack against the dry leaves beneath us. Nathaniel turns back to Selena, shaking his head.

I remember, suddenly, when we stood in the waves on the beach, the light creeping toward evening. How the water felt warm, welcoming, the air above it breezy and cold. We had walked out together, arms clasped, nothing but question marks between us. Somehow, though, between the two of us, we had enough. In that moment, I felt brave. Now I wish I could slip back into that water, salty and heavy and deceptively warm. It seems sweet, like poppies, deep as the woods. But then I hear Nathaniel's voice in a tenor I've never heard before. His hands a light touch, scanning over my shoulders, my back. Finally, he sinks onto his heels, takes my wrist in his hands, thumb pressing to look for a pulse. After a moment he sighs, presses his lips to my palm, ducks his chin to rest his face in my hand. I think I feel a tear on my palm. "Wake up," he whispers, pleading. "Tell me you're okay." I stretch my fingers, turn his cheek to face me.

"Y-yes." When I try to speak, I cough instead, then press my tongue against my swollen lip. I feel like my throat's full of gravel, making it impossible to speak, so I find his hand and hold on tight, feel its familiar calluses and warmth. I hear his breath of relief, see the spark come back to his eyes as he presses my hand in his. "Alright," he says. "Alright, we're getting you out of here." I reach for my brother.

"Dora," Nathaniel whispers. "He's gone. It's over."

"No." I move, now, shaking my head hard from side to side. Every muscle screams. Negotiating with the branches of the laurel hell around us, he angles his arm around my back and helps me sit up. I want to speak, to say I can't, but my voice has fled again. "You can," he says, as if he knows what I'm thinking. "One foot, and then the other, alright?" Though he doesn't spell it out, there's a yes or no question here. A choice is something that I can understand.

The movement it takes to get out of the thicket and to my feet brings tears to my eyes. It hurts even to be awake. When I crawl out into the light, I see the dawn is breaking, the sky violet and pink. I make it a few steps, his arm under my shoulders, before I hesitate, and, without waiting, he lifts me up in both arms, so that my head rests against his chest. We make our way back to where the police cars and ambulance are waiting. She gives Nathaniel a look, which breaks soon into relief.

"Welcome back, Dora," she says. She turns and, with a wave of her hand, summons a group of paramedics who wait nearby. Nathaniel hands me over, and I stand on my own for a few moments before I collapse into someone's arms. I'm reclined on a stretcher, a set of gloved hands examining my side, another looking close into my eyes, asking me to follow a little light. I feel a sense of relief, followed closely by dismay. I've dropped Miles' jacket.

"Get the jacket," I say. "Please." But I'm mumbling, barely forming the syllables. Nathaniel gives the medics space enough to work, arms crossed. I can see the tension in his shoulders, in the set of his jaw.

"How's she look?" he asks.

"She's going to be fine," one of them calls back. "Most of the blood isn't hers." I try to lean up on my elbows, looking for Miles, then remember. I try to speak, to tell someone I need the jacket.

"It's okay," one of the medics says. "You're safe now."

They're getting ready to lift the stretcher into the ambulance. I'm tired, so tired, but I'm afraid to close my eyes. Someone needs to be here who knows my brother for who he is. I can't leave him with people who only know him as a criminal. I don't feel anything, but my eyes begin to water. I choke out a breath and feel the world around me start to blur.

"Let him go with you," Selena says to one of the medics. She watches Nathaniel walk away from her. "I'll see you later, okay? Take care."

One of the medics nods and waves Nathaniel over. He climbs into the back of the ambulance and sits next to me. Someone's clipping monitors to my arm, placing an oxygen mask over my face. Pulling aside the torn fabric on my side and pressing something cool to the injury there. The pain I feel everywhere begins to fade into sleepiness. I turn my face to make sure he's still here.

"Hey," I whisper. I tug the oxygen mask off and hold it. The medic watches me uneasily, checking the monitor.

"Hey."

I look at him for a moment, then the medic places the mask back over my face. Something between us is different. Finally, for the first time, we can just sit together. There isn't anything between us that needs to be said. I close my eyes and find deep, dreamless sleep waiting for me.

CHAPTER FIFTY-EIGHT

I open my eyes to a hospital room. I know the feel of it, the smell. The noises of machines, the white walls. I blink once, and then again, and a surge of fear rises. Not this. Not again.

And then, like a tide rushing back in, I remember everything.

On the whiteboard on the wall, someone's written my name, Dora Bailey, and drawn cutesy little flowers and birds around it in dry-erase marker. I remember that one dove means peace, two, love. I'm cataloguing of the rest of it—my scratches, bruises, the patch of a bandage on my side, when a nurse comes in. Her face lights up.

"Evening, Dora." She smiles, and I realize it's Anjali, the nurse who cared for me when I was here before. "I don't know if 'welcome back' is appropriate here, but I'm glad to see you."

"Thanks. You, too." I smile faintly with gratitude as she looks over my arms, checks everything that she needs to check. I've always savored the feeling of someone taking care of me, whether it's just for their work or not. "Quite a summer, wasn't it?"

She grins. "I heard some stories about you." I sigh, realizing that I don't want to go over it right now. "I—" I want to tell her, but my voice catches.

"Sweetie," she says, turning to see my face. I look at her and hold her gaze.

"My brother died." The truth is that I want to tell somebody. Practice saying it out loud.

"I'm so sorry."

"Thanks," I say. She lifts the dressing on my ribs and looks over it. I realize it hurts.

"Sorry," she whispers. "How's your pain level? Do you need anything? We have—"

"Tylenol?" I cut her off. She nods.

"Kitchen's closing in an hour. You might get hungry."

"All I want to do is sleep," I say, adding as an afterthought: "Maybe just in case, though. Hey, what day is it?"

"You came in early this morning. You remember that, right?" I remember a blur of doctors and hallways, faces and fluorescents.

"More or less."

"They put you under to stitch you up," she says, as if apologizing. I shrug. They probably needed to, the way my teeth were chattering.

"You slept for—" Anjali looks at the clock. "Until just now. Almost fourteen hours."

So it's still the same day. That explains why I'm still sapped, still weary. I think Anjali sees the question written on my face when I sit up in the bed, look at the door.

"He was here all day," she said. "He never left. Every time I came in to check on you, he reminded me to keep quiet. Said you needed rest." She must see that I'm trying to hold myself together, because she continues. "Until visiting hours ended at eight, and I had to kick him out. You understand, right?" I smile back at her gratefully.

"I understand."

There's a part of me that's glad to be alone, that there's nobody to stay awake for. I need some time to inventory the wounds the machines, my body, couldn't register. I'm more tired than I think I've ever been. But sleep isn't what I want.

"Can I get you anything else? Just the Tylenol?"

"Do you have anything I could draw on?" I ask. "Any scrap of paper and a pen would be great."

*

Anjali brings a branded pad of paper and a ballpoint pen. I draw until I'm relaxed enough to rest. I want to count each hour that Miles has been dead. I realize I don't know exactly when it happened. But I remember his face, every detail. I remember more about him, too, but I don't have to hold all of it right at this moment. I tell myself that it's okay to put some of it aside for now. Sometime after midnight, I close my eyes, then wake what feels like moments later to find it is past nine in the morning. I don't think anyone will mind if I unplug the IV, so I do, and walk to the bathroom. I take a disposable comb from the packet and try to neaten my hair. My lip's still swollen, and I think more of my body is bruised than isn't. But I feel brand new.

When I walk back to sit on my bed, the morning nurse is knocking at the door. I don't know him, but he seems kind. He goes over the basics, asks me if I need anything—another Tylenol, thank you—and, I add, some breakfast. He's about to leave when his pager goes off. "You have a visitor," he says. "Someone named Selena. If you're up for it?"

"Okay," I answer, bracing myself for something unpleasant. "She can come in."

Selena's in uniform. She knocks, waits for me to call her in, and then stands lingering in the doorway, looking down at her feet.

"Morning," I say, slightly hesitant.

"How are you, Dora?"

"Better. I'll be fine."

"Do we need to talk about—" I trail off. "You know, a report or anything?"

"No. Nothing major," she answers, with uncharacteristic softness. "It can all wait," she says, unusually nonchalant. "You just get better. Forensics was able to put everything together as far as the major events."

"Can you tell me what happened last night?" I ask. "After I left with Miles?"

"Yep." She takes a seat on the edge of a chair. "Nathaniel had told me you'd left. That he was worried. It was a couple days after that, while you were still missing, that I put everything together. We finally had a name for you. And your brother. Knew that he was involved in some really dangerous stuff."

"You did?" I ask. "How? What'd you find?"

"The blue house, Dora. I… I knew from your reaction that you'd seen it before."

"Am I that bad a liar?"

"Pretty bad," she answers, smiling. "Yeah, you are. So, I sent for more records, but it took days to get a response. There was a CPS worker who was arrested the following year for working with child traffickers at that address. And then I noticed that the kid who was arrested for arson afterward was named Miles. You didn't tell me much about that, but you were always clear about his name. So, I looked a bit more, and I found out he had a sister."

"He got me out," I answer, guilt souring my stomach. "There was one other kid there, that I know of. I don't think she made it. I remember—" Selena shakes her head to cut me off and I'm grateful for the commanding tone in her voice.

"Dora, what they did, they did. You didn't do it." I have a sudden recollection of Miles, an arm around my waist, gun at my head, with a voice all the world like a loving brother's, making me repeat after him that it wasn't my fault. I nod.

"Anyway, so: when I tried to call back, and couldn't get an answer? I knew something was wrong. Came out right away. It took a couple hours, but we found the car. What happened?"

"He was driving," I answer. "I hit him in the nose and pulled the brake." She nods with something like admiration.

"Anyway, from there, we spent the rest of the night looking for you. It got a little easier once the morning came."

"Right."

"Can I do anything else for you?"

"I want Miles' jacket," I say. "He gave it to me, when—anyway, it's really mine, now."

"I'm so sorry," Selena answers. "I haven't seen it. Might be with evidence. I'll see what I can do, but don't get your hopes up. I'll let you rest, okay? I just wanted to stop in and check on you." I motion for her to continue. Selena walks a little bit closer to me. "I'm sorry. I'm so sorry for bringing those photos out when I did. That was some spectacularly bad judgment, and it was mean-hearted. If I'd listened, or been more thoughtful—"

I find I don't want to dwell on it. "It's alright."

"Dora, what you did was incredibly brave. I'm really sorry I misjudged you."

"Don't worry about it."

"Anyway. Take care," she says, turning quickly out the door. "I'll be seeing you."

I lean back on the pillow, thank the nurse when he brings me the Tylenol. I poke at my breakfast, eating just enough that my stomach will tolerate the medicine. I roll over, wince and wiggle onto my back, and close my eyes.

My thoughts return to Zenaida's missive on an abandoned desk and the place where she etched her initials. *A century's worth of sadness*, was how she put it. Sadness like that is enough to make you chase anything, even if you know it's capable of killing you. It's too much to think about. I sit up, blotting at my eyes with the sheets. I don't have the energy to hold it in anymore. Trying to rest is only giving me more to think on.

"Ms. Bailey?" The nurse taps on the doorframe.

"Dora's fine." Unashamed, I sniff and sit up.

"Oh—I'm sorry. Are you sleeping?"

"No."

"You've got another visitor. I know, it's been a busy day. You want to rest?"

I shake my head. "No. It's not doing a lot of good, right now."

"I get it." He returns my nod, then looks down the hallway, waving. "Come on in. She's up."

Nathaniel walks in and pulls a chair close to the side of the bed. I can't help it: despite all my worries, the moment I see him, I forget that I'm crying, seeing the smile on his face. I realize that I'm smiling too.

I sit up and lean forward, wanting with everything I am to be closer to him. He squeezes my hands. A moment or two passes that way, then we both begin to speak at once.

"How are you?" I ask.

"How are you?"

"I'm okay." I realize that I'm doing it again, pasting a billboard over how I really feel. "I'm okay," I repeat, sounding a bit different this time.

"Sorry I wasn't here when you woke up," he says. "I hoped you'd get to sleep in. Figured you'd have visitors in the morning, then maybe rest some after."

"It was something like that."

"So, I brought you lunch." He indicates a lunchbox on the chair by the door. "Mac and cheese. My mother's. I can't cook like she does."

"Thank you." The idea of something homemade jogs my appetite a little. I ask him again: "How are you?"

He runs a hand through his hair and looks at me almost shyly. "Yeah," he says, his voice low and soft. "Not too bad." But I see the shadows under his eyes, the self-reproach. "When I first saw you, this morning, I was certain you were dead." He squeezes my hand in his and holds it to his lips. Again, as I did this morning, I flutter my fingers, trace his brow, turn his cheek to face me. I think again, what might have happened if I hadn't led Miles to his house. The horrible situation I put him in. "I'm sorry for—"

"Don't." He touches my hair, traces my cheek, then the cut on my lip. Leans forward, kisses me softly. "We're good."

I breathe out slowly. Look at him and see that he means it.

As if remembering suddenly, he goes to the bench by the door, returns with something in his hands. "I brought your book."

"Thanks." He places it in my hands, the tattered sketchbook. I squeeze his arms, not just his muscles, the warmth of his skin, but the realness of him, of something certain.

"You're cold," he says, arms around my back.

"Hospitals are always cold," I answer.

"Oh: that reminds me. I also have your brother's jacket."

"Thank you."

I put the book down and hold his hand in both of mine, pressing my thumbs against his palm, pulling close for another kiss. He rests his forehead against my hair and sighs. "Dora, what are we gonna do here?"

I don't answer him right away. The silence that follows fills me with foreboding. I don't want to let go of his hand. I squeeze it tighter. I hear a voice telling me: *it will heal better if you let it breathe.* My eyes fill with tears. Can I go back to that house, where I lived so long in fear? Can I stand to leave it? And how do I make a decision of any scale, without Miles to reference? I'm forgetting her command. *Let it breathe.* I remember, now, where I heard that first.

"Take a breath," he says. "Don't worry about that now. Everything will be fine." So I do, taking a breath in, decide to leave this hanging and change the subject. "How's Lincoln?"

"He's good." Nathaniel looks at me with a bit of hesitation, or maybe it's admiration. "My mother came to stay with him last night. Dora—" He looks into my eyes, then quickly away, and I can see he's thinking about it again. I reach for his hand. "He didn't have his glasses on. He didn't see that there was a gun. He didn't even know that you were hurt." There's a pause, then he looks at me again. "He knew something was wrong, obviously, but not that he was in any danger. I don't know how to thank you."

"We're good. Where is he today?"

He grins back. "He's here, if you'd like to say a quick hello. I asked my mother to wait with him outside, but—"

"No, no," I insist. "Please, can they come in?"

Lincoln whizzes into the room, tailed by a sturdy woman with kind brown eyes, who I see right away is Nathaniel's mother.

"Sophie!"

"It's Dora," Nathaniel says.

"Fine. It's Dove Girl," Lincoln shouts, zipping around the room. He has his glasses on now. "What happened to your face?"

"I—"

"And you've got stitches?" He walks right up and stares at my side. "Dad, did Dora get shot?"

"Lincoln!" Nathaniel's eyes widen. "How did you—"

"That man." Lincoln adjusts his glasses as his mouth settles into a scowl. "He was hurting your feelings. He made you lie. He made you say that you wanted to leave us, but I knew you didn't want to."

"Oh, Lincoln." I cover my eyes, hoping he won't see I'm crying again.

"I'm glad you came back," he adds.

"Me too," I answer. Lincoln shrugs his shoulders, unperturbed.

"Well? Did you get shot?"

"I, uh."

"That's way cool," he exclaims.

"It is *not*," Nathaniel whispers, mortified. I share a look with his mother, and, though we haven't been introduced yet, we're both trying to hold in a laugh. I remember that, nearsighted or no, children are more perceptive than we give them credit for. "How long are you going to be in here?" Lincoln asks. "Where are you going to live? Are you going to stay with my dad?"

"Oh, that's a lot of questions. I—" I pause. I haven't even had time to wonder where I'd go, when I leave here. The memory of sitting in a hospital bed, unsure where I'll go when I'm patched up, isn't a pleasant one.

"Questions she doesn't have to answer right now," Nathaniel says, smiling at his son. But in the quiet moment that follows, his eyes find mine, and I know there's a question here. I look away. When I try to picture a future, images of scars crowd my thoughts. Lincoln, meanwhile, stands up on the seat of a chair, takes the marker from the dry-erase board. He draws a circle under my name, gives it two dots for eyes and a curved line of a smile. Lincoln's grandmother draws closer to us.

"I'm Olive," she says. "Glad to meet you, under any circumstances."

"You, too." I don't have the energy to talk, so I reach out and hold her hand.

"Lincoln, honey," Olive says. "Can you come and sit down over here with me? Dora's been through a lot."

"Thanks for the food." I look over at her, smiling.

"Anytime, honey. Nathaniel, Lincoln told me after she cooked dinner for you two, she put the red stuff in the mac and cheese."

"Oh, what's that?"

"Paprika," Olive says. "I knew Dora was a big deal the minute I heard that."

He laughs, and I think he almost blushes. "Come on, Mom."

Time passes, almost without my noticing it, and the four of us are just talking. Sometimes, a few moments pass where we don't need to talk, instead sitting quietly together. Even though I've only known Nathaniel and his son for a few months, and his mother a few minutes, I feel it's taken me an awfully long time, maybe most of my life, to get to where I am right now. By early afternoon, I'm yawning again, and it's clear that Lincoln is getting fidgety from having to be contained in one room for so long. Lincoln gives me a big, wincing hug, one that leaves me with a smile nonetheless, and Olive pats my head and gives me a kiss on the cheek, before the two of them file out. I open my sketchbook again, flipping over my pictures.

"I'll come back and see you," Nathaniel says. "If you don't mind."

"I don't know how long they'll keep me here," I answer, my hand resting in his. "But look at this." I nod at the phone on the wall. "You can call me now. I'm moving up in the world, see?" He kisses my hand, then walks to the door.

"Get some rest, Dove Girl."

"Fine," I answer, smiling around a yawn.

CHAPTER FIFTY-NINE

From my window, I watch the sun setting over Hazel Bluff. It's a strange feeling to remember that I have a name. Probably a credit score, a college degree—and most of all, nobody following me. That I could go anywhere I'd like to. Beauty aside, this place has been the site of a nightmare for me. Part of me would love to walk away and never come back. When night has fallen, I watch the stoplights changing.

"Feeling any better?" Anjali asks.

"Yes," I answer. "Thanks." She unclips my IV line and types a bit on a computer. "Doc says you don't need this anymore. Plenty of bruises, but you're healthy. Those sprains will heal pretty fast," she says. "In the morning, we'll put a sling on your arm. Shoulder should be fine within a week. Your knee, probably before then."

"Thanks. When do you think they'll let me get out of here?"

"I think it'll be in the next couple of days." She adjusts a few more things, then makes ready to leave my room. "Will you let me know if there's anything else I can do for you? I mean it. I'm going home for the night soon, but I'll be back in the morning."

"I will," I answer. "Thanks." She marks a couple of updates on the dry-erase board, then leaves the room. I study the board, and it occurs to me to wonder who drew the doves on either side of my name. Doves. *Zenaida macroura.* I breathe a parting sigh for that sad woman, lost in the forest, and recite the riddle once again. *Whether it should follow me down what remains of my path, or rest here, allowing me to walk away freed of it, I now go to find out.* That century's worth of sadness, I realize now, she must have left behind. That has to be why the pull to walk away into the forest and never come out is so strong. Still looking at the doves on my dry-erase board, my eyes fall on the date. My head spins: was it only two days ago that I was in that room up in the mountains, listening to Sawyer's voice through the door, saying July 30?

A century's worth of sadness.

August 1, 1910.

And today, August 1, 2010.

I lean back against my pillows, heart full of longing. If I do leave, I'll miss this place. My mind roves, seeking out any number of possible plans, looking, as usual, for the one where I don't get hurt. Where there are as few variables as possible. But I took every safe choice before I came here, sacrificed connection for safety at every turn, and it almost got me killed regardless. It doesn't matter where you run to, if the minefield's your own heart. Bodies heal, skin renews itself around scars, a strange miracle to witness. But I don't know how to tend the wounds I can't see.

I listen, search my thoughts, looking for the voice I've come to think of as Zenaida's, hoping she'll tell me one thing or another. The familiar, maddening singsong: *it will heal better if it can breathe.* But she doesn't speak to me. Instead, the voice I hear sounds a lot like my own. *Where*, it asks, *could you breathe better than here?*

I wonder if it's been my own voice all along. I press the call button and within a few minutes, Anjali is back at my door.

"There might be something you could help me with," I tell her.

"What is it?"

"When I'm cleared to leave, can you help me get a ride home?"

"Of course, Dora," she answers. "Whatever you need. Get some sleep, okay?"

"I will. Thank you."

CHAPTER SIXTY

So, a few days later, for the second time, I find myself lingering outside the iron gate. The gate is ajar this time, though, and I walk in as if I belong here. It's good luck, too, considering my left arm is in a sling, and my twisted knee is still a little tender, bound snugly in a brace that lets me walk. Just as before, the moment I'm on this side of the wall, I sigh with relief. I walk the grounds slowly, not only because my knee is still sore. Everything looks new. At first sight, this place answered my prayers, so isolated and shadowed, behind that wall of stone. But now, I'm seeing how it opens itself to the sunlight, how it draws my eye to the landscape beyond, reminding me that I'm still in the world of the living.

I find Nathaniel just where I knew I would, on the bench in the garden that looks up at the stained-glass window. I sneak up behind him, cover his eyes with my free hand.

"It's me," I whisper into his ear.

"I don't believe it," he says. I can't tell whether he's teasing me or not. "Let me see you."

"You know, I kind of like the look of this place. What would you say if I asked you to let me stay?" I move my hand from his eyes and he lifts his face to look at me, his smile giving way to an earnest stare. My pattering heartbeat calms and I rest my hand on his shoulder.

"I've watched you leave twice, thinking it was the last time I'd see you." Nathaniel scoots over and I sit next to him. "I don't want to do that again."

"I don't either. Not ever again." I know this in the way one always knows the truth: more than mere fact, solid as the ground under my feet. Nathaniel pulls me close and I can feel his heartbeat under my cheek.

"You shouldn't be walking on that leg, Dora," he murmurs, as if he's just thought of it. "How'd you get in, anyway? I could have sworn the gate was locked. Please tell me you didn't climb that tree in a sling."

"You must have left it open by accident," I answer. "So I let myself in. I hope you don't mind."

"Not a bit."

Sometimes you don't know a turning point for what it is until later. Then again, sometimes it's clear as day. Nathaniel seems lost in thought, and I follow his gaze to the woman in the window. Where before the figure in the glass appeared to glimmer with untold secrets, her expression now is tranquil, casting an air of peace over the gardens. The jewel-green shadows welcome me, just the same as the sunlit flower beds, like so many open doorways, all promises of days to come.

A LETTER FROM KELLY

Thank you so much for taking the time to read *The Silent Girl*. If you'd like to stay informed of my future releases, please sign up to my email list below. Your email address will never be shared and you can unsubscribe at any time.

www.bookouture.com/kelly-heard

This story has been an absolute joy to write. During a particularly turbulent year, writing Sophie's journey has given my long, quarantined days an element of adventure and indulgence. I'm elated to imagine this book providing readers with the same, or even just a few hours of pleasant distraction. However, before I found myself escaping into the setting and the plot, the story took shape from a very simple idea, which was a question about how people overcome codependent relationships. If you have ever felt like less than a main character in your own life, know that this book was written with you close to my heart.

While Dovemorn House and the Atwoods are fictional, I encourage anyone with an interest in spectral, opulent mansions hidden away in Appalachia to read about and visit Swannanoa in Afton, Virginia.

If you liked reading this book, or if you have any questions for me, I'm happy to hear from you. Please get in touch with me on Twitter or through my website.

Kelly

 @KHeardBooks

@KellyHeardBooks

 kellyheardbooks.com

ACKNOWLEDGMENTS

Jane—thank you for always giving the wisest advice and for always making me laugh. Whatever our souls are made of, yours and mine are the same.

John—you have always supported my writing: by believing that I could, by answering my innumerable medical scenario questions, by taking on more than your share of housework and childcare when I needed time to work. I'm the lucky one here, and don't doubt that I know it.

I'm incredibly thankful for the support and guidance of my editor, Cara Chimirri. Thank you so much for sharing this writing adventure with me, for seeing the potential in my ideas, and for graciously suffering through the endless run-on sentences in my drafts.

When this book was just a two-sentence idea ("I don't know where this might go, but there's a woman with amnesia, and I think there's a poppy field"), Leodora Darlington, who was my editor at the time, encouraged me to follow my passion, to explore it, and helped me develop it into what has become my favorite project to date. Leodora, working with you during your time at Bookouture was a joy and a privilege.

I'm grateful for the spectacular Bookouture team, and, as always, for my family, for the countless ways they have supported me.

Made in the USA
Columbia, SC
12 April 2021

36074629R00176